NIGHT ANGEL

NIGHT ANGEL

KATE GREEN

Delacorte Press

Published by
Delacorte Press
Bantam Doubleday Dell Publishing Group, Inc.
666 Fifth Avenue
New York, New York 10103

Library of Congress Cataloging in Publication Data
Green, Kate.
    Night angel / Kate Green.
        p.   cm.
    ISBN 0-440-50102-4
    I. Title.
PS3557.R3729N5   1989   88–17445
813'.54—dc19   CIP
    Manufactured in the United States of America
                    February 1989
            10 9 8 7 6 5 4 3 2 1
                        BG

For my California crew, with love:
Lea Earnheart, Bob Gold, Richard McCormack,
and Jon Nielsen

Prologue

She argued with her husband the day she died. The subject was money, the subject was love. Lora sat tense and quiet on the couch by the split-rock fireplace, her black hair draped over her thin shoulders. Dennis stalked the room, arms flailing. He implored her to come with him, begged her not to stay, if only for her own peace of mind. She refused to go. The back of his car spun up the dust as it sped down the road toward town.

The Pacific, metal gray in the flat light, took up the entire view from the front windows, the horizon a sure line between one emptiness and another. Lora wanted to be out on the ocean. Its pure and roaring quiet would swallow every confusion and fear. There she would feel safe and clear and calm.

She drove down through Stinson Beach in her new red Mazda RX7, heading north to Point Reyes. Winding through Dogtown, Olema, past small ranches and farms, the car's low headlights aimed streaks into the afternoon fog that drifted over the black pines and groves of eucalyptus. The car stereo blasted Tina Turner's "Private Dancer." That was the tape found later in her abandoned car.

*At Inverness she stopped for gas. The station attendant
recalled that she was alone, that she bought cigarettes,
that they discussed the weather. No sun in five days, wind
strong from the south, fishing season over. Not much of a
year for salmon.*

*The boat was moored at Drake's Bay. Most of the boats
had been moved down to San Francisco Bay or up to
Bodega Bay for the winter by then, the dock quiet by mid-
October.* The Sailfin, Rosie, Irena, Dancing Nightly *and*
The Deep Blue, *all of them gone. Only a few boats remained, a few fishermen coming out to tinker and repair.
Lora's husband's boat was not a pleasure craft, not some
yacht or sleek sailboat, but a thirty-foot commercial fishing boat, white with blue trim. It was named* The Pearl,
after Janis Joplin.

*There was no one at the dock that afternoon. The fisher-
man who'd been working on his boat earlier in the day
had quit about three, gone to Point Reyes to drink. No one
saw Lora drag the small skiff down over the rocks, launch
into high tide, and row out to the boat. No one saw her tie
off from the anchor, head out from the mooring east to
Chimney Rock, around the buoy and past the lighthouse
into the open Pacific.*

Lora knew how to operate The Pearl, *start up the diesel,
and hold the wheel steady, but she'd never been out of the
bay by herself. That summer she'd taken a sudden interest
in the boat after years of indifference, even hostility, ac-
companying her husband, Dennis, on fishing runs, trawl-
ing for salmon up and down the coast to Bodega Bay and
back. There'd been days of gray peace together, hooking
lines with anchovies and drinking black coffee, the only
noise the even, low rumble of the engine and crackle of
the radio.*

*When Lora was out several miles from Drake's Bay, the
engine sputtered and stopped and the weather turned bad
as the south wind picked up, the boat diving in the roll
and sway of the water. She tried the ignition again and
hoisted the cover to the engine case, looking down into the*

darkness with a dim flashlight. It was hard to stand without holding on to the edge, and sometimes the side seemed to dip straight down as the boat crested and fell. But Lora knew nothing about the engine or why it might have died.

In the cabin she pressed down the mike button and called on the radio to see if any of Dennis's friends would answer. Only static replied. Then after several minutes an old fisherman monitoring radio calls in a steamy kitchen on a fall afternoon heard her distress.

"Hey there, Pearl, Pearl. You having some trouble out there?"

"Yeah, my engine's died," she responded. "Can't get her going."

"What's the trouble?"

"I don't know. It's my husband's boat, I'm not sure what's wrong."

"He know you're out there?"

"Yes," she lied.

"What's your location?"

"Couple of miles north of Drake's Bay."

"That's it? Can't you give me a little more than that?"

"Sorry," she said.

"Yeah, then. I'll have the Coast Guard give you a call out there. What's your call number?"

"I'm not sure."

"You alone?"

"I'm alone."

"What—are you crazy or something?" asked the fisherman.

Lora waited for the Coast Guard call and straddled the engine case again, shining a beam down into it and cursing. Then out of the steady dip and swell came a movement from the deep ocean, a wave twice as big as the others. Fishermen called them sneaker waves, places where crosscurrents heaved together, shoving the surface up into a pointed crest. Without warning the wave slammed against the boat, nearly capsizing it. Lora slipped on the wet deck and was thrown out against the *edge. Her head hit hard on the wood. She tried to grab the ropes, the wedge of the trawler, but could not steady herself, and when the next wave came, slapping the boat down against the sea, she lost her grip, hitting the wave as it rose.*

The boat lifted toward her like a black rock. Her mouth and lungs full of salt water, eyes open in the green cold, she spun down in the spiraling pull, arms outstretched as if she were flying.

Chapter 1

That was how Maggie Shea pictured her friend's death. She needed to hold some final image of Lora in her mind. She tried different versions, filling in details based on conversations with Lora about the boat, long letters from Dennis explaining what had happened: the Coast Guard's report, the fisherman's recollection of the radio call. Maggie stayed with the known facts as much as she could, perhaps as a way to counteract all that was unknown about that day. The part about Lora falling overboard into the sea—yes, she'd made that up, but finally that was the scene that stayed with her, the one she'd invented so that she would know the end of Lora's story.

Maggie Shea leaned her head against the window of the plane. Fields of clouds below blocked any view of the mountains. They were somewhere over Utah now, due into San Francisco International Airport around eight thirty. Rob Garson, Lora's older brother, would be meeting her. She hadn't been able to bring herself to stay at Lora's house in Stinson Beach, for that was how she thought of it: *Lora's house*. It would have been too hard.

Pulling the scratchy blanket over her lap, she huddled

in her knit jacket. Her black jeans felt too tight, and her feet, in sandals, were cold. She was glad she remembered to bring a sweater—it was ninety-two degrees in Minneapolis when she boarded the plane.

August, ten months since Lora had died. Earlier that week, on a Tuesday, Maggie had received a package in the mail, found it on her front porch in the typical brown wrapping paper and masking tape. When she read the return address, her breath stopped for a moment, frozen in her throat. The familiar scribble read: LORA MAYHEW, P.O. BOX 3415, STINSON BEACH, CA.

"Lora's writing." She'd said it aloud. There was an envelope taped to the back of the package, and written on the envelope in red pen were the words READ THIS FIRST.

In his brief note, Dennis explained that he'd been cleaning out some things *(Lora's things,* thought Maggie. *Getting rid of her things)* when he'd come across a package that Lora had intended to mail. In fact, he went on, Lora had asked him to mail it for her, had left it for him to mail, but in all the trauma he'd forgotten. It had been stuck back in a closet and he'd only just now come across it. He had no idea what it was, probably a birthday present. Wasn't Maggie's birthday in November? "Anyway she wanted you to have this, whatever it is. Sorry this is so belated."

Maggie reached under the seat in front of her and pulled Lora's gift from a canvas satchel. The man next to her looked up briefly from his *U.S. News and World Report* and glanced at the object, then at her.

It was a shadow box, the size of a piece of writing paper, a shallow frame about an inch deep, divided into eight small squares and covered with glass. The kind artsy-craftsy types used to put dried beans and little plaid ribbons on, thought Maggie, when she first saw it. Lora had taken care to pack it in shreds of paper from the gallery where she'd worked. Still, it was amazing that the glass hadn't broken.

Each section of the box contained black-and-white photographs of a group of ten people who'd lived together in a house in Berkeley in 1969 and 1970. Inside the squares, held behind glass, were small objects that had belonged to each person: buttons, ticket stubs, jewelry. It had the effect of a small shrine, a collage of memorabilia.

In the upper left-hand corner was a snapshot of Lily, a wan flower child, and her boyfriend, Peter String, standing on a corner in the Haight-Ashbury. A picture of Sandy Craig playing the dulcimer was pasted in the upper right-hand box. The second row held pictures of Maggie's two best friends from college, Jesse Ryder and Lora. Beneath that were photographs of Rob, Lora's brother, and Cody, both of them wearing standard Berkeley uniforms for Vietnam vets, circa late sixties—field jackets and bandana headbands. The two pictures at the bottom were of Dennis Mayhew wearing a top hat and, finally, one of Maggie standing with an old boyfriend named Quinn.

The box itself was purple. Along its sides some sort of odd symbols, possibly astrological or alchemical, had been carefully inscribed in silver paint, and there was tiny, unintelligible writing that resembled Arabic on the thin wood pieces that separated the sections.

How eerie it was to have received a package from a friend who'd died nearly a year ago. Stranger still was the phone call that had come that same night. Dennis, his voice whirring across the long-distance connection, first inquired whether the package had arrived.

"Just this afternoon," Maggie said, and was about to tell him about the letter Lora had included in the package when Dennis blurted out, "It looks like they found her today, Maggie. Her remains."

Maggie sat down in a wicker chair next to the phone and snapped off the fan so she could hear Dennis more clearly.

"I thought the boat sank," she said quietly. "I thought it was washed out to sea."

"So did I. So did the Coast Guard. But I got a call this morning from the Marin County Sheriff's Office. Some

kids were climbing rocks down by Slide Ranch. You know
where I mean? Those steep cliffs between Golden Gate
and Stinson Beach, below Highway One. At the bottom of
a really remote area, totally out of the way, they found the
lifeboat for *The Pearl*. It's mostly splinters, but they made
out a few letters on one of the boards, P-E-A-R. It was
washed up into a cave that's usually above tide level but
floods with debris and seaweed during the winter storms.
They also found shreds of Lora's jean jacket and that diamond stickpin of Gram's. Remember? The one Lora stuck
on every jacket she ever wore. It was on the lapel." His
voice hesitated and he cleared his throat. "And they
found her remains. They're examining it—them—now,
trying to get a positive identification, but they're pretty
sure it's her. I knew you'd want to know right away."

Maggie could feel the pulse throb in her head, and she
felt shocked, as if she were hearing of Lora's death for the
first time.

Finally she said, "Was Lora just floating out there, then,
the whole time the Coast Guard was looking for her?"

"They think the skiff probably washed up into the cave
before the Coast Guard even started. You can't see in the
cave by air—and that was mostly how they conducted the
search."

"Dennis," Maggie whispered. "I'm so sorry."

He sighed, a long hiss of breath. "I'm glad they found
her, but it doesn't change anything."

He sounded withdrawn, his voice flat, without affect.
She recognized that stage of grieving, wounds opened
again, the system shutting down to avoid feeling pain.

They did not speak much longer, and Maggie sat in the
humid Minnesota night, that imagined scene of Lora's
death playing through her mind. She saw now the story
she'd made up was wrong, all wrong. Lora had been in a
boat the entire time. She might even have lived for several days in that boat, sure that someone would find her.

It wasn't until the next morning that Maggie decided to
go out to San Francisco. She booked a Friday afternoon

flight, called Dennis and then Rob, Lora's brother, who
told her how relieved he was that she was coming. "I'm
glad you'll be here for the funeral. We haven't set a date
for it yet—they have to finish the examination. It's been
one hell of a year, Maggie. The terrible part was not finding her. Then just when we started to come to terms with
that—" He didn't finish the sentence. "Everybody will be
really glad to see you, anyway. Maybe you can help us
through all of this."

Maggie didn't know how much help she'd be. For eight
years she'd been a family counselor for a hospice program,
but this summer she'd taken a leave, with the idea of
going back to school for a doctorate. She'd been taking
classes at the Jungian Association and had even toyed with
the notion of going to Zurich to study for a few months.
People were sometimes put off when they heard she
worked with death and dying. They assumed it was de-
pressing work, but it was a good field as long as one main-
tained a professional distance, kept those boundaries
clear. *Their* death, *their* dying. Maggie appreciated the
rich archetypal patterns that emerged, the stages of grief
that led to a healing transformation; but when it was
someone you loved, then it was different. She wanted to
tell Rob she was coming out so she wouldn't feel so alone
with Lora's death, so she wouldn't have to be professional
about it. Maybe she could offer some sympathy to Dennis
and Rob, but the truth was that she wanted some sympathy too. She'd lost an old friend, and even though she'd
known since last October that Lora was gone, she hadn't
been able to believe it until now.

The businessman in the seat beside her looked again at
the shadow box Maggie held in her lap. "Are you an artist?" he asked.

"No. I didn't make this," she explained. "An old friend
of mine did, this one here. And that's me." She pointed
first to the picture of Jesse Ryder, then to her own picture
—a young woman with long hair, wearing granny glasses,
bellbottoms, a tie-dyed T-shirt.

"I never would have guessed you were a hippie," said the businessman.

Maggie smiled. "We're all in disguise now."

She turned toward the window and closed her eyes. It helped in her work that her face was friendly, with a wide smile and a warm, direct gaze. Usually she talked easily, and under normal circumstances would have told this man all about her wild years in Berkeley, but now she hoped the man would get the hint. She just wanted to be alone. Lora had once given Maggie a hard time about how she kept men at a distance, didn't see her own beauty. *Maybe you were right,* thought Maggie.

She did have the Shea black-Irish good looks, thick dark hair with streaks of sun red. She wore it chin-length and curly, framing pale skin that burned easily. Her light blue eyes had a glint that made her look as if she had a good story to tell, another Shea trait. "You come from a long line of bards and liars," her father liked to tease. From her mother's side she'd gotten the thin-boned nose and the smoky voice, an inheritance from all that Irish drinking. She was tall like her father, though even at five-eight Maggie was diminutive among five towering brothers who had all grown up to be lawyers and judges in St. Paul. At times she wondered if there was any gene in her at all that wasn't Irish, if she was simply a variation on a theme of centuries of Colleen Brannigans and Sadie O'Tooles.

Maggie took a deep breath and consciously resolved to be quiet, to keep herself from spilling out the story of her friend who had died and sent her a gift from beyond the grave. She shuddered in the forced-air cool of the jet, pulling the blanket up over her shoulders. *But she's not even in her grave,* she thought.

It had been over a year since she had last seen Lora in the Cayman Islands, April of 1985. In the years since college they'd met on trips at least once a year, often to ski or go to the ocean. Maggie reached down into the satchel and found a small envelope of old snapshots: Maggie,

Lora, and Jesse in the dorm, Maggie as Lora's maid of honor. Here was the one she was looking for: Lora by the pool at the Paradise Manor, squinting into the sun. Flat straw hat, black bikini. *Goddamn it,* Maggie thought. *I miss you.*

The picture didn't do her justice; Lora had never photographed well. She'd always been thin, delicate yet boyish, her face pert. Her thick Texas drawl had been slightly muted by years at private eastern schools, and her brown eyes closed when she laughed, loudly and often, a funny, infectious sound that never seemed to come from her small, tense body. No one ever made Maggie laugh as hard. But it was her sense of adventure that Maggie missed most. Perhaps because Lora had always had money, she'd never gotten dragged down into a workaday rut.

And she'd been generous—to a fault, Dennis had claimed. During her student days she gave money away to leftist organizations and more recently to New Age concerns, to a holistic retreat near Sonoma, and to the publication of a book on socially conscious investments. Through the years she had helped her friends start up businesses that ranged from herb farms to demo tapes for rock bands, even a travel agency that booked trips to shamanistic power sites in Peru.

Lora's money had come from her grandmother, the famous Gram, who was just as much a soft touch as Lora herself. Maybe Lora had squandered some of her trust fund, as Dennis had complained, but she'd been a good friend. She'd even lent Maggie money for the down payment on a house the year after Maggie's husband died. It was Lora who put up the money for Quinn's art gallery in Sausalito, and then she'd worked with him, importing primitive art from third-world countries. That was why she and Maggie had met in the Caymans, to check out the dolls and the black coral sculptures there.

Maggie turned to one final snapshot: Lora in scuba gear, perched on the side of a boat. Maggie had stayed on the

boat reading while Lora dove the sheer wall of a coral reef
that went straight down two miles. Later Lora said to her,
"I'll never dive a wall like that again. You get to a point
where there's the light of the surface far above you, just
shimmering. Then there's all that pitch black below. And
you could just keep on going down. It pulls you. You can
choose—light or dark. And for a minute I didn't know
which way I'd rather go."

There was that side of Lora too: dark, unpredictable,
with wild mood swings and an attraction to trouble. Maggie didn't like to think about it and had once been blind to
it. Some of Lora's investments hadn't been so socially
conscious—she'd financed some drug dealing back in the
Berkeley days, made a few "loans" to people who didn't
deserve them. She wasn't always discerning in her judg-
ments of others, and it was usually during periods when
she herself was using drugs. It wasn't until Maggie's own
training as a therapist that she really understood the nature of Lora's chemical dependency, how it altered a good
person, and when that happened, things always went
wrong.

On the trip to the Caymans, Lora had urged Maggie
once again to come out to San Francisco for a visit. "How
come y'all never visit me? We've got this house a quarter
mile from one of the prettiest beaches in California!
Horseback riding, bird watching. Dennis'll even take you
out on his boat. Don't you have any nostalgia? You mid-
westerners are so damn rooted. You're worse than trees.
Even the Ice Age moved on, sister."

Lora had added that anyway there were at least one or
two "boys" from that Berkeley house that would be perfectly delighted to see Maggie now that she was available
again. She counted them on her fingers, "Big brother,
Robbie, for starters. Our old friend and business partner,
Mr. Quinn."

Maggie had laughed. "What about Cody? Don't leave
him out."

"Okay, throw him in too." Then Lora had scolded.

"Maggie, you're going to have to get over Mark sometime. It's been four years since that motorcycle accident and you haven't gone out once."

"That's not true."

"Well, been involved then. Look, I know Quinn is still in love with you. And my brother always asks after you. He pretends like he's a little bored when I talk about you, cleaning his nails with a toothpick or something. He says stuff like 'Yeah, what did she say?' "

Lora had mimicked the conversation she'd had with her brother.

" 'She asked about you, pinhead. I told her you're a hotshot lawyer, a spy for nuclear power companies, that you defend known criminals in court. I told her that ever since your second divorce the bottom line is the basis for your spirituality and you just bought a Porsche.' So he says, 'Since when are you such a Marxist? Anyway it's a BMW.' He threw the toothpick at me, of course. But I told him maybe she *is* interested. 'You *were* her first lover, Robbie.' "

Maggie could still recall Lora's voice, as if she were sitting right next to her on this plane. It just couldn't be that she was gone, that she wouldn't be standing at the arrival gate, wearing dark glasses and waving. It was Lora who'd always brought out that part of herself she associated with the Berkeley days, free-spirited, easygoing and slightly crazy. She and Jesse and Lora had made quite a trio, a sisterhood of sorts. Now, no one had heard from Jesse since 1970, and Lora was dead, her body washed up in a cave just a few miles from the Golden Gate Bridge.

Why didn't I come out to California to see you? Maggie silently asked the picture. *Were you in some kind of trouble again? Was there anything I could have done?*

She reached down into the satchel at her feet and pulled out the letter that Lora had sent with the shadow box package. She'd not had time to tell Dennis about it, nor had she mentioned it to Rob. It was this letter that

made her feel the most uncomfortable about Lora's
death. She opened it and read it again.

> *Dear Maggie,*
> *I dreamed of you the other night. Actually it was a*
> *nightmare. We were back in Berkeley at the old house.*
> *Someone or something was in the walls. You know, the*
> *way squirrels and mice get between the joists? I felt*
> *surrounded by this thing, whatever it was, and I kept*
> *looking for you all over the house. I knew you were*
> *there but I couldn't find you.*
> *I know what caused the dream—a month ago I was in*
> *Berkeley and on a whim went back to our house. The*
> *woman who owns the place now gave me something she*
> *found when she was cleaning the basement. It's one of*
> *Jesse's shrines. Remember when you and Jesse were into*
> *all that witchy stuff—spells and amulets and rituals?*
> *Well, ever since I got this thing I've been feeling like the*
> *wheel of my life is about to turn one big notch, a reac-*
> *tion to forces not really my own. It scares me. Maybe I*
> *never should have gone back there.*
> *Funny how we don't know how much time we have*
> *left. What if we did know—like an appointment? I*
> *wonder sometimes about the way String and Lily and*
> *Sandy died that summer in the Berkeley house. If we*
> *weren't all under some kind of spell then, just as Jesse*
> *feared. Maybe we still are. Where do we go when we*
> *cross over to the other side? Or is it like Gautama Bud-*
> *dha said, that beings born in time must disappear when*
> *time integrates. You of all people should have an opin-*
> *ion.*
> *Though I'm not religious. I feel sure there must be an*
> *afterlife and that I will see you there one day. I just*
> *hope it has palm trees, a nice pool, venetian blinds in*
> *the cabana, and an angel bartender who makes a great*
> *piña colada.*
> *So, sister Maggie, I'm sending this little shrine of*

Jesse's along to you. Call it a gift for the archives. Tell me if you understand what it all means. Love, Lora.

Then, in a different-colored pen, scribbled at the bottom of the page:

M. I think of you often. I'll always love you no matter what. Happy Trails.

There were things that bothered Maggie about this letter. For one thing, it was out of character, overly serious, even melodramatic, except for the reference to some tropical heaven. Lora usually made fun of things, even herself, unless she'd been drinking or was back into cocaine. Had she been using again? But Lora had gone through treatment back in eighty-three—Maggie had been the one to get her to check into Hazelden on one of her visits to Minnesota—and as far as she knew, Lora had been straight since then.

The timing was the second thing that bothered her. She fingered the date of the letter—October sixteenth, 1985. Two days before Lora took the boat out of Drake's Bay.

Finally there was the fact that Dennis had sent it to Maggie at all. It was definitely Lora's handwriting on the letter and the package. Certainly Maggie had no reason to disbelieve Dennis as to why he'd sent it so belatedly—but to receive the package the very day that Lora's body was found was too strange.

Why had Lora gone back to the Berkeley house in the first place and died so soon afterwards? Synchronicity?

The plane began its descent into San Francisco and she looked out at the hills around the bay, the point of downtown glittering in the sunset. As they circled out over the Pacific and came in toward the city of seven hills, Maggie acknowledged the real reason she'd never returned to California all those years. It wasn't inconvenience or lost love that kept her away. During that summer of 1970, three of their roommates in the Berkeley house had died

in the space of a few weeks, all of them from drug overdoses, one a possible suicide. What had been a magical
and important time in her life had gone very wrong. The
magic went bad and she'd tried to get it back, but it hadn't
worked. Maybe that was why she'd always feared that
darkness in Lora. Whenever it surfaced, it brought back
memories she'd rather forget.

Maggie glanced up as the stewardess asked the passengers to extinguish all smoking materials and place seat
backs and trays in a full upright position. God, she wanted
to love San Francisco again, but in that few seconds of
rumbling descent, the plane winding its landing gear
down, pulling into the vacuum before touchdown, she still
felt some shivering remnant of fear leftover, calcified by
fifteen years.

The plane bumped down once, twice, then the rush of
brakes pushed her back against the seat. Passengers began standing before they were supposed to, lurching in
the aisles as they gathered belongings from the overhead
racks. Maggie Shea took a deep breath, wishing she could
pretend she was only coming back to visit old friends,
walk in the Muir woods, go to Chinatown, or ride the ferry
to Sausalito.

As she stashed the shadow box back in the satchel, she
couldn't shake the thought that Lora's death was tied in
some way to those events long ago, that the arrival of the
package at the exact time Lora's body had been found was
no mere coincidence. She couldn't get over the idea that
the box and letter contained some sort of message Lora
had been trying to send to her. She'd received it ten
months too late.

Chapter 2

Maggie would have walked right past Rob Garson if he hadn't said her name. Leaning there against the wall by the line of telephones, he looked totally different. He'd lost weight, even seemed taller. His black hair was cut short, and his beard, neatly trimmed, sharpened his round features. He wore jeans, a wrinkled white shirt, no tie, running shoes, and a rumpled sport coat that looked expensive.

Rob smiled broadly, raising his hand in greeting. He was certainly better-looking than the scraggly vet he'd been back in Berkeley, and it struck her that although she had seen Lora any number of times since college, she'd not seen Rob since Lora's wedding back in seventy-one. *Your first lover,* Lora had teased. Though things hadn't worked out between them for long, Maggie had always thought fondly of Rob. She wondered briefly if he was with anybody now.

"Maggie! Over here!" He took the satchel from her. "Let me carry that. God, you look great. It's great that you could come out. Great, great—I sound like an idiot." He turned toward her and they hugged awkwardly. "I really am glad you came," he said.

"Lora's been—she tried to get me to come back here for a long time."

"You finally made it. She'd have been real happy." Still a hint of Texas in his voice, though he hadn't lived in his home state since grade school. Both he and Lora had been sent away to private schools from the time they had been twelve or thirteen.

Familiar stranger. That was how Maggie thought of him as they waited for her suitcase to come down the carousel, chatting about the flight, the weather in Minnesota, baseball. They avoided talking any further about Lora for the time being, as if the subject were too intimate. Their friendship would have to be reestablished before they could speak of her again.

As they drove back through the city, Rob stopped at Twin Peaks so Maggie could look over the panorama of lights below. It seemed a dream landscape, the postcard sky, the thin red line of the Golden Gate Bridge spanning the bay. Rob stood behind her in the strong wind, and suddenly she felt relieved by the beauty of the place.

She turned to him. "You know what? I was always afraid to come back here."

"I was always scared to leave. Why were you afraid?"

She pulled the jacket up around her neck. "The bad magic. That's what I called it. It stayed with me a long time. I can't help thinking about it."

Rob had a gesture of ruffling the hair on the back of his head. She remembered it from years ago when his long hair had strayed over his shoulders. He did it now. Lora in his face, their mother's good looks.

"All of it," she went on. "The drugs, the phone-tapping, messing around with witchcraft. That whole wild year. There was something about that house, wasn't there? Jesse used to say it had its own presence, that it turned against us. I guess I thought that was true. The things you believe when you're young." She laughed, but Rob's face was very serious.

"Let's go to my place. It's freezing up here."

It wasn't far to his house down in the Haight. "Welcome
to the gentrification of the Summer of Love," said Rob as
he parked on the steep hill. He pulled her suitcase from
the back seat and they climbed the steps of a red Victorian
with black trim, tall as a thin ship and flanked all the way
down the block by other houses painted colors no one in
the Midwest dared to use: coral with sky-blue trim, gray
with lavender. His was one of the few houses on the block
that had not been divided into flats.

Inside he carried Maggie's bag up the narrow stairway.
As she stood below in the foyer, the chandelier overhead
suddenly went dark, the room swimming in shadow.
"Rob?" she called out, feeling for the wall next to her.

"Sorry." Rob's voice came from above and the light
glowed on again. "Hit the switch by accident." He came
down to her jangling a set of keys in his palm. "House
key," he explained. "And this one is for that blue Impala
down the street. I keep trying to sell it, but then I think of
three more reasons why I need a beater. She's a lot better
than a BMW on mountain roads. The only thing is, she's
finicky—it's the carburetor. If she stalls, just wait a minute
and she'll start right back up again. You're welcome to use
it while you're here." Then he mixed them each a drink
while Maggie looked around.

Rob's living room was a hodgepodge of modern furniture—sleek leather couch, glass coffee table—and stately
antiques he must have inherited from his family. Bright
abstract paintings hung on the walls. In front of a bay
window at the far end of the room stood a large wooden
merry-go-round horse, its paint flaking. Maggie went over
to it and touched its carved mane.

"You like it?" asked Rob. "I'm storing it for a friend of
mine who went to New Zealand."

Next to an upright piano a saxophone leaned in a stand.

"Still playing?" she asked.

"For myself. For fun."

"Quite the place." She dropped onto the cool leather of

the couch, slipped off her sandals, and pulled her legs up under her. "I can't believe this is the Haight."

"Bought it cheap in seventy-four when there were still a lot of junkies. We've come a long way, haven't we?" He handed her a drink. "To the eighties." They toasted.

"In a few years it'll be the nineties."

"Please," he said. "Let's invoke a little Peter Pan energy around here."

"Never grow old?" Maggie asked.

Rob sat down next to her on the couch and handed her a photo album. "This'll make you feel even older," he said. "Pictures from the Berkeley house. Found it among Lora's things. Dennis let me have it."

"I was just looking at old snapshots on the plane. Let's see."

Maggie held the album for a moment before opening the cover and paging through Lora's album. Here were pictures she had forgotten were ever taken, caught moments stuck in time. She smiled, pointing to a picture of Jesse Ryder in a red chair wearing a tattered, sexy kimono.

"Isn't this typical?"

"Check out Cody. 'Sound Man.' What was the name of that band of his?" asked Rob.

"The first one was 'Dante and The Infernos,' wasn't it?" They both laughed.

"Yeah, that one lasted about a month," said Rob. "Now I remember the other one—'The Seventh Circle.' They weren't bad." He fingered faded shots of Cody on a mattress, mouthing a harmonica; Quinn at a rally, standing onstage next to the national secretary of SDS.

"Don't I look just like a farm girl in this one? Look at those overalls!"

Maggie turned to the next page, a large household portrait. There was a date written below the picture in tiny Roman numerals. It looked like Jesse's writing, her careful script: *VI/IX/MCMLXX*. A six and a nine; that would be June ninth. The year had to be 1970. She glanced at a few more pages, noting the dates written under the pictures in that small block script of Jesse's.

Rob had gone back into the kitchen for a moment when the phone rang. Maggie heard his voice, low, then he called out, "It's for you, Maggie. There's a phone on the table by the couch. It's Quinn."

Talking to ghosts: that's how it felt to be back here. Ghosts that had survived and were living new lives in rehabbed Victorians. *And some who didn't survive,* she thought. She closed her eyes. That old heart thud of past love; she could swoon off into it as if listening to an old Smokey Robinson song.

"Hi, Quinn."

"Say! Queen Maggie returns to recapture her throne in the Land of the Violet Ray!"

All Maggie could say was, "I can't believe it's you."

"How come you're staying with Garson is what I want to know. How does he rate?"

"He invited me, babe."

"Babe? Really? Even after all these years? You mean there's hope?"

Maggie heard the hiss of an inbreath. "Are you getting high?" she asked.

"This very moment. From talking to you."

"You are exactly the same, Quinn! Does that rap still work on women?"

"Like it worked on you?"

Maggie said nothing. Too much too soon. Quinn dropped the teasing tone. "No, actually it doesn't work. Actually it has the same effect it ended up having on you. Guess I'm just trying to fill up space. So I don't have to say—" He stopped. "You know all about Lora and everything then?"

"I know they found her. Rob and I haven't had a chance to talk much yet."

"We're all pretty screwed up over it. Dennis is really a mess. I guess he wants to have everybody out to his place

on Sunday. Did Rob mention it? Just think—we're all back
here now, even you."

"A reunion, then?"

"Let's call it a party. Lora would have wanted it to be a
party. Am I going to get a chance to see you before that,
though? Alone, I mean. I'd really like to talk to you about
Lora."

"Quinn, I'm not out here as a therapist, just as a friend."

"Analysis wasn't what I had in mind. There are just
some things you should know about what happened."

"Such as?" Maggie set her drink down as Rob lowered
himself onto the couch beside her.

"Is Rob right there?" asked Quinn.

"Yes," she said.

"Look, maybe we better have breakfast tomorrow."

Rob bent forward, flipping through the album. When
Maggie said, "Breakfast?" he turned to her, shook his head
no, pleading, then lifted upturned hands as if to say what
the hell—do what you want. She knew he wouldn't want
her to go running off with Quinn right away—after all, she
was staying with him—but she wanted to hear what
Quinn had to say. His hushed tone of privacy confirmed
her uneasy feeling that there was more to Lora's death
than she'd been told. *But there's time,* she thought. *I've
only been here an hour.*

"Quinn? Look—I don't know about breakfast. Let me
call you tomorrow and we'll make a date. I just got here
and I'm on Central Time. I'll probably have jet lag."

"Okay, Purey. You're the queen. Why don't you call
about ten or so. Maybe we can have lunch instead. Don't
let Garson hog you."

"I'll be here a week."

"A week? How can I make my move in one week?"

"You've already made it."

"Yeah, but it didn't work."

"Quinn?" she said softly. "I'll call you tomorrow." Maggie hung up, sipped her drink. *Purey.* She hadn't been

called that in so long. She turned to Rob. "Quinn sounds the same."

"Pretty much. Not quite as much hair."

"Don't tell me he's bald!"

Rob laughed. "I didn't mean to stop you from making plans or anything. It's just that—"

Maggie put up her hand. "You know Quinn. I'm not in a hurry."

"Great. Let's just hang out tomorrow in the city then." He was obviously relieved.

There were times in counseling when she'd sensed this with families—the anxious energy of feelings hidden and held in. People would maneuver to get off with her alone, to tell her what was *really* going on. It always signaled to her that there were family secrets that had long been protected. Death had a way of bringing them to the surface. It was important not to pry, to ask just the right questions. Not nosy, just concerned. She pulled the satchel over to her and lifted out the shadow box.

"Rob, I got a very odd package in the mail this week, the same day Dennis called about Lora's body. It was *from* Lora, actually." She explained briefly about Dennis's note and handed him the shadow box, sitting back to watch his reaction. He held it for a moment, then shook it, the trinkets clacking against glass. There was a dried flower for Lily, blue button from String's coat, tiger's eye for Jesse, and coins for Lora. By Cody's picture there was a ticket stub from a Grateful Dead concert. Rob's square held the broken reed from a saxophone mouthpiece. At the bottom, pasted onto Dennis's picture, were several miniature playing cards, a full house. For Maggie and Quinn, an imitation pearl necklace and a strip of camera film.

Rob read through Lora's letter twice, somewhat blank-faced, she thought, as if he were reading a legal brief. Without speaking, he fingered the intricate markings along the edges and under each picture. She'd forgotten how quiet and withdrawn Rob could be at times, way back in his brain somewhere. She tried to wait him out, then finally asked, "Rob, was there anything funny about the way Lora died?"

"The whole thing was funny," he muttered.

"Tell me about it. Was she using drugs again or drinking? Were she and Dennis getting along? Her letter is so foreboding, don't you think?"

Rob stood and walked to the bay window, long legs, quick movements. The sky had darkened and the lights of Noe Valley and the Castro were spread below. He stood with his hands jammed in his back pockets.

"She wasn't using that I knew of. Their marriage—they were always on each other's backs. I think that was half the reason Dennis had the boat in the first place, why Lora traveled as much as she did. You know they separated that spring for about two months—but then they got back together and things actually seemed better between them." He sighed and turned back to her. "She was really involved in importing all those crafts from the Caribbean."

"Yes, I know."

"Well, a couple of weeks before the accident, she started getting kind of spooked by it all. She told me she thought sometimes that these objects were made with people's 'personal power,' as she called it. That maybe she was violating something by selling them as mere artifacts.

"Now, I never knew about this firsthand—it was Dennis who told me—but the week before she died she got really scared. She claimed weird things were happening to her, that somebody was following her. I guess she got a couple of crazy phone calls, someone calling, not saying anything. Claimed a car almost ran her off the road when she was coming over the hill on Highway One. That would have been right about the time she wrote that letter.

"So Dennis planned this trip for her. A three-day weekend in Lake Tahoe at a cabin Quinn rented. The three of them were to go up and gamble, relax for the weekend, get away from the gallery. Quinn agreed that she'd gotten a bit obsessed with it all too. Maybe she was overworked. But she wouldn't go. She and Dennis had a big fight."

"Dennis told me they argued," said Maggie. "I gathered he felt pretty guilty about it, since that was the last time they saw each other."

"After they fought, he split for three days, went on up to Tahoe with Quinn—and when he came back Lora wasn't home. That afternoon he drove out to Drake's Bay and her car was sitting there and the boat was gone. He called the Marin County Sheriff's Office, they called in the Coast Guard, and that's when they started looking. They realized it was probably the same boat that had put in a distress call a couple of days before that—but they'd had no call number or location to go on. By the time the search was started she'd already been out there three days and now it looks like she was in that lifeboat by then, that it washed up into the cave.

"We wondered right away about whether or not she could have gotten into the lifeboat. It wouldn't have been hard to launch—it was rigged to a cable system and there was a lever in the cabin. If you pulled on it, the lifeboat automatically lowered into the water. Now it turns out that's what she must have done. But why didn't she use the survival suit?"

"What survival suit?" Maggie asked.

"It was always hanging in a little plastic pouch in the cabin, kind of like a rain suit. When you put it on and pull the tab at the waist the thing inflates like a life vest. It also sends out some sort of signal that the Coast Guard can pick up on radar. That's what's so sad. I know Lora was aware of these things. If only she'd used them, they would have found her within a matter of hours."

Maggie tried to visualize the boat from pictures Lora had showed her over the years. "Was that all their argument was about—going to Tahoe? There wasn't anything else going on?"

Rob tipped his drink back to his mouth, then set the

glass on the table. "Dennis thought that maybe Lora was seeing somebody else," he admitted.

"Go on."

"That's about all I know. She was traveling a lot, buying all that stuff for Quinn's gallery—masks, weavings, dolls, prayer flags, beads. Going regularly to Haiti, Jamaica, Mexico. Dennis suspected she had a lover somewhere or that someone traveled with her. He had no idea who it was."

Maggie held her empty glass up to Rob. "I think I'd like a refill," she said. When Rob went into the kitchen, she set the shadow box on top of the photo album, looking from the small pictures in the box's partitions to the group portrait in the album. Suddenly she glanced from the cuneiformlike inscriptions on the shadow box to Jesse's writing in the album. Rob crossed the living room and handed her the drink.

"Do you have a magnifying glass?" she asked him.

He went into a den off from the living room and brought one back. Maggie took it and leaned over the box. "Look, Rob," she said. "This is the same lettering as in the album, only much smaller. I thought it was Arabic or something, but it's Roman numerals. Probably dates, just like in the album."

Rob found a yellow legal tablet under some magazines. "Not every picture is dated," he observed. "Just the ones of Lily and Peter, Sandy, Jesse, and Lora." On the tablet he wrote their names. Beside each name he listed the Roman numerals and translated them. Maggie looked over his arm as he wrote, a black fear gathering in her stomach.

"Birthdays?" she whispered.

But there were two sets of dates for each of the five names.

Lily   IV/X/MCMLIV–VII/XXIV/MCMLXX
          April 10, 1954–July 24,1970

Peter XII/XII/MCML–VII/XXIV/MCMLXX
      December 12, 1950–July 24, 1970

Sandy I/VIII/MCML–VIII/V/MCMLXX
      January 8, 1950–August 5, 1970

Jesse XI/IX/MCMXLVIII–III/XVIII/MCMLXXII
      November 9, 1948–March 18, 1972

Lora VI/II/MCML–X/XVIII/MCMLXXXV
     June 2, 1950–October 18, 1985

Even before he completed the list, Maggie realized that the second set of numbers were dates of death.

"Christ," Rob breathed.

She covered her face with her hands. "What do you think that means, the writing on the side of the box? What language is it?"

Rob peered closely at the highly stylized inscription, turning the box in his hands. "It's upside down. Latin. Looks like some little kid's idea of a secret code. *Et hoc praeteribit. Et* means 'also, even.' 'This . . .'" He paused. "'This will also pass by,' or 'This too shall pass.'"

He handed her the magnifying glass and she peered at the writing, not understanding it any more than if it had been Arabic. Then she handed the box back to Rob.

"I don't like it." She felt chilled, and not just because she'd forgotten how cold San Francisco could be in summer.

He tossed it down on the coffee table angrily. "What in the hell is this thing?" he asked, raising his voice.

"Lora's letter said it was one of Jesse's shrines. Maybe it was some kind of hex or something. Maybe Lora got it from the Berkeley house and . . ."

Rob spun around, interrupting her. "Do you really believe that, Maggie? That Lora died because of a goddamn hex? It doesn't make any sense!" He was yelling. "So Jesse makes this thing, puts in dates of death for Lily and Peter and Sandy. But how could she have known way back then

when Lora would die, and why would she include herself
among the dead?"

"No one has heard from Jesse since then, Rob."

"But we don't know for sure that she's dead," he protested. "She just disappeared. Ran away."

"Last I heard she was in Mexico. Another rumor had
her in India."

"It's crazy," he shouted. "Crazy." Suddenly he grew
quiet. He picked up the shadow box, carefully set it on top
of the piano next to a pile of sheet music, and stared at it
for several minutes.

"I had a feeling right from the beginning there was
something wrong about the way Lora died. It's just that
there was nothing I could point to." He held his hand out,
palm up, as if offering an argument to a jury. "No evidence. Nothing specific. No boat to examine, no body.
Until this week." He rubbed his forehead with the ends of
his fingers.

"You don't think she did it on purpose, do you?" Maggie
asked.

"I considered that possibility. I had to. According to
Dennis, her behavior was pretty erratic right before she
died. But I just don't know, Maggie. Are you thinking she
might have put the time of her own death on this shadow
box thing? Did you ever think she was suicidal?"

She remembered what Lora had said after diving in the
Caymans. That pull toward the darkness of the ocean. Rob
held his fist tight, making little pounding motions in the
air. He seemed to be holding something back. *What?* she
thought. *What is it?* But she already knew. Unspeakable
thought, the one thing neither of them had mentioned.
His reticent silence seemed to have a sound of its own, a
hum. She had often felt something similar with clients
when they were about to cry, but Rob did not, would not,
cry. He'd always been very private, even when they'd
gone together back in the Berkeley days. She'd attributed
it then to his having been in Vietnam, some core of him
untouchable. She watched him struggling now, emotions

moving over his face almost imperceptibly, tic at the edge of his mouth.

"Could someone have killed her, Rob?"

"I always suspected that. But it's hard to prove someone's been killed when there's no body. That's what the police told me when I asked them a few months ago to investigate her disappearance as a homicide. You can't book anybody based on a goddamn hunch."

"Book who, Rob?"

He looked at her directly and his voice cracked. "Dennis, of course. Who else?"

Maggie stood and paced the room, holding her arms about her. "The police, the police," she stammered. "They know you suspect Dennis had something to do with this?"

"Of course they do!" He was shouting again. "I talked to them until I was blue in the face. 'No evidence,' they kept saying. No goddamned evidence, no motive!" Maggie backed against the piano at the force of his words. "Nothing that could be used in a court of law," he said bitterly. "Surely I understood that." He looked across the room at her. She could tell he was trying to restrain himself.

"Rob, I wish you had called me sooner."

"I can't talk about it anymore," he muttered and strode into the kitchen. Maggie came in behind him as he poured an inch of brandy into a juice glass and threw it down his throat.

"Is there anything I can do?" she whispered.

"No. Nothing."

Unreachable. Distant. Leave him alone, she thought. Finally Maggie left the kitchen and picked up the shadow box from the piano, the photo album from the couch. She climbed the stairs. The young faces of old friends looked up at her from under glass, stuck there, the living and the dead.

Chapter 3

J ust outside Fairfax in Marin County stood a small wood-shake house next to a grove of towering redwoods. It had taken her a long time to find this place, this particular combination of the domestic and sacred, this ramshackle house with its tilting front steps, its odd-shaped decks built out over the reinforced hillside.

The neighboring redwoods moved quietly in the wind, their tiny green-cone buds weighting the feathery branches. Throughout the grove, stands of trees grew from giant burned-out stumps next to bay laurels and eucalyptus. When she looked up at the redwoods in the dark evening sky, they seemed to lean toward a central point, all lines of vision converging. A power place, she thought. Good fortune to have found one right next to her ivy-covered yard, a rare flat stretch of ground in an area of brown hills. Luck left too much to chance; fate was after the fact. No, Jesse Ryder had envisioned this place, had drawn it into her life—but, as with all visualizations, she'd left the details open to the universe.

It was dark. Just off from a gravel driveway that wound in a circle through the grove, she stood barefoot on dirt

strewn with dried eucalyptus leaves. She was holding a
stick, she wore no special costume. Ordinary magic tonight. Plain old moon ritual but good to observe. Keep
contact with the sky. Don't ever forget your relationship
with the sky.

A long black sundress fell over the curves of her strong
body, bare arms muscular as she raised the wand. Occasionally she passed her hand through her short, red curls,
touching one long ringlet at the back of her neck, absentmindedly pulling it down.

She was alone. The others who might have been there
with her on this night were busy, but it was important to
her to observe the moonrise. In five days, it would be huge
and yellow and full. August moon: ripening, gathering in
of a whole summer's work. But her work had not been
gardening.

Empty sky, deep blue tonight high over the black
shapes of the trees, the smell of pine still warm in the air.
Dogs barked down the road. Jesse Ryder liked the dark,
standing out in it, hidden and unseen. Relating to dark as a
presence. A being, an atmosphere.

Begin by breathing, just aware of breath; ready. She
stood directly in front of some stones that had been set in a
circle eight feet in diameter. In the middle of that circle a
hole several feet deep had been dug, a mound of dirt piled
next to it.

With her cedar wand she greeted the seven directions,
the proper start to any ritual: sky and earth, above and
below. Supporting and receiving. East, south, west, north.
Brother and sister spirits. Whoever was in the neighborhood. And the center, of course. The present. She whispered incantations, then lay down in the damp grass,
hands over her head, the prick of pine needles on her legs
and shoulders. Waiting to hear the voice of intuition.

After a time she sat up and took three candles from a
basket that had been placed on the mound of dirt, stuck
them in the ground, and lit them. The first match sputtered out. Holding a cedar branch in the flame, she knelt,

spinning it in the air around her. Closed her eyes, picturing what she would like to see actualized in the arc of days between this moment and full moon. The ritual completed. That was what she wanted. Completion. Full circle. A coming home. Convergence of disparate points like the redwoods overhead.

One of the candles blew out in the wind. She lay back again on the grass, legs extending out onto the dirt drive. *Artemis, the invoked. Horned huntress. Give me the power to bring them all together, to complete the cycle once begun. Let all the circuits hold.* Then the other two candles blew out. Just black now.

Suddenly a bike wheeled onto the driveway from the shadows and skidded to a halt. Jesse jumped up to a squatting position and screamed a short "Oh!"

"Mom?" An adolescent boy straddled the bike, shouting though he was only a few feet away from her. "Jeez, I almost ran over you! What are you doing lying out in the driveway?"

"Greeting the powers of earth and sky," she said, mostly to herself.

"Mom, it's night out here."

"That's the point!" she said. "That's when you're most likely to glimpse the moon."

"How can you expect me to have friends over? What if I was coming home from a date or something and wanting to park here in front of the house?"

"You don't even have your license yet," she said.

"But I will next year! I'm almost sixteen and my mother spends her Friday nights lying in the driveway in the moonlight and there's not even a moon out."

"It's coming. It hasn't risen yet, Ben." She tried to lower her voice. "Why are you shouting at me? I've asked you not to interrupt me when I'm doing rituals."

She watched the boy—barely fifteen, not *almost* sixteen, she thought—wheel the bike to the house, shaking his head. He leaned it against the porch behind some bushes and slammed inside. From his bedroom window the flicker of blue-gray light appeared. He'd be up late watching music videos.

Jesse Ryder rose and walked back to the house, flipped on a light switch in the kitchen. Sudden fluorescence. Ben stood at his bedroom door, blond hair windblown, thin boy-body—yes, still boy, she could count his ribs through the Tom Petty and the Heartbreakers T-shirt. Big feet in red Reeboks, black sunglasses. He slipped the glasses up on his forehead.

"Did you see the message I left?" Ben asked. "I left a note by the sink."

Oh perfect, she thought. *Just where I'd be likely to look for a phone message.* Jesse turned to the kitchen counter and saw where Ben had left the note on the windowsill above the faucet.

"Sorry I almost ran over you," the boy offered.

"No prob." She smiled at him, picked up the note and read, in Ben's scribbled writing, "Friday 4:00. Back from fishing. Dennis."

All right, she thought. *Just as he'd promised. My spell is beginning to work already.*

It was after midnight when Jesse turned out the reading light in the living room. She knelt near the far wall, inserted a plug into a socket, and a single line of blue neon blinked on, suspended from the ceiling overhead. Reaching around on the floor for the wires, she plugged several more cords into a long socket box, one by one, and the walls and ceiling lit up in a strange tangle of swirls and curves, blue and violet, yellow, magenta and green, some static, some zapping like beer signs crowded on the white walls of the house. She smiled.

Ben peered out of his room, half asleep, still wearing headphones. "Mom, you should have worked in an amusement park."

She lifted one of the earphones away from his head. "Life *is* an amusement park, dear."

"*Our* life is." He yawned. "Why couldn't you just be a regular artist?"

"I paint with light, okay? Just think of it as my job, just think of all this as food." She lifted a violet stem of glass down from the wall and held it over her head. She could hear the sound of the neon humming in the tube. "Check this one out, Ben. I just finished it yesterday." She held it out in front of her like a fencing sword, swirled it in a small circle, then walked to the front door, opened it, and stepped out into the wooded darkness, pulling a long orange extension cord behind her. Holding the rod of neon, she whirled it above her head, and it spun a violet sheath of light. The tube made a soft whistling sound as it whirred. "Isn't it going to be perfect?" she called out. Ben gave her thumbs-up and disappeared back into the house.

Even in the Berkeley days, Jesse Ryder had always thought of herself as an artist. At first she'd been a painter —watercolors, acrylics, flat oil surfaces, hallucinogenic cartoonlike paintings, then intricate acid-paisley designs. Poster art. But what she'd always liked most of all was the hanging of the paintings. What a painting did to the light in a room, how it changed a wall. In the years after she left Berkeley, when she was still in hiding in Mexico, then afterwards in Vancouver and L.A, she'd taken to hanging things. Hundreds of nails from transparent fishing line. Viewers in a gallery had to push their way through the nails, which rang like tinny chimes. Great swaths of cloth dyed yellow and crimson, curtains, walls of gauze separating people in a room. Sashes to pull so that the cloth raised up or pulled over, people ducking under them or being enclosed in small circular rooms made of curtains of whiter and whiter material. She'd done one room all of lace, satin, and nylon, stitching and hanging odd pieces, stretching them on frames made of steel tubes like lingerie on a jungle gym. She liked to create art that was three-dimensional, that invited people to enter, to participate. To be inside the work, not an outsider, not separate from the thing seen.

She'd first started working with neon in L.A. in the late seventies. But neon sculptures were always mounted on walls. Passive, she thought. Boring. She liked the idea of a single blue line suspended from the ceiling on a white cord. In her last show she'd made a whole ceiling of pink and blue swirls and hung them horizontally at different levels. The gallery visitors had to stoop slightly or make their way carefully through the lines like paths drawn in air. "Choosing Gender," she'd called that show.

But this installation coming up would be the best of all. For one thing it would be outside, not in some stuffy white gallery. Multicolored neon wands would be hung from limbs of redwoods and bay trees all over the yard, if only she could get this wiring straightened out. The first night of the installation would be a private ritual with her coven. After that it would be open for viewing through the September full moon.

In the center of the yard, near to where she was standing, would be a pool lined with copper, just in front of a huge burned-out redwood stump the size of a small playhouse. Around the pool a circle of pressed-wood logs would be lit, a ring of flames, and with any luck—*no, conjuring*—the night would be clear, full moon directly overhead, reflecting in the pool, the woods streaming with neon, solid and blinking, the circle of fire blazing under the trees. The installation was titled "Real and Imagined Light."

Early next week the women from her coven would meet to finish digging the pool, to cleanse the air for a sacred place. Now, if she could only keep Ben from riding his bike across the yard.

Jesse wedged the violet neon tube onto a set of hooks on a tree and walked across the yard to observe it from a distance. She entered a small garage that had been converted into a studio and pulled tangled cords into the center of the room, inserting the cords into a long plug box. The studio, too, was hung with neon designs. The yin-yang circles, half-moons, palm trees and stars made up a lot of her custom business. A large restaurant sign she'd been commissioned to make was lying in parts on a work table. And out in the night, at various points in the yard, were more tubes of neon dangling from the trees over-head.

Jesse stood at the door and put her hand on the power switch that would light all of them at once. She'd been working on the wiring for weeks now. She shoved the switch up, glancing out the door into the yard. The studio and the house across the way immediately went black.

She heard Ben yell from the house, "Mo-om!"

"Damn," she whispered. "Not enough power."

Chapter 4

In the guest bedroom upstairs Maggie closed the French doors that led out onto a small balcony. The August night was cool. From downstairs she heard a low saxophone riff moan down the scale. Rob had told her he liked to play when he was down, put on headphones and breathe along with Sonny Rollins, blow it all out through the gold keys and be done with it. Maybe his playing was making him feel better, but Maggie was terribly shaken—not only by the revelation of his suspicions but by the violent force of his reaction, the shouting, the wild mood swing. It was as if he were a different person from the man who had picked her up at the airport. Even though she was exhausted she knew it would take her hours to get to sleep.

She changed into her nightgown and sat in a wing chair, turning to a group portrait in Lora's album. The picture had been taken on the porch of the Berkeley house. An American flag hung behind them in the dining-room window. There was Lora in her thirties-style hat with the black veil, wearing, Maggie shuddered to see now, the India-print dress later given to Lily, the dress Lily died in.

Dennis wore his magician's costume—white gloves, top
hat. Jesse had pressed her cheek to Lora's, her eyes hidden behind silver Peter Fonda sunglasses, red hair tangled out in a wild bush from her angular face. And Quinn,
blond hair waving past his shoulders. Mischievous eyes
and that huge grin. Cody, perched on the porch railing
like a lanky bird. He wore a leather jacket he'd gotten
from a biker friend.

On the steps sat Sandy, String, and Lily, the three of
them so soon dead by the end of that summer. Sandy, hair
in braids, baggy jeans, a little overweight, the first of all of
them to bake bread, eat brown rice. String, gangly in a
flowered shirt. Lily, nondescript, wistful, peeking out
from behind String's shoulder. Maggie looked again. Rob
must have taken the picture. He was not in the portrait.
Always the outsider.

The house itself had been a duplex, two separate two-
story houses joined together, sharing an inner wall and a
sagging porch that faced College Avenue, a five-minute
bike ride from Telegraph Avenue, a ten-minute walk from
campus. The front doors had been painted orange and
plum, a silver peace symbol inscribed in model-airplane
paint on the window. It was obvious that the doors were
the only parts of the house that had been painted in years.
Sunflowers sprouted in creative anarchy all over the front
yard. They'd sit around a table made from a huge wooden
spool smoking from a blue bong, or lounge in Jesse's room,
which had been painted a deep rose.

Jesse and Cody were the ones who rented the house just
after Maggie's freshman year; during the following year
Lora also moved in. Maggie went often to the house, to
parties or simply to hang out after class, sleep over on the
old couch, stay up late listening to Sandy play the dulcimer while Jesse discussed alternative realities, magic being the thread that connected them to the everyday or
the combination to some universal lock which, if opened,
would reveal a realm of mysterious secrets.

Rob moved into the men's side of the house shortly

after Christmas of sixty-nine, having just finished his tour in Vietnam. He and Lora were very close, even though they hadn't lived together as a family since they were kids. Maybe that was why they were close—they'd only had each other. Their mother had been an alcoholic and their father a distant businessman who sold real estate in Dallas. Lora said Rob had joined the army to spite his father—anything but go into business with his father. Maggie remembered the day Lora picked Rob up from the airport and brought him back to the house. Everyone surveyed his uniform with the ribbons and medals and Lora said, "I'm real glad you made it home alive, big bro, but I hope to God you got something else to put on. That outfit isn't going to go over real big here in Berkeley."

Maggie had long been infatuated with both Lora and Jesse. They were both romantic, wild characters, very different from anyone she'd known in high school back in St. Paul. Jesse was lively and brilliant, a sort of outlaw. Even at Berkeley she stood out, sweeping into the student union in a blue velvet cape, brocade vest, white cowboy boots, her hair ballooning out in a crown, eyes a clear green, skin lightly freckled. Her beauty was partly a product of restraint—braces, nose job, she confided to Maggie —partly some sultry wildness, dramatized and exaggerated.

Walking into her room was like entering a human heart. Lace curtains, dyed black, hung at the large windows. An old lace tablecloth, also dyed black, draped over the bed in a canopy. Jesse would sit by the window wearing her red kimono. A low table at her side was covered with candlesticks, silver, glass, fat sand candles, a menorah with rainbow-striped candles. When she lit them all, the table glowed like a birthday cake.

Maggie also got to know Sandy that year. A quiet girl, Sandy was the earth mother of the house. She was serious about her studies in a way none of the rest of them admitted to being. A premed student with honors, Sandy wanted more than anything to become a surgeon. Her

face was plain and round, wire-frame glasses balanced on
the bridge of her small nose. As if to take a role opposite to
Lora and Jesse's counterculture glamour, Sandy became
the one who cooked and cleaned, the only one of the
women who cared anything about domestic chores. In
fact, she was a bit obsessive about it.

Maggie also got to know "the boys" before she actually
came to live in the house. Dennis was good-looking in an
impish way, his wispy sand-colored hair tied back in a
ponytail. Bright gray eyes set far apart gave him a catlike
appearance. He was dreamy and sweet, a surfer from
Santa Barbara, just up at Berkeley taking a few classes.
"I'm going to major in sunlight," he said. In his room a
collection of magic artifacts lined a tilting bookcase. One
night Maggie sat mesmerized as Dennis donned top hat
and white gloves and put on a show at the dining-room
table, card tricks, ball disappearing under plastic cups,
scarves into which anything would dissolve—cigarettes,
money, a bottle opener. Hand is quicker than the eye
stuff, wise-boy grin and constant rap. "See this? No, you
don't. You can't see reality because reality is made up of
air. In between atoms what is there? Space, ladies and
gentlemen. The essence of the universe. The elixir of
nothing. And what do we have right here in Berkeley?
Our very own linear accelerator splitting matter into its
zero essence, the true nature of Life," all the time dealing
the cards, shuffling them and smiling.

The three Roberts were initially harder for Maggie to
get to know. Robert Garson, Robert Cody, and Robert
Quinn: odd how they all had the same name, all of them
called after their fathers. Quinn was a photographer who
worked first for the campus paper, later for *The Berkeley
Barb*. He was the witness, the recorder, always a camera
around his neck, another in an army-green backpack,
black beret pulled down over shoulder-length hair. Bird
of paradise embroidered on the back of a work shirt by
one of many girlfriends. He almost looked like a girl himself, slender build, curve of waist, hipbones sharp under

low-riding bellbottoms. Pale eyes, dark lashes. The man
was a beauty. At first he'd made Maggie uncomfortable. It
was probably just that he was too aggressive, cock-sure,
and pretty. Just the kind of boy her brothers warned her
never to go out with. That black box lifted to his face.
Snap. Time lock. The truth of image. "Film doesn't lie,"
Quinn always said. Students outside the office of the university president. Panhandlers in the Haight. A young
woman, wrapped in a plaid blanket, asleep in People's
Park.

Cody, "Sound Man," was tall and thin with muscular
arms and a hawklike, delicate face, long nose and intense
blue stare, eyes half shut as if peering from someplace
deep in his skull, about to laugh at some raucous joke
known only to him. His hair, shiny and brown, swayed to
his shoulders. He'd sit cross-legged in his room, walls hung
with India-print bedspreads, hookah on a low table like
the Caterpillar in Wonderland, cataloguing his books in
alphabetical order or organizing pot seeds into baby-food
jars, labeling them by type, date, and country of origin. A
contemplative and yet clownlike man, he'd also been in
Nam, two years before Rob. He'd appear for Saturday
pancakes at the women's side of the house with his face
painted, already several hours into an acid trip and
mouthing his harmonica while the rest of them sipped
coffee. He rode a Harley Davidson, and sometimes Hell's
Angels would come around asking for him.

From the outside Maggie watched the household's romantic loyalties ebb and flow with lunar regularity. First
Jesse went with Dennis, next with Bob Quinn. Lora was
suddenly paired with Dennis. Cody dated different girls, a
biker in black leather—the one who gave him the jacket
—then a poet who wore men's hunting boots under her
long skirts. Rob and Sandy both seemed to be loners.

Late in the spring of her sophomore year a space
opened up in the house and Lora urged Maggie to move
in. Over Memorial Day weekend she carted in cardboard
boxes, hung flowered curtains her mother had sent and

spread a patchwork quilt on a mattress on the floor. That
night there was an impromptu dinner, no one cooking
exactly but food anyway—apples, cheese, bread, popcorn,
an eggplant casserole that tasted like grease and tomato
juice.

Maggie was given the chair of honor and they toasted
her. Someone put on Jimi Hendrix's "Angel." A Chinese
paper lantern lit the living room in a red glow. Lora
swirled in a long dress while Dennis performed card
tricks at the table. Cody slid whining notes from a harmonica. Sandy washed the dishes. For the first time since
she'd left Minnesota, Maggie felt truly at home.

That night as she was getting ready for bed, Quinn
wandered in. He was shirtless though it was cool, his yellow hair swaying over his shoulders. He sat down next to
her on the mattress. Maggie always thought he was attractive although he was a flirt, came on to everyone—arm
around her shoulder, hand smoothing her hair down her
back. She asked him where Jesse was, as if to more clearly
define his presence in the room.

"Asleep down the hall," he said. Then added, "You
know what? I want to kiss you."

Maggie didn't say anything. She even thought briefly,
that's the stupidest thing anyone's ever said to me. Aloud
she said, "I don't want you to."

"Why not?" he asked. Taking her hand, he turned it
over, stared at her palm as if to see some message there
that she could not possibly know.

She shrugged. "You're going with Jesse."

"Yeah?" he said. Almost a question. "We're friends. I
have a lot of friends."

"Oh, you do," she said. "That's nice. You mean you
screw around."

He smiled then, big flashy grin. "You don't even know
you're beautiful, do you?"

"No," she said, blushing.

"Well, hey, I just wanted to welcome you to the house.
We're one big family here."

"An incestuous one?"

He kissed her on the cheek, head pecking quickly at her face. "How's that for brotherly. Okay?" Taking her chin in his hand, he kissed her again, his tongue reaching into her mouth. "Now, was that so bad?"

Cocky son of a bitch, she thought. *Really thinks he's something.* He yanked a black beret from his back pocket, pulled it down over his hair, and left the room.

In spite of Quinn's flirtation and Jesse's extravagance, Maggie loved the people in that Berkeley house. She guessed everyone must have in their gray cells some memory area allotted to an idyllic youth. Those first weeks in the house were hers. Living on her own for the first time in an era that seemed both historical and charmed, in the wake of Woodstock and the Summer of Love, every day seemed an adventure—the night Dennis did magic tricks on the front porch and a stranger appeared out of nowhere to juggle oranges, disappearing without a word. The night they all took windowpane acid and filigreed Quinn's room with Day-Glo symbols Jesse had copied out of some book on alchemical formulas. One night they all piled into Sandy's rusty VW, sat until dawn on the beach singing Baez and Dylan songs, Cody on harmonica, Lora playing bells and maracas. Maggie kept a scrapbook of mementos that summer and everyone teased her about being the keeper of the archives, nicknaming her "Purey" after those clear crystalline marbles when Jesse claimed on a trip one night that Maggie glowed with white light just like an angel.

She tried to recall when it was that Jesse got into the witchcraft. No one took it seriously at first. It seemed playful, a way to be outlandish. Maybe she collected witch paraphernalia as a way of competing with Dennis's magic collection—dagger in a sheath, candles in every conceivable color, tall staff of polished wood, pentagram painted in Day-Glo yellow on her ceiling. She claimed she was preparing to join a coven over in the Haight.

"Magic is a state of mind," she said. "What you see is what you get."

"Magic is a trick," said Dennis. "Illusion. It's fooled perception."

"It's creating perception," she objected. "Anything on earth you see come into being, first it's up here"—she pointed to her crown of thick curls. "Visualized, seen in image, mind photo." Quinn snapping a picture just at that moment. "And with the proper attention cultivated by word—chant, spell, if you will—and ritual . . ." She pulled out the dagger and inscribed a circle in the air. "What you want will be yours. Love, power . . ."

"Satan," said Cody.

"It's not devil worship, Cody. It's pagan. The ancients revered the animal spirits in their celebrations because they needed animals to live. So they'd dress to dance in horns and skins and revel around a fire and get high, singing in the moonlight. When the church made the scene they didn't like the animal ritual so they called it evil. Made the goat-man into a figure of Satan. He was only Pan! A wood nymph!"

"I don't mess with invisibles," said Cody.

"I believe in facts." Sandy wiped the table as she spoke. "Empirical knowledge. The scientific method."

"You sound like the Bank of America," said Jesse.

"There's no bibbety-bobbety-boo. The universe has laws," she argued.

Quinn leapt up from his chair, crying, "All power to Chaos!"

"What about you, Lora?" Cody asked.

"Love," she drawled, kissing Dennis on top of his head. "That's all the magic I need."

"She means sex." Dennis laughed. "Tantra. The Kama Sutra. Me? I like knowing exactly how things work. The logic behind the illusion."

"That's what I'm talking about!" said Sandy.

Maggie preferred Jesse's definition. Her Catholic upbringing had attuned her to ceremony and ritual, but women had always been left out unless they were virgins. Perhaps she'd seen Jesse as her first priestess.

Jesse taught Maggie to make tiny amulets out of chamois skin and leather cord. They gave them to people in the house and created altars and shrines, arrangements of disparate objects for a purpose no one could guess. They painted the dining-room table purple, with silver glyphs from a book Jesse had borrowed from her coven.

Maybe it was Maggie's discomfort around Quinn, coupled with her attraction to him, that made her sleep with Rob. It happened quickly within a few weeks of her moving in. She trusted him; he was her best friend's brother. Of that first time, Maggie remembered that he was tender and that his body was thick, more manly than boys she'd made out with in cars. He was, after all, several years older than she, all of twenty-two. Their brief love lasted three weeks at most. A mental picture still remained: Rob in Golden Gate Park playing his saxophone, wearing his field jacket, dark curls under a black cowboy hat to which he'd affixed a plume. Another odd memory surfaced. One night as she lay down with Rob, the sounds of lovemaking emanated very loudly from the next room. Rob put a pillow over his head. "It's Dennis and Lora. Jesus, listen to them. Our closets are connected. Look." They'd crawled over and peeked through over a pile of shoes and boots, stifling laughter as they peered in at the shape rising and falling under an old chenille bedspread. "In your half of the house," Rob told her, "it's Sandy's and Jesse's rooms that are connected. I'd kill for a wall."

And then one day for no apparent reason Rob simply pulled back. He'd have nothing to do with her. For a week Maggie moped and Lora consoled her. "He's funny since Nam. Don't take it personally." Looking back, Maggie realized they had all been such kids, everyone playing out extremes. And she had so wanted to be like them, their abandon, flamboyance, and drama—but there was a way in which she was just too straight, the "Purey" of the group. Even though she dropped orange sunshine along

with the rest of them she remained apart, an observer.
There were times Maggie thought she'd have been better
off at some small Wisconsin college, dating a hockey
player.

It was sometime after Rob broke up with Maggie that
Jesse invited her to a coven meeting. "Don't go," Cody
said. "One witch around here is bad enough. A man can't
compete with two witches."

"Yeah," Jesse teased, "because we got blood magic. Men
have always been freaked by women's magic."

"You don't know anything about blood magic. What do
you know about sacrifice? You'd cry like a baby if you ever
cut your toe."

"I'm not talking about men's blood," she said. "Your old
hunting, territorial killing kind of blood. I'm talking re-
generative blood, sexual blood. Life-giving blood!"

"You're dangerous, Jesse. You think magic is just some
kind of kindergarten game, ring around the caldron. In
Nam, people's lives depended on magic. Man, somebody
would have a talisman and nobody could kill him. Sometimes it was a word or a phrase on a helmet, everything
from 'Beaucoup Crazy MF' to 'Soldier of God.' Those that
didn't have some kind of magic had to be plain lucky."

Just then Rob entered the room where they stood talking. "What was your magic in Nam, Garson?" Cody asked.

"Must have been luck," he said.

"Mine was this." Cody yanked a curved wallet out of his
jeans pocket, extended to Rob a cracked photograph between two fingers. Rob passed it to Jesse, then to Maggie.
"That's disgusting," Jesse said. It was a picture of a Viet-
namese man's head, severed from the body, lying on its
side, blank eyes open, gazing off to the side.

"This picture belonged to a buddy of mine who fought
at Hue. He gave it to me right before he left for home. It
saved his life and it saved mine. I can't tell you how. I
don't keep it because I'm proud of it. I keep it so I remember the insanity. You've got to understand the exact nature of insanity that looks perfectly sane."

Rob lifted the needle off a record that was playing and
the room went silent. "Cody, why don't you just forget all
that. You're home now."

"You can't forget it, Garson. At best you just hide it
somewhere back in your skull and walk around half invisible. When I got back I was a ghost for about a year. How
long you been back?"

"About seven months."

"You're still a ghost."

Maggie was disappointed at first that the meeting they
attended was not a real coven ceremony but only an open
meeting for prospective members. She'd walked around
the flat looking at various artifacts displayed on long tables
—a black bowl, several knives, one with a mother-of-pearl
handle, a lurid purple-satin cape, and some handouts
quoting from *The Book of Shadows.*

"It's kind of hokey," Maggie whispered to Jesse.

"Not when you know what it all means."

"Do you know what it all means?"

Jesse shook her head, then pointed to a tall man who
had just entered the room. "That's the high priest, Henry
Loam," she explained. He was an astonishing-looking man
with a silver beard, standing well over six feet. He wore all
black, and a knife was sheathed to his leg.

He seemed a dark presence, forbidding, playacting the
powerful priest with his penetrating gaze and resonant
voice. She could see he was a magnetic, charismatic person, but suddenly Maggie felt uneasy, not sure she wanted
to get involved anymore.

Halfway through his lecture about raising etherics
through the sexes practicing together, tuning their minds
and bodies to achieve the greatest success, Maggie slipped
out and waited for Jesse on the steps.

"What's the matter?" Jesse asked afterwards. "Are you
okay?"

"It's not my style," she said. "It's too much like church.
The rules are all set. I imagined it would be more open."

"You take what you like and you leave the rest," said
Jesse. "Don't listen to Cody."

The magic continued for a time, Maggie and Jesse playfully experimenting with simple candle spells, amulets
filled with herbs and gems, Lora moon-eyed over Dennis,
and Sandy fastidiously cleaning out cupboards and closets.
It was a time that seemed innocent, a kind of garden
before the fall, but it wasn't long before the ripe summer
gave way to decay and it seemed to happen, now that
Maggie looked back, when Peter String and Lily came to
stay. They'd only lived in the house a few weeks before
they died and Maggie hadn't known them well, yet she
could picture them as she'd found them on that cool July
morning, a memory still intact as any mummy in a tomb:

*At first she thought they were sleeping, String facedown
on the faded rug in an upstairs bedroom. No shirt, shoulders a little broken out. Lily, in a paisley India-print
dress, sprawled on the overstuffed chair, her neck thrown
back. That's what seemed so strange. No one could sleep
that way.*

*Maggie was never able to get it out of her mind, the
angle of Lily's head. It was early morning. She was only
looking for her hairbrush, misplaced the night before.
Maggie went over to Lily to ease her into a more comfortable position. Later she thought it was odd, something
you'd only do to a child, the way she bent down, hands
carefully on Lily's neck to lift her, the skin cold, head too
heavy, eyes rolled back, mouth too slack for sleep.*

*She dropped Lily and let out a cry. "String?" she whis-
pered, knowing even before she turned him, pushed at his
thin ribs, the long hair covering his face, same empty look
in the eyes, but vomit dried on his lips. Sweet rotten
stench, his skin bluish, also cold. She'd never forget that.*

*For several minutes she just stood frightened, as horri-
fied as if she herself had done it, as if it were her fault, and
now, looking back, she knew that in some way that was
true. There was some way in which all of them were guilty
—Dennis, Rob, Cody, Quinn and Jesse, even Lora. Even*

herself. Maggie had not understood it then, nor did she really understand it now.

She snapped on the light in Rob's guest room—2:00 A.M.—and wondered if she'd slept some, a restless black-out that left her more tired than if she'd stayed awake. What could Lora have been trying to tell her with that shadow box? She slipped on a robe and descended the stairs, pausing to turn the dial, lighting the chandelier to a pale glow. The shadow box was still on the table by the couch, but where was the magnifying glass? Rob must have put it back in his office. She wanted to examine the box and the album again, looking for similarities she might have overlooked, other codified phrases she might have missed in the tiny hieroglyphics. Stepping around the corner into the den, she flicked on the green desk lamp. It appeared to be Rob's home office, legal books, files stacked neatly on the rosewood desk. *Now, where did he put that thing?*

Maggie sat at his desk, sliding open drawers of paper clips, rubber bands, stationery. In the last drawer she shuffled through a stack of *National Geographics* and some manila folders and felt the cold metal before she actually saw it—a small black pistol hidden at the bottom of the drawer. She reached down to pick it up but didn't, her heart loud in her chest.

An Oriental armoire took up the wall across from the desk. Maggie crossed to it and swung open the doors. An entire collection of shotguns and rifles was neatly displayed in racks. On the wall next to the armoire gold and silver medals for marksmanship were mounted on a black frame. *So what,* she told herself. *So he's a gun collector. He was in the army. There's no law against someone having a gun.*

She leaned back against the desk. It was just that she was so tired, everything seemed so complicated and opaque. She glanced down at the stack of file folders and saw one marked LORA MAYHEW ESTATE. The typed pages

and scribbled notes inside were full of confusing legalese,
but there was one sentence that loomed out at her from a
small white pad: "Amount in Lora's estate if codicil admitted, $1,879,473 as of 8/1/86." But Lora had told Maggie in
the Caymans that her trust fund money was running very
low; that was why she'd been working at the gallery.

Maggie shivered as she shut the doors to the armoire
and snapped out the light. It was clear Rob had so much
more to tell than he was letting on and she was tired of
being the subtle questioner, the good listener. Tomorrow
she wanted him to tell her everything he knew. If he
wouldn't, maybe the police would. *And another thing,*
she thought. *I want to go back to the Berkeley house.
Lora's letter suggested she knew something about those
deaths, or at least was connecting her own fears back to
the bad magic.* Maybe the people who owned the house
now could tell her something about Lora's visit there.

If Lora had been murdered, Maggie wanted it all out in
the open. *What was that children's rhyme? No more
secrets, no more lies?* She'd always disagreed with the
biblical myth that knowledge was a sin. She'd seen in her
practice that what was hidden and denied was the real sin,
a kind of lying that sometimes killed.

Chapter 5

In her dream Maggie wandered the white corridor searching for Lora. She knew Lora was behind one of the blank, closed doors. When she found her in a hospital bed, she pulled back the white sheet, but Lora was already old, her face creviced with wrinkles, white hair tangled as angel hair, eye sockets sunken to bone. The doctor came in and prepared to give Lora a shot. As he leaned down to inject her, Maggie saw that the doctor was Dennis. She reached to knock the hypodermic from his hand; he lunged at her, pushing her down, holding her arm, pressing the needle against Maggie's forearm. She tore away from him, ran down a tunneled hall. At last she found the fire alarm lever and yanked it down, the bell screaming into the emptiness.

Maggie jerked awake, tangled in the sheets. The phone at her bedside was ringing, and down the hall she could hear the spray of the shower. Rob was up, but he couldn't hear the phone.

"Hello?" she said. The web of the dream was still stuck to her thoughts. Her words felt thick in her mouth. "Hello?"

But no one spoke. "Rob Garson's residence," Maggie prompted. There was only silence followed by a soft click, the dial tone humming back on the line. Maybe it was a wrong number, Maggie thought, but as she rose to put on her robe she remembered what Rob had told her last night, that before Lora died, she'd started getting odd phone calls just like that. A coincidence? But there had just been too many of those in the last few days.

Rob was out of the shower now; she could hear him dressing, slamming drawers, then rattling around in the kitchen downstairs. She got in the shower, and as she let the hot water lash her face, she resolved to talk firmly and directly to Rob this morning, no tiptoeing around the subject. But her stomach felt anxious, thoughts whirling loudly in her head, and she knew when she'd last felt this. Obsessive thinking, unable to get out of the endless circling. It had been after Mark had died.

They'd been married since 1975, most of it happy, only the usual ups and downs of any close relationship. Mark had been a commercial artist, but the year before the accident he'd received a grant to pursue his first love: pen and pencil drawings, large-scale images on beautiful handmade paper, natural objects blown out of proportion, curled leaves, broken shells, stones. He'd taken the year off to draw and was riding to a cabin a friend had lent him up near the Boundary Waters Canoe Area when his motorcycle left the road on a straightaway. He'd been found shortly thereafter by a farmer. The doctors said he died instantly.

Maggie had just begun the hospice work at that point, and it was nearly impossible to maintain a professional distance from her clients. Yet in some way Mark's death helped her understand the people she worked with much more deeply. *I'm going through this too,* she told them. *I understand.* But there was so much she didn't understand. Therapists could not always see their own predicaments as clearly as those of their clients. But one thing she had been able to observe about herself was that her grieving had taken the form of an almost obsessive desire to know what had happened to Mark. Why had the bike left the road on a clear day on a good road? Had a bug gotten in his eye, had he swerved to avoid an animal, had he fallen asleep? Could he have done it on purpose? Over and over the thoughts multiplied, like horrible insects crawling through her waking hours, infesting her dreams. *I have to be careful,* Maggie thought, *because that's just how I feel this morning about Lora's death. I want clarity, not obsession.*

Rob sat in the kitchen, drinking coffee. He wore black jeans and an oversized blue chambray shirt. He offered her a cup of coffee and she took a deep breath, preparing to question him, preparing for his best trial attorney evasiveness too.

"Rob, I was up half the night thinking about Lora," she began.

"Wait a minute," he interrupted, setting his cup in the sink. "So was I. And I realized that I was very rude to you, Maggie, and I'm really sorry. I didn't mean to be. It's just that this whole thing has been such a strain. And what with her body turning up . . . Please understand—I haven't talked about this to anyone but the police. I guess I was torn last night because I wasn't sure how much to say to you. It isn't that I don't trust you, believe me. I don't want to jeopardize their investigation and I don't want Dennis to know what's going on. I'm afraid he might bolt or something."

"Please tell me what you know."

He held up his hand. "I'm going to tell you everything. I can't keep this in anyway. Sometimes I feel like I'm going to explode with it all."

Rob suggested they go for a walk, and they slipped on jackets, heading down the incline of the street toward the Haight. He began talking immediately.

"At first the case was classified as a missing-person's file. The Marin County Sheriff's Office was very thorough, very professional. The detective in charge of the case is a guy named Sergeant Tom Beale. A very good man, very sincere. Throughout the entire search and investigation no one even mentioned foul play. All the evidence pointed to an accident." Rob rattled off the information and observations as if they were facts he'd gathered for a trial. "Lora had gone out on the boat before. She had Dennis's permission. She had access to the keys, so it wasn't a theft. A man at a gas station in Inverness was the last person to see her alive—he said she was alone. When she radioed in that she was having trouble, the fisherman who picked up on the call asked if Dennis was with her. She said no. She was having trouble with the boat, but she said nothing that indicated anyone was with her or that anyone was threatening her. She was alone out there, Maggie. She went out there by herself, under her own will. Dennis reported her missing as soon as he knew about it. He had an alibi, he was with Quinn all weekend. He cooperated fully in the search."

Rob's steps kept pace with his rapid-fire speech. They crossed over Haight Street, a strange mixture of time-warp sixties memorabilia and already-dated eighties punk. There was a shop selling Nehru shirts, dove medallions, John Lennon glasses. Video stores and The Gap were right in there with Uganda Liquors and St. Vincent de Paul. A man with long Rasta locks stood contemplating a pyramid of tomatoes. A woman with pink cotton-candy hair strode by wearing an old bridal dress and ankle-high tennis shoes. Maggie and Rob continued down toward the Panhandle, that strip of green boulevard that ran all the way to Golden Gate Park.

"With no boat to examine, no body," Rob went on, "there was no evidence to support a homicide investigation. I talked to Beale about it, I told him about Lora's strange behavior in the weeks prior to her disappearance, told him to check Dennis out, but I had no proof or anything. Neither did they. No motive: they kept stressing that."

They found a wooden bench and sat down. Near them a man in shredded jeans worked the grass with a metal detector. "Surely the difficulty in their marriage was a motive," she said. "The possibility of her having a lover . . ."

"I told Beale all of that, but he pointed out that couples fight all the time. Discord in their marriage was not ample evidence to classify Lora's death as a homicide."

"What about a life insurance policy?" Maggie asked.

"Zip. The strange thing was that Lora didn't leave Dennis much money at all, only about fifteen K." *Right,* thought Maggie, thinking of the file on his desk. Rob went on. "Neither of them had life insurance and their house had a second mortgage on it. The boat had a business policy, though. Dennis did get a new boat, but he gave it a different name this time—*Grace.* After Slick, of course."

Maggie decided to bait him a little. "I thought Lora still had quite a large trust fund coming to her, Rob. She talked about it when we met in the Caymans. Wasn't she to have inherited something like a million dollars when she turned forty?"

"Yes. Gram established trust funds for me and Lora and our cousin, Andrea. We got some of the money at eighteen, another chunk at thirty, and the remainder was set to come to us at age forty. Well, Lora and money—you know, Maggie—she basically spent it. Trips, cars, the beach house, the boat. She gave half of it away. Turns out she didn't have much left. Neither did Andrea. They went to Gram and tried to talk her into changing her will so they could have access to their trust funds sooner. Gram never did anything about it. Then Lora died. About three months later Gram died. Stroke. Last January."

Okay, he's coming clean. She felt relieved. "I'm sorry to hear that," she said. "First Lora and then Gram."

"Yeah, it was hard. Is hard. Anyway, Andrea and her husband were cleaning out Gram's house and they found a codicil to the will changing the last age of the trust fund payments back to thirty-five—just what Lora and Andrea had lobbied for. The codicil just surfaced a month ago. It would have been found sooner, but it was months before the house was cleaned out for the estate sale."

Maggie mentally calculated Lora's age. "And Lora was thirty-five when she died."

"That's just the thing. She'd already turned thirty-five, so legally, if the codicil is honored, that million—actually it's more than that, closer to two—has to be considered part of her estate."

"Which Dennis will inherit," said Maggie, continuing his thought. "But why didn't Gram just go ahead then and give Lora the money on her birthday?"

"I don't know. Gram was pretty spaced in those last months. The stroke that killed her was actually her second. There's some question of how lucid she was and whether the codicil will be admitted to probate."

"Did Lora know about the codicil? Did Dennis?"

"That's what I don't know. If she had known, I think she'd have pressed to get the money the second she turned thirty-five. If Dennis knew, he had one terrific motive for murder."

Maggie put her hand over her eyes and shook her head.

"There's more," Rob continued. "Without assurance of death he couldn't inherit the money. Had her body not been found, Dennis would have had to wait seven years until the presumption of death could be affirmed. That's the law."

"So first the codicil surfaces, then Lora's body turns up."

"Rather coincidental, I'd say."

"What do the police think?"

"They're resisting the idea of classifying the case as a homicide. Or hesitant about it. It's so slow, so bureaucratic. They're waiting until they finish examining the remains. That's why I was so closed-mouthed when we talked last night. Everything is so up in the air. I just don't want anything to go wrong."

"But how does the shadow box fit into all of this? I was

thinking that I'd like to go over there, back to the Berkeley house, to talk to the woman who gave it to Lora."

"Okay," he said, "but you can't breathe a word of this to anyone—not the woman at the house, not Quinn, not Cody. They're both still close to Dennis—Quinn especially so. Promise me you'll keep this in complete confidence, will you, Maggie?"

"You have my word," she said.

They headed back up through the Haight, past old houses with flaking paint and newly painted Victorians, geraniums dangling from the roofs. As they neared the house, Maggie realized that she had now been pulled into the secret-keeping. It felt almost conspiratorial, and she wondered how it would be when she saw Quinn and Cody later that day and Dennis tomorrow. *It will still be important to try to be objective,* she thought. *And almost impossible.*

Chapter 6

Maggie opened the car door and stepped out onto the shaded sidewalk facing the old house across College Avenue. She used to imagine that she would come back here someday and see her young self looking out the window at her. She'd always wondered how she'd turn out. Maggie suddenly saw herself from the outside, pushing up the sleeves of her cotton sweater, baggy beige pants slim at the ankles, a small leather bag hung over her chest, dark curls blown across her face in a sudden gust.

She was both more and less than she had hoped to be at thirty-six. Her life was more serious and interesting, perhaps, what with her practice, her studies, and travels. She was more independent—a homeowner, an investor. But she was also a bit less—maybe less happy, maybe too alone. She'd always assumed that by this age she'd be surrounded by a flock of curly-haired kids in a big house on Crocus Hill in St. Paul. It wasn't a question of feeling complete or not—she certainly rejected the notion that one had to have children. It was just that she'd found herself longing more and more for the complications of intimacy again and for the comfortable noise of the big family she'd grown up in.

Rob came around the side of the car and stood next to her. "Well, there it is."

"For so long I thought it was just a place in my head," she said.

The house had been painted gray with off-white trim, the old porch removed, a cedar deck built on the side. The wild garden that had sprawled through the yard had been sodded over. It looked like a regular house, not the strange Day-Glo palace of ruins she remembered, American flags in the windows, Jesse's black lace curtains. Mao was gone from the front door. In its place there was a blue-eyed police-protection sticker and a brass knocker.

Maggie crossed College Avenue and waited for Rob to follow. She stood for a moment on the deck, feeling the odd dislocation of present and memory, then knocked. Inside a dog barked and a woman's voice called, "Settle down, Max, settle down." The door swung open. "Yes?"

She was not much older than Rob and Maggie, her hair cut short, peppered with gray. Her torn sweatshirt fell off one shoulder and a young child hid behind her knees.

Maggie introduced herself and Rob, then told her, "We used to live in this house, years ago when we were students. Back in sixty-nine, seventy."

The woman laughed. "You won't believe how often people come by saying that. I ought to charge admission. This house must have been pretty historic."

"It was," said Rob. "As a matter of fact, one of those other people might have been my sister. She mentioned that she stopped by here. It would have been last fall. September, wasn't it, Maggie?"

"You'd remember her," said Maggie. "Her name was Lora Mayhew, long black hair, probably braided down the back. Texas accent, beautiful, small features . . ."

"Wait, I have a picture," said Rob. He opened his wallet and took out a cracked, dated picture of Lora. "It's pretty old," he said.

"You gave her this," offered Maggie, extending the shadow box to the woman, who by now had picked up the toddler and was cradling him on her hip. She took the box and glanced at it.

"I remember, yeah. Sure. We'd just bought the place and I found that in the basement. But something about it looks different now."

Maggie looked at Rob, then back at the woman. "Like what?" Maggie asked.

The woman shrugged. "I can't put my finger on it. But she just loved the thing, kept telling her friend about some girl she'd known in college who was a witch."

"Friend?" asked Maggie.

"Yeah, a big guy, not tall but big. Big in the chest. He had short brown hair, a beard. At first I thought he was a professor, he had that kind of look. But he said he was an importer, just like she was. That's it. I remember because they got to admiring some of the things we'd brought back from Thailand and Burma when we were there two years ago. No—three years, now." The woman gestured behind her at a large Asian tapestry on a wall. "Your sister gave me her card. So did her friend—said if we ever went back to the Far East we should contact them. Maybe we could do some buying for them. What's all this about anyway?" she asked.

"She's away on one of her long buying trips," Rob lied. "We found this at her house and just got curious."

How easily that little lie slipped out, Maggie thought. He wanted to keep the investigation a secret; it wouldn't have done to have told the woman the truth. But even though he had finally told Maggie what was really going on, she noticed how smooth he was in deception, his voice intelligent, assured.

"You wouldn't still have those business cards, would you?" asked Rob.

"Sure. Oh, sure I do. Hey, come on in. Would you like some coffee or something? Yeah, I kept the cards because after they left we started tearing down walls and renovating and I found some more old stuff I thought she might be interested in. Wait here, I'll get it."

Rob and Maggie stood in the living room of what had once been the women's side of the house, and Maggie was surprised to feel possessive about the room, almost angry that it had been changed. The window sills, stripped of blue and red paint, were now a beautiful blond wood, walls painted a dusty mauve, ivory Berber rug, Levolor blinds, low gray couch, lots of books. It was fine, really. Quite nice. The big front window had been replaced by French doors, grilled panes. A glass table stood where their spool-table had been, where they'd sat night after night eating those bowls of lentil soup.

Maggie shook her head. "It's like seeing some ancient relative that you thought was a monster, meeting him years later, realizing he's just some scrawny old man. Harmless."

The woman returned carrying a large shopping bag, which she set on the coffee table. "Yeah, we were tearing some more walls out upstairs. My husband is an architect —he can't leave a house alone. We gutted the whole second floor. God, we found all kinds of stuff in a wall between two rooms. Do you remember how some of the bedrooms were joined together by a closet? Over the years someone had built walls to close them off. We were hammering away, sledging everything down, dust everywhere—and here was this cache of . . . God, everything —old books, jewelry, snapshots, and another of those little boxes. I kept all the stuff we found, I don't even know why. I can't throw anything out. Look." She lifted out a second shadow box. "Maharishi, a mounted butterfly, banana rolling papers, a masthead from *The Berkeley Barb*, and a 'Hell No—We Won't Go' button. Real sixties souvenir. If my husband wasn't such a fanatic about design, I'd have put it up somewhere."

Rob was going through the shopping bag, pulling out books: *Be Here Now, Siddhartha, Childhood's End*, a

poster of Sitting Bull. The child had taken a string of
meditation beads from the bag and was sucking on them.

"What about the business cards?" Maggie asked.

"Oh, yeah. Right over here." The woman fumbled
through a desk drawer and found them tucked into a
small address book. She handed them to Maggie. Lora's
card read simply, "Quinn Gallery, Folk Art Imports, Sausalito. Lora Mayhew, Buyer and Consultant." On the second card was a name Maggie didn't recognize. "Phillip
Dodd. Third World Imports." The card listed a Berkeley
address and phone number. Maggie handed it to Rob,
who read it and shrugged.

"I don't remember Lora ever mentioning him," he said.
"If he's an importer, Quinn might know him."

"That's about it," the woman went on. "Honey, put
those back." She grabbed the beads from the child and
tossed them in the bag. He started to cry. "I'd better feed
him," she said. "Here—it's all yours. I like to trip back too.
Same era. University of Colorado, Boulder, sixty-nine. I
remember when the SDS chapter took over the student
government and voted to change the Glenn Miller Ball-
room in the student union to the Ball Karl Marx Room.
Those were the days, right?" She handed Maggie the bag
stuffed with junk and said a friendly good-bye. They
walked out to the car.

Maggie crossed College Avenue, set the bag on the sidewalk, and squatted down, fingering through the layers
until she found, at the bottom, a portfolio tied with brown
string. As she opened it, Rob looked over her shoulder.
Polaroid snapshots—small, square pictures, slightly out of
focus.

"Are they Quinn's?" asked Rob.

"I don't know. Quinn always shot with a thirty-five mil-
limeter, didn't he?" Maggie stared at the one of Lily,
asleep on the chair, her head tilted back. "Jesus," she said.
"I could swear this was taken the morning Lily died. That
dress, the way she's lying back on that chair. I swear it is,
Rob." The next picture was of Peter String, his cheek to

the ragged Oriental rug. The angle of the camera close down, aiming directly at his face.

Maggie handed the shapshots up to Rob and looked at the next one: Sandy, mouth open, eyes rolled back in her head.

"Sandy too," he breathed. "So somebody took pictures of them after they were dead and hid them in the walls? I don't get it. You're right, though—I don't recall Quinn having a Polaroid."

"That doesn't mean he didn't have one. But why? Why would anyone take these?"

He shook his head.

"We should give them to the police, Rob. Along with the shadow box and the letter."

"But what will they make of them?"

"I don't know, but it's their job to figure that out. And what about this 'friend,' this Phillip Dodd? Could he have been Lora's lover? Maybe we should stop by this address and talk to him. It can't be too far from here."

"Slow down," said Rob. "We've got no business going to this guy's house, even if he did have something to do with Lora. We might screw up the whole investigation that's going on now. Look, tomorrow we've got this brunch out at Dennis's. Monday morning I've got a meeting with Dennis and the lawyers about this will business. Then let's go talk to Beale, together, Monday afternoon. Until then I'd like to just watch Dennis, without him being aware of it."

"Monday seems too far off. Couldn't we at least call the police and tell them what we've found?"

After a moment he nodded in agreement. "Yes, we could. I just don't want to get in the way. They might have enough evidence to arrest Dennis after they finish the forensic examination, and I don't want to throw in something that's completely extraneous."

"I don't see this as completely extraneous," she argued. "These deaths might all be tied together in some way. Anyway, you can't keep holding things back. The police

should have every bit of information they can possibly get
their hands on, even if it seems insignificant."

"You haven't been working with them, Maggie," he
said. "They're earnest and everything, but they're not
interested in every single detail. I told you, they totally
rejected my initial suspicions about Dennis until this will
thing started to point toward a believable motive. That's
why I'm trying to be so careful. Do you understand? I just
don't want to blow it."

Maggie set the bag in the car and shut the door with a
clank. Maybe it was just that she'd never talked to the
police herself. She really had no idea how they'd proceed
with this, but it all sounded so slow, overly cautious. She
would feel better when she'd talked to them, but she
supposed she could wait until Monday. "Okay," she said.
"Let's go down to Telegraph Avenue as long as we're
here."

As they walked, Maggie thought about how difficult it
was to read Rob. One minute he was confessing his deep-
est suspicions, the next minute he seemed ambivalent and
secretive. She wondered what it was that Quinn had
wanted to tell her. Even though she'd pressed Rob to tell
her everything he knew, she still felt there was something
more that he'd neglected to reveal. At the same time
she'd have to be careful in questioning Quinn. What if it
was Quinn himself who'd taken those photographs?

From the corner house they headed down toward the
avenue, then toward the campus past bookstores and cof-
feeshops, Moe's, Shakespeare's. Street vendors tended tables laden with earrings, pottery, crystals, handmade
clothing, and shawls. Maggie stopped to buy a violet scarf
shot through with metallic threads and tied it like a head-
band around her flying hair. She didn't care if she looked
like a thirty-six-year-old therapist who'd once dropped
acid at a Grateful Dead concert and would never recover
no matter how much she had in her money market fund,
no matter how many aerobics classes she took. Her
shadow self walked beside her like a dream, young and

frightened, high and in love, committed to the self-determination of all third-world peoples. She was gladdened by the man begging for spare change on the corner, the scruffy students staring into the window of a comic-book store. She walked slowly next to Rob, thinking of Jimi Hendrix, Diane Di Prima, Grace Slick, Ram Dass, all their lost heroes and heroines, saints and patrons, their poets, their muses.

Nasturtiums, pine smell. They walked the campus with its peaceful white buildings, passing through the green gate with the naked male and female figures cast in concrete, and the fishbowl lamps at the tops of the pillars, and it all seemed smaller somehow, smaller and much more steady in her vision than when she had walked here so long ago. Stopping back at a café, they took a window seat and ordered espresso. Rob rested his arms on the table. Maggie looked at her watch.

"So we're meeting Quinn and Cody for dinner in Sausalito?" Rob didn't answer, simply stared down at the salt shaker, distracted. "What is it?" she asked. "Is there something else, Rob?"

"There is, but it has nothing to do with Lora." Rob cleared his throat, and a waiter set two small white cups before them. "I've thought about this a long time, but I never had a chance to tell you. I never saw you—I kept thinking you'd come out here to visit Lora. . . . There's no right time, so I'll just make a fool of myself and get it over with. I just wanted to say I'm sorry I was such an asshole back then. Running away like I did, back when we were—when we were lovers. Maybe you don't even remember." He laughed nervously.

"Of course I do." Maggie dropped a sliver of lemon peel into the espresso.

"I guess I wasn't ready." He was quiet awhile. "Anyway, I acted badly. I always wanted to apologize. I had a long talk with Lora about it once. I wanted her to tell you for me but she refused. It was hard for me to get close to anyone because of Nam. It wasn't because of you. I just wanted you to know, for whatever it's worth. I was numb back then. Maybe I still am to some degree. At least I know it now." He looked down into his cup, relieved, his cheeks flushed.

Maggie sipped the espresso, embarrassed in some way by his urge to apologize for the inadequacies of his young self, but she, too, felt a little relieved, suddenly closer to Rob in a way she had not been before. Maybe the vacillations in his moods went far deeper than she really knew, the reticence part of the very fabric of his being, not an intentional evasiveness.

"Robert, I accept your apology. But I want you to know it was all your fault that I ended up almost marrying Quinn!"

"Hey, I'm not taking credit for that fiasco!"

They both laughed then.

"I do feel better," he said. "That's been in the back of my mind for ages."

"Are you a free man now?"

"Very free, very easy. Very much a Berkeley kind of guy."

"What about your other relationships?" she asked. "I feel as if I know so much more about you than I should. Lora told me everything about your divorces. I hope I'm not being too snoopy."

"No," he said. "It's actually good to talk. Lora was about the only one I ever confided in. Yeah, I've been married twice. Great track record, right? My first wife, Kathy, was the interior designer for the house. She fixed it up and moved right in. That lasted about four years. I guess I was preoccupied with work. She claimed I was emotionally absent. Within months of the divorce, I married Sheila. She was just graduating from law school. I see now that I rushed into that one trying to fill the proverbial void. You know, I think I always married the idea of marriage, not really a specific person. I had some fantasy of married life, but I never really knew how to do it. My family always lived apart. When things got rough, I never knew what to do, how to work anything out.

"But it's not like I'm a basket case or anything. I actually like single life. I play sax in a little jazz group now and then. I still like target shooting, doing some hunting in the fall out in Montana—Cody comes along once in a while. And I do go out—I'm dating this woman who owns a kite shop. She's been out of town for the last week—actually she was supposed to get back in last night. It's nothing serious, but it's nice."

"Maybe that was who called this morning," said Maggie. She explained about the phone call with no one there. "Maybe she thought you had a woman over."

"I did." He smiled.

He was quiet for several minutes, then said, "You know, after my folks died, Lora was all the family I had. Every holiday, Thanksgiving, Christmas, we tried to re-create some kind of closeness we never had as kids. Dennis was part of it too. That's why this is all so fucked up. Dennis and I were like brothers." He held up two fingers pressed together. "I can hardly look at him straight now. Not only have I lost Lora, but I've lost Dennis too."

"What would Dennis do," she asked suddenly, "if he knew you suspected him?"

"I don't know," he said. "I get the feeling sometimes that he does know. Like he's watching me too." Rob shot a glance over his shoulder through the café window as if he thought Dennis might appear in a puff of smoke on Telegraph Avenue. Then he looked back at Maggie and stared down into his cup. "I'll tell you one thing though," he said. "I'm ready for him."

Chapter 7

"**Y**ou look like you were talking to a ghost," said Ben.

Jesse had just hung up the phone. "Something like that," she said. "Some old friends of mine are getting together for a party."

"You sound real excited, Mom," said Ben in a flat, teasing tone.

She turned around to look at her son. "It's hard to explain. Sometimes you try to leave things behind, but they stay with you a long time."

"Mom, please don't start talking about karma, okay?"

It was Saturday and there was a lot to be accomplished. Jesse dressed in tight black sweatpants cut off at the calf, flat boots, and a blue satin T-shirt. She drove down into Fairfax in her dusty red pickup. The town was just far enough north of the city to feel nearly rural at times, at least for the Bay Area. As she came down out of the shaded hills into the sunny streets, she smiled. *Sun,* she thought, *what goddess do I have to thank for this?* For three weeks northern California had been blanketed in fog, and now the damp weight had finally lifted. Clarity boded well, the ritual only a few days off. She hoped the sky would stay open for the full moon.

Jesse went on her errands, stopping in at Patrick's Bookshop and Café, stepping over a German shepherd asleep in the doorway. She picked up croissants at a bakery. At the hardware store she spoke with a man who knew a trick or two about outside wiring, but she couldn't get her mind off what Dennis had told her when she'd called him back that morning: *Maggie Shea was in town.* All of the old group were back and Dennis was having them out to the house tomorrow—why didn't Jesse drop in, he suggested, unannounced? "Surprise the hell out of everyone. Lighten things up."

But Jesse wasn't sure she wanted to go. Certainly she'd love to see Maggie. But she'd fled that group, that life, and the person she'd been then, fled in shame and fear years ago. Perhaps it had been silly to have run away, maybe nothing would have happened. Maybe no one else would have died; maybe no one would have blamed her.

Still, if she was going to continue to date Dennis, surely she'd be seeing Quinn and Cody and Rob sooner or later and the brunch tomorrow might be just the right time. See them all at once and be done with it. Dennis confessed he'd already told Quinn he was going out with her anyway. What was there to hide?

Ben had arranged to spend Saturday night with his friend Milo. Jesse had called Zoë, Milo's mother, to make sure it was all right. "Sure," said Zoë. "You've got enough on your mind with the ritual coming up and everything." Zoë, a lawyer who had a small practice in Mill Valley, was also in her coven. So as Jesse headed home, on impulse she turned west and drove the winding road through Laguanitas toward the ocean. She wanted to talk to Dennis in person. He said he'd be up at the house most of the day or down at the wharf in Bolinas, working on his boat.

It had been strange enough seeing Dennis again in the first place. A couple of months ago when Jesse and Ben

had gone over to Bolinas on a Sunday to check out a flea
market she'd run into him. He was perched out on the
porch steps of the bakery beside a fat man in overalls.
When he saw her, he leapt up, astonishment lighting his
face, and came down the steps to embrace her. "Jesse
Ryder!" he nearly shouted. "I never expected to see you
again. Goddamn!" He stepped back from her. "We heard
you were living down in Mexico."

Dennis had changed very little. He had a rough,
friendly face, each feature just slightly off center, and he
appeared rumpled in a blue flannel shirt and jeans. His
body was still that of a young man, slender, almost
bouncy. He seemed so energetic, shifting from foot to foot
in red sneakers, and when he took off his baseball cap, his
sandy hair spiked up in a short cut, though he'd left it long
in the back. His skin was deeply tanned, his cat-eyes
gleaming. He was obviously delighted to see her.

"Whatever happened to you?" Dennis asked. "You just
disappeared. Where have you been all this time?"

"I was down in Mexico for a while. I moved around—
Canada, L.A. I had a kid." She gestured toward Ben, who
stood down on the sidewalk balancing on a skateboard.
"Meet Ben. Ben, this is Dennis."

They nodded at one another. "Married?" Dennis asked.

"No, I never did get married. I heard you did though. Is
Lora here?" Jesse glanced past him through the bakery
door.

Dennis suddenly seemed uncomfortable, and the fat
man clapped a hand to his back, saying he'd see him later
at the dock.

Dennis turned back to Jesse and said simply, "Lora's
dead."

She shut her eyes for a moment, thinking he had to be
kidding, but no one would make a joke of his wife's death.
Not Lora, she thought. She'd seen enough people die
young back in Berkeley, and it was always difficult to
believe.

As he told her about the accident she took hold of his

hand. "Dennis, I'm so sorry. I don't even know what to say."

"There is nothing you can say. Everyone who could say something has already said it and it doesn't change what happened. Let me buy you coffee," he offered. "Something for your boy?"

But by that time Ben had wheeled off through town toward the wharf and the beach. Jesse nodded. "Ben'll be back. He knows where to find me."

Dennis had seemed so attractive to Jesse that day that she briefly experienced a strange hope and elation for which she immediately felt immense guilt. It was just that he seemed so vital—and yes, sexual—strong brown arms and sunburned neck, the old magician reappearing out of nowhere back into her life. Presto chango. Even his sadness about Lora's death made him seem attractive, a depth there that almost radiated.

He brought her a mug of coffee and they settled onto a worn couch on the bakery porch to talk about the years that had passed since they'd seen each other. The first thing he asked was, "So tell me, Jesse. Are you still a witch?"

"You know I am," she answered.

That had been June, just two months ago. She hadn't consciously conceived of them being lovers. They'd gone to bed easily, old friends. It was comforting. That old intimacy, earned years ago, still passionate and intense, now came to her like a gift. No courtship dance was needed. No Quinn around to confuse things. Maybe that was another reason she'd not jumped right back into a social circle that included people from the Berkeley house.

It was probably the second or third time they slept together that she asked about Lora. Dennis, sprawled naked on the bed, was smoking a joint. Jesse lay beside him, her head on his flat stomach, and she thought how much this place was still Lora's. How many men had dressing tables in their bedrooms? In the bathroom hung a wom-

an's robe. Jesse slipped it on once after a shower and
Dennis looked at her oddly. Once or twice she'd walked
into his kitchen or living room, with its floor-to-ceiling
windows, stone fireplace, dhurrie rug, all the vases and
mirrors and silver pitchers that were so Lora—and she'd
just stopped cold, expecting Lora to be sitting right there,
smoking a cigarette and filing her nails. Jesse didn't want
to say ghost exactly, but still—what was it then? Just wind,
a cold movement across her face, a whisper? Only wild
rose branches blowing up against the house, she told herself. Shut the window against the chill. So when Dennis
stubbed out the joint in a cut-glass ashtray and turned
back to hold her she asked him, "What about Lora?"

"You say that like I'm cheating on her."

"I guess I feel her here, her presence. Something."

"You saying my house is haunted?" he asked.

"Don't make fun of me, Dennis. You know what I mean.
You were married—what?—thirteen years?"

"Fourteen."

"So? Go on."

"I don't want to talk about her, Jess."

"I do. I need to hear something. It's like there's this big
hole between us, something we're not supposed to talk
about. Walking on eggshells. Even though I hadn't seen
her—or you—all these years, still she was my friend too.
Now here we are, lovers again, as if she never even ex-
isted. It makes me feel a little weird, that's all."

Dennis flipped over on his stomach and sighed into the
pillow. "It was hard when she died. What more can I say?
Of course I loved her. But I'm not going to lie to you—
things weren't that good between us. We were separated
a few months and we were trying it back together but it
wasn't working out. She'd gone into treatment but she
was back doing coke on the sly, spending all kinds of
money. I thought maybe she was seeing someone. I
couldn't be sure. If she'd lived, we probably would have
split up. Does that make you feel any better?"

Jesse said, "No, actually."

It was odd being back in Dennis's life. Jesse sensed it would not be wise to fall in love with him again, although it was happening anyway. She saw that he would not be rid of the burden of Lora's death for a long time. He seemed pregnant with it. He carried it in him, it grew. Still she felt the old passion for him—that had never diminished—and more than once she'd wondered what would have happened if they'd stayed together since college.

But she was older now and could see his faults. Yes, he was a dreamer, a starter of projects that he didn't finish, sometimes volatile in his moods. But he still loved magic —only now, instead of tricks, it was the magic of the natural world he loved. The wildlife of the lagoon, white horses at the ranch. Maybe he was too laid-back. Jesse wondered if a simple life—his stated goal—was enough of an ambition. But in the weeks she'd been seeing him again she'd come to think of the simple life as something of an achievement in these times.

Plus, Ben liked him. Dennis had kept Ben over a weekend in mid-July when she'd attended a neon workshop in L.A. "He's fresh, Mom," Ben had reported.

"Is that the same as cool?"

"He's like the old man and the sea on that boat. He *knows* stuff. I caught three black cod and one ling cod. You should have seen Dennis nail those suckers on the head with a sledgehammer!" Ben had been impressed. Usually he remained quite aloof from the men Jesse dated, knowing on some level that they wouldn't last long. With Dennis, Jesse could tell, Ben was becoming attached.

Dennis had only mentioned Lora once more. "I know this might sound funny," he said over a beer one night at a bar in Olema, "but I feel like I only just now grew up, in the months since Lora died. I mean, all those years were such a party—living off her trust fund and all. Neither of us had to get serious, you know? When she died and there was so little left—it was the first time I ever really had to think about working. I always loved the fishing, but if you

want to really make a living you're up in Alaska, not down
here where the rivers have all been dammed up and the
salmon population has been almost completely killed off."
He'd gone on to say how much he loved working two days
a week with a local rancher, training new mares, and his
other part-time job with an environmental agency, working to protect the balance of sea life in the Bolinas Lagoon.
"It's too bad it took all this before I got my life together,"
he said. "Maybe that's what death is for—to wake you up
in your life."

Jesse turned south onto Highway One, passed the hidden Bolinas turnoff, ranches pastoral with white horses,
then drove along the lagoon where egrets stood one-
legged in the water. She wondered if Dennis would have
any advice about the wiring problem she was having with
the neon. He'd always been good with the mechanics of
things. Back in Berkeley both he and Cody had been the
ones they would call on to fix stereos, TVs, even clocks.
Anything with wires.

That phrase that had come to her last night: *Not enough
power.* That had been wrong, Jesse thought. Incorrect.
There *was* enough power. It was simply the connections
that were wrong, the plugs, the sockets, the wires. The
question was not the power, but the managing of power,
the direction of it. That was what she loved most about
being an artist—the functional, everyday difficulties of
achieving a goal, actualizing a vision, were what yielded
the most wisdom. Sure, there would be that final moment
in the woods when the wands of neon were lit and the
witches all entered humming, but this was where the
energy and meaning were centered for her: how to splice
this wire or thread that circuit so that the whole damn
thing wouldn't blow out. You had to refine the means for
channeling power. Power would not flow to one not ready
for it.

Dennis lived up on a wheat-brown hill overlooking Stinson Beach. Set back into a grove of old cedars, the house

was the farthest one up a narrow hairpin road, and although the road continued up another quarter mile, no one lived above him. The modern house was all wood and stone, redwood beams. Its carved oak door faced directly out over the Pacific. She pulled up into the drive beside the house, got out and knocked on the door. No answer. She opened it a crack and cooed, "Mr. Mayhew, Avon calling." Then she thought, *How stupid. His car isn't even here. Must be at the wharf. I'll leave a note for him.*

For a moment Jesse stood there in the kitchen, listening. The last time she'd slept here she'd thought almost certainly that she'd seen Lora's ghost. She knew ghosts didn't appear in the twentieth century as they had in damp castles three hundred years ago. No rattling chains, no lacy see-through damsels. It was far more subtle, the pervasive presence that had chilled her that night. She'd been in bed with Dennis and a fog had come up over the hills, a strange singing moan floating through the cracks of the house. Dennis had said it was just the wind. The house always did that.

When she'd gotten up at around four in the morning to pee, she'd seen an odd shadow made of light down at the far end of the hall and she'd followed it. Just outside the closed door of the room she'd felt a terrible cold. As she reached to open the door, it sucked open and the whole room was white with fog. She had hissed, "Dennis, Dennis, come here," but he slept and she had walked through it, shutting the windows on three walls and wondering why they'd all been left open. Maybe it had just been fog after all.

But today, just now, as she came into the house, she felt it again, out of the corner of her eye, a glimpse sliced through the light—Lora just sitting over in the low cane rocker by the fireplace. When she turned her head to look there had been nothing there. Of course not. You couldn't look a ghost in the eye.

She didn't really know if she believed in ghosts, but she'd never had any reason to believe or disbelieve one way or another until now. Secretly she'd always thought ghosts were the projected thought forms of a frightened person. Thick grief. Something still clinging to someone, blocking his life. But if that were true, why had it been she who had seen Lora's ghost and not Dennis? While she was very sad about Lora, it was he who was truly grieving.

Jesse hurriedly scribbled out a note—"Stopped by with croissants. Love, Jesse"—and was glad to be out of the house. She drove down to the wharf in Bolinas to see if Dennis's boat was docked there. He didn't bring it into the lagoon much, he'd told her once. It was too hard to get it in and out of the narrow channel. But as she came through the main street and parked near the beach, she saw it bobbing out on the bright water. In a smaller boat anchored down by some pilings, she spotted the fat man who'd been with Dennis that day at the bakery.

"Do you know if Dennis is out there?" she called down to him.

"Just about ready to head out, I think. Yup."

"Could you give me a lift out there? I'll give you a croissant."

"Hell, anything for a bribe. Come on down." He motioned for her to climb down into the wet boat and she was glad she'd worn boots.

"Ahoy!" she called as they came up alongside Dennis's boat, its new lettering in black stencil: *Grace.* Wearing his baseball cap, Dennis emerged from the cabin and waved, then helped her up into the larger boat as waves slapped between the two. She tossed the large man a croissant and shouted her thanks as he put-putted back to the wharf.

"This is a nice surprise." Dennis kissed her. "Cold?" He pulled off his sweater and tossed it to her, his cap nearly blowing off into the water. *Kind man,* she thought. *Nice man.*

It took her a few minutes to become accustomed to the sway of the water.

"Just happened to be in the neighborhood?" he asked.

"I broke into your house, looking for buried treasure."

He gave her a strange look.

"I stopped up to your house first," she explained. "Left you a note."

"Are you coming tomorrow?"

She looked out across the lagoon at a pelican arrowing for the water, scooping a silver fish in its beak. "I might as well. I'll see them all sooner or later. I don't know why I'm being so furtive about it. Old vibes, I guess. Anyway, I'm dying to talk to Maggie Shea."

It was good to see Dennis out on the boat sitting on the engine case in jeans, high rubber boots, and a black T-shirt that read UNIVERSITY OF MARS. He was sunburned, his hair bleach-streaked. He looked healthy and relaxed. Suddenly she understood—the beach house was not his at all, never was. That had been Lora's domain, this was his. He smiled at her then, slipped on dark glasses. Jesse took it all in—her first time on the boat—the high outriggers sticking straight up, squeal of gulls circling around them smelling bait, static nasal voices on the radio. White pails neatly stacked, coil of rubber hose. He kept it much neater than she had imagined. In the small cabin, under the windshield, a digital clock, compass, paper towels, box of toothpicks. Pack of cigarettes. Even a little propane cook stove and cache of food. Beneath the bow was the reel house where he slept sometimes, two bunks built against the sides of the boat. A sleeping bag and roll of maps lay on one of the bunks. This, she realized, was Dennis's true home. Here was where the dreamer, the disappearing magician who loved solitude, and the caretaker of the natural world all came together in one man wearing a red baseball cap, staring out to the open Pacific.

Jesse straddled the doorway of the cabin and peered down the shore toward Stinson Beach. "Can you see it from here—when you're farther out?" she asked. "The place where Lora was found?"

Dennis hopped down from the engine case and began coiling a length of rope around his arm. "Why are you always bringing her up?"

She shrugged. "We go back a long way. I still think about her a lot, I guess, whenever I'm with you."

"Well, the hell with that."

"Why are you so angry about it? You should talk about her more. It's healthy to get it out."

"Don't therapize me, Jesse."

She stepped down into the cabin and leaned against the steering wheel.

Dennis continued. "Why, on a perfectly nice day, do you have to throw Lora up in my face?"

"You don't think anyone is going to mention her tomorrow?" she called back to him.

He lit a cigarette, cupping his hands to the wind.

She squinted into the sun, then blurted out, "Look, Dennis, I've been thinking. We can pretend to pick up where we left off in college, but that's trying to make fifteen years invisible. Here we are in totally different bodies than the ones we had back then. Don't you know we replace all our cells every seven years? We're different people, Denny. We can pretend to know each other from the old days, but what do we really know? It's all new. Why do you keep pushing me away every time I bring her up? She was here, she was real."

"Fuck off, Jesse. There are some things people don't want to have a goddamn discussion about every other day."

"Fine. It's been sweet, old D. We gave it that old college try. Why don't you give me a ride back in, okay?" She swung down into the reel house and sat on the bed. After a few minutes Dennis crawled down next to her.

"I'm sorry," he said quietly.

"You are sorry."

"Don't push me. I said I'm sorry. There's a whole lot you don't know about Lora and me."

"I'm picking up on that, I guess. I'm assuming we're closer than we are. Forget it, I'll back off."

"No I don't want that. It's just that it hasn't even been a year. They just found her body last week, for Christ's sake.

I'm still screwed up over her, okay? I think I deserve to be screwed up for at least another year. Instead of wearing black I'll be neurotic and touchy."

Jesse felt bad then. She covered her face with one hand. "I'm an idiot," she whispered. "I've been so insensitive. I have a hard time staying on the surface, that's all."

"I know. That's why I need you around. You keep me honest."

He tried to kiss her. She pulled away, smiling. "Liar," she said.

He pulled her down on the bed and kissed her, then rolled over toward the side of the boat, hands behind his head. "Look, another reason I'm upset about Lora is that the cop who helped me out when the boat disappeared came to the house last night asking a lot of funny questions. 'How could Lora have launched the boat by herself? How could she have gotten the lifeboat into the water? Had I ever gone out looking for her myself in a boat? When did I get the new boat and how much did it cost? When did I take out the business policy on the boat? What about Gram's will, was I aware at the time of Lora's death that Gram's will had been changed?' "

"What did he mean by that?" asked Jesse.

Dennis explained quickly about some cousin of Lora's, a will codicil, lawyers, meetings.

"So I'm nervous," he admitted.

"But why?"

He rubbed his hands over his face. "Isn't it obvious? They're checking out the old foul-play angle, that's why."

"No. They can't think that."

"But they do," he said quietly. "Well, screw 'em. I'm innocent until proven guilty, right? Isn't that the goddamn beauty of America? Jesse, why don't you come out and fish with me? Just for a couple of hours. We'll catch a salmon for tomorrow. Cheer me up."

"I've got a lot of work to do in the studio," she told him.

He kissed her again. "Come fishing," he pleaded.

"Oh, all right."

Jesse sat on the engine box and pulled Dennis's sweater over her head. He hauled up the anchor, fired the diesel engine, then swung around and out the channel to the open water, rocking and splashing across the waves. As they made their way farther and farther out, Jesse thought again about the strange feelings she'd had at Dennis's house. Maybe it really was Lora's ghost she'd felt. She'd have to be open to that possibility. Not some Casper sheet-draped spook but a thought form. A memory trace rising up because of the police inquiry and because of Dennis's fear. Yes, a cleansing ritual at Dennis's house. Good idea. But she'd have to find a way get in to do it when Dennis wasn't there.

Chapter 8

As they drove over the San Rafael Bridge on the way to Sausalito, Maggie wondered how she would manage to get off alone with Quinn for a few minutes. She sensed that Rob was going to be protective, if only to make sure she mentioned nothing of his suspicions about Dennis or what they'd discovered in Berkeley.

"I hate coming here on weekends, especially August. Apex of the tourist season," Rob muttered as they exited off Highway One. They sat in grid-lock traffic, slowly inching toward the main plaza, where tour buses and ferries were depositing hordes of people hungry for shopping and photo opportunities. Still, it looked lovely to Maggie. Downtown San Francisco gleamed dusty white—an Oz mirage across the bay and a bleached light made the hills of cedar and cypress look hazy. Mount Tamalpais loomed behind them in blue shadow.

"Why don't you get out here?" suggested Rob. "I'm going to have to park up on the hill, it's too crowded down here." Maggie hopped out at a corner and Rob pointed out Quinn's gallery up the block, then drove slowly off. *Good*, she thought, envisioning a few minutes alone with

Quinn at the outset. On the way to the gallery, Maggie
paused briefly to watch an Asian boy, surrounded by a
throng of tourists, land a giant stingray. Then she hurried
through the crowd to "Quinn Gallery: Folk Art, Photogra-
phy and Paintings of Distinction."

Lora had told her once that Quinn wanted it to be a real
gallery, not just a tourist showcase for sailboat watercolors
and predictable landscapes. Apparently her idea that the
gallery carry folk art from around the world had been
timely and profitable. Maggie remembered her saying
that it was Cody who'd provided some of her initial contacts. He had business connections all over the world.
Maggie's news of Cody, as with the others, had come
through Lora's friendly gossip. Cody had started out selling small shipments of reel-to-reel tape recorders and
small radios sent to him by friends in the Far East, old
Nam buddies who'd remained overseas. In the early seventies he'd opened an electronic specialty store in Berkeley, one of the first of its kind in the country, Media Electronics. Within a few years he owned a chain of stores all
over California and then the West Coast. His were among
the very first stores to offer personal computers and soft-
ware at reasonable prices to the same people who were
charging cassette tape decks and VCRs on their new Mas-
terCards. His business had been successful far beyond
what any of them had imagined for the lanky Sound Man
with his Hell's Angels buddies and harp-blowing mania.
Lora had reported that Cody wore shirts that cost over
two hundred dollars, lizard-skin shoes, Giorgio Armani
sweaters, that he drove a Mercedes and was with a different woman every time she saw him, which wasn't often.
"They all look like starlets," Lora had reported. "I think
he works too hard to settle down."

Maggie stood for a moment in the doorway of the gallery, allowing her eyes to adjust to the dark. The gallery
walls were gray, the black ceiling hung with track lighting. Though the glass door stood open, street sounds were
muffled by thick carpeting. Television screens, suspended

from the ceiling, displayed videos of artists at work. Silver micro-blinds on the high front windows slanted up to deflect the late daylight.

When Quinn spotted her, he came toward her, imitating Dylan in a nasal rendition of "On Maggie's Farm." Then he stopped and grinned widely, arms outstretched. "What can I say? That I still adore you, that you're more beautiful than I remember, that I'm so glad you got rid of Garson!" She laughed in spite of herself and accepted his embrace, familiar even after so long; the ache of it stunned her, a longing like some dormant thing only he could wake in her. *O Prince Charming.* She laughed to herself. He wore a pale gray sweater over white pants, pink leather tie. No shirt beneath, just the tie. He put his hand on the back of her head. "When can I see you alone?" he asked.

"Now," she said.

But behind him in the second room of the gallery she saw Cody in a low chair, long legs extended before him. His thin face was tanned; a shock of silk-brown hair fell across his eyes and he shook his head back, smiling, hand uplifted.

"Look who descended from his palace in Tiburon to grace us with his regal presence," said Quinn. Then Cody, too, rose and came over to her, bending to kiss her cheek. "Welcome back, Maggie," he said.

Excitedly Quinn gestured around the gallery. "What do you think?" Elegant black-and-white photographs lined the wall behind the receptionist's desk. They appeared to be close-ups of rocks or bones. It struck her how like Mark's pen-and-ink drawings they were, and she immediately knew they must be Quinn's work. Quinn introduced her to his assistant, Kathleen, a small woman with very short black-dyed hair wearing a strapless sundress, and was just explaining to Maggie about a shipment of pieces due in from Haiti this week that she simply had to see when Rob came in, looking very hot.

Rob greeted Cody, firm handshake, grip to the upper arm.

"Hey, man," Cody said to him, straightening his suit coat, a pale mauve tweed, dark green tie. "Quinn just told me they found Lora's body. I hadn't heard." He looked down, grimaced. "That's tough, man."

"Yeah. I guess we can go ahead and have some kind of funeral now," said Rob. "I'll let you know."

"Do that," Cody said. "What's the cliché? You can put her to rest now." Cody glanced at his gold Rolex.

Just then Quinn put his arm around Maggie's waist and guided her to a small room. "I thought you'd want to see this first," he said. "Lora's pride and joy." The walls were hung with childlike tropical paintings, dolls and the glittery banners Lora had called prayer flags. They were the size of paintings, fabric designs made of sequins stitched into hearts, spades, clubs, snakes, with names embroidered in glass beads, names like Aïda and Lenore. Maggie felt sad in the room. The last time she'd seen Lora in the Caymans, she had showed her some of these very pieces.

On the wall beside a pink prayer flag there was a short explanation in typeface: "The word *voodoo* means Life Force or Spirit in certain West African languages. In the voodoo religion, signs and images are thought to hold power in the spirit world. Dolls, prayer flags, even paintings contain visual images that are believed to affect the lives of those who make the article as well as others for whom the piece is intended. The prayer flag Aïda is a fertility flag. The purpose of the flag titled Lenore is to ward off illness. Names are often worked into a piece. If the prayer flag is intended for another person, that name will be incorporated into the design; if the artist intended it for herself, the design will feature her own name. It is interesting to note how modern technology continues to modify and change folk-art practices. For instance, in many regions of the world polyester is now preferred to cotton for quilt making because of its bright colors, which will not fade in washing. Photographs have begun to appear instead of drawings, paintings, or embroidered names in voodoo prayer flags."

Maggie paused at that. "Did Lora write this?" she asked. Quinn nodded.

On a low table in the center of the room stood a small folding screen about a foot and a half high. It looked something like an icon, but instead of a picture of the Madonna, three photographs of the same woman were glued to wood panels along with locks of hair, ribbons, a rosary and dried leaves. Maggie stared at the piece for several minutes. The materials were different, but the similarity to the shadow box was uncanny.

"Quinn?" she started, but Rob appeared at the door then, gesturing for them to come into the back room. She was not going to get a chance to speak alone with either Cody or Quinn—she could see that now. It felt a bit claustrophobic suddenly, as if Rob were trying to keep track of her, an unruly child.

The back room was filled with large oils, one wall entirely covered with masks—gargoyle faces of plaster, carved faces with hinged jaws, Balinese smooth-moon faces in black mahogany, a tray with faces for handles, tiny animal faces painted wild colors like three-dimensional cartoons. On another wall, staffs and spears were mounted every few feet, as were tall wooden rectangles with faces carved at the top. These resembled totem poles.

"Those are wonderful," said Maggie, viewing the masks. "It's like they're all looking at you."

"If you think this is a good collection, you should see Cody's. His living room is wall-to-wall masks—it's a third-world costume shop. What are you going to do with all that stuff, anyway?"

"Mark them up and sell them to you, buddy." Cody's eyes glittered. "Business as usual."

"What are these?" Maggie asked Quinn.

"Those are effigy figures."

"What does that mean?"

Cody answered. "Grave markers."

"You mean someone took these from graves in Africa somewhere?" she asked.

Quinn shrugged. "Let's just say that the buyers don't always mention exactly how they acquire the things they bring back. Those particular ones are Nigerian. I guess sometimes there's an old cemetery that's moved to make way for a road or something. Then again there are craftsmen who just carve the things. They're in demand now. Designers love them."

Cody had cornered Rob back by the effigy figures. Maggie caught snatches of conversation, Cody questioning Rob about some stock. Then she realized they were talking guns, target shooting; still the vets with their private male language of munitions and marksmanship. Two of her brothers hunted. She'd gone with them once as a kid and waited all day in a deer blind, praying no deer would come. Now was her chance to talk to Quinn alone. She took his hand and led him back into the prayer flag room.

As soon as they were alone, he turned and kissed her, his mouth opening hers. *Not now, baby,* she thought. Palms to his chest, she gently pushed him away. She remembered the teasing tone necessary to keep him at bay.

"Darling," she said, "we've only just met."

He dropped his hands, bit his lower lip. "I couldn't help it," he said. "The last time I saw you I had to be all proper and everything. You were married." Maggie looked down for a moment and Quinn continued. "I was real sorry to hear about Mark. Lora told me all about it."

"You sent flowers to the funeral. That was very kind of you, Quinn."

"You're an old friend, Maggie."

"You do have a streak of kindness behind those fangs—I always forget."

"Duly noted," he said. "The knight errant moves back two squares and waits for an opening to get to the queen." He smiled.

"I did drag you back here for a reason, Quinn. What can

you tell me about that Haitian piece with the photographs of the woman and the hair?"

Quinn straddled the arch between rooms. "That was one of Lora's favorites."

"Did she ever make things like that?"

"No, they're all authentic Caribbean collector's items. One of a kind."

"That's not what I mean. Did she ever make things like that for her own use?"

Quinn lifted his hair back from his forehead. "I don't think so. But I know somebody who could probably tell you—the woman who turned her on to Haitian prayer flags. She's an expert on voodoo images, and it's not all that pins-in-dolls stuff, either. When you get into the spiritual aspect, it's pretty fascinating. Do you remember that secondhand store in the city where you and Jesse and Lora used to buy dresses and jewelry back in college? It's in a new location now. Freda is the woman who owns the place. It's not far from where Rob lives, actually."

Maggie vaguely remembered Lora mentioning it.

"Yeah, Freda," Quinn continued. "She's from Port-au-Prince, speaks French. She's the one who got Lora going to the Caribbean in the first place. Her husband is Henry Loam. I know you remember him—the sorcerer of Haight Street, Jesse's high priest? Small world, isn't it? He and Freda own the shop where Lora first saw the prayer flags."

Maggie looked again at the iconlike shrine. *Another connection to the past,* she thought. She was cataloguing them now. "How did Lora happen to hook up with them —just through this shop?"

"I think Freda contacted her, actually. She was looking for West Coast buyers; she had relatives in Haiti she wanted connections for."

"Do you know many other importers, Quinn?"

"Sure," he said. "Tons. They're kind of a network."

Just then Rob grabbed her elbow from behind and spoke closely to the side of her head. "It's after six." Maggie caught herself from breathing in sharply. Why was it that she felt like a child stealing coins from her father's dresser? Had Rob heard what she was asking Quinn? She couldn't be sure.

Quinn announced, "The Laurel Inn. Six o'clock. We're late already."

Maggie walked beside Rob out into the dazzling light. "How are you doing?" she asked.

"How are you doing? It's your vacation." He slipped his arm through hers, and again she felt as if he were trying to restrain her, keep her from walking ahead to join Quinn and Cody.

"I wouldn't exactly call it a vacation. But I'm trying to act cheerful. Don't I look cheerful?"

"Yes."

"Come on," Quinn called back to them.

As they climbed the back streets to where Rob had parked, he handed Maggie an information sheet on gallery letterhead that listed the paintings and photographs of selected artists whose work Quinn was showing that month. "Check this out," he said.

She glanced at the sheet. The date, August 23, 1986, had been written entirely in Roman numerals.

Chapter 9

At dinner Maggie sipped her white Zinfandel, watching the bay light on the marina go rose, blue, then black. Their table was nudged beneath several hanging ferns and a ficus tree lit with white Christmas tree lights. In the skylight overhead, stars appeared.

She listened as Quinn made fun of the restaurant's paintings of seagulls and surfers and talked about art as corporate investment, the private sector from Michelangelo to Jennifer Bartlett. Rob brought up the Rehnquist nomination, then asked Cody how he thought certain proposed tax changes would affect the export of goods to South America. Cody touched briefly on Central American politics and the funding of the contras. That was the only time the conversation veered anywhere near the romance and idealism of their bantering years ago. When it was her turn, she felt as though she were compressing her life into an advertising jingle, an article in *Reader's Digest*: "Surviving Widowhood," in twenty-five words or less. "Seven Reasons I Became a Shrink."

"I'm not surprised you chose the hospice field, Maggie. Weren't you reading Kübler-Ross even back in college?"

Cody asked. "I always wondered why you were drawn to
the study of death."

"I'm not sure," she said. "Maybe some part of me always
wanted to be a priest and I knew I never could. When you
work with death you connect with the sacred, you have
to. I guess I was attracted to that spiritual aspect, the
healing potential. It's not as dark as you might think."

"But you always liked that dark side, you and Jesse."

Maggie smiled. "You mean our forays into witchcraft?
That was no darker than your interest in masks. Both are
connected to archetypal images, right? There's a lot of
power in those ancient images and practices. They come
up through the collective unconscious, much bigger than
we are. Maybe that's why modern life feels so empty
sometimes. TV is our most powerful image."

"And our most powerful ritual," added Rob.

Around nine Cody stood to leave, saying he'd see them
all tomorrow at Dennis's. "Can we have dinner this
week?" Cody asked her. "It's so good to talk to somebody
about a subject other than bytes, superconductors, and
the value of the dollar, I can't tell you."

Rob looked over at Maggie. "We should go too," he said.

But Quinn touched her elbow under the table. "So
soon? Hey, it's Saturday night. Come on." Then to Maggie. "Why don't you stay?"

After a moment Maggie said, "I think I would like to
stay for a while, if you don't mind, Rob." There was an
uncomfortable moment. Quinn broke the silence with an
offer to drive her back to the city in a few hours.

After Cody and Rob left, Quinn ordered another bottle
of wine and slid his chair over toward hers with that dazzling, elfin grin that took up his whole face. She knew Rob
was worried that she'd ask the wrong questions of Quinn
and word would leak to Dennis about his suspicions. She
decided to wait until Quinn brought the whole thing up
and then use her best therapist questioning techniques,
neither blurting anything out nor betraying Rob's confidence.

"I'd forgotten you were so midwestern," Quinn said.

"And you're just so California. *Très* West Coast," she said. *"Darling."*

"Hey, it wasn't meant as a criticism. I meant, well, solid. Scrubbed."

"Just out of the sauna, *ja*? *Uff da.*"

He threw back his head and laughed. *"Uff da!* I haven't heard that in so long! I used to think it was Swedish for 'fuck you!' "

"Actually, you seem solid too. More solid than I remember."

"I should be. I'm thirty-six," he said.

"I still feel about twenty-seven."

"Not twenty?"

"No, I was still stupid at twenty." Maggie sipped the wine.

"Yeah, you were with me."

"Yes, I was."

"We should have gotten married," Quinn said suddenly and Maggie blushed. He would go and make a joke out of it. Somehow the subject was too tender for that, even after all this time. They'd been engaged for a few months the year after the Berkeley house, but Quinn had slept around and Maggie was already beginning to tire of the drug scene by then. She'd broken it off.

Quinn went on. "We could be yuppies by now, have our kids in private schools. You could play tennis and have your Christmas card address list on a home computer."

"I do play tennis and have my Christmas card address list on a home computer."

"But you're not like them."

"Who?"

"The zombies. The blank-skulled consumers of the world."

"In a lot of ways I am. You'd be surprised. I have a Cuisinart, an Apple IIe, a VCR. I make good money. Even have investments, zero interest bonds, shares in Cray Research. Maybe I am a yup. Maybe we all are. Cody sure seems to be prospering, anyway."

"You dropped acid, Maggie. You can't be a yup. You're cracked open, you'll never recover. You were in Berkeley in sixty-nine and seventy. That'll always be with you."

"Maybe I ought to wear a red *A* for 'Acid.' How about a big *B* for 'Berkeley'?"

"Maggie, believe me, you're not like them."

"What about you?"

"I'm in the arts, as we like to say. That keeps me close to the fringe."

"Is it a stance?"

"Sure. Everything is a stance."

"You were always like that, Quinn."

"Like what?"

"Fronting. Personas. It's fitting that you sell masks."

Then he asked, "Do you think there is anything behind my mask, or have you really always thought I was a complete airhead?"

It was the first authentic thing he'd said all night, dropping the rogue play acting for an instant. "I always thought there might be something to that gray matter of yours. Back then you were like an exotic travelogue, a museum of esoteric information, a sprawl of libido. Then every once in a while there was a glimpse of the real Quinn in there, somewhere at the core under all the bullshit. Like just now."

Quinn tilted the wine bottle to his lips and blew a staccato of hollow notes. "Now I remember why it didn't work out between us," he said. "You saw through me, Maggie. You brought out the best in me and even I couldn't stand it."

"Well, hey, when you grow up in the Midwest eating a lot of cheese, what can you do?"

"You're really grown up," he said.

"I was a baby when we met. You were worldly wise. The great radical artist. You were stunning."

"We should have married, huh? Paid off a mortgage?

Taken parent effectiveness training courses? It would
have been swell, babe."

"It would have been swell, Quinn. Yeah."

In some way, Maggie was astonished that she still found
Quinn so attractive. Didn't she know better? Quinn had
always liked not so much particular women as he liked
Women, she thought. He sincerely liked them, not only
their skin, round curves of breast, sway of back, their hair,
the smell of them, faint musk, soap and sweat, but he liked
their anger and assertiveness, their declarations of self-
hood. Over the years Lora had reported back on the many
women who'd fallen for Quinn. He was always with a new
one and they were always beautiful, smart, divorced.
They had money, interesting jobs. They were tired of
men without feelings and along came Quinn who acted
the part of tenderness so well. He could shed a tear over a
good French film and he was committed, goddamn it:
belonged to the Freeze movement, defended whales.
"None of them can believe," Lora had once said, "that
they've gotten so lucky to find such a man, unattached,
without child-support payments, heterosexual, solvent,
and free. But he's always free. That's his gift, isn't it? He's
a great sexual pal." Moths to the flame, Maggie thought.
She wondered if Lora had ever been sucked into that
flame, ever been burned.

Arm in arm, Maggie and Quinn walked through Sausalito, looking into darkened shop windows. Downtown
glimmered across the water. Maybe her doubts about
Quinn were right. He had nothing further to say about
Lora, no family secret after all. But if she wanted to be
sure, she would have to ask him. It was clear he was not
going to bring up the subject.

Back at his house in Mill Valley several miles away,
Quinn poured ginger brandy and built a fire in the wood
stove. His house was comfortable and rustic, rough wood
walls, old furniture. She looked out the large glass doors,
the whole back wall of the living room like a treehouse

hanging out over a wooded hillside. He came into the room behind her, and as she turned to face him, he snapped her picture, the flash blinding her, then quickly again.

Her hand flew to her face. "Quinn, don't," she protested.

He snapped again. Her thoughts flew back to the Polaroids, the sleeping and the dead, and suddenly his picture taking seemed a terrible invasion. She grabbed the camera, threw it on the couch. He wrestled her for it and it went off again, the flash strobing at the ceiling. Playfully he bit at her hand, her shoulder, then leaned down over her, his mouth hard against hers, hands gripping her hair, whispering, "I just want to touch you, Maggie. All the way through dinner I just wanted this."

This time she gave in to his mouth, his kiss like a signature. His hair was coarse in her hands. She knew it all, even the mole on the back of his neck. Fifteen years ago it all seemed so easy; well, perhaps, not so easy after all.

After a few minutes she turned her head to the side and his body relaxed. He put his head on her chest and she listened to him breathe. It wasn't just that she had doubts, a legacy of old hurts. It was the photographs she and Rob had found that morning. The date on the gallery letterhead. There was too much going on.

"The queen retreats," he whispered into her hair.

"It's not a game, Quinn. Actually I was thinking about Lora. Wondering what it was you wanted to tell me."

He got up and arranged logs in the fire, then sat on the floor across from her, threw a scrap of paper into the fire. "I didn't know if I should bring it up. You seem so chummy with Garson. But there's something you should probably know before you see Dennis, before this hoopla tomorrow. It might not have been an accident. Dennis has a feeling that Lora might have been murdered."

Maggie was shocked to hear him say so directly what Rob had finally admitted in such a roundabout way.

"Lora acted bizarro for a couple weeks before she

died," Quinn explained. "Paranoid, jumpy. She kept having nightmares, said she was afraid in the house alone. She wanted to move to Haiti for the winter, get out of the country. Dennis thought she was going overboard on the voodoo stuff, just a bit too obsessed. After a while she claimed outside forces were controlling her. Dennis also thought she was back into the white stuff. The week before the accident she wouldn't leave the house. It was like she was hiding out. They had a huge fight about her going to Haiti. He accused her of getting carried away with all that stuff and he refused to let her go. They were supposed to meet me up at Tahoe for the weekend but only Dennis showed up. When he came back—that's when he discovered the boat was missing."

"What does he think happened?" she asked.

"At first he thought maybe she actually did go down to Haiti. He even flew down there last December to look for her, told Rob he was vacationing in Mexico. But since they found the remains he thinks possibly someone drugged her, set her out in the lifeboat alone, knowing there was a storm coming."

"But who? If there was somebody else on the boat with her, what did they do with the boat? If they wanted to kill her, why would they leave her in a lifeboat; why not just throw her over?" Her voice had grown loud now. "Why would anyone want to kill her?"

"I'm no detective, but who would benefit the most from her death? Financially."

"He would. Dennis."

"I don't know how much you know about their grandmother's will." Quinn repeated to her essentially the same story she'd already heard from Rob. She tried to calm herself. *Just listen. Objective questions. Let him speak, don't interrupt.* But then he told her some things Rob had left completely out of his story.

"Did you know Rob is the executor of Gram's estate?" Quinn asked. "Of course he favors the first version of the will. Why, you ask? Because then the estate will only be

divided into two parts—half the money to Andrea, half to
Rob, each on their fortieth birthdays. Lora wasn't forty, so
according to that first will, her estate is zilch."

Maggie stood now, looking down at the fire. Quinn lay
on his back on the rug, arms behind his head. Rob had
seemed withdrawn, yes, but she'd never thought he could
actually have had anything to do with this.

"But Rob is devastated about Lora's death," she said.
"And he's going to inherit a lot of money himself anyway.
It wouldn't be worth murder, would it? He loved Lora."

"Ask Rob about his portfolio sometime," said Quinn.
"Ask him how it's possible to lose a shitload of money in
tax-shelter oil investments. Ask him how much he makes
as executor and how much he'll lose if two million is taken
out of the kitty and given to Dennis. Call Andrea in Dallas,
ask her how she feels about dividing that estate in thirds,
instead of halves. She might not want that codicil favored
either."

"But if what you're saying is true, doesn't Andrea have
about the same motive you're claiming Rob has?"

"Except she's not executor. But yes, that's right," he
said.

Maggie walked to the glass wall, looked across the way
into the houses on the next hill, yellow boxes illuminating
domestic scenes. Though her back was to him, Quinn
went on. "Dennis doesn't know how the coroner could
ever have reported accidental drowning as the cause of
death." She could tell he was studying her, waiting. Then
he asked, "Rob didn't tell you about the remains, did he?"

"What about them?" asked Maggie.

"They only found half of her."

Maggie spun to face him. She put her hand on the cool
glass. "What?" she whispered.

"What they found was a smashed-up lifeboat, a shred of
Lora's jacket with a diamond stickpin in the lapel, and
some bones. No skull. Only a torso, one arm, and a couple
of leg bones, a tibia or something. Rob didn't tell you any
of this?"

She shook her head.

"The remains were found almost ten months after Lora disappeared. The coroner said the flesh was probably eaten away by birds and crabs. They've been studying the remains all week for signs of cutting, knives, forced dismemberment. They think the body fell apart or was torn apart—it was not hacked up or sawed or anything. Presumably it was smashed around on the rocks by the waves, or taken apart by animals. *Accidental drowning.* Dennis doesn't believe it. Where's her head? She could have been hit over the head. She could have been shot, right? They can't prove a damn thing. How convenient. They can't even get a positive identification. No dental records."

Quinn shut the cast-iron door of the wood stove with a small clink. The room darkened. "I just thought you'd want to know when you see Dennis tomorrow. He's damn freaked."

Maggie didn't want to believe any of this: first Rob was accusing Dennis, and now he himself was a suspect.

Quinn came over to her at the window. Now that the lights were out behind them, they could see the moon arcing through the low clouds over the bay. "I'm bringing up questions, that's all," he said quietly. "You are pretty tight with Garson, aren't you?"

"Of course I am. Like you said earlier about me—he's an old friend."

"Well, so is Dennis. Look, I'll admit all of this is conjecture. It's just that you get to wondering. Shit, maybe Lora did have a lover. It could have been just an accident. That's what the police thought at first. She could have been out there floating around in that skiff for weeks and been picked apart by birds. It was all so goddamn strange. I guess you just start thinking. I had to listen to Dennis grieve all winter for her, and then all this crap about the will started up. Somebody's got to play devil's advocate."

"What about Phillip Dodd, Quinn?" She knew she shouldn't be bringing this up—she'd promised Rob. But she couldn't help it.

"What about him? I buy stuff from him sometimes. How do you know him?"

"Was he Lora's lover?"

"I never thought about it. I doubt it, he wasn't really her type."

"And what about the hex?" she demanded, having abandoned all her restraint and objectivity. There was a trembling in her chest as from too much caffeine, and her voice sounded shrill.

"What hex?" asked Quinn.

"Jesse's hex. Her spells."

"You mean all that black-magic bullshit?"

"She said that there was a hex on the house, don't you remember?"

"Well, there was, in a way. It did get pretty bizarre."

"That's what I mean—and look what happened. Peter and Lily died. Sandy died. Jesse disappeared . . ."

"So the myth goes."

"Now all of this."

"What's the connection?"

"I don't know. Maybe *I'm* the connection. Do you realize I'm the only woman left from the Berkeley house?"

He blew out a sigh. "The only hex on that house was chemically induced. It was a shipment of bad drugs. Rat poison. Just wait, I bet old Jesse'll even turn up one of these days." He put his arms around her, and she knew he could feel her shaking. "Hey, Purey, what happened to Lora was awful, and no one really knows what went on. That's why it's important to ask questions, even uncomfortable ones. But believe me, there's no hex. Come on, you're not on some demon's hit list, okay? You're midwestern. You're protected."

Chapter 10

Maggie watched the lights of the Golden Gate Bridge flick past the car window. She and Quinn rode mostly in silence. As he pulled up in front of Rob's he said, "I still wish you'd stayed with me tonight."

She smiled thinly and opened the door. "I'm sorry. It's just that I'm really upset about this whole thing."

"Why shouldn't you be? Everyone else is." He took her hand. "Can we try again?" He leaned across the seat and kissed her. His mouth was soft and tentative, the way small children kiss.

"I'll see you up at Dennis's, all right?" she whispered.

She did not feel much like sleeping. Though her body was tired, her mind hummed anxiously. Rob had left his shoes by the couch, a *Sports Illustrated* fanned open on the table. He must have gone up to bed early when he returned from Sausalito. In the kitchen she looked for some tea, pulling open cupboard doors, several of them almost empty, a small broom closet next to the stove, finally finding some chamomile. As the water boiled she looked through the photo album left open on the counter, the plastic pages clicking together as she flipped them one by one. When she got to a picture of Sandy in her flower-stitched Mexican blouse, she stopped. Why were both Rob and Quinn playing down the connection between the deaths in the Berkeley house and Lora's death when the shadow box and her own letter seemed so obviously to connect them? She wanted to think back, to examine the past the way the police were examining Lora's bones. Where were the cracks and fissures, what was broken? What was missing?

It was after Peter and Lily moved into the house that the spell of that green summer had been broken, but it was hard to remember what the elements of change had been. Maybe it was all chemical, as Quinn had suggested, a bad shipment of acid and speed in a month dry of marijuana. Suddenly Jesse had been gone for days at a time without telling anyone where she was going. Quinn went looking for her in the Haight and came back sullen, slamming doors. When Jesse returned, she looked unhealthy—skin yellow, eyelids shadowed by lack of sleep, her great halo of curls frizzed dry. She slept for a day and then staggered out, only to be zipping an hour later after endless cups of coffee or whatever else she was taking. She rarely ate, and bickered constantly with Quinn.

One night Maggie went to Jesse's room, lay across her bed while Jesse paced the room and talked. "I've been initiated. Henry brought me into the coven. All this time, the shrines, the amulets, those herbs hanging on my curtain rods, all my abracadabra—I was making it up as I went. But this is for real. They celebrate the witches' Sabbath, Lammas, Beltaine, they have new-moon rituals, everything." Jesse sounded entranced, and her enthusiasm both attracted and scared Maggie.

Quinn grew increasingly paranoid that the FBI was watching him because of his antiwar activities and his work with *The Barb.* He stopped making phone calls from the house and kept his cameras and film locked in his closet, padlock on the door. The offices of *The Barb* had been broken into, film stolen, name-and-address lists taken away. The movement was in chaos, he said, in a long discussion with Cody about the harassment, infiltration, firebombing of underground papers and Black Panther headquarters. Since Kent State, Cody admitted, he sometimes carried a gun.

One night Maggie stayed up late talking politics with Quinn. After she confided to him about Rob's betrayal, Quinn told her that things were breaking down between him and Jesse, too. "She's in over her head with all this witch shit. That priest dude—I've met him, he's strange. There are powers that should never be touched. Humans are just too stupid."

Quinn took Maggie out for breakfast. Without Jesse around, he seemed relaxed, less manic. She listened to him talk about his disillusionment with politics, how he might go up to Canada, start over. Back at the house he lay down next to her on the mattress and apologized for coming on so strong the night she moved in. He didn't try to kiss her or touch her, just her hair. He kept stroking her head until she fell asleep.

Again Jesse returned after several days in the Haight. She slept through one day, then cleaned the house, snatching a whole winter's worth of posters and postcards off a bulletin board in the kitchen and tacking up pictures of each of the girls. Yes, that was it. That was where Maggie had seen it for the first time—photographs and objects like the shadow box, blowups of snapshots Quinn had made when they hadn't been looking. Around each picture Jesse tacked locks of hair, ribbons, tickets, a necklace.

"What is it?" Maggie asked her.

Jesse turned to her, red-eyed. "Protection. You control the material plane from the astral. Charms, okay? We're charmed now. We've got to create our thought forms more consciously. What we think will come to pass. Thinking is the beginning. Don't you see?"

"I'll tell you what I think," said Lora that night. "I think it's the beginning of her being strung out."

Once when Jesse had gone again into the Haight, Quinn crept into Maggie's room. He whispered that he was lonely, cold. "Can I sleep with you?" he pleaded, touching her, sliding his hand down her belly, between her legs. She was glad she was on the pill and not a virgin; so her brief liaison with Rob had at least been good for something. She wondered if he wanted her only because Jesse wasn't there, but decided not to ask. Maggie knew it wasn't right to sleep with him behind Jesse's back, yet in some way that is exactly why she did it. Quinn was so goddamned beautiful, he was forbidden, and he was Jesse's lover. That meant he was chosen.

Quinn promised he'd break it off with Jesse but he did not. This for all of a week or so; it seemed like years. Each night Jesse stayed over in the Haight, Quinn came to Maggie. Maybe it was that week that Peter String and Lily arrived. They said they'd met Jesse in the Haight, that Jesse said there might be a place for them to stay. No one knew who they were, but they said they knew Jesse so it was all right. They hung around, hung out, *man, be cool, just passing through.* At that time no one seemed to mind some strangers sitting in your kitchen eating your food. *Go with the flow, don't get uptight behind it.*

Maggie remembered several other odd things that happened then. None seemed connected at the time but all seemed portentous, something about to break open. The first was this: one night they were all sitting around smoking and listening to "It's a Beautiful Day" when red lights whirled at their corner—cop cars, three, four of them. There was the tramp of footsteps and Cody leapt up, grabbing a box of hash. "Shit," he hissed. "Hit the can, folks."

"Wait," whispered Jesse, holding up her hand. Footsteps on the porch. She closed her eyes. All of them were silent, held breath, fear clapping in their chests. Then the police simply left. Turned and left. "Maybe they got the wrong house," Dennis said.

Jesse just said, "They were sent away."

The other thing that happened was that Jesse had an argument with someone who came to buy a lid from her, sharp voices behind her closed door. The man stalked out, bells on his jacket jingling at the end of leather fringe, and when Maggie peeked out of her room to see what was up, Jesse stood in her doorway shouting, "You don't short-change a brother, you don't cheat on your own sister! All your big talk about a better world and you're no different from any fucking imperialist, capitalist, military-industrial prickhead. Tried to rip me off," she added to Maggie. "Slime."

A few days later Quinn announced that the man had been busted. Four people in his flat had also been arrested. He pointed at Jesse. "You better lay low, princess."

"I'm protected, your highness."

"This is a glass house," he said. "Grand Central Station."

"He brought it on himself. He created it with his vibes."

"Yeah? What are you creating with yours? Bat wing stew? Good karma casserole?"

The look she gave him Maggie would never forget. Not a mean glinting cut of eye, but glossy, transparent, her eyes taking up the whole of her mind, windows all the way open, air blowing through. She just said, "It's coming, Quinn."

"What is?"

"The end."

"You're right about that."

"I'm not talking about you and me."

"I am," he said.

Several days later Lora and Maggie found Jesse shivering in front of a mirror. "Pull me away," she whispered. "I'm stuck. I've been in this mirror for hours, I can't get out."

"Look at her eyes," said Lora. "Dilated. She's tripping for sure." They dragged her away as Jesse stared at them through bottomless black pools, swimming eternity back in her brain, ego dissolved.

"Something terrible is going to happen," Jesse cried.

"Honey, it's just the acid," Lora said. "Do you want something? Some downers or something?"

"It's not the trip. It's this house. I've been in the mirror and I know now. I know that we're all going to die."

"That's just cosmic truth," said Lora. "That's what's at the end for all of us. But not now. We've got our whole lives ahead of us."

"It's all around us. I've seen it. This house will eat us. It's hexed." Jesse chanted like an oracle. "It's coming. Maybe it's already here. You can't turn away from what you know. When your body knows a thing, you have to believe it. You have to act or you'll be stuck forever." Jesse pulled away from them, ran to her room, and did not come out for two days.

One hot afternoon Maggie answered a knock at the door to find Henry Loam standing on the porch. Up close he was even more massive and dramatic-looking. The only thing small about him was the steel points of his eyes. He did not seem to recognize Maggie from the meeting, and she was glad. "I'm looking for Jesse," he said.

"She's not here. Hasn't been around in a couple of days."

"I'd like to leave a note for her."

Maggie didn't know why she didn't trust him. Don't trust anybody over thirty? He must have been in his late thirties, and everyone that age seemed ancient to her. Inside the house he peered around as if he were looking for something, then scribbled a note about a party that night, an address in the Haight, signing it "Love, Henry."

Maggie read the note. "I'll give it to her," she promised.

When Jesse returned later, she urged both Lora and Maggie to come with her to the party. They dressed in tripping regalia, Lora in her black-veiled hat, Maggie in a thrift-shop lace dress. They drove into the city in Sandy's VW. At the crowded flat, a loud band blasted in the front room, and Maggie spotted a familiar face in a corner with the biker contingent. "Cody's here," she shouted above the music. Jesse put her arm around Maggie and said, "I know all about you and Quinn, okay?" Maggie looked away, then back at Jesse's cool green stare. "It's all right, really it is. When we love someone, it binds us together. It's like we're related. Besides, I'm with Henry now." Just then Henry Loam appeared and led Jesse away into the smoky throng.

Lora was dancing by herself in the jerk light of a flicking strobe. Maggie watched for a while, flattened against a wall, later wandering back to a bedroom to get away from the piercing whine of the electric guitars. In a shadowy room, a man sat on the floor fiddling with what looked like equipment from a high school chemistry lab.

"Cotton," he said to a young girl. "Give me the cotton."

The girl fumbled in a purse. "I don't have any."

He slapped her. "Don't tell me you don't have any!" he barked above the screeching music.

"Here, I have a Tampax, how's this?" The girl was crying.

He lunged at her, knocking her over.

Maggie cringed. Someone handed him a fistful of cotton. "Be cool, be cool." Words rippled through the black light and her eyes adjusted to the violet dark. She saw that the girl was Lily. The man placed a needle to his arm. The one who'd handed him cotton left the room—wasn't that String? Maggie was sure it was. Suddenly she felt light-headed. It was one thing to smoke an occasional joint, but the sight of that needle scared and sickened and disgusted her. It looked like something out of all those health-class movies on drug addiction she'd seen in high school. *Too far down for me,* she thought, and left the room. She searched the still-crowded flat and couldn't find Jesse, but discovered Lora out on the back steps. Together they drove back to Berkeley.

She was surprised to find Quinn and Sandy up making tea for Lily and Peter. They were discussing what made a person cosmic. Quinn came over to Maggie and draped his arm around her shoulders. Sandy continued talking. "I think it's service. I don't think you have to know God or even have any idea of what or who God is. It's just doing things for people."

"I think it's when you know for sure you're nothing," said Lily. She looked as if she was about to fall over, a rag doll in a ripped dinette chair. "You've got nothing in your whole life so all you really have is God but since you don't get it, I mean you don't understand, it's really nothing. God's there but you're empty. You're shit." Suddenly she began to cry.

"It's the drugs," Quinn spat. "Bad fucking chemicals."

Maggie took Lily up to the room where she and Peter were staying and brushed her hair, talking her down, singing lullabies and child songs to her.

When Peter came in, he set a roll of black cloth on the nightstand. "I'll take care of her now," he said. "It's going to be okay, Lily. You're going to feel better in a minute."

"I could run a nice hot bath for her," Maggie offered. That was when she saw it next to the bed, the cloth fallen open, syringe, needle, rubber strap.

Peter glanced up. "She'll be fine."

Quinn and Maggie left the house, walked all the way up to the Lawrence Science Museum to watch the sunrise. In the morning they hitched a ride down with a janitor. It was nine or so when Maggie went searching for her hairbrush, touched Lily's neck gone flaccid, damp-cool. Peter asleep forever on the faded rug.

Immediately Maggie called the police. Quinn rushed toward her screaming as she hung up. "You didn't call the fucking pigs, did you? Maggie, don't be stupid! Give us time, for God's sake!" They ran from room to room shouting at the others to get rid of all drugs and paraphernalia. When the police pulled up in front of the house, Quinn was gone, out the back door, between the houses, across the quiet Berkeley streets. Maggie assumed it was his FBI paranoia that made him bolt like that. To Quinn, federal agents and police were the same thing.

Rob came into the room where Lily and Peter were and he looked Maggie in the eyes for the first time since they'd broken up. Sandy and Lora were crying. The bodies were placed on stretchers. They had no identification, no wallets, no names, no money. Maggie glanced around as the police riffled through their few clothes in a tattered backpack. She noticed that the syringe and black cloth were gone. She tried to remember if they'd been there when she first found the bodies. She tried for many years to remember that.

Long into the morning they answered questions for the police. Instinctively, none of them mentioned Peter and Lily's connection with Jesse. To protect Jesse was to protect themselves.

"They were hitchhikers," said Dennis. "They just showed up at the house a couple of weeks ago and said they were from—where did they say, Lora?"

"Kansas."

"I think it was Kansas. They needed a place to crash for a couple of weeks. They were traveling. They were on their way to—where were they going, Lora?"

"Oregon, I think."

Maggie remembered the other man who stood about the room as they answered the questions, a thin man in a gray suit who only listened.

Jesse had said in one of her diatribes, "Thinking makes it so, images are magic, watch your thoughts. The universe is listening. Now we are protected." But whatever she'd been doing back then did not seem to have anything to do with protection.

Maggie and Lora were sent to track Jesse down in the Haight because the police wanted to talk to her. Maggie remembered Jesse sitting in the living room wearing straight-leg jeans, pink button-down blouse, hair pulled back in a ponytail. She looked like a completely different person, one who had removed a costume that Maggie had mistaken for her real self.

"Were you aware they were using drugs?" asked the officer.

"No, sir. No idea at all."

"Were they selling drugs?"

"If they were they sure kept quiet about it."

"How did you know them?"

"I guess I really didn't. Sir."

What struck Maggie as saddest was that Peter and Lily's bodies remained unidentified. Who were they, really? Maggie guessed it was the times. The Haight, Berkeley, all of San Francisco was still filling with kids from all over the country searching for the remnants of the Summer of Love in the city of seven hills, on the steep hillsides and in foggy corners, between the pale buildings and along the seedy wharves of the bay.

For a week or so Maggie wouldn't make love to Quinn, just lay beside him. He said she was too sensitive, taking too much of it on. What was the death of two kids in Berkeley who had a drug problem compared to thousands of innocent Asians napalmed by U.S. forces? You had to keep death in perspective, he said.

Within a few days Quinn finally broke up with Jesse for good. Maggie went to Jesse's room later that night. "Maggie, he really loves you. We all love you. I was never any good to him anyway." Jesse's voice broke and she cried, no sound, just a throaty rasp. "You're clean, you're pure. That's why he loves you. You're so goddamn pure." Maggie didn't know what she meant.

"Listen," said Jesse, wiping her eyes with her sleeve. "I've become aware that a spirit has come to this house. It's up to us to clean it out. We make some kind of a current, you and I. You with your light. And me—I'm the dark."

Maggie could see now how stupid it was to have remained in the house. Why didn't she just move out then, find a room down the street with some girls from Ohio who dated fraternity boys? But it was 1970, not 1956. She could not have abandoned Jesse. Even though she could see Jesse was a bad angel starting to fall, Jesse and Lora were everything Maggie thought she wanted to be—mysterious, powerful, utterly romantic.

* * *

It was late, the men's house dark. Jesse packed odd
things in a basket—candles, incense, vials of herbs. From a
large envelope in Quinn's room she lifted some contact
sheets, cutting out a picture of Lily and Peter. Quinn slept
in a curl on his bed.

In the room where Peter and Lily had died, they swept
the floor, washed it with an herbal infusion—angelica, said
Jesse. Mandrake root. She lit three candles in a triangle at
the center of the room, set them on a piece of white cloth.
When she opened the windows, salt air blew in, smell of
fog. With chalk she drew a pentagram on the floor, lit
incense, waving it in the corners. She gathered up stray
papers, ashtrays, towels, dirty clothes, and put them in a
brown paper bag outside the door.

Maggie had the strange sensation that they were being
watched. Maybe it was the feeling of blasphemy connected with the witchcraft. *God was watching. Her
mother was watching.* They sat cross-legged on either side
of the candles, and Jesse handed Maggie a tiny photograph of Lily, while she herself picked a small picture of
Peter. As they held the pictures in the candle flame, the
paper wrinkled black. They dropped them on a cracked
china plate, where they burned to ash. The door opened
slowly several inches, whining on the hinge. Breath held,
hot—Maggie's heart leapt in her chest. Jesse tiptoed to the
door, glancing out in the hallway. No one was there.

"It must be the spirits leaving," Jesse whispered.

Just then the window catch gave and the frame
slammed down, cracking the glass. The small fires
squeezed out.

"This room is cleansed," said Jesse. "Spirits be done
with this house." She poured a cup of water from the jar
onto the plate, and the ashes sizzled. Dipping her finger in
the wet ash, Jesse smeared it into her palm, then reached
over to Maggie, dotting the mixture on her forehead.
Maggie wiped it away.

"Don't," said Maggie. "I don't want it on me."

"It's on you anyway. It's on all of us."

"I thought you said we were getting rid of the spirits."

"Maybe we are, maybe we are."

It was after that that Jesse became obsessed with her altars and amulets. Perhaps they had all known that Jesse was flipping out, but it happened so very quickly. They were pulled in. From her understanding now, Maggie wondered if Jesse hadn't experienced a psychotic break from too many amphetamines, too much acid. She claimed once that voices on the radio had information for her, and her behavior became ritualistic. Doors must be shut three times, she claimed—once for humans, once for angels, once for demons.

The first altar Maggie noticed was constructed out of the spice rack in the kitchen. One morning the shelf was taken over with jars of herbs, odd signs from Dennis's alchemy book. Next, a shelf in the bookcase was cleaned off, dried flowers placed there and a jar: of ashes, Maggie noted. Photographs of each of them leaned on the shelf. The more chaotic things became in the house, the more Sandy cleaned. She was always sweeping, dusting, even washing the floors in the men's rooms, her hair in a kerchief. "It's filthy around here," she snapped.

One night Maggie woke late and Quinn, who had fallen asleep beside her, was not in the bed. Maggie waited for him to return, but when he did not, she stole out into the hallway, stood there naked in the darkness when she heard what she thought were sounds of crying. She pressed herself against the wall so they would not see her and peered in from the black hall. Quinn was moaning, hands over his face. "I love her, Jesse."

"But you need me. You need me more," Jesse whispered.

Maggie flattened against the wall, listening in shocked secrecy.

"Jesse," Quinn said, "I can't. I don't want there to be any more hurt."

"You don't know anything about hurt," she said bitterly.

"You'll always love me. You'll never get rid of me. I'm going to haunt you for the rest of your life. You don't know the half of it."

"You're evil," he whispered.

Maggie didn't know why she stayed there, crouched in the dark, listening to them making love. When she was sure they were asleep, she took Quinn's camera from his backpack in her room, the one with the zoom lens, and in the dawn light she leaned in and snapped a picture of them wound together like snakes. She left it in the camera for him to discover among his contact sheets.

The first part of August passed under a tense truce. Jesse stayed more and more in the Haight with Henry Loam. On a Sunday, Lora surveyed the kitchen, dirty dishes stacked on every available surface. "Look at this pit," she complained. "Why is it such a dump in here?"

"Sandy must be on strike," observed Dennis. "She's the only one who ever cleans up around here."

Lora stopped, clanked down the coffee pot. "Where *is* Sandy?" she demanded. "Has anybody seen her? She's usually up by now. I didn't see her last night either." Lora stomped up the stairs, holding her jean skirt up to her knees. Maggie heard her clogs on the wooden steps and minutes later, Lora screaming.

They all clambered up to the room, where Lora leaned over Sandy's bed, shaking her violently. "Get up. It's Sunday. Oh, God, get up, Sandy, please." Then she fell on her, sobbing, "No, no, not again."

Dennis pulled Lora off, put his hand to Sandy's cheek, then her neck. "Christ almighty," he choked. "She's dead." He crossed himself. Maggie had never seen him do that.

Rob and Cody were sitting stunned on the couch by the time the police arrived, the same two officers who'd come several weeks before. They recovered an empty vial under the bed. The last entry in Sandy's diary, left open on her desk, read, "I'm sorry, I'm sorry, I'm sorry," the

phrase repeated over and over down the small, lined
page.

This time Quinn did not leave when the police came.
Maggie sat out on the front steps with him while the
police continued their search. Suddenly Quinn jumped
up, shaking his head as if he were silently arguing with
someone. He gestured, waving a hand before his face.
"Gnats," he said under his breath as a police officer
stepped out through the front door.

When Sandy's parents came to collect their daughter's
body, they asked that Lora pack Sandy's things and ship
them down on the Greyhound bus to Tucson. Maggie
helped, emptying the contents of neat dresser drawers,
bookshelves, packing up papers Sandy had just completed
for a course. On impulse they decided against shipping
the things and drove all the way to Arizona in a single
night in a van Cody had borrowed. No one could get in
touch with Jesse before they left. At the last minute Maggie left a note for her explaining what had happened.

All of them stayed in one room in a green stucco motel.
The family hardly spoke to them, averted their eyes, lace
over their heads, white Stetsons.

Within days of their return from Arizona, Lora announced that she'd just had it and was moving out of this
freak show, getting a place with Dennis. She let Maggie
know she'd be open to having her and Quinn come with
them. Maggie said she didn't know, she just wasn't sure.
She knew she was afraid to go on living in the Berkeley
house though.

She remembered the night before they moved out.
Dennis's room was already empty; all that remained were
the remnants of the cleansing ritual, the ashes and the
cracked plate. Cody said he was going to stay on, that he'd
keep Jesse's things in her room for a couple of weeks, then
store them in the basement. Maybe she just went gypsy-
ing off somewhere, he said. Once last year she took off for
two months and on rent day there came a check from
New York City. "Jesse and I were the ones who got this

house in the first place. I ain't scared of ghosts anyway. Not after Nam."

Jesse Ryder never did return. Maggie went home to Minnesota after summer school finals, and when she returned in the fall to live in the two-bedroom flat with Lora, Dennis and Quinn, Lora told her that the police had come around searching for Jesse. There was the question of how Sandy had gotten the drugs she'd taken and the police said that Jesse had been under surveillance, that it was known she sometimes sold drugs on campus.

After she disappeared, it seemed to Maggie that Jesse had been a totally fictional character they had dreamed of in a blur of weed, revolution, and rock and roll. A hallucination. Briefly glimpsed paisley in the design of a tree, then gone. Maggie tried several times to contact her. She knew Jesse had a stepbrother who lived in Indianapolis. When he finally returned her calls, he told her in a Hoosier drawl, "Jesse? Oh, you mean Lynn. Is that what she's callin' herself nowadays? I'll be damned if I know where she is. I got a postcard from her from Mexico darn near four months ago. No return address or nothing." Jesse's mother had remarried and moved to Florida; Maggie didn't know her new name.

Lora was the one who told Maggie several years later the rumor that Jesse was with a Rasta man in Jamaica, up in the hills somewhere, that she'd had a child by him. A third source said India, living at an ashram with a guru who manifested holy ashes out of tears on a picture. Maggie liked the last stories better. Jesse would have liked those particular versions of her life, wherever she was.

Maggie snapped off the light in Rob's kitchen and watched the skyline glimmer below in a grid of neon and streetlights. She believed to this day that Jesse's witchcraft had not been intentionally evil, not any more so than any other brand of dime-store revelation or universal soothsaying in the Golden West. She'd never really thought Jesse had been responsible for the way Peter,

Lily, and Sandy died, either. Even if Jesse had done some
dealing, it was only grass, sometimes orange sunshine or
windowpane. Surely, she'd thought back then, it had all
been a terrible accident. *Just like Lora's "accident."*

Now she knew differently. They'd been killed, all three
of them, she was sure of it. Someone had documented
their murders with a Polaroid camera. Though she could
not tie those deaths clearly to Lora's, she was certain now
that there was a connection. Lora had known something
about the deaths in the Berkeley house. She had information or was getting close to information that had long
been hidden.

She was going to have to be discreet in what she told
Rob. He'd not been forthright with her about Lora's remains. If Lora had been shot in the head or beaten—
Maggie shuddered to think of it—it was very convenient
for her skull to be missing, just as Quinn had said.

Unconsciously Maggie let her hand rest near the phone
on the counter, remembering how this long day had
started, that phone call, no voice, white air. After Lora
had gotten the shadow box, she'd begun receiving strange
calls. Soon after she was dead. Maggie felt like a caught fly
on a thin web. Her own movements might entangle and
trap her and the pattern, if there was one, was too close to
see.

Chapter 11

The moon was obscured. It was damp in the black woods. She hoped that it wouldn't rain or cloud up on the night of the full moon. She had visualized it so clearly, had seen it, had asked that it be so. But if the moon chose not to participate, that would be all right too. Jesse Ryder would have her own light.

She unrolled the extension cords out across the grass into the woods as if she were preparing a stage for a rock concert. Rods of neon were already hung from branches on dowels and frames she'd constructed earlier in the summer. There were eleven violet wands, each four feet long, curved like parentheses, and seven straight blue rods. The yellow rod was a seven-foot-long squiggle. The others, nine white lines, hung vertically like small slashes of lightning.

The blue wands, suspended at odd angles around the grove, were lit now, glowing eerily. Moths and gnats hovered in a flurry, orbiting the light. A neighbor who stopped over when Jesse first turned on the lights tonight expressed the hope that she wasn't opening a bar. He didn't think the property was zoned for commercial use.

Jesse stood back and thought, *good. It is good.* Other
titles for the installation came to mind: *Ascension Electric.
Moon With Unnatural Daughters.* One in the coven had
criticized the idea of using electricity. It should all be
done with candles, she said. Jesse told her, "This is the
twentieth century. The goddess comes in many forms."

There. She stepped back to the studio, surveying the
circle coming into form out there in the darkness. When
she pulled the power switch back down, black flowed in
again. *Maybe that's how it should end,* she thought. *Cut
the power. Natural light of the stars and moon and our
own singing. The oracles at Delphi would be proud of us.
No white pillars of stone. Our temples are temporary. The
sacred is a slippery thing.*

Now if only she could be sure no fuses would blow
during the ritual. She might need a higher voltage. A
generator or something, she thought.

Jesse sat out on the deck listening to the wind in the
redwoods. The house was so quiet without Ben. He had
called to ask if he could go up to Bodega Bay camping
with Milo and his father. "We'll be back Monday morning,
Mom. Don't worry, I'll be there to help with the installation," he'd promised. She was a little disappointed. She'd
entertained the thought of dragging him with her to Dennis's. The idea of seeing everyone again made her nervous. *Old patterns, old fears. And karma too,* she thought.
What she knew about that household had always haunted
her. And now this trouble with Dennis. Horrible that the
police suspected, even minimally, that Dennis had anything to do with Lora's death.

It would all be worth it, though, to see Maggie Shea
again. She and Maggie and Lora, what a triumvirate
they'd been. She felt bad that because of the awful circumstances she'd had to cut off contact from all of them so
completely. *Over. Done with,* she thought. *Ancient history.*

*   *   *

It was during the Summer of Love that Jesse had realized she would have to invent herself. She'd left home in June 1967, hitchhiking across the South and West, up the California coast, arriving in the Haight-Ashbury along with thousands of other wandering souls. She'd left her mother and new stepfather in a small cement house in Florida and never looked back. With each person she met she made herself more fictional. It wasn't that she was a con artist; it was herself she deceived. She created the story of her life, refined it and found it more believable than her real past. Circus performer? Oh, sure. But not a far cry from her mother's real job. Until her mother married the real-estate agent she'd been a divorced pet groomer. Specialty: poodles, Lhasa apsos, cockapoos. Dip baths for fleas. Actually, it was Jesse's childhood dream to take Mom and the dogs out on the road. That summer in the Haight, that's what she claimed to new friends. It was a marriage of myths: Kerouac and Barnum and Bailey. *Yeah, I grew up with the circus. My mom was "Mary Lee and the Wonderful Wonder Dogs."* It was years before Jesse realized how solid and comfortable all her lies had become. Besides, she wasn't the only one—everyone she knew was digging out a place on that crazy anthill, busy inventing *themselves* out of their middle-class backgrounds, all living on the rhetoric of dreams.

In sixty-eight she crossed the bay to Berkeley, living here and there, crashing in an unused room in the dorm where she first met Maggie and Lora, eventually renting the house on College Avenue. Even though she wasn't registered, she attended classes regularly, figuring it was the only way she'd ever get to college. She fell in with the movement, more because it was a wave that pulled her under than because of any intellectual or moral decision.

But after a while Jesse became disillusioned with the left. She couldn't articulate it then—she was not enough of a movement heavy to argue her position correctly—but she was searching for Eros, for Art and Spirit, a quest then thought of as terribly bourgeois. It was poetics, imagination, and sexuality that interested her, not political paranoia and the increasingly violent urges of the left to take up arms against a fascist state.

She missed Woodstock in sixty-nine, did not drive east with Cody, Quinn, Dennis, and Lora but stayed back in Berkeley with Sandy Craig. In fact it was during that summer that she met Henry Loam at a bookstore in the Haight, first talked to him about the solstice and equinox celebrations once instigated by the Diggers, now continued in a small Aquarian coven, "a practicum for ritual work," Loam called it. A call to the etherics for aid and comfort. He invited Jesse to attend a newcomers' meeting.

By the time Henry Loam initiated Jesse into his coven, it was the only thing that made sense to her. An act of human imagination against a repressive world that denied magic. *Cleanse the air. Create images of charged power, visualize what you want to see actualized. Protect yourself. Pay homage to the invisibles.*

Of all the people in that house, it was Maggie who seemed untouched by the troubles of the times. There was something so good about her. Like everything else in that house, they mythologized her midwestern earthsolid purity, and Jesse came to depend on that the further she delved into the dark world. She'd asked for Maggie's help when she did the cleansing ritual so the spirits wouldn't eat her up. Maggie didn't know it, but she was white light, both talisman and shield.

That was why Maggie had become so important to Jesse, even though they'd tugged a bit over Quinn. Maggie was the only one she could talk to about her interest in magic, the only one who'd play it with her. Maggie also had qualities that Jesse had deeply envied, and when they became close Jesse felt she had access to those qualities too. For not only was Maggie grounded and practical, she seemed to have an inherent feeling of self-worth—she'd come from that big Irish family where she must have been loved and wanted in a way Jesse never had. Finally,

though she only knew it years later, it was Maggie's deep
and unwavering faith in God that she'd most admired.
Sure, Maggie rebelled against her parochial school upbringing, but Jesse knew that at her center Maggie had
God's ear, and for years, until her own faith took hold,
under all her wild seeking there was a hole of doubt and
emptiness.

Jesse had been so involved in her own fantasies then
that it had taken her a long time to understand some
things about that house, secrets she wished she'd never
known. Some information could kill. Bite into the apple,
fall from grace or sleep for a hundred years. Jesse felt as
though she'd done all of them. When she'd been told that
Peter and Lily had died of a heroin overdose, it didn't
occur to her at first that they might have died because of
drugs they'd gotten at the party she'd invited them to.
But when the police had grilled her for hours, she'd gotten sick to her stomach at the imagined scent of death in
that house, terrified she'd be tied in with their deaths in
some way. But it was not uncommon in those days, a drug
overdose in San Francisco, Berkeley, or Oakland. Two
unidentified kids, one only sixteen, one maybe twenty.
They went into cold storage with tags on their toes, unidentified, and the members of the Berkeley house at-
tempted to resume their crazed, ordinary lives.

Jesse pushed it away, the thought that their deaths had
anything to do with her. It was people's own responsibility
what they took, how much and in what combination. She
didn't sell class A narcotics, anyway. Only candy drugs
and mostly to friends. Looking back, she could see what
she did with her fears. She turned them into a darker
magic, an underworld casting of spells and charms, amulets against the death she felt not only in Peter and Lily
but in the whole decline of the sixties into a chemical and
political sinkhole, the death of the world. It was, as they
said in those days, a bad trip, one from which Jesse did not
return for a number of years.

Yes, she became a witch. She idealized the powerful

Henry Loam, even fell a little in love with him, and she
felt, through him, that she was in on some great secret,
some unfolding of meaning about the Ultimate Nature of
Reality. Once she had felt that the salvation of the world
was in political work, but slowly she began to feel that the
political leanings of the household were on the wrong
track. Their social pronouncements lacked transcen-
dence. She imagined that Loam's coven both knew the
secrets of reality and kept them from all the world. She
began to think of Henry Loam as some sort of God-em-
peror who, with his spells, could single-handedly bring
Nixon to his knees. Jesse laughed now to realize how the
world went down on its knees all by itself, without direction from any god other than the natural gravity of human
ignorance, greed, and deceit.

A few weeks after Peter and Lily died, Jesse had heard
someone rustling around in the basement and had gone
down to see who it was. Sandy gasped when Jesse appeared behind her. Sandy's face was pale and drained.
She'd been dusting—the heating ducts of all places—
when she'd come across a wire that led in through a basement window, a small copper clip fixed to it.

"Look," Sandy whispered. "Our phone is tapped, just
like Quinn said it was."

Jesse unhooked it, yanking at the clip until it broke off.

Then Sandy had beckoned Jesse to her room. "I can't
keep this to myself anymore," she whispered. In her bedroom Sandy fumbled in her closet, emerging with a small
envelope. Inside were several Polaroid photographs,
blurred and artless.

"These were taken of them after they died," Sandy
whispered. "I found them in the basement, too, hidden on
top of one of the ducts. Do you think they're for blackmail
or something?"

"Or somebody documenting for an FBI file," suggested
Jesse.

"Should I take them to the cops?" asked Sandy.

"Hell no," she said. "They're probably in on it. Who

planted the wiretap anyway? Sandy, what if someone in this house is an informer?"

"But who?"

Jesse shuddered, shoving the pictures back to Sandy. "I think you should just hide them someplace where no one would ever think of looking until we know what's going on. And Sandy—don't tell anyone else about this, promise me."

Jesse had gone that night to the city to see Henry Loam, and the next day, when she'd returned, police cars were lined up in front of the house, their red lights spinning in the sunlight. Jesse watched from the shadows across College Avenue. It was then that Quinn stepped out onto the porch with Maggie. Seeing her, he raised his hand and waved her away.

Two days later, in the middle of the night, Jesse went back to the house and found Maggie's note. She sat trembling, reading the note over and over. Somebody must have known that Sandy found that wiretap, those pictures. *And they must know I'm aware of them too,* she thought. Maybe the whole house was bugged, Sandy's room too. God, they should have gone to the police. Even FBI pigs didn't go around murdering innocent people. Or did they? That's what Quinn was always claiming in his diatribes, and Cody, too, in his tales about Vietnam. Innocent people were murdered, tools of fascist powers. Jesse didn't stay around to figure it out. Sick with grief and guilt, she sobbed in her room, holding the sheets to her face.

They were watching the house. Possibly she'd been followed there. They knew everything. The room was bugged, there was a man in an empty car out there on the street. She grabbed a few things and ran from the house. The next day she withdrew a few hundred dollars from a savings account in an Oakland bank and bought a one-way bus ticket to Mexico City. At the border they asked her name and she almost didn't answer because for so long she had pretended to be someone else. "Lynn Janet Resiewski," she said.

Of those years in Mexico, she could only say this: she had a vision of a dirty beach in an orange sunset. For the first time in many years she perceived no alternative reality, only the absolute present, the light of the world and the littered shore. That was the truth of it. She stopped all drugs and nearly died of diarrhea, vomiting, and dehydration. When she began to bleed heavily and then to hemorrhage she knew it was not a period. In a hospital she miscarried the child she'd been unaware she was carrying. Though she had no idea who the father had been, she grieved the loss of the unknown child. She might have made a family, become a family. Motherhood might have been the only thing that could redeem the evil that Quinn had seen in her.

Jesse Ryder watched the stars come in and out of the low clouds over the redwoods. For all those years she had lived with that regret and fear, wondering if she was indirectly responsible for Peter and Lily's death but feeling for certain that she could have prevented Sandy's. They should have gone to the police in the first place, but she'd been too afraid. She hid in Mexico, worked as a waitress, then as a maid for a man named Alegria. It was during that time that she conceived Ben. His father was a boy she'd slept with a few times on a trip to Baja, another American hippie on the road. Ben spent the first three years of his life in Alegria's garden chasing chickens. Jesse hung clothes out on the line to dry.

That's when she started to hang things, cloth and folds, hanging and washing. All her art had its seeds in women's chores, even this bizarre neon forest she was creating. For wasn't worshiping the moon and sun women's work, their bodies' homage? She didn't know. Maybe it was all new dream rhetoric, another form of fantasy and deception. Yet she believed it. It was the only grounding in her life other than Ben.

She just prayed that it wasn't a mistake to see all of the people from the Berkeley house. Maybe Sandy's death had been a suicide, an accidental overdose of sleeping pills and speed, as Maggie's note had said so long ago. But Sandy had been the only one among them who'd never done drugs at all. She thought of her old friends: surely none of them could have killed Peter and Lily and Sandy. Surely she'd only thought that in her drug-induced paranoia. For a moment, though, she wasn't sure.

And tomorrow she would see them all at Dennis's house. Quinn, King Rat, her lost love. Cody, Sound Man, who'd always warned her that her own magic would do her in. Rob, Mr. Saxophone, wounded in some way but with no outward scars. Dennis, former magician and man of the sea. Maggie, Purey, Our Lady of the Corn Fields. *And Lora's ghost,* Jesse thought, *watching over us all.*

Chapter 12

M aggie woke with a dense pool of fear just under her breastbone, the feeling in her chest of not enough air, the morning sky outside the French windows hazy, blue and promising light. *All wrong,* she thought, pulling on jeans, a long purple T-shirt, and sandals she'd bought a week ago in Minnesota before . . . *Before I knew,* she thought. *Lies and concealments and half-truths. Omissions like erasures on a page. Hold the paper up to the light, read through the vague smudges.*

Running fingers through her thick hair she came quickly down the stairs to the living room. She wanted to take the shadow box out to Dennis's. She wouldn't exactly hide it from Rob, she simply wouldn't mention it. Besides, it was hers—she could do with it what she wanted and she wanted others to see it. White drapes pulled over the bay window muted the room in gray half-light, and as she approached the coffee table she saw Rob cross his office with quick sure steps. She froze, still as an animal in shadow. He swung open the carved doors of the armoire and took a boxy black handgun off the inside of the door, pulled the slide back and let it go forward again with a quiet clack, then lowered the hammer and shoved the gun into a briefcase. He did not see her. She took several steps back toward the stairway as he bent over his desk examining something. Her leg brushed a side table, a lampshade rattling softly. A magazine slid to the floor.

"Maggie?" he called, and she knelt to pick it up, her heart rushing as if she'd been caught at something. *But it's him that's been caught,* she thought.

"I didn't know you were up yet," Rob said, stepping toward her.

Maggie tossed the magazine down and smiled, she knew, too brightly. "Just got up. Thought I heard you down here."

"Did you have a good time with Quinn?"

Good time. Very nice, thank you. "Oh, yes. We talked about old times."

"Are you all right?" he asked.

"Some coffee." Her voice was high and thin. "Coffee would help."

"Great," he said, walked two steps to the kitchen, then turned back to her. "Are you sure?"

"With half and half if there's some left."

"No, I mean are you sure that you're okay?"

She straightened a couch pillow. "Probably a little hung over." She forced herself to look at him directly. "We drank another bottle of wine after you left."

"I'll make the coffee strong then," he said. He hesitated a moment, then turned toward the kitchen.

I'm a lousy liar, she thought, *My father was wrong. Stories, okay. Lies, no.* She didn't know why she didn't say something, even a joke. *Oh, I see you're going to do some target shooting today. With your brother-in-law as target?* But she'd said nothing; the moment had passed. Her furtive observation had become one more little lie of not-saying.

But perhaps it was better. A silent watch. The advantage of the seemingly innocent observer. *He doesn't know I'm watching him, too, just as he is watching Dennis.* Last night as Quinn had driven her home, she'd wondered briefly if it was wise to continue staying with Rob if he was in any way implicated in this. But now she thought, *Stay. Stay close in, listen and see.* Amazing what a receptive attention could draw out, the essence of good therapy.

And in that moment Maggie made a deliberate decision about what had only been happenstance until then. She was going to consciously investigate Lora's death, and from her vantage point as Purey, their old pigeonhole of her, the good midwestern girl, she'd learn plenty. She already had. They all trusted her far too much. Today she would see all of them together—all of them that were left, that is. And surely she'd learn more. *Tell me if you understand what it all means,* Lora had written in her final letter. *All right,* thought Maggie. *For you, I'll try.*

They drove along Highway One past Green Gulch Zen Center, small ranches and cliff-hung houses. The early fog would recede as the sun burned it off. Rob pointed out the sheer drop of brown cliff that fell to the ocean below. "That's Slide Ranch down there," he said. "Where they found the boat." Maggie noticed that he mentioned only the boat, not Lora's body. Then he asked, "So what all did you and Quinn talk about last night?"

"Don't worry, I didn't say anything indiscreet." She swallowed hard, hoping that was true.

"You didn't tell him about going to the house in Berkeley?"

"Of course not, Rob. I said I wouldn't." *Go ahead,* she told herself, torn between the urge to confront him with what Quinn had told her and a fear which said *Keep quiet. Don't let him know what you know.* But without some questioning, she knew Rob would offer little.

"Quinn told me some things, though," she added after a silence. When she glanced over at Rob, his eyes were fixed on the winding road, the rock-drop of cliff hundreds of feet below to the Pacific. They drove slowly behind a yellow pickup.

"Such as . . ."

"He told me about Lora's remains for one thing," she offered. "With a few more details than you mentioned. That there was no skull, for instance."

Rob kept his eyes straight ahead, and she wondered again if she should be mentioning this at all. The unspoken rule to keep silent in some families was so powerful you could feel it like a threat. *Speak truth and die.* That's almost how it felt. "I wish you'd told me that, Rob. It seems pretty relevant to what we've been talking about."

Nothing. Numb again, icy quiet.

When he spoke, his voice was dry, slightly sarcastic. "I didn't mention it because it was so horrible. Dennis went in to the coroner's office and couldn't bring himself to look at the remains. I went. Have you ever seen a person's ashes, how awful it is to think a human being can be reduced to that—white powder and a few chunks like stones? Well, that's how it was, only worse. She was nothing but a bunch of bones laid out on a stainless-steel table. Talk about identifying the deceased. Pardon me for not going into the details for you."

Defensive, she thought. She decided to press on.

"Quinn also talked about the will some. He seemed to have the feeling that you're the one who would benefit most if that codicil is not admitted to probate, that it would be to your advantage both as an individual and as executor."

"Is that right?" Rob gunned past the pickup on a short straightaway, swerving toward the edge of the narrow road, jerking the car back into the right lane as a van sped toward them honking.

He sniffed out a short, angry laugh. "So that's going to be Dennis's stance. Very nice. Very very nice. I should have thought of that. I can't believe I didn't. Thanks, Maggie. That's a very helpful bit of information. I can use that tomorrow with the lawyers," he said. "It helps to be forewarned of a strategy. I can't believe how well Dennis has thought this out. I'll give him credit for that." He made a fist in the air. "And to think all that's needed to keep him from a conviction is reasonable doubt. See, that's what he's working on. Throw the blame onto me, sure. Create a diversion. He's always been good at that. You know that's the essence of trick magic. Keep your eye busy over here so you don't see what's really going on. And I'm sure he's got Quinn convinced of his innocence. That makes perfect sense. Quinn's already his alibi for the weekend she disappeared, so that fits. I wonder if Cody's in his stable too. Great, great," he sputtered, words rocketing forth. "Well, this is going to be one hell of a pleasant afternoon. You'll excuse me if I don't stay long. And if I do stay it will be only to try to catch that son of a bitch at something, because he's going to make a mistake. He's going to make a very big mistake, and I'm going to be ready for him."

By the time they dropped down into Stinson Beach the fog had lifted. They drove up the gravel road onto a brown-baked hill that faced Bolinas Lagoon and the ocean beyond. As they pulled up in front of the house, Maggie thought, *It's stunning.* Lora had often described its weathered wood, high-slanted windows and front door, the wood carved into the shape of a curved fish, some Oriental figure for a knocker. She didn't know how much Lora had received for her initial trust fund payment but this house must have eaten a good bit of it. Houses had a way of requiring money, and the taxes here couldn't be cheap.

Rob hopped up several steps to a deck that surrounded the house, then disappeared around a corner and Maggie followed. Dennis sat in a weather-beaten lawn chair reading a warped copy of *The Village Voice.* He wore shades with red frames, his flannel shirttails hanging out over jeans torn at the knee. Flower beds that Lora must have kept full of petunias and poppies were dry, a few succulents hanging in the crumbling earth. Half a joint balanced in a full ashtray on a large wooden crate being used as a table.

Dennis stretched to standing and Maggie went to embrace him, his growth of beard prickly against her cheek. She had to pull back to keep from giving in to the thick grief gathering again in her chest.

"Maggie," said Dennis, "you look like a million bucks! You girls just don't age."

"Girls, Dennis? Girls?" She forced the cheerfulness.

"Sorry. I mean Amazons. Female warriors from the matriarchy. Feminine principle incarnate, how could I have forgotten?"

She tried to relax, overwhelmed by the feeling of Lora —more than specific memories, the force of her remembered presence. "I can't believe I've never been out here. If I'd known this was where you lived I might have moved in."

"Want to buy it? I'll give it to you cheap just to keep it in the family. Then you can rent me a room. What do you say? I'll probably need the money—right, Rob?"

Dennis said it lightheartedly, but Rob nearly snarled, "Save it for your lawyer, Dennis."

"I thought you were my lawyer." He looked at Rob straight-faced and innocent.

"I think there's going to be a little conflict of interest, Dennis."

"Is that right? Now what has Andrea come up with?"

"Tomorrow," said Rob. "I said save it for tomorrow, okay?"

Dennis shrugged and went into the house, calling back for Maggie to join him. He put the Layla album on and circled the open kitchen, cracking eggs into a bowl and wrapping a loaf of bread in aluminum foil. Rob sat out on the deck, fuming. Dennis ignored him.

Before long Quinn and Cody arrived in Cody's sleek gray Mercedes. Both men bent to kiss her, Quinn brushing Maggie's cheek, then kissing her mouth.

"Does your brain feel like waxed paper?" Quinn asked. "Are we resuming our romantic interlude?"

Maggie shook her head, laughing, relieved he was here. "You," she said. "I know you from someplace."

"I could fall right back in love," he said, "in two seconds. I figured it out. It's because you reject me. It's irresistible." He reached for her as if to kiss her neck.

"Later," she whispered.

"See? It's pure technique."

The talk bantered and ruffled on the sunny deck, cars, travel, the ecological balance of the Bolinas Lagoon, and then Maggie heard the gravel churn again and a truck pulled up into the yard. *Who could this be?* she wondered. *We're all here.*

A thin woman with short hair hopped out of a truck holding a bottle of wine and a bunch of wildflowers. Cody stood slowly and whistled. "Damn if it isn't the sorcerer's apprentice." It wasn't until that moment that Maggie recognized Jesse Ryder.

Quinn had just been about to take a picture. Lifting the Nikon, he snapped. Jesse put the toe of her pink sneaker down behind her, sweeping into a deep bow like a courtier.

"Hi, everybody!" she called out. "Heard there was a party. Maggie, get over here and pose with me, this is historical."

Thoroughly astonished, Maggie ran over to her and threw her arms around Jesse's thin shoulders. "You don't know how glad I am to know you're all right," Maggie said. She'd have been elated to see her in any case, but one thought kept going through her mind: *The shadow box is wrong, then. Jesse's alive.*

"Look at you," Jesse cried. "You're gorgeous. Tell me you live in a big house in St. Paul and have six kids."

"That's my mother you're thinking about. All I've got is an aquarium."

"Christ," she said. "How could I have stayed out of touch for so long?"

"I looked for you."

"I heard about that. My brother told me. We've got a lot of catching up to do."

Just then Dennis emerged from the house. "Look who I found!" he shouted. "The good witch of the west!"

"And her assistant," said Cody.

By now Quinn, Cody, and Rob had come out to join Jesse and Maggie, all of them embracing in reunion, holding each other's faces in their hands as if examining a mask for clues to who they'd been. It was the same warm greeting Maggie had received yesterday at the gallery, and for a moment she could almost have forgotten the dark undercurrent swelling beneath the music and the bell-like laughter.

"Where did you ever find her?" asked Cody. "She's an apparition. Dennis, tell me you pulled her out of a hat."

"Found her at a flea market in Bolinas a couple of months ago," Dennis answered.

Jesse threw him the bouquet of flowers tied with a piece of string.

"How much was she?" asked Cody.

"Real bargain. Reduced rate."

"Shut up you sexist son of a bitch!" Jesse laughed. "I was *free*! Surely you all knew that. Cody, I can't believe you're wearing a suit!"

He grinned, holding his hands out like a runway model. "This is no mere suit, girl. This is Italian sportswear."

"I suppose that's your car, too, boy. You used to wear biker leather, ride a raggedy old Harley, and your boots had holes. What did you do, Cody, rob a bank?"

"It was insider trading," said Quinn. "But be nice to him, everybody, he's going to start up a foundation and make donations to all of us."

Jesse raised her hand. "I definitely qualify—I'm already a nonprofit organization."

She walked over to Dennis and took the beer from his hand, swigged on it. "Listen, all of you. Dennis lies. It was me who found him on that day in Bolinas. I'd been back in

Marin about a year—moved up from L.A.—and I made
him promise not to tell any of you I was back here. Now it
seems stupid, but I had this feeling I still had to be incognito. Didn't you ever feel like if you started hanging
around with people from your past you'd somehow get
stuck in who you were back then?"

"Yeah, especially if who you were getting stuck with
was Dennis!" laughed Quinn.

Maggie felt a chill as Jesse spoke. Quinn had predicted
last night that Jesse would reappear. *Just like magic,* she
thought. He must have known Jesse was around. Why
hadn't he told her? And while she was tremendously relieved and happy to see Jesse, it was yet another coincidence that fit with almost orchestrated timing. Will, body,
shadow box, Jesse. Jesse and Dennis together. What did
that add up to? She could not find the pattern of meaning
that would knit this tangled skein of facts into a reason for
Lora's death.

Rob was leaning on the deck railing, standing back,
watching as he always did. Jesse strode over to him,
brushed a kiss across his cheek. "Hi, Robbie," she began.
"I'm so sorry about—"

"Not now," he interrupted, shaking his head. Jesse put
her arms around his neck and gave him a quick squeeze.

Dennis called for them all to come into the feast—
scrambled eggs with cream cheese and chives, organic
sausage from the coop in Bolinas, bagels, muffins, a slab of
grilled salmon, Greek olives, a pasta salad Cody had
brought from a deli in Tiburon. They gathered around the
large oak table, trading tales with no apparent chronol-
ogy, everyone talking at once, what had happened to all of
them in fifteen years. Dennis told fishing stories, Rob
seemed to emerge from the gloom to discuss jazz with
Quinn, Jesse launched into a long explanation of her work
with neon and ritual as performance art, and Cody promised he'd come up to her house in Fairfax to help her with
some problem she was having with her wiring—Sound
Man to the rescue. She said it would definitely be a bad

omen if the lights failed at any time during the ritual. They poured down margaritas and wine while Quinn clicked pictures with a zoom lens the way he always did, documenting the bright day with the dark core at its center that no one mentioned at all.

During a break in conversation Quinn turned to Jesse. "Why did you go away, really?" he asked suddenly. "Why did you disappear like that?"

Jesse sipped wine from a tall tulip glass. All of them were quiet, waiting. "Wasn't it obvious?" she asked. "I thought I was going to get busted. You're the one who warned me, Quinn. I was scared. When Sandy died . . ." Her voice trailed off. "I guess I thought they'd try to nail me for it. You know that house really was bugged? It wasn't just your paranoia, Quinn." She seemed to hesitate. "I—I found the wire in the basement. For a while I even thought one of you could have been an informer." Jesse blurted out a laugh. "Maggie, tell me it wasn't you!"

"Hey, there's the Freedom of Information act now. We could all get our FBI files and read them to each other!" said Quinn. He slanted his eyes in mock interrogation and spoke in a fake German accent. "Maybe vun of us really vas a spy. . . . And, Maggie, you could find out the truth of the Great Berkeley Hex!" He winked at her and she pressed her foot hard against his under the table. Very slowly she shook her head.

"All that dealing karma," Jesse continued. "It's just coming to light now, isn't it? How screwed up we all were then. Flower power was chemical dependence. At least mine was. So what the hell, I figured if the pranksters went south of the border, I could go too. I ended up staying for a long time. I even had a baby."

"Far out!" said Quinn. "The only one of us who reproduced."

"*Far out?*" said Dennis. "How about *groovy*, Quinn? Better yet—*psychedelic.*"

Jesse turned to Maggie. "You never forgave me for splitting, did you?" she asked quietly.

Maggie took her hand. "What can I say? You were your own mystery tour. I'm just amazed to see you, all of you, again. To see how we all turned out."

Cody jumped up from the table. "Well, this is not the end of me!" he shouted. "I'm still cooking. I'm still getting ingredients together. This is not the finished form. I'm in alchemical transformation. As long as I'm sucking air I'm in process. Until the last lights go out. You talk like we're all corpses or something, preserved for hundreds of years in some time-capsule tomb!"

"Take it easy," said Quinn. "She's talking memory lane, not mummification."

There was an uneasy silence then and they all stood slowly and began clearing plates to the sink in respect for the dead who, it seemed, could not be spoken of.

In the early afternoon, after the dishes had been cleared and another round of joints passed, Dennis invited everyone to drive over to the wharf in Bolinas to check out his new boat. As Maggie brought empty wineglasses into the kitchen, she came on Dennis and Jesse leaning by the sink, arms wrapped loosely about each other's waists. They did not pull apart or seem in any way embarrassed.

"I'm going over the hill tonight with Quinn," Dennis told Jesse. "There's that meeting with the lawyers tomorrow. When can I see you?"

"I'm going to be pretty busy with the wiring for the installation."

"Well, I'll call you."

"Let me know how the meeting goes," she said.

Maggie exited into the sunshine. Across the yard she saw Rob pulling his briefcase from the trunk of his car. *No,* she thought. *Don't take that gun out here.* She crossed quickly to him, gravel kicking up in the soles of her sandals. Cody's tall frame bent over the open trunk beside Rob. Maggie touched Rob's arm.

"Rob, please—I saw you put that gun in there this morning. Don't do anything you'll regret."

He straightened and looked at her and she swallowed hard. "What, this?" he asked. He lifted the gun out of the briefcase and extended it to Cody, grip first. "It's Cody's," said Rob. "I took it to a gunsmith shop in the city for him. It needed a trigger-pull adjustment and they put a new sight on it. This little place down in the Castro. It's been there for years. What . . . you thought . . ." He started to laugh.

Cody took the gun and stared, slit-eyed, down the length of his arm. "Fantastic," he said.

Rob motioned Maggie away from the car. "You didn't think I was going to threaten Dennis or anything, did you?" He kept shaking his head. "Hey, I'm not some avenger, okay? I only want to understand. Maggie, relax, will you?"

"I can't," she said.

"I'm going down to the boat," he said. "Are you coming?"

But several minutes later, as the men climbed into Cody's car, Maggie touched Jesse's arm. "Stay," Maggie whispered. "I want to talk."

"Come on, women!" called Dennis.

"You go on ahead," Jesse answered. "We're going to stay up here and gossip about all of you!"

"We'll be back in an hour or so," he cried through the dust as they rolled down the driveway, car wheels crunching on gravel.

"They had quite a place here, didn't they?" asked Maggie.

"Did you know you said that in the past tense?"

Maggie sighed and looked at her old friend, the same beauty, aged now, leaner to the bone, a magical gleam in those green eyes. "I sure wish Lora were here."

"Yeah," said Jesse. "It's sad." She hesitated. "I guess you can tell I'm seeing Dennis now. Can you believe it? I don't know where it can go. He was so lonely, so devastated by this whole thing with Lora. Dennis is complicated, but he's familiar. I guess I still love him. It's like I have this second chance with him. Sometimes I wish I'd never gotten so swept away with Quinn."

"Did you know I almost married Quinn? We were actually engaged."

"Good God! What happened?"

"He fucked around and smoked too much dope and I went back to Minnesota. But you know what? It doesn't seem at all odd to me, your being attracted to Dennis again. I mean, my feelings for Quinn after all this time . . ."

"Jesus! We should double!" Jesse laughed.

"Maybe it's just comfort, the safe old past. But nothing lasts, does it?"

"The big deals don't. Then things you thought were over suddenly surface. Not just love but old friends. You . . ."

Maggie sat on the deck steps and stared out over the ocean. The surface of the water seemed to slant up to the far horizon.

"Jesse, what really happened with Lora? Does Dennis talk about it?"

Jesse picked up a handful of gravel, let it fall through her long fingers.

"It's pretty tense. The police have questioned him since her body turned up. There's this meeting tomorrow about her will. I guess they want to make sure it was an accidental death. I don't know—he's pretty closed-mouthed about it and awfully upset, I think, underneath."

Maggie went over to Rob's car and pulled her satchel from the back seat. She lifted out the shadow box and Lora's letter. As she handed them to Jesse, she explained, just as she had to Rob, the circumstances of Dennis's mailing the package to her.

"Jesse, tell me the truth. Did you make this thing?"

"It looks like something I made back then, but it's been changed. These pictures weren't in here, although the doodads were. It's definitely been added to. I didn't put all this silver writing on it either. What is it anyway?"

"Roman numerals," said Maggie.

"Really, it looks as if Quinn could have made it. Aren't those his pictures? And Roman numerals—that's the way he always used to date them."

"I thought that's how you dated pictures. It's that way in the photo album that Lora passed on to Rob."

"Sure—I picked it up from Quinn. You know I was a sponge. Always stealing somebody else's style," she said.

"Jesse, that's not true. You were a total original."

"What does this say?" Jesse asked.

"It's Latin for 'This too shall pass.' "

"That's the truth."

Maggie stopped then, unsure how much else to tell. Surely everything she said to Jesse would get right back to Dennis. "What about Henry Loam? Are you still in touch with him?"

"Henry? God no. I haven't even heard of him in years. Why?"

Maggie shrugged and explained briefly about Lora's imports of Haitian crafts and her connection with Freda Loam. Jesse stared down at the box with renewed interest. Haltingly, Maggie added, "So you don't think Dennis had anything to do with Lora's death?"

"Would I be sleeping with him if I did? No, the whole thing is just some bogus police procedural because of the big bucks in her will. They've got to go through their bureaucracy, that's all. But I'll tell you one thing—sometimes I feel her ghost here. Don't laugh. I mean in the same way we felt Peter and Lily in the Berkeley house after they died. In fact, I'm going to do a cleansing ritual here. You wouldn't want to help me, would you?"

Maggie shook her head. "No, but it's not a bad idea. It might clear the air."

"Dennis is very locked up about the whole thing. He was doing all right until they recovered her body. That really threw him. I think for Dennis, it's as if she died twice."

Jesse picked up the shadow box again and looked at Lora's picture. "It's like she's a mist hanging around here, waiting. Uneasy. A good burial is what she needs. That and some righteous magic."

Chapter 13

"Do you think I'm just obsessed?" Rob asked. He and Maggie had driven into the city and were nearly back to his house. "This is what happens. When I see Dennis, it's like I remember who he really is. My brother-in-law, one of my oldest friends. Then I think maybe I'm just nuts."

Maggie was silent, staring out at the odd shops along Haight Street. There, suddenly, nuzzled between a shoe repair shop and a bookstore just off Clayton, was the crowded window of a second-hand store. "Island Antiques" was painted in flaking gold letters on glass. When Rob had parked in front of the house, she excused herself, saying she just wanted to wander a bit, spend some time by herself. After he'd gone inside, she slipped the handle of her satchel over her shoulder and walked down toward the Haight. As she neared the shop, Maggie felt overwhelmed by the fact that the person she had assumed was the creator of the shadow box was still alive and still, from her own description of her artwork, involved with witchcraft and magic. And the fact that Jesse was seeing Dennis knocked her out too.

A tattered awning sheltered the front window of the store. At first it appeared that no one was in. It was late Sunday afternoon. But as she neared the door she saw someone inside. As she pushed the door open the late-day light streamed across old bureaus, mirrors, and cane chairs. The walls were cluttered with worn suitcoats, beaded twenties dresses, neck furs, hats with veils, a glass counter stacked with rhinestone jewelry. A row of fringed lamps was lined up under an Elvis poster. In the window, patent leather high heels stood on faded hatboxes, and at the back of the shop, inconspicuous among the ratty stoles and deco lamps, hung three or four beaded prayer flags exactly like the ones Lora had brought back from Haiti.

A black woman stood behind the counter dusting the jewelry. Her hair was wound in a patterned silk scarf. She had a round, moonlike face, her lips painted a wet burgundy.

Maggie approached the glass counter. "Are you Freda?" she asked. "Mrs. Loam?"

"C'est moi." The woman smiled. "Do I know you? Do I have something here on consignment for you?"

"No, it's my friend you know. Knew. Lora Mayhew. She imported folk art for a gallery in Sausalito. I'm told that you helped her identify some pieces a while back, last year sometime. And that you made some buying contacts for her."

"That's right. She hasn't been in for a while. How is her business going?"

Maggie hesitated. Almost under her breath she said, "She died last fall."

Freda Loam finally looked up. "Oh, no," she said. "This is very sad. I am sorry to hear this news." Her voice was low, and she spoke slowly, with an accent difficult to place. French, patois, British English. "I hope it was not while she was traveling in Haiti."

"No, it wasn't, but why do you say that?"

"Things are chaotic in the islands right now. I believe we spoke of it the last time we met. Not a good time for a

white woman out in the countryside. Lora made her contacts there, you know. She went out to buy directly from
the women themselves. Beautiful things, they were—
flags, like these ones I have here, and dolls. . . . I even
helped her to find a dollmaker, a cousin of mine. But I
have heard of foreigners having difficulty over there. It is
not a good time for tourism."

Maggie took the shadow box from her satchel and
placed it on the counter. "Did Lora ever show you anything like this?"

Freda Loam looked at it and frowned. "I've seen things
like it. Little shrines with photographs. Ribbons and rosa-
ries. Usually they are used for ancestor worship, such like
that."

"Could something like this ever have a hex on it? Could
it be a way of sending negative energy to somebody?"

Freda Loam examined the box, tracing her long fingers
over the silver writing. "This is exactly the conversation
that I had with your friend, Mrs. —"

"Ms. Shea. Maggie Shea. I should have introduced myself. Could you tell me more about that conversation?"

"We talked many times. I don't know if it is one particular conversation I recall. We talked often about images—
the power in words and mental signs. This is the core of
the voodoo religion in Haiti. The prayer flags, the dolls,
the shrines, the herb balls—all of that is a way to create an
image in the mind of the maker. The spirit world then
follows. In the islands it is a way of controlling life for
those whose lives have no control at all, those in extreme
poverty whose leaders have no connection to the lives of
the people. There are images for love, fertility, finding a
husband, making a baby, preventing a baby, making your
mother-in-law move out, making a man fall down sick in a
cane field for sleeping with another woman. Any excuse
will do. You see them all. Not all of them are pretty or
harmonious. But I have never seen a shrine like this. This
is not Haitian."

Maggie explained to her about the dates, the Roman

numerals. "What I want to know is whether this thing could be a hex, something that could have caused Lora's death or something that she might have believed would cause her death. A way to prophesize a death—"

"The whole point is that the image is in the mind," Freda interrupted. The one who believes, the one who has it in her mind. That is the power, not the image itself, but the mental thought that carries and sends the power. In a church, is God in the crucifix? No, He is in the image, in the word. He is on the cross in the mind of the faithful.

"Now, I would say this is not made in Haiti but in America by an American. I would say it could well be a death image, a hex, if you will, very dangerous to send because like begets like. A love potion will bring love to the maker. Likewise, they say, with a death wish, the sender is in much danger."

Freda Loam held the shadow box for a long time, regarding the strange writing and counting silently to herself. "You know, I am noticing something here. You say that Lora was born in 1950 and died last year in 1985?"

Maggie nodded.

"Then this is mistaken in some way. This date of her death is not 1985 but 1986. You see this small line? At first I thought it was just a scratch. But no—VI—six—not V."

Maggie felt bewildered, and she peered at the tiny lines of the numerals. Rob had transcribed the dates and she'd not checked them to make sure they were correct. "Then maybe the whole thing means nothing. This one is also wrong." She pointed to Jesse's picture. "This woman is alive, not at all dead, as the dates indicate. Only these three are correct." Maggie pointed to the pictures of Lily, Peter, and Sandy.

"I will tell you why this is not Haitian," said Freda. "Numbers, dates—all of this is very American. No one tries in Haiti to control the time of anything to happen in the future. It would be folly. Asking far too much of the gods. They don't know clocks. Time is our realm, not theirs. The gods would laugh very hard at a voodoo image asking for a baby on such and such a date, or for a person to die on a particular day or even a year. The spirits do not have appointment calendars. Yes, now more and more I see. Perhaps these are not dates of death at all, since you are now finding discrepancies in them. Perhaps, if Lora made the shrine, they are dates only when she knew and then lost a person."

"But then why did she include herself?"

"Perhaps she became unknown to herself."

Maggie shook her head. What an incredible thought. The poetry of it seemed accurate beyond any fact she'd been able to uncover so far. "But at any rate, you think it was not made in Haiti. It is not really voodoo?"

"I say it is not traditional Haitian voodoo. Voodoo is a living method of spiritual practice, so you cannot say. It is always changing. I say this. It is an image, and, as such, it creates a pattern in the mind. Perhaps, as I said, Lora made it herself. Perhaps she thought to die in a certain year, but the gods took her earlier, one year before. Sometimes your wish comes before you are ready."

Just then a man emerged from the back room, carrying some boxes of jewelry which he began placing in the display cases. Immediately Maggie recognized him as Henry Loam. She saw that he did not recognize her. His hair had receded, and he wore it cut short, but he still had a full beard, trimmed closely now to his face. He was dressed in jeans and a white shirt, sleeves rolled to his elbows and, while he was still striking, he seemed like a character in a play, seen offstage in ordinary life.

Freda continued. "Once an image is created, it continues to act in the world of form, you see. You cannot control it. It will come about eventually. Then it, too, shall pass."

Maggie started at her words. "That's just what this says, in Latin. 'This too shall pass.' She pointed to the words along the side of the box. This picture is me. Do you think I'm in any danger because of this thing?"

Freda held her chin in her hands and thought for a

moment. "Its power should be undone is what I think," she said. "Just to be safe."

"But how?"

"Burn it. Alter what it says. Scratch out the numbers and words. Make your own magic against it. Or have the person who made it undo the hex."

At this Henry Loam looked up and came over to look at the shadow box. Freda introduced Maggie to him. "This is a friend of a woman I had conversations with in the past about voodoo and prayer flags. The woman has now died. Her name was Lora Mayhew. She was a buyer for the gallery in Sausalito."

Loam picked up the shadow box.

"You wouldn't recognize any of the people in these pictures, would you?" asked Maggie.

Henry Loam shook his head.

"This one is named Jesse Ryder. My friend, Lora, told me that you people knew her years ago. They were at Berkeley in the late sixties."

Maggie kept her eyes down but caught Henry Loam as he glanced quickly at his wife. Freda picked up the feather duster and began to whisk it over the patent leather shoes.

"Freda," he said, "there are some things in the back room that I would like you to catalogue." Freda slid by her husband into the back of the shop.

"You say that this Lora Mayhew is now dead?" Loam asked.

"That's right. She drowned in a boating accident last fall. Before she died, she sent me this shrine. I'm curious whether the thing was . . ." Maggie shrugged. "A hex."

"Last fall? When last fall?"

"Mid-October. October eighteenth."

"A boating accident, you say? Did this have anything to do with her business, her importing?"

"I—I don't know. It was on her husband's fishing boat. The entire boat disappeared."

"I see. She wasn't transporting a shipment of goods, then."

"Goods?" asked Maggie.

"And you are . . ." Loam extended his hand. Maggie realized suddenly that she'd come to question them; now she was being questioned. Loam seemed intensely interested in Lora's importing. But why would she have used Dennis's boat to bring in dolls and prayer flags?

"Maggie Shea," she said, taking his hand. "Lora was a dear friend of mine."

"Of course," he said. "I am sorry to hear of her death. Thank you for letting us know. We wondered what became of her."

"You wouldn't have known another importer, a friend of hers—a Phillip Dodd?"

With that Loam straightened behind the glass counter. He simply nodded. "And whatever became of him, do you know?"

"No. I thought you might know."

"Importers come and they go. We can't keep track of them. They move around a lot and stay out of the country for months at a time."

"Were they lovers?" Maggie blurted out suddenly.

Loam's hands were large on the glass spread over the glittering costume jewelry. "I really have no idea," he said. He stared at her curiously until Maggie felt an odd chill.

"And this woman here, is she around in the Bay Area now too?" Loam pointed to Jesse's picture.

Maggie nodded. "You do know Jesse, then?"

"It's very curious," he said, shaking his head. "I'm sorry to hear about your friend. Now, if you will excuse me, it's past closing time. If I hear of anything, is there somewhere I can reach you?"

For some reason, Maggie said simply, "No, no, that won't be necessary. I'm just staying for another day or so and then I'll be leaving California." As she left the shop, a bell on the door rang once overhead. Loam's eyes had looked right through her.

She turned the corner and began walking up Haight Street, when Freda Loam bolted suddenly from an alley and rushed toward her. "Tell me one thing," she whispered, touching Maggie's arm. "I was assuming as we spoke that possibly Lora made this shrine, this little bit of American voodoo. Some dabbling on her part. She was very interested in this sort of thing. But you mention the name of one of the others in the photographs—Jesse Ryder. Could she have been the one to have made it?"

"That's what I thought at first," said Maggie. "But when I asked her, she said no."

"Say nothing to my husband of this, promise me. We know her from many years ago. All I can say is this: If Jesse Ryder made this thing, you must surely burn it or turn the magic in another direction. She is a powerful witch. Once her images are created, they will come to pass unless undone."

"So you do know Jesse Ryder?"

"That's all," she said, and turned back into the alley.

"Mrs. Loam," Maggie called after her.

"Don't come to me about this again," she warned. "Just do as I say. Burn it."

Maggie stood alone on the bright street as Freda Loam disappeared behind the clapboard building. This afternoon she had trusted Jesse intuitively. She hadn't told her everything but she hadn't mistrusted her either. Now she saw that it wasn't so much any particular person she mistrusted as it was all of them—the dark synchronicity of that household that had been reunited at Dennis's today —the whole of them was what she feared. That was what she'd always feared. There was an alchemy among them gone to something frightening beyond any of their control. For the first time it occurred to Maggie that in sending her the box, Lora had consciously pulled her into this. Maggie couldn't even trust Lora, though nothing remained of her but a pile of bones—with the head missing.

Chapter 14

When Jesse got home she stood in the kitchen and listened to the messages on her answering machine. Zoë had called to say the witches had been there all afternoon and finished the pool. Some woman wanted a neon Star of David for her son's bar mitzvah, and a guy was checking on his order for a red sign that would read PLEASURE in caps. He wanted to make sure it blinked.

Then Ben's message clicked on through the slight static of a long-distance connection. "Hi, Mom. We made it up here safe and sound. Milo's dad is making me call so you'll think I'm a thoughtful son. Hey, I had this wild thought. Is there any chance that after the installation on Tuesday you could take up cooking again? Love, your starving child who will be home tomorrow morning."

Jesse went out with a flashlight and looked at the copper pool, now welded in place in the center of the altar beneath the redwoods. Perfect. Tomorrow she'd put the last touches on the wiring and the sound system. She had gotten Sound Man to promise to come up and help her. Then she could spend the twenty-four hours before the ritual simply clearing her mind. She wanted to go into the ritual with all channels open, no blocks, no fears, nothing welling up from the shadow of the unconscious.

She climbed into the huge charred stump of an ancient redwood that stood just behind the reflecting pool. Ben had made a fort out of it when they'd first moved in. Apparently previous tenants had had the same idea. Someone had nailed small boards onto the inside wall of the stump, providing steps that led to a sort of platform halfway up. Jesse scurried up and checked the pulley for the large yellow rod, then climbed down.

Dennis had said he was going over the hill to stay at Quinn's tonight, she thought. Ben was gone too. The moon was almost full, and there'd be plenty of light. The cleansing ritual might even clear the way for Dennis's meeting with the lawyers. All signs said the cleansing should take place now, tonight. She only wished that Maggie had agreed to come with her. Maybe she could convince her to take part in the full-moon ritual. Jesse gathered the materials she needed, put them in a basket and headed back over to Stinson Beach, watching the moon rise through scattered clouds above the hills.

She parked in the driveway for a moment and sat in the dark, deciding that it would be better to walk up to the house rather than drive to it. That way she'd have time to prepare herself before entering the sphere of energy. So she backed out and drove farther up the gravel road to a turnaround under a stand of cypresses. There she meditated a few minutes and checked to make sure she had everything: spring water, salt, a large quartz crystal and a bell.

She walked down the hill to Dennis's house through silver shadows. Below the mountain the surf growled in the distance. The back door was open, as she knew it would be. She stepped into the dark house, waiting as her eyes adjusted to the black. Even standing here she could feel the ghost-presence strongly. It was like the knowledge of a large animal near her in a room, the feeling so strong that Jesse nearly turned and fled but forced herself to push forward. The presence seemed to float above her in the air. She had thought it would be enough to cleanse only the large open space of the main floor. The bedrooms were off from a hallway that overlooked the living room. Maybe she'd have to cleanse them, too. Moonlight helped, thin zinc light. She fumbled in the basket, took out small bags of herbs, the crystals, and set them all on the glass coffee table. A vial of water from a spring in Ojo Caliente, New Mexico, for sprinkling on the floor. Then she realized she'd forgotten to bring a candle.

"Damn," she said under her breath. Then whispered, "No—blessed. Blessed be." It was important to watch your language when you were in a ritual space.

She felt her way up the stairs to Dennis's room. She knew he kept a candle on his dresser just inside the door. As she made her way up the stairs she felt a wave of nausea pass through her, and she stopped, leaning on the wall. Hadn't realized she was so frightened. Not right, not clear, this cleansing. Secrecy had always gotten her in trouble. She stood, listening. It was as if the shape of a thing was gathering itself out of the darkness. Feeling around the corner, she knocked the candle with her hand, caught it, then ran quickly back down the stairs. As she lit the wick, the flame light drew thinly up into a spiral and shadows played on the walls.

Jesse sat for a moment in the rocking chair where several weeks ago she'd almost seen Lora, a corner-eye vision, transparent as gauze. She breathed quietly, visualizing what she would do. *Always begin by clarifying your intentions and making sure that what you ask is for the good of all. That it harms no one and benefits others, rather than merely yourself. Cleanse the atmosphere with a bit of burning incense or a sprig of sage or cedar. Inscribe an arc with your wand around the working space.*

Old witches used a white-handled knife. She'd tried that and found the metallic edge left a swath in the air, a

cut edge to her circles that she did not like, although
sometimes during rituals she still wore a knife sheathed to
her leg just in case it was needed. Mostly she preferred
wood or fire or electricity. To each witch her own. In fact,
that was the whole point of the neon rods, to act as energy
fields around the circle in the forest. Tonight she'd chosen
a cedar wand, carved with the Hebrew letters *beth* and
tsade, corresponding in the Kabbalah to the High Priestess and the Moon.

"Powers that be," she whispered, rising from the chair,
feeling the urge to speak prayer come over her like an
old-time preacher in a backwoods church. Then she said it
in a clear calling voice, "Powers that be," and took the
wand in her hand, pointing it to the east. "I welcome the
beings of beginnings, of risings and arrivals and first
thoughts." To the south, she called quietly, "I welcome
the sun, spirits of light, growth and transformation, the
changing fire, Beings of starlight and thought." She
turned to the west. "Of culmination and completion, of
return to the underworld, I welcome Beings of the west
wind. Of ocean and water, of unconscious, of the cup and
chalice, of all that is receptive, I welcome you." She
turned and faced north. "I welcome all spirits of darkness,
of that which is before and that which is after, Beings of
unbeing and Beings of the formless world. I welcome
purity and clarity of ice and radiant darkness."

At last she dropped her hands and held them cup-
shaped before her heart. "Lastly I greet you, Beings of the
Center, mandala eye, conception seed, spun wheel of the
present upon which we turn, head of needle and all angels
who fit on this point of the moment, I welcome you all.
And I ask that you gather into this conscious space to assist
me and support me in what I ask, that the spirit of this
woman be released to travel on and this house be cleansed
of her."

Just then Jesse heard, unmistakably, a cough from the
bedroom upstairs where she had just been. She froze, fear
pulsing through her like a stain. *But Dennis said he was*

going to Quinn's. Had he not gone, then? Quickly she fumbled her things back into the basket as she heard the rustle of bare feet above her on the bedroom floor. Back door, she thought, but the stairs came down right at the entrance to the kitchen where she would have to pass. The front door would be locked. She stepped backwards behind an Oriental screen that stood at an angle behind the couch and she crouched there quietly. She had not imagined it. Then a woman's voice called, "Dennis?"

Maggie, she thought. *Dennis must have asked her to stay on for a couple of days. Spend time at the beach, time to talk. That was it. Surely that was it. In a moment she'd come down into the living room.* Jesse could hear her coming.

She drew a breath in sharply. *The candle.* She'd left it burning on the coffee table.

A car's lights swung up into the yard, sweeping across the wall, and a stripe of light fell on her chest through the crack in the screen. In a flick all was black again except for the flighty shadows of the candle in the wind. She heard the rattle of an engine, a door slam. Slam again. That was Dennis. His car door never shut properly. His boots on the gravel walk, up the steps of the deck. *What was he doing back here?*

"Have I got some company?" he called. He pushed open the kitchen door and light flooded the room. "Jesse? Is that you?"

Everything in her wanted to leap out, cry, *Yes, Dennis, it's me—up to my old tricks! I'm sorry, I'm sorry, really I am, it's just that I—*

From her hiding place she had a clear view of the foyer where the stairs came down, so Jesse must have seen her at exactly the same moment that Dennis did, as she stepped down into the living room and untied her hair.

"Hello, Dennis," Lora said in that still-familiar drawl. "I'm home."

Dennis staggered back against the doorjamb, one arm

holding a loop of rope, the other arm held in front of him, hand raised as if stopping traffic.

"Christ almighty," he whispered. "Jesus Christ almighty and all the angels in heaven."

Lora touched her own cheek as if checking to make sure she was still there. "I'm sorry," she said, her voice cracking. "I'm sorry. You don't ever have to forgive me for what I've done, but I need help real bad and I didn't know where else to go."

He still leaned back against the door as if he might fall. Jesse pressed her hand to her own mouth to keep from screaming. *Alive, alive. No pile of bones in a cave.* Lora looked thin and tired, old, but then Jesse hadn't seen her since 1970. She wanted to bolt from her hiding place and run to touch her, apparition of pale flesh risen from fog.

Dennis slowly put down the coil of rope. "Lora," he whispered. "What in God's name is going on? I'm drunk, that's it. It's a goddamn flashback. I just came from having a few beers with Cody and Quinn in Olema. We toasted your ever-loving memory. I was supposed to go over the hill with Quinn but I changed my mind. I—I can't believe it's you."

He walked toward her, hesitated, then took her in his arms. His cheek against her hair, he looked absently over the top of her head in Jesse's direction at the candle burning on the coffee table. He patted Lora's back, the movement almost brotherly. Then she backed away.

"Funny," she said, "I feel shy to see you. I'm scared you'll be angry with me."

"I'm sure I will be when I come out of shock. Lora, where were you? Why? Why did you . . ." He never finished the sentence.

Lora stepped into the living room, walked over to the candle and looked at it quizzically. She bent, lit a long Benson and Hedges, and blew the candle out. As she slumped on the couch, she knocked the screen slightly. Jesse crouched lower, pressing her hand against the wobbling screen, Lora so close she could have touched the back of her head. Lora watched the smoke rise from her cigarette while Dennis just stood waiting, dumbfounded, shaking his head.

"South America. Bogotá," she began, coughing again. "I flew in this afternoon. The man I was with rented a car and drove me up here."

"The man you were with," Dennis repeated. "Figures."

"It's not what you think. Please listen. Just hear me out, will you, baby? I'm in real big trouble. Someone might be trying to kill me."

He put his hands in his jeans pockets.

"I don't even know where to start. I wasn't importing just prayer flags and dolls. There was some dealing. I got in over my head. It was small at first, I didn't know what I was doing. I got sucked in. The trust fund was running low, I thought we needed the cash. I let some stuff come in with my shipments, weed at first, then coke. Mostly I carried information, I helped make some contacts in places where I traveled. It seemed like a big game, I thought I was some kind of two-bit spy or something, having meetings in Rio and Mexico City. I thought it was a movie. And I started to use again, too. The whole scene."

She stubbed out the cigarette, reached over to the coffee table and picked up the quartz crystal.

"Give me that," he whispered, turning it over in his palm. "Where did you get this?"

"It was just sitting right there."

He studied it for a moment.

"Do you want to hear the rest?" she asked.

"I don't know. I really don't know."

"It turned out I was being watched by federal agents for some time. There was this secret grand jury investigation and my name appeared on a list of possible witnesses. Then someone leaked the witness list to West Coast organized crime. I don't know who they are. Big business, real big. And they put out a hit on anybody who was competing with their territory. Meaning small potatoes. Meaning me. Meaning snuff the small dealers."

Lora covered her face with her hands.

Jesse leaned back against the wall in the shadow of the screen. She almost didn't want to hear any more either. Distance, space. Out of there into the silver moonlight was what she wanted. Not this. She wondered if Lora was crying.

Finally Dennis spoke. "So that was what was going on last fall. The weird phone calls, the car that tried to run you off the road."

"And I was shot at, I was! Dennis, you didn't believe me."

"I knew you were nuts, that was all. I knew you were probably using and I was just fed up. Don't you remember, I didn't want you to stay in the house alone? I didn't know what to believe, but I was afraid for you. I thought you were flipping out again. But why didn't you tell me what was really going on? Why did you leave me out of the whole thing?"

Lora took a sudden deep breath like a swimmer pulling through riptide to get oxygen. She lit another cigarette, her hands trembling slightly with the match.

"Just like I said—I got sucked in. People were giving me advice—"

"What people?"

"What difference does it make? People I worked with, other importers. I suppose I could have gone to the police or the FBI at that point and asked for protection in return for turning state's evidence, but I was too damn scared. Plus the way things were with us. I couldn't face some horrible divorce, Dennis. I had this idea I'd just start a new life in South America. New name, everything. It was impulsive, stupid—I know. I was scared to death and I just wanted out."

"Why couldn't you have let me know you were alive, at least that, Lora? Do you have any idea what I've been through?"

"You have every single right to hate me."

"I don't hate you, I just want to kill you." He laughed, a forced cry, then sat down next to her on the couch.

"You're hot," he said. "Feverish. Look at you—you're shaking. Are you on something now?"

"I'm not in good shape. That's the other reason I had to come home. I need treatment, Denny."

"What are you using?"

"Coke, Quaaludes . . ." Lora turned to him and bent into his arms, curled inward, a small child, her voice muffled against his chest. "Dennis, I did want you to think of me as dead, at first. Maybe I had some dumb notion of protecting you in case anybody came around asking about me. The FBI, the goddamn mafia. Then you wouldn't be implicated. And after a while I just got caught in my own lie, couldn't tell the difference between my own fantasies and what was real. Maybe I still can't."

He put his hand to her forehead.

Go away, thought Jesse. *Go out to the kitchen for God's sake, let me get out of here!* Their close presence almost made her sick. His forgiveness of her, his caretaking. Jesse put her head against her knees. *Admit it then: his touching her. Wife back. Pretend and real, another love down the drain.*

"So now what?" he asked.

"They're after me. They found us down there."

"Us?"

"Me. They found out where I was. It wasn't safe down there and I didn't know where else to go. Dennis, I don't want to die."

His voice was almost imperceptible. "But you're already dead."

She stood suddenly and lurched toward the kitchen. "God, I need a drink or something." Lora grabbed the open bottle from the counter, slamming out to the back deck, and Dennis followed after her into the darkness, calling her name.

Jesse waited until they were gone, then crept in a low crouch from her hiding place, unlocked the heavy wooden door, pushed it open and ran out. She darted among the trees until she was out to the road and on her way up to her car hidden in the cypress grove above the house. *Lora alive,* she thought. *And Dennis hadn't even suspected. Dupe. Wool over his eyes, blind spot. Turn and she's gone. Abracadabra. The woman in the disappearing act, just like one of his old tricks from years ago. But he wasn't the only one who'd been duped.*

When she got to the car, Jesse fumbled for her keys in the shadows. Even strung out, Lora was vulnerable and persuasive as ever. Beautiful, romantic, and dangerous. The bad girl drama had always drawn her. Jesse knew because it had drawn her once, too, pulled her all the way to the edge and back. But she quit all that years ago; Lora had continued. Come back home for help.

Jesse slipped into the car, pulling the door shut with a click. She had this terrible feeling that home was the worst possible place for Lora to have come to. Maybe she ought to call Maggie and let her know what was going on. "Damn," she breathed out. Then drove down the dirt road by moonlight without turning her car lights on, wishing she'd remembered to grab her crystals from the table by the couch.

Chapter 15

Maggie awoke Monday with one thought—she wanted to go talk to Detective Sergeant Tom Beale by herself. Last night after returning from the Loams' shop she'd told Rob she was exhausted and was going upstairs to take a hot bath and go to bed early. "I'll be done with my meetings by about two or three tomorrow," he'd promised. "Then we'll go straight over to the Marin County Sheriff's Office."

She'd agreed, but knew this morning it was imperative that she go visit Beale by herself.

This whole thing brought to mind those paint-by-numbers kits she used to get as a kid. She'd color in all the twenty-nines and then the seventeens, the thirty-twos. Eventually it would truly begin to look like a picture. *Ah, the purple becomes the shadows. Oh, I see, the brown marks the contours of a face.* She wanted this picture in focus; more numbers, more colors. But she was no professional investigator and there was no way she had the skills to check into the probate files of her friends or find out what Loam's connection to all of this was. There were things that had turned up in the last three days that the

police should know about, and one of them had come to
her out of the blue as she was falling asleep last night.

Back in 1978, she and Lora had met in Vail one Thanksgiving to ski. The conditions had been icy and difficult.
Lora had fallen and broken her leg; it was only a hair-line
fracture that caused her right leg to swell near the ankle.
Maggie was sure it had been the right leg because she'd
had to do all the driving after that. If the remains included
that part of Lora—Maggie shuddered to think of her that
way—perhaps that could be used as a basis for a positive
identification. There had been no cast. Lora had just put
on an Ace bandage and spent the rest of the vacation in a
bar with a ski instructor named Jean-Michel.

She'd even gone off with him for a day or two to another
ski area, Copper Mountain or Breckenridge, and hadn't
even told Maggie she was going. Yes, now Maggie remembered: it was the pre-Hazelden days, the sudden changes
in mood or plan or lover. Lora out-of-control. And she'd
simply showed back up at the hotel in Vail after she'd
dumped Jean-Michel, innocent, hung over. Not even that
morose, just that naughty-me smile. *I'm sorry, I really am.
I guess I should have called. It was just one of those
things!*

Maggie checked to make sure she had the keys to the
Impala, gathered up the photo album, the pictures they
had gotten from the woman at the Berkeley house, the
shadow box and letter. She called the sheriff's office in
Marin County, made an appointment to talk to Sergeant
Beale, and drove up to the civic center in San Rafael.

Sergeant Beale didn't look anything like he sounded.
On the phone his voice was gruff and curt, and she'd
expected someone cool, efficient, and in a hurry. Instead
he greeted her with a smile and a warm handshake, his
demeanor gentle and well organized. He was fortyish,
shorter than she, with graying hair and a thick mustache.
Lean and wiry, he wore clear framed glasses, a blue shirt,
navy slacks. In spite of his gray hair, he looked like a young

law student or a broker. His eyes were very blue against
his deep tan. As he spoke he removed a gold pen from his
shirt pocket and clicked it open and shut, then leaned
across the desk and folded his hands.

The desk was in a room with other desks, and several
other men sat talking on the phones or filling out forms.
On Beale's desk was a picture of a wife and two children,
and a red Swiss army knife. He saw Maggie eyeing the
knife. "Great for pulling out staples." He smiled at her.
"So," he began, serious now, "you were a friend of Lora
Mayhew's."

"And her husband, Dennis, and her brother, Rob. Also
Robert Quinn, her partner in the art gallery. We all knew
each other in college. We shared a house in Berkeley in
the late sixties and early seventies. I live in Minneapolis
now—I flew out on Friday after I heard that Lora's body
had been found."

Beale simply nodded, waiting for her to go on.

"As I mentioned on the phone, I've been feeling very
confused about her death and I just have some questions. I
thought that if I really understood what happened, I'd
feel better. I probably won't but at least I'll have tried.
Does that make any sense?"

"What would you like to know?"

"I guess the main thing I'd like to know is why this isn't
being investigated as a homicide."

She watched Beale blink quickly several times in succession and refocus his attention on her. Then he stood.
"Let's go talk about this somewhere else." He showed her
into a room down a tan hallway, opened a file and looked
over his notes for a few moments before speaking.

"Do you have some reason to believe that Lora
Mayhew's death was a homicide?"

"It's not so much a 'reason to believe' as it is a number of
reasons that make me want to ask the question. I know
that Rob Garson has pushed for a homicide investigation
and I'd like to know what's preventing that from going
forward."

He rubbed his mustache with his forefinger, put the gold pen behind his ear. "Lora Mayhew was first classified as a missing person for a number of reasons. First of all, she went out on the boat herself, she had access to and permission to use the boat. Her husband reported her missing as soon as he was aware of her disappearance. That there was a space of several days is not odd in cases of domestic disappearance. In fact, if it hadn't been for the missing boat and finding her car, we would have told Dennis Mayhew to go home and wait a week or two before we would begin any investigation. People walk out on their spouses and come back every day. Happens all the time.

"There was no evidence of a struggle in the household, anything that would indicate she had been forced from her residence. Her husband was very helpful in the investigation—and quite candid, I might add. He told us they had argued, that she often went off for days at a time. She traveled quite often on business. He told us that he suspected she might have had a lover, but he had no idea who it was or even if it was someone who lived in this country. What I'm trying to say is that until the boat was discovered to have been missing it could have been assumed that she ran off with someone."

Maggie shifted in her chair and listened. He spoke kindly, with an official tone, a man making a report.

"Where there is no body recovered, no autopsy to confirm the cause of death as a homicide, we have to go by the people involved. In this case Dennis Mayhew cooperated fully in the search and investigation, and there were no red flags to arouse our suspicion—until several months after her disappearance. Now I stress that term *disappearance* because until the remains were located last week—and there is yet to be a positive ID on that—it could not be assumed she was dead. There was no proof of death. Her brother did come in to say he felt Mayhew might have had something to do with her disappearance. But there simply was not enough evidence to warrant a

homicide investigation. No money involved, no body. You
see what I'm getting at?"

Maggie nodded.

"Of course, in the last month, with the changes in the
probate situation and the body turning up—possibly—"
Beale raised one finger and repeated, "possibly—that situation may change. Have you been informed about the
circumstances of the remains?"

"I know the body was only partially recovered. That's
one of my concerns."

Beale cleared his throat. "Yes. Well, without a skull it's
very difficult to get a positive identification. A forensic
investigation was done. The coroner looked for signs of
damage that would indicate beating, knife or bullet
wounds and so on. Nothing was found. It was not a very
conclusive examination, I can tell you that. If the body
hadn't been discovered at that point, it probably would
never have been found. Nature had taken its course, a
high storm could have easily washed the whole thing
away. But I'll admit, the fact that there was no skull is one
of the factors that does tilt the case toward homicide.
Actually, there is a strong push within the department to
classify the case as a homicide, and if you have any information that would be useful to us I'd certainly appreciate
hearing about it."

Maggie opened the satchel and placed its contents on
the desk. She handed him Lora's letter and the shadow
box, pointing out the Roman numerals and how the dates
corresponded to the deaths of several, but not all, of the
people whose pictures were in the box. She explained that
she and Rob had gone to the Berkeley house and discovered photographs that could have been pictures taken of
people after they died. She told him about Lora's interest
in voodoo, her travels in the Caribbean, and her connection to the Loams, their odd interest in the news of Lora's
death, about the correspondence between the way Quinn
dated his acquisitions at the gallery and the numerals on
the shadow box, and the fact that he was a photographer.

She tried to explain about Jesse Ryder turning up alive after all these years and being involved in witchcraft, that when questioned she denied ever having seen the box before.

Beale listened intently to her monologue, occasionally making notes on a white, lined tablet. When Maggie fell silent, he continued scribbling with his pen for several minutes. Finally she asked, "What do you make of all this?"

"Well, first, I want you to know that I really appreciate your coming forward with your concerns," said Beale. "I guess the thing we have to look out for is jumping to conclusions. Witchcraft, voodoo, that sort of thing—it usually turns out to be a hoax. You can't discount it, there's a lot of crazy people out there. But you have to be careful, especially in California. As far as the connection to these three other deaths back in Berkeley, I'll have to do some checking on that with the police over there. We'll certainly look into it and it may give us an angle for future questioning.

"Now what I'd like to do is make a duplicate of this letter and I'd like to keep these photographs for identification purposes with the Berkeley police. Why don't you keep this?" He slid the shadow box across the desk to her.

"You don't want to keep this for evidence?"

"At this point it's really not evidence of anything. Besides, it's your memento. If I need it, I'll let you know."

Beale made a photocopy of the letter, noted where Maggie could be reached both in California and at home in Minnesota and the two shook hands. At the door she turned around.

"Did the coroner, the one in charge of the forensic examination, take X rays of the bones that were found?"

Beale said yes.

"Will you check to see if there is a hairline fracture on the right lower leg? I can't remember if it was a tibia or a fibula or what. Lora had a skiing accident out in Vail back in seventy-eight. A doctor at a clinic there took X rays. I even remember her name: Dr. Hill. We thought that was hilarious at the time. Would you just check that for me? It might be nothing. She didn't even have to wear a cast."

"Certainly!" he said, suddenly animated. "Now that's just the sort of thing we can use. This other information is interesting but tangential. I hope the physician kept good records. Again, Ms. Shea, I really appreciate your coming in."

Out in the car Maggie sat in the shade of a laurel. What *was* the thing that tied Lora's death to the deaths in the Berkeley house? If Peter and Lily and Sandy were murdered, if Lora was murdered, was the shadow box the only thing that connected them? The only other common denominators were all the other people in the Berkeley house and drugs. She stared across the road at Mount Tam, tapped her fingers on the steering wheel. *Drugs.* The thought had been facetious, but she didn't know why she hadn't thought of it before. And there was one other last thing she'd forgotten to tell Beale.

She walked back into the civic center and requested to see the sergeant again just for a few minutes. Soon he emerged from the glass doors and sat next to her on a Naugahyde couch in the lobby.

"Something else?" he asked.

"Just something I'd like checked into a bit more. For my own information more than anything else. Back when we all lived together in Berkeley there was a lot of drug activity—you know, the typical late-sixties scene. I always wondered about the people that OD'd in that house—if the house was under surveillance at all, if there would be any narcotics records on any of the people . . ." She trailed off, not exactly sure what it was she wanted.

"I'll have to talk to the FBI about that."

Maggie thought of something Quinn had mentioned yesterday at the brunch. "With the Freedom of Information Act, wouldn't those files be open to the public now?"

"Yes, but it would take you several months to get through the red tape of acquiring access to them. I've got a friend who was on the drug task force back in those days who's still with the bureau. I'll definitely give him a call."

"And one more thing," she added. "This fell to the bottom of my satchel and I forgot to give it to you." She handed Beale the importer's card, the one the woman at the Berkeley house had given to her. "This Phillip Dodd —he was a friend of Lora's. Quinn knew him, and so did Henry Loam. Maybe it's just another tangential . . ."

"Look—when I said that, I didn't mean new information isn't important. I meant the witchcraft, the voodoo angle, that kind of thing. Information like this is actual, it's physical. We can use it."

"Good," she said. "I hope so."

Maggie drove back to the highway but instead of continuing south toward the city, she headed up to Fairfax to see Jesse Ryder. The directions Jesse had given her yesterday were sitting right inside her purse. As she drove, she understood much more clearly why Rob had been so reticent to speak of Lora's death as a murder, why he had seemed so withdrawn about it. Without the shadow box and letter there was nothing suspicious except the missing skull. And Beale considered the shadow box "tangential," a "memento," while Maggie still thought it was central and important, though its true meaning was certainly veiled. Most of all she wondered if Beale himself didn't *want* this case to be classified as a murder. That's what she felt from him. There was "a strong push" within the department, he'd said. Which he opposed because there was nothing cut and dried about Lora's death? No boat, no skull, no clues, no evidence, no killer. *No homicide.* Or so he seemed to have concluded.

As she turned off the highway toward Fairfax, Maggie felt a catch in her breath, a moment's doubt about seeing Jesse. Freda Loam's reaction to her name had been so extreme—but maybe it was just that Jesse had once been her husband's lover. Anyway, she wanted to see the site of Jesse's current magic. And Cody would be there. Perhaps she'd show him the shadow box. Quinn had mentioned that he knew a lot about third-world art. Maybe Cody knew Phillip Dodd as well.

Green light flecked with sun-pattern fell on her windshield as she headed up the steep road cut into a hill above Fairfax. Near the top the hill flattened out. She pulled into the wooded driveway and parked up close to the house, next to Jesse's dusty pickup. Cody's Mercedes was pulled up beside it. She knocked at the red door of the house and peered through the open screen, calling out, "Anybody home?"

Another small building stood on the far side of the circular drive. As Maggie approached she could see Jesse through a window, bent over a workbench twisting some wires with a pair of pliers. The door was open and she stepped in.

"Hi," said Maggie. "Hope I'm not interrupting anything."

Jesse looked up, startled, and pulled the Walkman earphones down around her neck. "Am I ever glad to see you." Jesse hugged her but didn't smile. She was wearing a large white T-shirt over black tights cut off at the ankle and gold loafers. Around her neck were several silver chains, all hung with clear quartz crystals. Maggie had carried the satchel in with her, and as she set it on the workbench the shadow box slid out. Jesse glanced at it briefly.

"Rob had meetings until midafternoon so I'm out exploring. I probably should have called first, you're working. Is this your studio?"

"Please. I wanted you to come up. Yeah, this is it. Electric Lady, Incorporated. Executive producer, chairman of the board, chief designer, glass bender, office manager, cook, caterer, tax accountant, secretary, and janitor. Not to mention mother! Yours truly."

"What are you working on?"

"The installation I told everybody about at Dennis's yesterday. Cody's been here since about eight thirty.

What a dear! Mr. Electronics himself. I kept having prob-
lems with the system blowing out—I guess it was this
power switch on the wall here. Cody said there was too
much juice going through one system. He's almost completely rewired the whole installation. He walked down
into town with Ben, my kid, to get some things at the
hardware store." Jesse glanced out a window at the back
of the studio. "They should be back soon. Ben wanted to
show him his secret path through the woods. I don't see
them yet."

Jesse seemed strained today, a bit reserved. "Look,"
said Maggie. "I can come back another time when you're
not right in the middle of . . ."

"No!" Jesse protested. "Please stay. I need to take a
break anyway." She pulled off her gloves and set them on
the worktable. "I just wish I had two more weeks to pull
this thing together. You're going to come, aren't you?
Look, Maggie, I wanted to ask you this yesterday but you
seemed hesitant about the cleansing ritual. I'd love it if
you'd participate in the moon ritual for old times' sake. It
would mean so much to me."

"No, I couldn't, Jess. I wouldn't know what to do anymore."

"Yes you would! It's half-improvised, just like it was back
then. It's easy. Greet the directions, help me to ground
the space. I'll fill you in."

Jesse took Maggie's hands, almost pleading with her.
Maggie noticed that her eyes were red and slightly swol-
len, as if she'd been crying. "The truth is, your energy was
always so important to me in the magic, Maggie. Don't
you remember our old current?"

"Yeah, but look what it led to!" She tried to laugh.

"Come on. It's a moon ritual, a celebration for light. You
were always my balancing power, my night angel. Think
about it, okay? I could really use your support." Jesse
sighed deeply. "I'm kind of a mess today. This thing with
Lora . . . it's just getting too weird."

"Do you think so too?" Maggie hesitated, but intuitively

she felt she could trust Jesse. She had to talk to someone
about this. "I wasn't going to say anything, but I've just
come from talking to the police, a detective from the
Marin County Sheriff's Office. I want them to investigate
Lora's death as a homicide. I feel that something's been
glossed over, it's all too pat, it's . . ."

"Maggie." Jesse took her by both arms, eyes wide, even
a bit frightened. She spoke slowly, almost in a whisper.
"Listen: *Lora's not dead.*"

"What?" Maggie felt as if she'd been hit in the stomach,
the world falling away behind her.

Jesse paced the workroom, gesturing with her hands in
expansive circles. "Oh, God, this is so hard to explain.
Remember I said I wanted to do a clearsing, like in the old
days? I went back over to Dennis's last night after everyone was gone. He said he was going to stay over at
Quinn's. I just kept sensing Lora's presence there. It was
so thick yesterday I could practically see her. No wonder!
She was there. Maggie, I heard her come down the stairs
and I hid behind that Oriental screen in the living room.
In she walked, the whole flesh and blood apparition. She
looked like hell, real thin, chain smoking. Then who shows
up next but Dennis, pulling into the driveway."

Jesse related her story to Maggie, who leaned on the
edge of a high stool, bending the pliers back and forth. At
first all she felt was shock, and then the thought rose up in
her: *I want to see Lora.*

"I guess I can't blame Dennis, but I feel so betrayed,"
said Jesse. "I should be glad to know she's alive. The part
that hurts the most is that Dennis and I were—" She
broke off. "It was clear that she wants to go back with him,
try to cut her losses. I feel so selfish, only thinking about
my relationship with him. And she seemed pretty messed
up—coke, she said. Quaaludes. She talked about wanting
to go back into treatment. But the thing that scared me
was this talk about people being after her. I mean, she's
really taking a risk coming back here at all. But it was all so
strange. It could have just been her paranoia too."

Oh, Lora. Maggie closed her eyes. *Not again.* "Did she talk about this shadow box at all?"

"No, neither of them mentioned it."

Maggie picked up a folded sheet of legal paper from the satchel and handed it to Jesse. "I didn't go into this at the brunch, but those Roman numerals on the box are all dates—dates of births and deaths. It even has your death on it Jesse—1972. And it says Lora's death is in 1985. It's all wrong. I don't know what to make of it."

Jesse read over the sheet and shook her head.

"Who else knows about Lora turning up?" asked Maggie. "Did you tell Cody?"

"I haven't told a soul but you. I've been too upset."

"I've got to talk to Rob." Maggie looked at her watch. It was almost noon.

Just then Cody appeared at the open door, holding an armful of brown paper bags. He was wearing gray designer jeans, creases ironed in, a black cotton sweater. A tall blond boy entered behind him, his fine hair blowing over his face.

"Madame, your lunch has arrived: Brie, pâté, French bread, pears . . . Maggie! When did you get here?" Cody slipped his arm around her and kissed her cheek. Jesse threw a glance toward Maggie and a quick, almost imperceptible shake of her head that said *silence.*

"Maggie, this is my son, Ben. Ben, Maggie was an apprentice witch with me back in the Berkeley days."

Maggie rolled her eyes. "That's stretching it a bit."

"She said she might help with the installation. Right, Maggie?"

"Might."

"Ah, the joining of the forces," said Cody. "And what is this?" he asked, picking up the shadow box from the worktable.

"Oh, nothing," said Jesse. "Just a little spell left over from our legendary past. Isn't it cute? Look, Cody, there's you with your ticket to the Dead."

"Where did you get this?" he asked.

"Lora sent it to me," said Maggie.

"Man, you really played with Jerry Garcia?" Ben asked Cody.

"I did the sound for the Dead a couple times, yeah."

Jesse broke in. "Ben, look, he probably blew into a microphone, okay? He probably tripped over a cord and plugged it back in. Don't adore him or anything." She cast a glance at Cody. "Don't encourage him."

"Hey, I descended into the Seventh Circle and lived to tell about it, didn't I? That was the name of my band," he told Ben. "Jesse, look, I've got this wiring problem all figured out. You don't have to worry about a thing."

Jesse bent down to untangle a loop of orange extension cord under the table and her eyes met Maggie's.

"Really?" she asked. "Not a thing?"

"It's all going to work out fine," Cody told her. "Just like magic."

Chapter 16

Maggie stood for a moment inside the charred redwood that Jesse had pointed out. She could feel that this was the center of Jesse's ritual space. The black walls had an almost silken sheen. Before leaving Jesse's, Maggie went to the house and hurriedly dialed Rob's office. "I'm sorry, he's unavailable for the rest of the day," said his secretary. There was nothing to be done then but to meet him back in the Haight around two as they'd planned and tell him the news. Maggie left Jesse and Ben climbing aluminum ladders up into the redwoods, raising and lowering neon rods on thin ropes held by an intricate system of pulleys as Cody dug holes in the soft ground, burying cables and switch boxes, somehow managing to keep his beige oxfords immaculately clean.

As she drove south, she thought how strange it would be to see Lora, and for some reason she felt afraid. Jesse was right. If Lora's life had been threatened before, if somebody had wanted her dead last fall, surely she wouldn't be entirely safe now. What had she gotten herself into? Maggie felt her heart drop at the thought of Lora using again, involved in some big drug dealing operation, after her treatment at Hazelden had seemed so successful. But that was Lora's decision, her choice, Maggie would have to watch that she didn't get sucked into codependence with Lora's drug problem. Still, she realized, like Jesse, that she felt betrayed by her friend. And it now occurred to her how very cruel Lora's scheme had been. Cruel to have sent Maggie the shadow box in the first place for whatever reason, drawing her in some inexplicable way into her plan. To Dennis and Rob, who had both suffered and lost each other's friendship as a result. Maggie felt an odd mixture of tremendous relief and incredible anger, with an edge of anxiety underneath that she couldn't name.

And then she realized what it was. The body, the remains that had been found—if they were not Lora, then whose bones were they, and how had it happened so conveniently that they were found with the remnants of the lifeboat of *The Pearl*? "Proof of death" indeed. Someone had wanted Lora proven dead. At least as close to proof as they could get without having a skull. And it certainly would have been handy for Dennis to have had that proof. Maybe he had nothing to do with Lora's disappearance in the first place, but Maggie felt pretty sure he was not entirely innocent in this mess. He stood to gain too much.

Twelve thirty. Yesterday she'd promised to meet Quinn for lunch at noon; she was late. Perhaps it would be better to forget it, but on impulse she exited at Sausalito. She couldn't just go back to Rob's and pace for two hours. As she pulled up onto the hill above town, the Impala suddenly died on a winding residential street. "Damn," she breathed, remembering Rob's instructions about the car's faulty carburetor. She waited several minutes, listening to a glass wind chime clink from the eave of a pink house. For some reason it only added to her sense of unease. The car started up on the next try. Maggie parked and half-ran down the hill to the main street of town.

The sidewalks were just as crowded on a Monday as they'd been over the weekend. Tourist buses unloaded in

the square near to where the ferries docked, and pushy
flocks of women brandishing purses dashed toward the
storefronts. Lovers stopped in midstreet for a picture.
"Can you get that mountain in?" A woman with a New
Jersey accent exclaimed, "Lettie, forget the café already.
There's a building up there that has forty different bou-
tiques. We can shop until we die. Then we'll eat."

The glass door to Quinn's gallery was propped open
with a small statue of a mermaid. Inside it was dark and
cool, a ceiling fan slowly wheeling overhead. Quinn's assistant was perched on a high chair behind a podium-style
desk.

"Hi," said Maggie, out of breath. "We were introduced
Saturday. I'm Maggie Shea. I'm running awfully late—"

"Quinn just left!" said the woman, dark red lips in a
theatrical pout. Then she smiled. "He said he was absolutely sure you would come but he wanted to deliver
some photographs he had developed for a client and he
said for you to wait and he'd be back in a flash. Would you
like to just look around? Or you can wait in his office if you
like."

Maggie walked back to the prayer flag room through
the dolls mounted on one wall, the masks on the other.
They seemed to be staring at each other, and she felt
invisible between them.

She wandered back to the front room. "Do you have a
private phone I could use?" she asked.

The assistant motioned up the stairs. "Why don't you
just go on up to his office—do you know where it is? Up in
the loft, it's the door on the back wall that's painted to look
like a window. Would you like some coffee while you're
waiting?"

"No, thanks," said Maggie. She climbed the carpeted
stairs and crossed to the window-door.

Quinn's office was surprisingly neat, white desk and
shelves, Elfa white-grid storage units, chrome track lights
and a high-tech desk lamp that elbowed sharply over a
pile of invoices. Quite different from the rustic house in

Mill Valley with its wood stove and stained glass. Black-and-white framed photographs hung on the wall. Glancing at the signatures, she saw they were his own. A black vase held a single calla lily.

She sat at his desk and debated about calling Beale. His office wasn't far, just over in San Rafael. Maybe instead of waiting around for Quinn she should just drive over there. Absentmindedly Maggie riffled through a pile of bills, pulling out a Pacific Bell statement for the month of July. Her eyes moved down the list of cities where calls had been placed or received: Los Angeles, Los Angeles, New York, Miami, Chicago, Cincinnati, Miami, Bogotá, Rio de Janeiro, Bogotá.

She stopped cold and read the entire list again. South America: Jesse had reported that Lora had been down in Bogotá. She jotted down the Bogotá number on a slip of paper and put her head in her hands.

Goddamn it, she thought. *I'm calling Beale.* She still had his number on the scrap of paper on which she'd drawn the map to Jesse's. When his voice snapped on the line he sounded breathless. "Ms. Shea, I can't believe what a help you were this morning. This whole thing may be much bigger than any of us thought." He spoke quickly without a break. "Phillip Dodd, the importer whose card you gave me—the Berkeley police sent an officer over there an hour ago to question him and the man's apartment had been broken into. Door wide open. The place was ransacked. They found him dead in a closet—shot in the head—and get this: there was a Polaroid snapshot of him, taken after he'd been shot, and pinned to his chest. I'm not talking about his shirt. The pin was pushed in like the guy's chest was a bulletin board or something. So this business about pictures of people after they're dead no longer seems the least bit tangential, and if it hadn't been for your visit this morning that clue would have held absolutely no meaning whatsoever."

"Sergeant Beale, I . . ."

He interrupted and went on. "Furthermore, the coro-

ner's X rays do include a shot of the right leg. There is no
sign of a break, hairline or otherwise, and Dr. Hill is supposed to return my call after she locates Lora's X rays.
Now I'm on my way to meet with the FBI about these files
of your old pals, and if I come up with something interesting I'll contact you as soon as I can. Many thanks again, Ms.
Shea. You can't know what a help you've been. Now what
was it you called about?"

Maggie sat stunned, not breathing. Now it seemed extremely urgent that Lora be found and protected—but
she simply had to get to Rob first. She owed him at least
that much. She decided to wait an hour or two to tell
Beale that Lora was alive until Rob knew. They could go
up and talk to Beale together as they'd planned.

"I . . . I didn't leave a package there this morning
. . . of French bread, did I? A white bakery bag?"

"Not that I know of. I can look around."

"You've got enough to worry about, Sergeant. Never
mind."

"As I said, if anything else opens up on this, I'll let you
know." He hung up and the dial tone hummed flatly on
the line.

She couldn't wait for Quinn now. As she hurried down
the narrow stairs, she called to the assistant that she simply had to be going.

"Oh, no!" The woman seemed alarmed. "He told me I
was to strap you to a chair and under no circumstances to
let you escape until he got back! Can't you wait just a few
more minutes?"

Maggie shook her head and turned to go.

"The dolls!" the assistant cried out. "He really, especially wanted you to see these dolls. They're from Haiti.
They just came in. It was something Lora ordered before
she died. Oh, please, stay just a few more minutes. I know
he'll be right back!"

The woman showed Maggie to the back of the gallery.
The door to the storeroom was nearly invisible: a tall
rectangular painting of a fish was mounted on it.

"Just help yourself—they're right in that crate. He really wanted you to see them!"

The room was not large. Stacked floor to ceiling were boxes and crates, paintings leaning against walls, some of them high as the back door, which stood open, slightly ajar, facing an alley. The return addresses on the crates were from all over the country, all over the world: Kentucky. Pennsylvania, Bali, Port-au-Prince.

At the back of the room beside a stack of large paintings wrapped in brown paper were several small wooden crates. The lid of one crate was partially lifted. These crates looked familiar—where had she seen one before? Dennis had used one for a table out on his deck. Yes, that was it. It had seemed odd next to the elegant porch furniture that Lora had obviously picked out. She yanked up the top of the crate and put her hand into the shredded paper, pulling out a thin, tube-shaped doll with a tiny straw hat and a plaid dress, red bead eyes. When she lifted the doll's skirt and pressed her finger into its hard belly, it gave slightly as if it were filled with sawdust or sand.

Why would Quinn be so anxious for her to see these dolls? Or was that only an excuse for keeping her there? Jesse had said that Lora had begun to mix the import of arts and crafts with dealing. Taking a utility knife from the counter, she sliced the doll open beneath its plaid dress. Shredded newspaper leaked out, scraps tiny as if a mouse had chewed them for a nest. She took another, larger doll, fingered its carefully stitched face, then slit it too, neck to legs. The same tightly packed newsprint was packed inside. Forget it: that was too obvious anyway. Maggie pulled the doll's skirt back down over the cut, stuffing the doll deeply into its shredded paper nest. Suddenly she felt cold and afraid, as if she were looking at something entirely familiar only to have its meaning completely hidden from her. The crate reeked, and she shut the lid, shoving a clump of excelsior paper back inside.

Carefully she tore the mailing label from the side of the crate, but as she stood to leave she heard voices approaching. Quinn and another man. She took a step back toward the open alley door, as the interior doorknob turned.

Maggie slipped quickly out the alley door, pressing herself against the warm stucco.

"This new shipment is very good," she heard Quinn say. "The quality really seems quite superior."

"What have you got in from the islands that's interesting?"

"Over there—that gray box and those crates by the back door. I haven't really unpacked things yet. Some of the prayer flags are wonderful, but there are a bunch of those small ones of fish that have no spiritual imagery whatsoever and were made just for *turistas.* Check out the ones with the snakes, though. There are some dolls, too, but they're not that good."

"These dolls are becoming a lost art," said the second man. Maggie knew she would not have recognized that deep baritone if she hadn't just heard it yesterday: the man with Quinn was Henry Loam. "Dolls are getting to be touristy, too. Everything is. Oh no, look at this one—a Cabbage Patch Rasta man. I'm going to have to talk to Freda about this. It's her cousin who gets the dolls for her. She runs a sort of craft guild in her town like that one in Bogotá you spoke of. I wonder if you couldn't actually provide more quality materials for them. You'd have a better chance of maintaining the old craftsmanship. Now what about those prayer flags?"

Maggie leaned her head back against the building, then turned and hurried to the main street. Here another world went about its business, looking across to Oz over the pleasant water. She stood for a moment, watching an Asian family fishing down on the rocks. So Lora's travels had never been purely for finding lovely third-world folk art. South America, Central America, Mexico, Haiti, Jamaica. What a great front for a tidy bit of drug trafficking. She wondered how they did it: were the drugs shipped in beautiful carved boxes or hollow masks? To what extent were Quinn and Dennis aware of Lora's activities? It seemed naive to think they knew nothing. Quinn knew Phillip Dodd; so did Loam.

As she walked back up the hill to her car, she glanced at her watch: 1:30. She'd get back just in time to meet Rob. Suddenly she realized she was exhausted and hungry. How long ago this morning's talk with Beale seemed. She felt for her purse to rummage for the keys to the Impala— then stopped in the middle of the street and groaned, "Oh, no."

She could picture it exactly, her purse left behind on the counter in the back room of the gallery, car keys and all. She would have to return now and face not only Quinn but Henry Loam.

Quinn spotted her as soon as she strode through the gallery door. He lifted his arm, grin sliced across his face. "Maggie! Kath said you were here but that you must have snuck out when she wasn't looking. You bum!"

Maggie offered her cheek to receive his kiss. "Could you believe seeing Jesse Ryder yesterday?" he asked.

Maggie looked about, relieved that Loam seemed nowhere around. She quickly offered an excuse for not staying. "Sorry I'm so late, I was up at Jesse's all morning, just can't stay, must have left my purse in the back." But as she followed Quinn to the storeroom, there he was, sitting at a small table looking at a portfolio of photographs, his long face as haunting as any of the masks behind him.

"Say, Henry," said Quinn. "I'd like you to meet Maggie Shea, another old friend from Berkeley. She's out visiting from Minnesota. Remember you were asking me about Rob Garson? Maggie's staying with him. Maggie, you remember the old magician, Henry Loam, don't you?"

She flashed a fake smile, hoping her fear was not transparent. He was still the dark sorcerer from the bad magic days, and something about his silvery eyes made her feel small.

"Ah. We've met, we've met," Henry said. He rose, extending his hand to her. "And now we meet again. We seem to know many of the same people."

Maggie's throat felt thick and dry, and she coughed slightly as she spoke. "Of course. You and Mrs. Loam must have done business with both Lora and Quinn."

"Of course," he said, his voice lyrical. "Quinn here is always one of the most committed supporters of indigenous crafts from the islands. Small world, small world."

"It's even smaller than you think, Henry." Quinn chattered on. "Your old protégée Jesse Ryder is back in the area, and she's having a performance-art installation cum full-moon ritual at her place up in Fairfax tomorrow night. You should come!"

Maggie grabbed her purse from the storeroom and thanked Quinn, breathing out, "Rain check for lunch, babe. So nice to see you again, Henry."

"Perhaps we'll meet again," he said.

"Perhaps." She exited into the too-bright sunshine.

As she fumbled in her purse for her sunglasses, Quinn came up behind her and slipped his arm across her throat, pulling her gently back against his chest. It was meant to be affectionate, a playful wrestling hold, but she shuddered stiffly in his embrace, wanting to break away.

"What's up, Maggie?" He put his cheek to her hair. "Is everything all right?"

She spun out of his hold, taking his hand from her throat, holding it for a moment before letting go. "I'm fine, Quinn. Just in a rush."

"Is something wrong? You seem upset."

Again she lied. "It's Rob, I guess. I'm worried about him."

"Garson can take care of himself. Don't let him spook you. Come and stay with me if he gets on your nerves."

She nodded, then nodded again.

He spread his arms wide, and flashed that grin again as she backed off down the sidewalk.

"Maggie," he called out, "you know you're breaking my heart."

* * *

The Impala was parked at a curve in the road next to an ivy-covered fence. Maggie looked out between the trees at the blue view below, then reached to unlock the car door, but it was already open. Not only open but slightly ajar as if she'd not fully shut it in her hurry to get to the gallery. That was strange. She could have sworn she'd locked it, for she'd left her satchel in the back seat on the floor. She glanced in through the side window—it was still there—then looked quickly around at the reclusive houses. Had someone broken into the car? But nothing was missing. Maybe that was all. She just hadn't slammed the door properly or the seat belt had gotten caught in the door. She tried slamming it now. It banged closed just fine. She shrugged and got in behind the wheel.

As she pulled out into the road, a delivery truck veered past her, honking loudly. She plunged her foot on the brake pedal. With that, the hood of the car jolted straight up, blocking her view.

Maggie swallowed hard, put her head on the steering wheel. A black car swerved around her, the driver honking and raising his middle finger. Shaken, she got out of the car, shoved the hood down, and drove out to the highway, praying Rob would be home when she got there.

Chapter 17

Nearly three o'clock; the house was still. Maggie changed into jeans and a sweatshirt, tying worn tennis shoes over thick socks. Perhaps the meeting had run late. It was all pointless now anyway. In the silence she could hear the rumble of the white city below and every car horn, creak, or tick of the clock made her turn, look over her shoulder at an empty room. *Dodd murdered; Lora back. If what Lora said was true they'd be looking for her now. They, they—but who?* When she heard the metallic click in the lock downstairs she felt a sudden relief wash through her. *Rob home.* Hurriedly she tied her other shoe.

She called out his name as she came down the stairs, but there was no answer, only movement back in the kitchen, clink of glass and running water. As she eased past an ironing board left out in the hallway, Maggie saw the face she thought she'd never see again except in memory or obsession. *Living ghost,* she thought.

Lora was startled when she saw Maggie, her mouth fell open, a curl of smoke coiling from her lips.

"Maggie," she whispered. "What in creation are you doing here?"

"I came out for your funeral."

Lora bit her lower lip, walked over, and put her head against Maggie's shoulder. They held each other tightly.

"I fucked up real good this time, girl," Lora whispered. "You don't even seem that surprised to see me."

Maggie hesitated, not wanting to mention Jesse just yet. "I already knew you were alive."

"So Dennis called here. Then Robbie must know too."

"Not yet." Maggie held Lora at arm's length and surveyed her. She was thinner than she'd ever been, even after one of her water-and-grapefruit diets, and her skin had a gray pallor. Even so, Maggie had never been so relieved to see anybody in her life, though just under her relief was a knot of fear: this was not just Lora back from a trip to South America, but the shadow Lora, the one she'd driven out to Hazelden years ago, the side of her old friend she always wanted to forget.

"Please don't lay a judgment trip on me, Maggie. I can explain this whole thing."

"You know, for months I prayed this would happen, prayed you just took off in the boat and landed on some island, living on coconuts. Or piña coladas, as you suggested in that last letter to me."

Just then the front door opened, quickly slammed, and Rob's voice, angry, called, "Dennis, is that you? I thought we said all we had to say at the lawyers'. I haven't got time to discuss this with you any further and I'd appreciate your returning my house key."

"I parked Dennis's car out front," Lora whispered.

Rob appeared at the entrance to the kitchen. He glanced over at Maggie incredulously, as if she had everything to do with Lora's being there, and he seemed unable to speak. Finally he said, "Little sister," and she ran to him, crying then, her thin shoulders shaking against him.

At last she pulled away, wiping at her eyes. "I need a drink," she drawled.

"I'm sure we all do," said Rob. "I've just been in meet-

ings all day going over your damn will." He poured Scotch
into three glasses, and they all drank. "I just don't know
what to say. But you've got some explaining to do, Lora. I
don't know whether to kiss you or slap you."

"That's about the way Dennis put it." She gulped her
drink and closed her eyes.

"You look half dead," said Rob, pouring a second shot,
tipping the glass to his mouth. "He didn't have you hidden
away someplace, did he?"

"Robbie, don't even bring Dennis into this. I swear he
didn't have anything to do with it." She swayed past them
into the living room, nearly falling onto the couch. Maggie
remembered what Jesse told her about the cocaine and
Quaaludes.

"Robbie, get out one of your legal pads, because I already told Dennis all this and I'm not going through it a
third time."

"How long has Dennis known you're alive?" Rob asked.

"He just found out last night. I made him promise not to
tell."

"That son of a bitch. All day in these meetings . . ."

Lora proceeded to tell them what had happened, much
the same story Jesse had repeated earlier to Maggie but in
much more detail. Rob questioned her in true trial-attor-
ney fashion.

"The reason I didn't come to you in the first place,"
Lora explained, "is because you're Mr. Law. You would
have made me go to the cops, and at that point all I
wanted was to disappear.

"Yes, I had help," she went on. "I can't tell you who, I'll
only get in bigger trouble. Besides, I want to put him
behind me. Okay, yes—it was a lover. *Was.*"

Lora reached down into a leather bag beside her and
tossed Rob a passport. "My fake name—Maria Consuela
Hernandez. It was all arranged by him—everything."

Maggie noticed that while Lora kept her voice calm
and quiet, her words seemed slurred.

"And what about Gram's will?" Rob asked. "Are you

saying this whole thing had nothing to do with your inheritance?"

"I swear it. Dennis told me about the will codicil last night. That was the first I heard of it. Lord, I didn't even know Gram was dead." Lora put her hand to her forehead.

Rob spun toward her, his voice strained. "What, you two didn't meet up behind the pearly gates?"

"Rob," Maggie interrupted.

"Don't protect her, Maggie." Then, to Lora: "Why should I believe you? You know what I think? I think this is some sort of scam with Dennis, and all this organized crime and grand jury crap is a big lie. There's no way you can come back and get your hands on that money— you've defrauded the estate. Neither you nor Dennis will get a penny out of it. And I won't get a penny either if I don't call the police this very minute and turn your ass in —I'd be a party to your ridiculous plan."

Maggie stood then and Rob held up his palm. "I said stay out of it, Maggie."

All that held-in anger, hissing out now, she thought, *snakelike. Under the surface, coiling, waiting. Time bomb.*

Lora's voice was shaking. "That's why I didn't come to you in the first place. I knew you wouldn't believe me."

"Well, I do," said Maggie. "Rob, I know you're upset. You've been focusing on Dennis as the responsible party in this for so long you can't see it any other way, but I did some checking around on my own today and I found out some things. Lora, your lover—was he Phillip Dodd? Is he the one who helped you with all of this?"

Lora looked shocked. "He's . . . he's not my lover— but he did help me. He's a friend who was down in Colombia with me, the one who helped me get away from my lover. We flew back into the country together yesterday."

Maggie continued, facing Rob. "I talked to Beale this morning and I told him all about the Berkeley house. I gave him Dodd's card. They sent someone to check him out and he was found dead, shot in the head."

"No!" Lora cried. *"Not Phillip* . . . Then they know I'm back for sure. Phillip was on that grand jury witness list, too. We both were. I told you I was in danger!"

Rob went on with his questioning as if he hadn't heard about Dodd at all. "And what about the body that was found?" he asked Lora.

"My lover arranged all that too—he did it to offer up some kind of public proof that I really was dead so no one would come looking for me. But now they must know I'm alive. They killed Phillip and I'm next. Can't you see?"

Rob stuffed his hands into his pockets. Maggie could tell his reaction was still one of disbelief and rage.

"Robbie, I'll go into treatment. I'll do whatever you want. You can arrange for me to get some protection in exchange for my testimony to the grand jury, can't you? Can't you do that?"

"Why doesn't your lover help you out now?"

"Give her a break, Rob," Maggie said quietly.

Lora said, "I can't make it with him, that's why. It's over with him. He wasn't good to me. He's mean, okay?" She rolled up her sleeve and revealed track marks on her arm. "Oh, yes—and Mister Monkey, my bad friend, compliments of my so-called lover. You know, I woke up one day down there and I couldn't understand a word anybody was saying? I was wasted on every goddamn substance, my boyfriend was roughing me up, and I thought back to my dear old home and said to myself, Baby girl, you didn't have it half bad up there. I saw that I probably still loved Dennis too. I missed him. Rob, I want it to end. It was a mistake!" she cried. "A mistake in judgment. Everybody makes mistakes!"

"I'm telling you, you're jeopardizing my whole career. I'm managing Gram's estate."

"Well, manage to fix things," she whispered.

"No!" He was shouting. "You've pushed too far. You

broke me when you died, you bitch!" He knocked over a small table and kicked it across the room.

"Who took care of you after Nam when you were a shell-shocked black hole in space, brother? Who took you in when you had nothing and you couldn't even talk to a human being for six months or look anybody straight in the eye? Who loved you then, Robbie? Mommy and Daddy? Gram?"

Lora reached for her leather bag, and the contents tumbled out onto the floor, change and loose bills, Bic lighter, scattered pills, a gold key ring with the initial *R*, a plastic syringe in cellophane, and a small handgun.

Maggie grabbed Lora's arm as she bent to pick up the gun and Rob scooped it off the rug, held it in his palm.

"You gave me that gun a long time ago, Robbie," whispered Lora. "For protection."

Maggie stroked Lora's hair. "Call a treatment center, Rob. You can see she needs professional help."

"And that is going to be her only out," he muttered, calmer now. "If she's diagnosed as mentally incompetent or chemically dependent or suicidal, that'll be her defense in case anyone brings a fraud suit. Especially if this lover of hers was supplying her with drugs. Okay. Okay."

Maggie couldn't believe that his main concern was still the money, the will. Maybe he was in shock too. People acted strangely under stress. He leaned against the piano for a moment, then went into his den and closed the door. She could hear his voice, low, on the phone.

"Maggie," Lora said into a pillow. "I'm so sorry. You know this isn't the real me."

"I just wish you'd come out to Minnesota when you were in trouble. I'd have helped you."

"I couldn't. You would have been in danger too."

"It's going to be all right," Maggie whispered. "The main thing is you're alive. I missed you so much."

"I missed you too. When this is all over and I'm better, we'll go to Paris, okay?"

"Lora, what in the hell was that shadow box all about, that thing from the Berkeley house?"

"I got involved with Haitian artifacts, images. I was studying with someone—"

"Freda Loam."

"You knew that too? After I agreed to go away—one day I made up that box out of old pictures that woman in Berkeley gave to me. I remembered how Jesse painted dates on her altars in Roman numerals—so I made it up like a little shrine, a little voodoo. It was like a ritual for my own death. I put in everyone who died or disappeared from the Berkeley house and then I got the idea it would be some kind of smokescreen, that my death would be seen as tied to theirs. Don't you remember how we used to think there was a hex on that house? I was afraid Dennis would just throw it away, so I set it out before I left and asked him to mail it to you. I wasn't in my right mind, Maggie. Everything seemed so unreal. Maybe it was some way I could avoid facing what I was about to do. I made it all into some kind of magic."

"And what about Quinn? Did he know about all of this?" Maggie asked.

"No, the gallery is totally clean. Quinn did not know about the dealing. God, I need an aspirin so bad. Do you think Rob has any upstairs in his bathroom?"

"I'll go look for some. Just take it easy."

Maggie ran up the carpeted steps, trying to detach from Lora. Costumes, veiled hats, and witchcraft: they'd all lived in some kind of fantasyland back in Berkeley. Some of them had never come out. How hard it was to sort out the person from the chemicals, the human being in need from the crisis she'd created. How hard it was to admit she loved Lora, yet hated this side of her. In treatment she'd be better off—and Rob could sort out the legal stuff once he'd settled down.

She'd just opened the medicine cabinet when she heard the front door open and the rap of footsteps on the front walk outside. Maggie raced down the stairs and into the street just as Lora screeched downhill toward the Haight in Dennis's car and was gone.

Again, the hood on the Impala had stood straight up, and as Maggie went over to slam it, the bright afternoon light made her feel dazed.

In an instant Rob appeared on the steps. "Where is she?" he shouted. "She's gone!"

"Gone, yes," muttered Maggie, approaching the car.

"Which way did she go? She's got to be heading back up to Dennis's over the bridge. I can catch her!" He bolted for his car. "She might come back. Wait here for her. I'll call you. Maggie, she's got that gun. Like an idiot, I set it on the piano."

Maggie cried out, "Don't leave me here alone!" But his car shot past her down the street. She leaned against the open hood of the Impala, holding the sides of her head.

Tangled in the maze of black pipes and machinery before her was a coil of copper wire, black and red clips fixed to the battery. She reached in and pulled the cables from the engine. They were not jumper cables but similar, the wires more delicate. She examined the rest of the engine, even peering under the car. Finding nothing else, she sat on the curb, the thin wire gleaming in her hands. Someone had broken into the hood this afternoon while she was at the gallery and tampered with the engine. Not just hot-wiring. No, someone had been rigging an explosive into the car. She must have interrupted the attempt, returned too soon.

Maggie glanced up and down the street. No one suspicious-looking, only a woman with a grocery bag, a man walking a dog. She shuddered as she slammed the hood down and hurried to the open front door. Inside the house it was cool and dark and silent, as it had been before.

Chapter 18

"Testing, testing." Jesse stood out in the grove, a cordless mike clipped to her shirt. "A little less volume, Ben!" Her voice came back at her from speakers hung in the surrounding trees. "Try some reverb. Perfect."

"Do you want to try a tape?" Ben called from the studio. Within seconds the sound of gulls came washing through the trees, the ocean like a roaring breath or a pulse recorded inside an ear. She held up her thumb, though Ben couldn't see her in the dark grove.

"Where's the whale tape?" he asked.

"Isn't it right there? I'll have to look for it. Maybe it's in the truck."

Ben snapped off the tape, and wind-silence came in after the waves. Jesse shivered. She could feel the space gathering energy. This afternoon she and Ben had put the last touches on the pool that would reflect the moon when it centered directly over the grove. They filled the six-foot pool with water, then spread sand around it, raked it close to the lip. Above the pool hung the long yellow rod. A ripple of light snaked across the water below. They'd set three gardenias to float in the pool. Already dry needles pricked the mirrored surface.

Ben strode out of the studio on thin legs, his blond hair spiking up from his forehead. He stood beside the pool and looked at the water light rippling off the copper.

"Mom, I've been wondering. Isn't magic supposed to be a trick like making something appear out of nowhere? Shouldn't there be some kind of outcome to this ritual? I mean, couldn't we get a bunch of doves to fly out of a box or something right at the end?"

Jesse sat on the soft ground and stared up at the first stars pocking the blue overhead. "The point is not a trick, Ben. That's stage magic. Real magic is about attention. The point is how you focus your mind." She put a finger to her temple. "Magic is a way to bring your attention to a very fine point. It allows you to practice that kind of tuning. Some do it through meditation, some pray. Tribal people focus on the drum, bringing all the energy right into the vibration of the air. I do it through ritual. This one is an homage to light. There is no product but the process itself."

"Seems like it's more of an homage to darkness," he said.

"Well, to honor a thing you have to include its opposite. An offering to the shadow gods."

"Where are they?"

"Down under," she whispered. "Down under."

The phone jangled back in the house and Jesse rose, running across the yard. She banged into the kitchen, slightly out of breath.

"Hello?"

"Jesse," said Dennis.

She could hardly hear his voice over the clatter of glass, a jukebox booming in the background. "Dennis, is that you? Where are you?"

"I'm at the bar in Olema and I have to see you. I have to talk to you," he insisted.

But she already knew his secret. Everything would be

different now. She pictured their last afternoon on the
boat before putting the fishing lines in, making love on
the narrow, hard bunks. *Grace* adrift on the swaying water. "Do you want to come over?" she asked.

"I can't, I don't have my car." He paused. "Jesse, it's an
emergency. Not the car—me," he stuttered. "Will you
just please meet me here?" His voice had an edge of
panic.

"I'll be right over," she said.

She told Ben she'd be back late and took the road
through Laguanitas toward the ocean. As the truck
bumped under the black shapes of the trees, she fumbled
on the seat next to her for a tape, then pushed it into the
tape deck. An eerie whine filled the cab. There it was, the
whale tape, sad underwater cries. The round moon rose
through a low bank of clouds. As she neared Olema, the
strange animal calls suddenly stopped, the tape hissing
silence. She knew it wasn't over—there were at least
thirty minutes on this side.

She knocked at the tape deck with her palm and a
voice, whispering, filled the cab, asking her name. "Jesse?
Jesse?" As she pulled over to the side of the road, she
continued to listen. Every few seconds a hoarse whisper
raked the air, the words barely audible. *Male,* she
thought. *Maybe not.* She couldn't be sure and had no idea
who it could be, saying now, "Whose magic is stronger?
Whose shall come to pass?"

Jesse yanked the tape out and opened the door to turn
the cab light on. It was certainly her tape. She inserted it
again, rewound it, and listened again. The strange
whisper was in no way familiar to her. It occurred to her
briefly that it was a prank, Milo, perhaps, or another of
Ben's cronies—but they all seemed honestly delighted
with the ritual. Some of their mothers were in her coven.
His friends wouldn't sabotage the installation, Ben
wouldn't allow it. Then the last phrase again. *Come to
pass.* Where had she heard that? She jerked the truck

door shut, the dim light blinked off, and the sad whale-mother voice resumed calling her young.

"That shadow box," she said aloud. Almost the exact words. The moon glowed behind an arm of cloud, and Jesse rested her head on the steering wheel. Who was trying to block her magic, blacken the light-energy of the ritual? All week the tape had been either in the truck or her studio, neither of which she ever locked. She had no idea who would do this to her, this mind game or power trick to distract attention and create fear. One more dark sign along with Lora's return. She ought to cancel the whole ritual. Then it came to her: *That is exactly what they want.*

The tape snapped off and Jesse ejected it, clicking open the glove compartment to see if any other tapes had been tampered with. She reached in, gasping as a small clutter of dried bones spilled out onto the floor of the truck.

Dennis sat in a booth at the back of the tavern, staring down at one inch of beer in a curved glass and doodling on a paper place mat. Jesse slid in across from him. He kept rubbing the pen around and around on the place mat until it tore through, then set down the pen, reached over to touch her hand. She cleared her throat, wanting to blurt out that she knew, she knew everything, she knew it was over between them again, she'd always known it was impossible. "How did the meeting go?" she asked above the jukebox music.

"Horseshit. But that's not what this is about. Jesse, the weirdest thing in a million years just happened. I found out Lora isn't dead. The whole thing was a hoax." He didn't look at her as he spoke but kept his hands folded, his eyes on the clear rim of the now-empty glass. Jesse listened carefully as he told her everything about Lora's reappearance. He left nothing out, not even his own confused feelings.

"It's so bizarre to have a thing you've wished for come true—*God, don't let her be dead, let her be found alive somewhere, God, please*—and then to find out that you don't know if you want it. I'm not saying I didn't love her once, Jesse. I just want you to know—we would have kept on going from here, you and me. I know it. At least that's what I wanted. And we still can, I want you to know that. When this thing settles down, when . . ." He stopped in midsentence. "I wanted you to know from me. Please don't leave."

"I'm not leaving. I just got here."

"I mean don't leave me."

Jesse studied the wood table carved with initials, hearts and arrows. *Bob loves Harmony. Lois was here.* Now it was her turn to confess. She explained about the cleansing ritual, how she'd hidden and seen everything. "I should know by now that anytime I try to do something in secret, sneaking around like a goblin, it always turns back in on me. Some ghost," she said. "Where is she now?"

Dennis simply shook his head. "When I got up this morning she was gone. She took my car. I got a ride into the city and back with a guy I know who commutes from Stinson Beach every day. I thought for sure she'd be back this afternoon. I waited around awhile, then walked down the hill and hitched here. I tell you, now that I know she's alive the house really does feel haunted."

"So you told Rob then—at the meeting?"

"No. Maybe I should have. I'll call him tonight. I guess I was waiting until she showed back up."

"At least now you won't be a murder suspect, Dennis."

"Little Miss Rainbow," he said. "Hadn't even thought of that."

Jesse got up and came around to his side of the booth. "Whatever happens . . ."

He put his mouth to hers, cutting her off. "Maybe I should call Rob now," he suggested. "Will you stay with me? I could use the support. What worries me is the whole thing about this hit list. I'm nervous about the wrong people knowing she's back. She wants to offer to testify in

the grand jury proceeding and get some kind of immunity
or even protection. Rob could help her with that."

"Let's go, then," she said. "Call him from your place,
and then I've got to get back. Ben's home from camping
with Milo."

Dennis put his arm around her and light fell on his face
from the Miller Lite sign on the wall above them. They
kissed hard, as if they were saying good-bye. She put her
hand on the rough denim of his jeans.

When Dennis opened the truck door he stepped up
onto the scattered chicken bones, crunching them with
his shoe. "What in the hell is this?" he asked.

Jesse started up the truck and told him about the tape,
the whispered phrase that matched the shrine Lora had
sent to Maggie, that she didn't recognize the voice.

"What shrine?" Dennis asked. "Why didn't Maggie
show it to me?"

She played the tape for him, and the road before them
glowed.

"Maybe it's a coincidence," said Dennis.

"Nothing is coincidence," she said.

By the time they pulled up in front of the house, the
moon had risen into a single blot of cloud and its light,
silver-black, permeated the yard. "Maybe she's not coming back," he said. "I thought for sure we'd pull up and see
the car sitting here." Jesse left the motor running and
Dennis leaned over and kissed her again.

"We've never been able quite to get it together, have
we? Lora's always gotten in the way somehow or other,"
he said.

"Or Quinn."

"Will you stay with me tonight?"

"And chance her coming back? Forget it, Dennis."

"You could finish your ritual."

"Hey, I do want my crystals back."

"I knew those were yours," he said. "Come on in. I'll get
them for you. Then let's call Rob and get this over with."

Dennis shoved the truck door shut as Jesse turned off
the ignition, leaving her keys in the truck. She followed
him up the wooden deck stairs, and he held the back door
open for her. As she stepped into the kitchen, she kicked
something with the edge of her foot. It rattled across the
floor, cracking into the leg of a chair. Jesse bent down,
feeling in the dark for it.

Her fingers closed around the cool metal and it took a
moment to realize what it was. "Turn on the light, will
you, Dennis?" Jesse dangled the pistol out in front of her
as if she'd picked up a small dead animal.

"Dennis? This was on the floor—my foot hit it."

"Shit," he whispered. "So she was here." He glanced
over his shoulder as if she still might be, then seemed to
shudder. "Put it there on the counter." Jesse set the gun
by the sink. He took a gulp from an open bottle of whiskey
that was on the table.

Jesse held very still, the feeling of darkness on her skin,
electrical. "She had a gun?"

"I didn't know she had it with her—but it is hers. Rob
gave it to her years ago."

Dennis crept into the living room, turning on an overhead light. He did a pirouette and Jesse felt suddenly
exposed.

"I'm going to check the bedrooms," he muttered.

She followed him upstairs and down the shadowed hall.
As he reached in and turned the light on, Jesse saw over
his shoulder that Lora was stretched diagonally across the
comforter, facedown. Her black hair tangled, unbraided,
covered the side of her face. Dennis went to her side and
touched her shoulder. "Lora?"

Jesse stood in the doorway. She took it in but it wasn't
until she faced the dresser and looked back in the mirror
that she knew Lora was dead. It wasn't anything obvious.
Her body knew it before any of her senses confirmed it.

As Dennis turned her, a smear of red stained the comforter and bloomed out of her chest, black hair strewn
over the clumped pillow.

Jesse put her hand to her mouth and leaned back against the door frame, light-headed. The scene grew small to a pinprick before her and she thought she might faint. Dennis put his hand to Lora's forehead, her throat, her wrist, looking for a pulse. It was then that Jesse started to scream.

"Shut up!" shouted Dennis. "Shut up!"

She swallowed hard, stepping back as he let Lora flop across the bed. He sat down then looked at his watch. His voice broke as he said, "I've got to get somebody."

"She's dead, Dennis."

"I've got to get a doctor, an ambulance," and he bolted down the stairs. Jesse clambered after him into the kitchen as he slammed the phone against the wall. "Line's dead," he yelled, and tore out of the house, running for the truck. He backed out, then shot forward, throwing gravel dust up into the light from the fully illuminated house.

Jesse glanced about the yard, the high shadows flailing from the pines. She thought about chasing after him, then turned back to the house. *He'll be right back,* she told herself. *Right back. Just went down to town to call, though it's useless. It's stupid. She's dead. Couldn't he see that? The flop of her arm, the way her mouth was twisted to the side.* She walked back to the house and stood still just inside the kitchen door.

Just then she thought she heard something scrape against the floor upstairs. She looked toward the wooden ceiling and slowly moved toward the counter where the gun lay and took it in her hand. She'd only held a gun once before; a small rifle that belonged to an old high school boyfriend. She had no idea how to use this, but held it anyway, held it out in front of her with two hands as she'd seen in TV cop shows, listening, listening but there was no second sound, no squeak of floor plank or click of door, only silence and the stillness of death.

In the quiet of the brightly lit house the immensity of it came over her, of Lora's return, of finding her this way.

Looking at her hands trembling, holding the gun, Jesse saw there was blood on her palms. Blood on the doorknob Dennis grabbed as he flew out. *Where was Dennis?* Slowly she backed toward the door. She couldn't stay here. She'd walk down after him and meet him as he came back up the road.

Just then the red-spun lights of a squad car whirled into the yard. Jesse ran out to the deck, holding up her right hand, left hand still clutching the gun. "Thank God!" she cried. Two policemen leapt from the car, swinging guns out before them, one crouched low, the other leaning over the hood.

"Drop it!" one of them shouted, but she kept on toward them, four steps. Five.

"Thank God you're here!" she cried in a choked voice.

"Drop the gun, lady!"

Jesse stared at the gun as if it were a third hand she'd suddenly grown, then set it on the deck rail as the policemen came toward her. One of them took her roughly by the arm and spun her toward the house into the kitchen.

"Put your hands on the table," he commanded. He patted her down, squeezing chest, waist, legs, ankles.

"Listen," she said. "Didn't Dennis tell you? She's right up there. She was dead when we found her. It's the first door on your right as you go up the stairs. We found her, I'm telling you. I heard a noise and I was scared. I took the gun and I was running out. I was scared, I swear. I don't even know how to shoot it." Her voice sounded high and rhythmic, almost a chant. "Where's Dennis? Is Dennis coming?"

One of the officers ran up the stairs, two at a time. The other stayed with her. "Where's Dennis?" Jesse asked again.

"Who's Dennis?"

"Her husband."

"Whose husband?"

Jesse realized her legs were shaking and she was having trouble getting her breath. She fell into one of the wooden chairs at the table and tried to be coherent. "I'm telling you, we came back here from the bar in Olema. We found her lying up there. Dennis went to call a doctor because the phone is dead. Maybe the line's been cut." She heard her voice from far away and could not seem to stop talking. "Didn't Dennis call you? He went down into town to call you."

"A neighbor phoned in. Reported a burglary in progress."

The officer came back downstairs. "Dead all right," he muttered. "You say you know the victim?"

"Her name is Lora Mayhew. I'm a friend of her husband's."

"Don't touch anything, please, ma'am," he said. The officers conferred quietly for a moment, then one of them went out to the squad car, lights still blinking red around the yard, and Jesse could hear the nasal static of the radio clearly as he reported Lora's death. "Apparent shooting. An involved party is present, not resisting," she heard him say. "The weapon has been confiscated."

Jesse kept glancing out into the yard, but Dennis did not return. The policeman came back into the house and looked down at her hands. She cringed at the sight of the brown-red blood on her palm. "There's blood on the doorknob," she whispered. The man took her arm and led her to the squad car. She stumbled on the gravel.

"Am I being arrested?" she asked.

"Detained for questioning. We'd like you to wait for the detective from the sheriff's office."

"I swear I had nothing to do with this. I'll answer any questions you have." He shut the car door with a clink and leaned there smoking. Several minutes passed before two other squad cars pulled up into the yard. Brief conversations, muffled voices.

The men seemed to move slowly, thick bodies in a dream. Molecules between seconds swelled and Jesse felt as if she were sinking very slowly under water. Still Dennis did not return.

He had not called the police. He had abandoned her
here with Lora. A neighbor had called in a burglary. She
went over and over it in her mind in the stuffy car, the
officer leaning against the door, smoking. She had held the
gun, she had been found with the gun. She was the lover
of the dead woman's husband. A woman who was supposed to be already dead but who had just returned. And
slowly, slowly, like a person interpreting a dream, dumb
to the obvious symbolism, she began to realize that Dennis was not going to come back, that it was possible that
he'd arranged this whole thing, planned for her to be here
when the police arrived, her fingerprints on the gun, on
the door.

It was nearly forty-five minutes before two Marin
County Sheriff's Office cars pulled up into the yard. She
wanted to call Ben and let him know what was going on
but the phone was out of order. Perhaps she could have
one of the officers radio to the police department and
someone there could call Zoë for her. They opened the
squad car door and led Jesse back into the kitchen. A man
in a navy blue nylon jacket, gun at his belt, went upstairs.
After several minutes he returned to the kitchen.

"Body's in pretty good shape for a woman dead nine
months," he muttered to one of the uniformed officers.
"Or maybe she's got two bodies. Split personality."

In a monotone he introduced himself as Sergeant Beale,
sat down at the table, and began methodically asking her
questions, jotting the answers on a tablet in a leather
portfolio. *What time did you enter the residence? Who
was with you? Where is he now? Please describe the vehicle and state the license number.* He handed that information to another officer and asked him to call in an all-points
bulletin on the truck. *Was the residence locked when you
arrived? Were there any lights on?* Again she described
kicking the gun, going up the stairs, Lora's body crossways
on the bed.

"Now let me get this straight," Beale asked. "How do you know Dennis Mayhew?"

"He's an old college friend of mine."

"You all lived together in Berkeley, right?"

"How did you know?" she asked, incredulous. It was as if he were psychic.

"I suppose you know a woman named Maggie Shea too."

"Oh, that's right. You talked to Maggie." She felt out of breath as she spoke, an aching throbbed behind her eye.

"You're the witch then, the one who made up that shadow box?"

"No," she protested. "That's not exactly right. I told Maggie yesterday—I made that box up years ago, but someone changed it, put in those pictures and painted on that crazy silver writing. Not me."

One of the officers came into the kitchen and whispered something to Beale. They exchanged a few more words in low voices and then Beale turned back to her.

"Ms. Ryder, we're going to give you a lift over to San Rafael to the sheriff's office, where we can talk a little more comfortably. They're going to seal the crime scene now, and it will just be a whole lot easier if we go down there. I'm afraid this is going to take some time—this questioning."

"But I've told you everything I know!" she protested, knowing at once that was not true. She hadn't mentioned the cleansing ritual or the voice on the cassette tape or the bones in the car. She didn't know why she hadn't told them everything. Fear, of course. And suddenly she realized that she could not afford to protect Dennis by withholding anything and that it was important for her to remain calm, very calm.

"Do I need to call a lawyer?" she asked.

"Officially what we're doing at this point is detaining you for questioning, Ms. Ryder. You can call a lawyer if you wish."

The second officer pulled a small white card from his

pocket and handed it to Beale. Beale began reading her
the Miranda statement. "You have the right to remain
silent. Anything you say can and will be used against
you. . . ." Then he took her arm and led her out through
the living room, where she saw that her collection of
crystals remained on the table in front of the couch.

Chapter 19

When the phone jangled in the dark room, Maggie woke with a start and felt around as it rang insistently and rang again. At last her fingers closed around the receiver.

"Hello?" She cleared her throat, fumbling for the bedside lamp. The light snapped the edges of the room into shadow. The small alarm clock read one twelve. "Hello?" She repeated. For a moment she was afraid this was the same silent caller from yesterday morning.

"It's Quinn, Maggie. I know it's late. I woke you, didn't I?"

She rubbed one eye with her finger, and though she had fallen asleep in her clothes, she was cold. She pulled the blanket over her legs, felt the sharp jab of the car key still in her pocket. "Where are you?" she whispered.

"At home. Mill Valley. Maggie, listen, I got this call from Dennis."

"What? What is it?" She sat up quickly, the day's events coming back into focus through sleep-fog: Loam, Lora's return, the wires on the engine of the Impala.

"Is Rob around?"

"He went out, I didn't hear him come back. I fell asleep. He drove up to Stinson Beach earlier to—"

"Then he knows. He must. I didn't know if the cops would call or what."

Did Quinn know too that Lora had turned up? Did Beale? She said nothing and waited for Quinn to speak.

"Dennis just called me. I know this is going to sound strange." He rambled out the disconnected story, by now like the child's game of telephone, facts altered slightly each time, blurred, diminished or magnified. Bogotá, the boat scheme, the grand jury, threats to Lora's life. Her sudden reappearance like an assistant in a magic show. But Quinn continued, the story gone now into myth or fantasy as he repeated what Dennis had just told him: "Jesse drove Dennis back to the house. They found a gun on the floor in the kitchen and got scared somebody was in there. They found Lora on the bed. Shot. In the chest. Maggie, this time she really is dead."

Maggie whispered *"No"* inaudibly, her hand clasped so tight around the phone that it hurt. And then she thought, *Not again,* as Quinn went on describing how Dennis bolted, leaving Jesse there because he was sure they would blame him, arrest him on the spot, but swearing, swearing to God he had nothing to do with it, nothing at all. He hadn't meant to keep going. He'd meant to call for help and go back, but instead he'd just kept on driving.

"I don't know where the hell he was calling from and he wouldn't say. Probably heading for Mexico. He was sure she was killed by people in organized crime, people who didn't want her to testify and somehow knew she was back in the country. I told him not to run, it would look even worse, but he was scared shitless. I just want to make sure Rob knows what's going on. It's the least I could do."

Maggie felt her breath go hot in her chest, her heart clamped on a core of fear. To have seen Lora this very day, her face miraculous and sick, it didn't matter. She'd believed all would be well, as in some fabulous fairy tale where the good rise from the dead and are given a second chance. She had touched Lora's hair and held her hand. Maggie closed her throat to the fears and locked them down in her chest.

"Quinn, Lora was here today. She sat right downstairs and told Rob and me everything. Rob was making arrangements for her to go into treatment and she ran." Her eyes blurred, wet salt on her cheeks and mouth. "How much did you know about all of this, Quinn? You knew she was down there, didn't you?"

"Come on, Maggie. Why would you think that? Give me a break."

In the back of her mind she knew she should be silent, but the words spilled out of her. "What about those calls the gallery placed to Bogotá, Quinn? And you knew Phillip Dodd, that importer she was involved with. Did you know he was also murdered this morning? Goddamn it, Quinn—" Her voice broke.

"Shit," he muttered. "Dodd was dealing too? Hey, I call Bogotá several times a month and I did before Lora ever went out on that damn boat. There's a native craft guild down there that I'm a member of. Check with Kathleen. Call the number if you want."

"What about Henry Loam, Quinn? How does he fit into—"

Just then there was a click on the line.

"Maggie, are you there?"

"I'm here," she said. "Rob?" she asked into the receiver. Then to Quinn: "It must be Rob picking up the extension downstairs. He must be back after all. Rob?" she asked again. No answer.

"Maggie, are you there alone?"

"I don't know. Rob should be back by—"

But Quinn could not have heard the rest of her sentence. The line went dead, no dial tone, only a flat silence. Maggie rattled the buttons on the phone, then hung up.

She stood at the doorway a moment before calling down the hall. The house was dark, she'd been asleep for hours. If Rob had driven up to Stinson, maybe he already knew about Lora. Maggie crept to the top of the stairs, listening to the still house, street sounds muted and far. When she'd gone up to sleep, hadn't she left a light on for him? Even if she hadn't, he would have turned it on when he came in.

She tiptoed down two or three steps then froze, absorbing the black silence, trying to calm herself. *Lora's been killed,* she thought. *And someone tried to kill me earlier today.* She never should have let Rob go off by himself. She'd called to report the wires in the car to Beale, but he'd been gone. He'd not returned her call. Now it was clear why.

Again she called out. "Rob, is that you?"

She should return to the bedroom and call Quinn back. A minor disruption in the line, something wrong with his phone. Sometimes a dial tone resumed after a moment. Better yet—call Beale again. *Now.*

Slowly Maggie backed up the steps. Feeling along the wall with her hand, she found the round dimmer switch for the chandelier. As she wound it, light rose in the foyer below. Again she descended, taking the room in—leather couch, piano, the oddly cheerful merry-go-round horse. No movement, no hidden presences that she could see. Her eyes scanned the long curtains over the bay windows, everything still. If Rob had come in, he'd say something. And even though Quinn had just told her otherwise, everything in her body told her Lora should be sitting on that couch down there, smoking a thin brown cigarette.

Then Maggie's eyes were drawn to the front door directly below her and fixed there just long enough to see two things. The chain lock was pulled into place in its brass slot—she knew she had not locked it when Rob left and she'd never seen him lock it when he was in the house. The second thing she saw was a pearl necklace on the marble tiled floor. That image stayed in her mind, lit there intensely as a camera flash, and she could still see it, an afterimage, even as the chandelier overhead dimmed and went black.

Instinctively, she crouched low next to the banister and held her breath. Pictured the layout of the room below, parson's table, overstuffed chair. She heard muffled footsteps and creak of a stair above her. In the dark she swung over the banister and hung down, feeling for the table below her, the crack of a lamp knocked over as she thumped to the floor and ran stumbling toward the kitchen, pushing the ironing board over behind her as she passed. At her back, the slow crack of steps—boots or rough shoes. She heard someone trip over the ironing board, kick it aside.

She tore through the kitchen around the L-shaped corner past the island, reached for the back door, and yanked it open. Remembering the small broom closet, she slipped into it, drawing the narrow door closed, swallowing her breath. No noise, no breath, just still. She could feel the damp wind coming in the open door. Careful footsteps, quiet now, heel to toe. A man's presence, the weight of his steps. From where she hid she could feel him pass, watching, crackle of linoleum underfoot. *Go out in the yard,* she prayed. *I'm out there, look for me out there.*

Behind her she fumbled for a broom handle, her hands closing around the slivered wood of a small shovel. By the sound she could tell he'd gone out onto the back steps. *Now,* she breathed out, throwing herself out of the closet at the back door. Ramming it shut with her shoulder, she zipped the bolt lock into place, the chain lock slipping out of her fingers, finally sliding into place with a clink.

Still leaning there, she felt the thud as he kicked at the door once, twice. Then nothing. A moment passed. Not even the sound of a step. Above her in the window by the sink a thick shadow passed and a black-gloved fist shoved through glass, the small pane shattering into the metal sink, an arm reaching upward to the window latch.

Maggie raced out of the kitchen, falling over the ironing board, dropping the shovel as she fell. Behind her, the window slammed up, glass breaking. The fist rammed through each pane in splintered explosions. She reached

the front door and frantically pulled at the chain lock. At
last the door flew open and she half fell down the steps to
the street, running for the car.

Throwing herself behind the wheel, she shoved the key
into the ignition of the Impala, and glanced up just then to
see in the mirror a figure at the open door above. For a
moment she thought she recognized Rob's face in the
black shape and almost stopped to call back to him. Perhaps he had thought *she* was an intruder. But no—he'd
seen her on the stairway when the chandelier had been
lit, he'd known she was there. Who else knew she was
there? Dennis, Loam . . . Maggie turned the key, flinch-
ing as she remembered the wires found earlier under the
hood. He was coming down the steps toward her now,
holding up the shovel she'd dropped. The engine fired up
—no bomb, just the roar of the motor. She yanked sharply
at the wheel and squealed out into the dark street, down
the hill, the figure a shrinking outline of shadow behind
her now. Down toward Haight Street she sped. Even this
late there'd be traffic, a lit-up liquor store, a phone booth,
a cruising police car.

Maggie turned left on Haight, glancing again in the
rearview mirror. No one seemed to be following. She
gunned through a yellow traffic light, then breathed out,
"Damn," as she passed a phone booth at the corner. On
impulse, she wheeled right, down toward the Panhandle,
and continued out through the park toward the Golden
Gate Bridge, through the black pillars of the trees.

As she crossed the bridge, she kept looking behind her
at the double stream of lights snaking in both directions.
She began to relax, to trust that whoever it was had not
been able to follow.

"That couldn't have been Rob." She said it aloud and
her voice surprised her. But why had she thought of him
at all? Who else had a key? The door had been bolted from
the inside, pearls from the shadow box strewn on the floor.

But that made no sense. There were other ways into a
house besides doors and keys. Maybe whoever it was had

been there to kill both her and Rob, anyone who had
known Lora was back in the country. *But we all know,* she
thought. *Quinn knows, Jesse knows. Does Cody know?*
Killing those who know, those who know. What had Peter
and Lily known? What had Sandy known?

She had to talk to Beale. Would he still be up in Stinson
Beach investigating at the house? She exited at Mill Valley
to find a phone booth—she'd call him from there. If he
was at Dennis's she could take the Mount Tam road over
to the other side.

At a corner in front of a darkened gas station, she spotted a pay phone and pulled up beside it. She fumbled in
the glove compartment through wrinkled maps, old re-
ceipts, pliers, a flashlight that didn't work, searching for a
coin to make the call. She bent over, feeling along the
floor for money that might have been dropped. Nothing.

When she sat up, bright headlights glared into the car, a
van or truck directly behind her, its lights burning into
the rearview mirror. Maggie slid back into the driver's
seat, put the Impala in gear, and rocketed out onto the
street. Just then the Impala stalled. *Not now,* she whispered. Against instructions, she tried the ignition again.
The engine whined once, twice, then turned over. As she
raced up the street, the vehicle jerked out after her,
squealing out of the lot.

Maggie spun left onto a residential street, then circled
back toward the highway. *Quinn's house,* she thought.
He's only blocks from here. She wheeled up the steep hill,
ascending the narrow road banked by ivy and roots of
trees, then screeched into Quinn's driveway, praying that
he was still there. Quickly she climbed out of the car,
waiting to see if the van or truck would follow, its high
beams arcing around the corner. Only then did she realize that her hands were shaking, her legs flaccid and wob-
bly.

It was just some kids out cruising in their parents' car,
she told herself. There were lights on in Quinn's house.
Why should you trust him either? But she knew he hadn't

been the one at Rob's, the arm through the broken window, the figure on the stairs. She'd just been talking to
him on the phone. Still, perhaps it would be better to just
go on up to San Rafael. Even if Beale wasn't there, she
could just wait for him.

But just then, Quinn's front door fell open, a slant of
light zigzagging across the steps. He squinted, not recog-
nizing the car at first, then calling out, "Maggie! How did
you get here so fast? Are you okay? What was with the
phone? I thought you hung up at first. Then I called the
phone company and they said it was the line. I was almost
ready to drive in myself to see if you were all right."

Maggie brushed past him into the house. She leaned
against the wall, breathing deeply, trying to control the
shivering in her chest. "I think he wanted to kill me."

"Who?"

"Yeah, who? Real good question. Some mafia thug?" She
explained about the front door, the pearls on the floor,
and the broken window.

"They didn't break in?"

"I didn't have time to check all the windows."

"So it could have been someone who had a key," Quinn
pushed his hair from his forehead. "Are you sure it wasn't
just Rob?"

"Just Rob? This guy was tracking me through the house
like an animal. Lora had a key this afternoon—maybe
Dennis took it from her. Where's the phone, Quinn? I've
got to call Beale right now."

"Look, why don't you stay here tonight. You'll be safe
here. In the morning I'll go with you first thing."

"Quinn, Lora is dead. Phillip Dodd was murdered this
morning in Berkeley. Somebody just tried to kill me and
they probably tried to wire a bomb into the Impala earlier
today but I came back too soon from visiting you at the
gallery and I'm not about to lie down and get a good
night's sleep."

"I don't want cops up here," Quinn said. Finally he shut
the front door, put one hand over his face. "I guess I'm

trying to protect Dennis. Give him enough time to get to Tacoland. Wire him some cash."

"That's very generous of you, Quinn. Also illegal. Doesn't that fall into the category of aiding and abetting? I hate to suggest the possibility that it really was Dennis who killed Lora—and tried to kill me."

"Why? Why do you keep saying that?"

"Because I don't know otherwise. And what about our old friend Loam? Does he just happen to drop in to the gallery on a regular basis inquiring about your recent acquisitions?" She told him about her visit to the second-hand store and of Freda's agitation. "Maybe Loam is the connection, Quinn. Does he deal? Does he have anything to do with organized crime?" As soon as she'd blurted out these questions, she regretted it. She trusted Quinn and she did not. She couldn't seem to stop.

Quinn leaned his head back against the wall, silent for a moment. "You know, I always did think it strange when Freda pulled Lora into the Haitian thing. It was like a hustle or something—as if Freda bewitched her. She became so obsessed with all the voodoo stuff. I mean they worked on her until she was hooked, even wanted to go to Haiti and study. I never quite understood it. And I hadn't seen either of them since before Lora first disappeared." He was quiet for a moment, then added, "The Loams might very well have gotten Lora involved in some kind of dealing. They were sure at the center of that whole scene back in the late sixties. I don't know why I never thought of it before."

A car passed just then, rumbling up the hill, and Maggie huddled closer to the wall. She shook her head. "I'm going to talk to Beale myself—if for no other reason than that I don't feel like dying."

He pulled at the edge of his mustache. "I'd better go with you. I don't want you out there alone. Just wait a second. I was down in the darkroom when you came and I've just got to finish up one last thing."

He opened a door that led to a lower level. Maggie

followed him down, watching as he pulled strips of film from a solution and hung them from small clips on lines, the thin banners of plastic swaying.

"I do developing for people sometimes," he muttered. "They drop film off at the gallery. Students mostly. . . . I probably just ruined these—haven't even had a chance to look at them yet."

He hung up the last strip, dried his hands on a towel, then flicked off the lamp overhead and strode up the wooden steps two at a time. Maggie remained below in the red light he'd forgotten to turn off.

From the kitchen he called down, "Are you coming up, Maggie?"

She bent close to the filmstrips, turned on the overhead lamp again, and peered at the small squares: outlines of flowers, splayed tulips, orchid stamens. The next strip was nudes, slightly abstract, closeups of breasts, a curve of buttocks.

Quinn appeared at the top of the steps, holding a beer. "You want a drink before we go?" he asked. Then, "Forget those," he said. "I told you they're not even mine. I'd like to show you some of my stuff. I'd like you to stay for a couple of days when this whole fucking mess is behind us. I'd like you to stay here with me." His voice suddenly sounded very tired. He moved into the kitchen above her, still talking, though she couldn't quite hear him.

She let go of the strip and it swung gently on the line. As she lifted the last ribbon of film, she ran her eyes down the frames, each one identical, snapped over and over and over. It was Lora, her face turned slightly to the side, lips parted, eyes unfocused but open, dark hair spread out on a checkerboard surface, half black, half white. *A picture of Lora dead.*

Maggie pulled the string of the red bulb, snapped off the overhead light, and shivered in the close wet dark. It could not have been Quinn at the house tonight because she'd been talking to him on the phone when the line went dead. But of course he could have been calling from down the street, or from a car phone for that matter. He could have been calling to make sure she was there, he could have been setting her up. She felt light-headed and leaned against a shelf of photographic supplies. Or perhaps he'd been telling the truth and really had been here all along in Mill Valley. What had ever made her think that there was only one person in on all of this?

Again Quinn called down into the darkness, "Are you coming up now, Maggie?" he asked. "Are you finished?"

Chapter 20

"I'm coming," she said, her voice weaker than she'd intended. Maggie unclipped the length of film, folded it once, and put it in her jeans pocket. *Rational,* that was her trouble. She'd been trying to be rational. Each known fact would narrow the possibilities. Instead it had increased them. Demonic logarithms, network of lies, interlocked. Perfect, perfect web and she, the black widow, climbing. *Leave,* screamed the voice in her head. *Just leave. Tell him you left something in the car. Anything.*

"Ah." Quinn nodded. "You looked at the negatives."

She just stared at him.

"I told you," he said, "they're not mine. People drop their film off at the gallery and I make up prints for them. I take no responsibility for the content whatsoever. Hey, I'm not even into nudes. In fact, I've been photographing sand. Microscopic closeups, particles . . . Maggie, why are you looking at me like that?"

"I left something out in the car. My purse." As she turned toward the door, he grabbed her arm.

"Stay," he said. "Have a drink first. I'm as upset about

this as you are." He handed her the Scotch, the brown liquid swirling in the short glass.

"Please. Have you never believed anything I've ever said? I guess I exaggerate. I omit things, okay? I lie sometimes. It's not meant to be evil. I find reality so dull most of the time. Yes, some of those pictures are mine—but the flowers, not the nudes. The tulips. Are they too sentimental? What do you think?"

He had not let go of her arm, and his fingers pressed into muscle. She touched his hand and he released his hold.

"I want some ice," she said calmly. He went on talking and she kept watching him as she backed slowly into the kitchen area that was open to the living room and the glass wall beyond, separated only by a waist-high counter.

"And that's another thing," said Quinn. "Under pressure I start making jokes, bantering about trivial subjects. Monkey mouth. It used to pass for charm. Intimacy avoidance, right?" He followed her into the galley kitchen. "I guess I did suspect in some way that Lora might be dealing. It makes sense, now that I think about it. She'd have these sudden infusions of cash for the gallery, she'd take great trips to Haiti when I knew damn well from Dennis that they didn't exactly have it in savings. I guess I thought Gram would always provide. I thought Lora could always hit the old girl up. The pot of gold. And I always felt the issue about the will was bogus, that Rob was behind it somehow. That's what seems strange to me now—all along I'm thinking Rob is behind this, he's going to somehow benefit from his sister's death. I know you thought I was a son of a bitch for even thinking it—but look, Lora turns up alive and in the course of twenty-four hours she really *is* dead. Don't you see what I mean? The organized crime bit is so handy—who can finger an anonymous hit man, you know? As a setup you can't beat it. That's why I've got to pull for Dennis. Okay, I'm biased. I never trusted Garson, that's all. I never forgave him for

being in the army, I guess. Am I crazy?" His words came
rapid-fire, staccato.

Maggie opened the freezer door, lifted out an ice tray,
and set it on the counter.

"Except for Dodd," Quinn continued. "It doesn't fit
that Rob would kill him. Unless Dodd just knew too much
about Lora, about the grand jury thing . . ."

As Quinn went on, she opened a drawer, then one next
to it, full of ladles, spatulas, large knives. Yes, she thought.
Ready to grab one if he came anywhere near her.

Quinn moved up next to her and she backed away from
him.

"But Maggie, I swear this mess has nothing to do with
me."

Hand shaking, she reached for the ice tray. A cube
slipped from her fingers, clattering across the floor. As
Maggie squatted down behind the counter to pick it up, a
crack blasted through her mind and the room was suddenly snowing glass. As if in slow motion, the glass spread
outward like fireworks blooming in all directions. She
could feel the sound of the shot through her bones and she
fell, not knowing if she was hit or not. As the second shot
came, Quinn's body seemed to lift into the air, fly back
against the refrigerator, and slump to the floor beside her,
his head at her feet.

"I'm shot," he whispered, his voice astonished and stupid. "I'm really shot." He touched his arm. Blood appeared, a red blot on flannel, then on his chest, the color
itself throbbing. The shots had come from outside. She
grabbed a broom leaning in the corner and jabbed it up at
the light suspended above the counter, smashing the
bulb. The room went dark.

"Maggie?" Quinn whispered. Her eyes adjusted to the
dark. "Come here. Touch me. You've got to get out of
here. Hide, babe. They know you're here, don't they?"

"Who, Quinn, who are they? What about the pictures of
Lora, why do you have those pictures?"

His voice cracked. "Even though I'm bullshit I've always loved you. That's fucking corny. Please, Lord, don't let those be my last words. Look at all this blood," he said.

"Oh, God," she whispered. "Don't die on me, Quinn. I've got to get you to a hospital."

She reached up on the wall to pull the phone down and a third shot blasted through the house. It was closer now. The phone dangled on its spiral cord and she squirmed toward it, pushing 911. Quinn was breathing in short, shallow gasps, his chest bubbling. She reached back to shove a dish towel over his heart, and his mouth went slack. Maggie set his head on the hard tiles.

"We've been shot at," she cried into the phone. "I don't know the house number, I don't know. There's a blue Impala in the driveway. Seaview Drive or something! And a van. Quinn Gallery, it's white—"

"Seventy-four Seaview Terrace," the voice said as if to someone else. "We've already traced your location. Ma'am, we have your location, the police are on their way. Tell me what's going on there. Is there someone there with a gun?"

Maggie heard footsteps outside on gravel. A light played across the window and the door creaked open. She shuddered, covering her head. "He's here now," she whispered.

"Quinn? Hey, Quinn did you hear some shots?" The room was suddenly lit. "It's Berman from next door. Anybody home? Oh, my God!" the voice cried.

Maggie cringed next to the cupboards, shielding Quinn's still body. From down the hill the whine of sirens rose. Tires on gravel, the slam of car doors and crackle of CB radios.

"Police!" shouted a man's voice. "Hold it right there!"

"I'm a neighbor!" yelled Berman, throwing his hands in the air.

Footsteps clattered into the house. Then more voices. "Call for an ambulance. Jesus Christ."

A policeman bent over Maggie, gun still in his hand. She did not know if she could move, but stood anyway, noticing for the first time that she was covered with small particles of glass, her clothes wet with Quinn's blood. She touched her head, and glass fell from her hair. When she told them about the shot coming in through the picture window they instantly snapped the lights off. An officer ran out to his car and radioed for assistance. She heard the words *telephoto, hills, set up a perimeter, net.*

Two others bent over Quinn while Berman flattened himself against the wall. Someone took Maggie's arm and led her away from Quinn.

A Rescue Unit van squealed up behind the squad car outside, quickly followed by several more squad cars. Two medics rushed into the house carrying IV equipment, clear tubes, a red case the size of a tackle box. She watched as they hovered over Quinn.

"Chest wound. Got it in the lung."

"There's still a pulse."

Their hands moved over his body, and one of the medics looked over his shoulder at Maggie, at the blood on her hands and shirt. "Are you all right? Were you hit?"

"I don't think so."

They placed Quinn on a stretcher and rushed him out to the open back of the ambulance. She ran out after them. "Please let me come," she begged.

The two officers consulted briefly. One almost shoved her in, then climbed in behind her.

"Can he talk?" the cop asked the medic. "Can I try to get a statement?"

"He's out, man," said the medic. "It's going to be touch and go. He ain't talking, I can tell you that."

The officer sat back and the ambulance screamed down the winding road, its red light whirling strobes across the black trees.

Maggie slouched on an orange Naugahyde couch in a bright fluorescent-lit room. The table before her was strewn with Styrofoam coffee cups and tattered copies of *People* magazine. A nurse came in with a white lab coat draped over her arm. She took Maggie's pulse and asked her if she'd like to just try this on. Maggie slipped the coat on over her blood-stained clothes. A police officer appeared at the door with a man in a gray suit. "Miss, this is Detective Bob Seymour of the Mill Valley Police Department. He's going to ask you some questions about what happened up there if you're up to it."

The detective sat down next to her. On the TV suspended from the wall Bryant Gumbel was interviewing a Saudi prince.

Maggie said, "The man I need to talk to is Sergeant Tom Beale—he's with the Marin County Sheriff's Office. He's known about this case from the very beginning. I tried calling him from the phone out in the hall but he's either at the scene of another shooting or interviewing suspects and can't be reached. These shootings are all related—that's why I've got to talk to him before anything else."

"Slow down, slow down," said the detective. "Why don't you let me ask some questions. Try to answer just exactly what I ask and only what I ask."

"But I need Beale," she repeated. "I talked to him just yesterday."

"Well, this shooting is under the jurisdiction of the Mill Valley Police Department. Sergeant Beale will be notified just as soon as possible and he'll have access to any information that's pertinent to his case, but we have to conduct our own investigation of this particular situation."

"All right," Maggie whispered.

As he questioned her, she answered slowly, listing the complicated and dislocated facts. She told it all—Lora's drug trafficking, the FBI surveillance, the grand jury investigation.

"Do you have any idea who shot at you?"

"Someone who thinks I know too much about Lora," said Maggie. "At first I thought it was her husband, Dennis, but I don't think Dennis would try to hurt Quinn unless he's gone completely crazy. I think it's probably someone in organized crime. For a couple of minutes

right before the shots I was even afraid Quinn was in on it.
I found these in his darkroom—pictures of Lora taken
after her death. That's the pattern—pictures taken after
the murder. Ask Beale, ask the Berkeley police about the
Polaroid of Phillip Dodd. I don't know if Quinn took these
himself or if they were taken by someone else. He developed pictures for other people, so they may have been
planted at the gallery."

Maggie's throat thickened with words and she couldn't
go on. The detective scribbled down some notes, then
said, "Pictures taken after a murder—that's pretty weird.
Like keeping evidence against yourself. It doesn't sound
at all like organized crime to me. They don't document
their crimes. I can't figure that one."

Maggie simply shook her head. The detective finished
writing, then stood. "Would you like some water?"

"I'm so cold," she said.

"You might be in some kind of shock. Let me get a
nurse."

Maggie's entire body ached. She lifted the lab coat and
looked again at her clothes. If only she could go somewhere and lie down, change into clean clothes. She knew
she would not sleep, but at least she could rest her body.
When Beale got in touch with her the questioning would
begin all over again.

Just then, the *Today* show cut to local news. A reporter
stood with a microphone before a white van with blue
letters printed along the side: QUINN GALLERY.

"In the early hours of dawn, three shots from a sniper's
rifle shattered the peace of this quiet Mill Valley hillside.
The area has been cordoned off while police search the
heavily wooded neighborhood. One man is reported in
critical condition at Marin General Hospital. Neighbors
say that Robert Quinn, owner of Quinn Gallery in Sausalito, is a friendly, well-liked man, active in the community
and a supporter of the arts. Meanwhile, the Marin County
Sheriff's Office has apprehended a suspect who is being
held for questioning in a shooting last night in Stinson

Beach. There is word that the two incidents may be related. We'll have more on this story on our eight A.M. report."

Who have they apprehended? Maggie prayed that Beale would get the message she left for him to call her here at the hospital.

She pictured again the image of Lora in the darkroom negatives. It was so awful, the thought of someone taking pictures of the dead. Some horrible fascination. What was that called? Necrophilia, attraction to or fascination with the dead. Erotic attraction to corpses. Suddenly Maggie felt sick to her stomach. She thought of the room in Quinn's gallery filled with death masks, effigy figures, grave markers, the sequined banners from Thailand that were coffin covers. The giant photographs that were close-ups of bones. The shadow box with its pictures of those thought to be dead and those who were next, photographs from the Berkeley house.

Quinn could have taken them—but if he'd known those negatives were there, would he have left her alone in the darkroom to find them? People brought film in for him to develop . . . Loam, she thought. He was there that day. Made a special trip—but when she'd seen Loam there, Lora was still alive.

She had just rested her head back against the couch when someone called her name and she jerked awake, realizing she'd dropped off into an aching sleep. Cody and Rob stood over her. Cody sat down beside her and brushed her hair from her forehead. Rob looked weary, dark growth of beard, his eyes red-rimmed.

"I saw it on the morning news and came right down," said Cody. "The nurse told me you were here. Are you all right?"

Rob perched on the coffee table, shoving aside the tattered magazines. He clasped his hands between his knees. "She's dead, Maggie."

Maggie only nodded. "I know."

"I've been with Beale all night," he said. "When I drove

up to Stinson yesterday afternoon to look for Lora, there
was no sign of her. I was checking around town and in
Bolinas and Inverness, friends' houses and bars—then I
came back over the hill and called Beale. He'd just gotten
the call that she'd been found dead up at the house, so I
drove back over Mount Tam."

"Why didn't you call me?"

"I did. It was busy. Busy every time I tried to call. I got
to wondering if there was something wrong with the
phone. They took Jesse into custody for questioning but
she's just been released pending further investigation.
They picked Dennis up in her truck just south of Merced.
They'll book him when they get him back to the sheriff's
office."

"But if Dennis was driving south all that time then who
shot at me and Quinn?" she asked.

Cody glanced over at Rob, waiting for him to go on.
"Beale has only just spoken with the Mill Valley police.
Dennis was about four hours south of here when he was
picked up. Almost exactly four hours from the time Quinn
was shot."

"But what about this hit list Lora was supposedly on?
What if some hit man killed her—and Dodd?"

Just then Sergeant Beale swung around the corner,
leather shoes on the sleek linoleum. Though he too must
have been up all night, he didn't look it. "There you are."
He nodded greetings toward Rob and Cody and bent
down in front of the couch.

"They told me you didn't look good but you're doing
okay." Beale surveyed her stained clothing under the
white lab coat.

"You've arrested Dennis, then?" she asked quietly.

"Yes—but there is much more going on here than a
domestic murder, as I'm sure you're aware. Of course
we'd never have known that without your cooperation.
That murder in Berkeley yesterday, Lora, and now this
shooting. I've just come from meeting with the Mill Valley
police and I'm going to want to go over all of this with you

again—but you'd better get some rest first. I can't meet
with you until later today anyway, what with Mayhew
being brought in." Beale looked at his watch.

Cody spoke. "I checked in on Quinn just before coming
down here. They've got him on a respirator. He's not
stable yet but they're doing all they can. Maggie, my place
is only minutes from here." He picked a shard of glass
from her hair. "Why don't we all go up there and I'll make
some coffee. You can get a change of clothes and take a
shower. We can come back here in an hour or so if you
want."

Rob stood immediately. "I could use a cup of coffee.
Then I've got to get back to the funeral home." Cody rose,
too, and they both helped Maggie to her feet. She still felt
light-headed and for a moment the Emergency Room
waiting area looked hallucinatory and dirty, like the tail
end of an all-night acid trip. Maggie glanced over at Beale
for approval.

"Fine," was all he said. "I'll check back here for you,
then, a bit later on."

She fell in beside Beale as they walked out, Rob stopping to let one of the nurses know they were leaving.

"Detective Seymour filled me in on what happened last
night," said Beale. "Now confidentially, we do feel there is
an organized crime element here—with possible ties to
some of the Berkeley activity you told us about. For instance, FBI files reveal that one of your former roommates was a paid informer for the Northern California
Drug Task Force—Peter String. The FBI is checking into
that angle now. We're not discounting Mayhew's connection. Apparently someone involved in the operation was
looking for Lora at Garson's last night and found you
instead. I don't want you going back there, understand?
I've asked Garson not to, either, not for a day or two. Is
there somewhere else you can stay?"

She thought immediately of Jesse—but how would that
look? Jesse was too closely involved. She said she wasn't
sure. "Maybe Cody's," she whispered.

Cody stood several paces away and she gestured toward him, introducing him to Beale. Cody jotted a telephone number down on a piece of paper and handed it to Beale. "It's an unlisted number," he explained. Beale shook his hand and said to Maggie, "I'll get back in touch with you later this afternoon—either here at the hospital or at this gentleman's house."

The three men walked ahead of Maggie through the glass doors of the hospital into the utterly clear morning. As they approached the parking lot, Rob put his arm around Maggie. "It's all over," he said.

Cody called out, "Follow me up there. I'll see you in a few minutes."

Maggie leaned into Rob. "I hope so." She sighed.

Chapter 21

Maggie sat at the table in Cody's kitchen waiting for a cup of tea to cool, holding the phone to her ear as Jesse's line rang again and again. There was no answer. She was exhausted past sleep, her chest full of weeping held in. Finally she hung up.

"Not home yet," she said. "Rob, I thought you said they released her."

"They did, but Dennis took her truck."

"Surely someone would drive her home."

Cody asked if either of them was hungry and she said no. In spite of what she knew about his success, Maggie was surprised by Cody's house, its grandeur and size. The house—"compound" she recalled Lora once saying—must have been worth well over a million. Hung in the woods on a steep hillside overlooking San Francisco Bay, the house was built on terraces down an embankment. It was starkly contemporary, gray tinted glass, black leather furniture, glass and black metal, black-and-white photographs—some of them by Quinn, she noted. Everything black and white, even the refrigerator polished ebony, the kitchen floor black and white tiles. To enter the com-

pound, they'd gone through a locked wrought-iron gate
and down two flights of steps to reach the front door.
Maggie stared out toward the living room at the long
white wall entirely covered with masks.

Quinn had been right—Cody must have been his best
customer. She was sure he had one of the finest private
collections anywhere in the country.

"Coffee's ready, Rob," Cody called across the room.

Rob spun suddenly and looked at his watch. "I guess I'll
take a rain check. I'm going to go back over to the funeral
home. The coroner should be done by now. I want to start
making arrangements. If I don't start doing something, I
think I'm going to go crazy."

"At least have a cup of coffee," Cody insisted, but Rob
blew past them and out the door, a pained look on his face.
The closest that he would ever come to tears, Maggie
thought.

Cody sat down across from her at the table. "You should
sleep," he said.

She nodded. "Cody, did you see Quinn a lot, or Dennis?"

"Quinn," he answered. "Fairly often."

"Were they ever lovers—Lora and Quinn?"

"A long time ago. I don't know how serious it was. You
know she played around. I knew about it but I kept quiet.
What good would it have done? I think Dennis suspected
but he didn't really want to face it. What people do is their
own business. Like I said, it was a long time ago."

"Did Quinn know about her dealing, did it ever involve
the gallery that you know of?"

He shrugged. "I think so. Quinn's not entirely innocent.
That's why nobody spoke with total honesty when she first
disappeared."

Suddenly Maggie remembered what Lora had once
told her in passing—that it was Cody who'd arranged
Lora's initial contacts through "buyers" he knew in the
"import business."

"So you knew about her dealing. Were you involved?"

"I helped her to launder some of the money she made but I'll deny it if you tell that to the police. My books are impeccable."

"What else did you know?"

He shrugged. "Not much else. She was on her own. She went too far with it. She wasn't careful. That was her big mistake."

Maggie felt as if Cody were speaking from across the kitchen, from very far away. Her own voice sounded as if it were coming through deep water. "You know more than you're telling me, don't you?" she asked. She placed both her hands flat on the table, and all the energy in her body seemed to flow down, out of the soles of her feet, out through the palms of her hands. She lowered her head onto the cool surface of the white marble table. "I think I'm going to pass out," she whispered.

Cody helped her up, put his arm around her, guiding her down a short hall into the bedroom just off the living room. As she lay down on the king-size bed, he swam above her. She felt strangely detached, as if she too were dying, leaving her body along with Lora, trailing along after him into an unknown world.

"Just rest," he said. "For now, just rest."

"I want to talk some more."

"We'll talk."

"Cody, will you call the hospital and see how Quinn is doing?"

He nodded, standing so far above her that his head seemed very small and his hands huge.

In the kitchen she heard him dial, ask for the doctor, then wait, tapping something metal against the counter. She listened to his voice around the corner.

"I see. I'm sorry to hear that. A coma?" he said. "No, she's all right, just exhausted. She's sleeping now, doctor."

Coma, thought Maggie. She wanted to talk to the doctor. She tried to sit up but the room seemed to float below her, miles away.

A cordless phone sat on a table beside the bed. Care-

fully she picked it up and listened to Cody, to the words
he was speaking intermingled with the Bay Area time and
temperature that kept repeating itself on the other end.

Maggie set the phone down against the pillow. Leaning
forward, she could see across the wide living room to
where he was standing, deep in conversation with a non-
existent doctor, and then it came to her with such force
that she nearly fell back against the bed. What she had
seen in the kitchen, the black and white floor tiles. The
negatives of Lora at Quinn's, her face outlined against
black, against white. Lora on that floor. The pictures had
been taken here. It was Cody who'd planted the negatives
at the gallery to implicate Quinn. So Quinn had been
telling the truth after all. He had been set up just like
everyone else. Like Dennis. Like Jesse. Like Lora. Like
herself.

Cody stood with his back to her, staring out at the blue
bay. Maggie tried to stand but her legs felt drained, soft.
She felt so dizzy, so tired. He must have put something in
the tea, some drug. Perhaps she'd already been poisoned.
Maggie knelt down on all fours and felt her way out of the
room, hoping Cody would stay turned toward the window, continuing his conversation with the time and temperature in low tones she could not make out.

She tried to stand, pressing herself against the wall for
balance. Just then the doorbell rang, chiming through the
house. *Thank God,* she thought. *Someone's here. Maybe
Beale coming to check on me. I'll say I'm in shock, I need
an ambulance.* She heard Cody exchange words with the
visitor on the intercom and in seconds the door opened.

"Forgot my briefcase." Rob's voice.

She moved along the wall, trying to keep from falling,
but her knees buckled under her and her scream dried to
dust in her throat.

"How's it working, Cody? Have you had a chance to try
it yet?"

Maggie crawled to the corner of the hallway as Cody
said, "Not until now, bud," and lifted the gun. Rob bent to

pick up his briefcase from the couch and he saw her reaching out to him.

"Maggie?" he asked.

Cody shot once. Rob jerked backwards, arms flying up, red appearing in blotches on the white wall between the masks, and Rob's face as he sunk down was a mask, an instant of confused recognition or maybe not. Maybe he'd never known.

Maggie staggered back down the hallway to a flight of stairs, black metal like a fire escape, one level down, then two. *There must be a door out of one of the lower levels of the house.* She did not hear him above her. Perhaps he thought she was safely passed out in the bed upstairs. Movement was difficult, the floor liquid beneath her. It was very dark in the lower hallway. She'd gone too far. This was not a split level open to the hillside but a basement, dug in underground. She felt along the wall for a light switch and came upon a door slightly ajar. Only silence above her.

For a moment she thought she'd be sick. The picture of what she'd just seen rocked through her. Cramp in her side as she doubled over. Still on hands and knees, she made her way through the door, listening. Hearing nothing, she slipped into the black room, slid her hand around searching for a light. Finding it, she flicked the switch on and turned to face the room bending and swaying before her.

The room was entirely filled with masks, devilish, toothy and grimacing. Some had huge fangs, others brass or ivory teeth like knives. Animal faces, their mouths open in silent roars. Those tall figures from the gallery, the effigy figures, grave markers, leaned against one side of a wall. Along another wall an ancient Asian coffin, black and red enamel, open and filled with hundreds of small white bones.

She took in the room in horror. It was a miniature gallery, a perverted collector's secret display, and though there was so much she didn't understand, Maggie knew deeply that here in this room was where all the disparate parts merged and met, originated and returned.

Across the room, between a giant wooden spear and a large African mask with ratty black raffia hair, was the purple shadow box hanging slightly askew, the glass cracked, the pearls gone. *Of course. Cody in the house last night.*

Facing right, she saw them arranged on a low table as an archeologist might place his finds after a day's digging—bones of a human skeleton, white and rough, one arm, one leg, one hand, the skull set on its side, empty eye holes black and vacant. *The other half of the body found in the cave. Among the ruins of the boat. The missing parts.*

As Maggie reached behind her for the doorknob, the door was pushed firmly shut. A metallic click sounded against the wood. She rattled the knob hard, put her cheek against the door—but this one locked from the outside.

"Just rest, like I told you to." His voice was muffled through the door. "I just want you to have a nice, long rest."

Chapter 22

$\mathbf{M}$aggie's head ached, she felt hung over, thoughts slurred like a half-remembered dream of falling. Not sure at first where she was, she rolled over once, knocking against a table. Objects cracked to the floor, scuttering across the room. She reached for the wall, found the light switch, and pushed it up. Bones were strewn across the cement, masks leered from the walls. *Death shrine,* she thought. Her breath felt hot and sick. No air. Deep in her chest, a shudder of realization, black fear crawling the back of her neck. The image returned full-force: Rob falling away from her, the sudden spasm of his head. Why did she have to remember at all, see death in her mind's eye, obsessive with final scene, last bead of a rosary, last breath? She thought of her dead husband and said his name like a prayer: *Mark, Mark . . . God.* A cry rose in her throat and she swallowed it back.

She noticed a cot along the back wall of the room and crawled over to it, pulled herself up to a sitting position, rubbing at her forehead and eyes. Balancing on the cot, she jumped with one fist upraised to jam against the lowered ceiling, trying to knock a panel down, but it only dented inward. She dragged the cot over to where a small heating duct entered near the ceiling, but it was screwed tightly in place. She had no idea what time it was.

Palms pressed against cement block, she felt along the cool walls, but there was no other door, crack, closet. Why hadn't he just killed her, turned toward her after he'd shot Rob? She slid down against the wall, hugging her knees. *Panic, I cannot panic,* she thought. *I've got to be ready for him in the split second he opens that door.* There was some reason he had not acted, some crack in his mind, and she had to find that crack and open it and run out.

A large ebony spear leaned in the corner, its point whittled flat and thin. When she lifted it, she was surprised at its weight, tried thrusting it forward over her shoulder, two hands holding it firmly straight at Cody's imagined heart. She might have one instant of surprise, one clean moment in which to act. What else might be used as a weapon? She picked larger bones out of the coffin, but they were too light, porous.

On a low table sat a black metal strongbox the size of a small filing cabinet. It opened easily, gold key left in the lock. She fingered through the papers, organized impeccably, dated, alphabetized, with file cards clipped to them, detailed notations in a tight, slanted hand. Everything was precisely, obsessively arranged, just the way Cody did everything, his clothes, even his bookshelves back in college. There were photographs, newspaper clippings, articles from magazines and tabloids. As she went through them she saw that many were news articles about Vietnam circa 1966 and 1967. A body facedown in a dirt road. Several bodies piled on a truck. A man draped backwards over a barbed wire fence, head on a fence post, several bodies on several fenceposts. A soldier kneeling next to a corpse. He held a large gun, a prize, a trophy. *Bagged one.* Cody grinning with a friend, guns at their shoulders, just a couple of guys out for a hunt. Picture after picture, she flipped through the box, incredulous, remembering the day back in Berkeley that Cody had pulled from his wallet that picture of the severed head of a Vietcong, the ragged cut of the neck, the picture crinkled and yellowed, well-worn from touching. She put her hand to her mouth as she continued through the files, newspaper accounts of murders, the inevitable Polaroid snapshots of people slumped over in wooden chairs and in trunks of cars.

From overhead she heard footsteps echoing on metal. She swept the rest of the bones from the table and lifted the strongbox to a corner, dragged the table quickly over by the door, climbed up on it and hoisted the spear. She would have more of a chance if she was above him in the dark. He'd be reaching for the light, ducking as he entered. She flipped the light off. Gripping the spear in both hands, she waited as the lock clicked open and the door slowly swung in. A dim light shadowed the room. Maggie held still, pressed against the wall.

As Cody leaned in, she brought the spear down as hard as she could against the back of his neck. He cried out in a a low guttural growl, doubled over, and staggered, holding on to the spear as he fell. She heard the clink of metal, the gun spinning across the polished floor. Maggie released the spear but it was too late, and she stumbled from the table. There was no time to try to get the gun. Pushing up, she rushed toward the open door. His hand grabbed her ankle and she slammed down, hands slapping the floor, breath blown from her chest. He pressed down on top of her, turning her over. Even in the darkness she could see he was smiling. Familiar face, old friend she saw now she had never known. *Who was the enemy? Who had the enemy been for years?*

"Good," he said. "That was good, Maggie."

"Get the fuck off me."

"Good," he said again.

Then he dragged her back into the room and threw her against the far wall, kicked the door shut behind him, and turned on the glaring fluorescent light. He picked up the gun and sat back on the floor, leaning back against the

wall, the gun pointed loosely in her direction. Maggie
thought it odd that she did not cringe but only waited for
the shot with eyes open in a strange, stunned stillness.
After a moment she saw he was not going to shoot, not just
yet. *Talk,* she thought. *Talk to him. Stay familiar, stay his
friend. Talk is the only thread of connection. Stay human.*

She spoke quietly, words clear and spaced and slow.
"Cody, what is this place?"

He just stared at her, his eyes not wild at all, but cool
gray, detached. "Let's just call it a memorial. Beautiful,
isn't it? Every culture in the world has celebrated it, the
passage to the other world. Egyptians were the best at it.
Preserving death for centuries, whole cities founded on it.
The Aztecs weren't bad—they threw virgins into the fire.
Slaughter of pagans, Christians to the lions, the Inquisi-
tion, burning of witches—in fact, all of history has proceeded by death advancing, overpowering, so you see
there is a precedent.

"The spiritual *is* death. It's the shadow of God, the most
sacred act, because that is when you get loose of the
bonesack, the skinbag. You exhale, expand—poof! You're
gone. It's universal. Every shaman in the world knows it.
Every priest. Priestess. Every witch, right, Maggie?"

"I'm not a witch, Cody. You know that."

He laughed. "Ah, the modern-day shaman-healer. Rattle the bones of psyche, call on the spirits of the unconscious, exorcise the mother-father-family-of-origin demons. But you are a demon-healer, aren't you, Maggie?
You deal in dispelling darkness. You guide people through
the underworld until they emerge transformed. That's
witchcraft! Come on, now, you and Jesse, yesterday morning up in the woods together? Just like old times, right? I
was there the night of your initiation. Surely you remember being up in Dennis's old room, sweeping it out, burning those pictures. I was watching from the closet when
Jesse touched the black ash to your forehead. I saw you
take your vows."

"I was a kid, Cody. It wasn't a real initiation. It was play."

"You never took it seriously enough. That was your trouble. You never took the darkness seriously. I see that I made a mistake. A bad mistake. I should have acted sooner. *Et hoc praeteribit. This too shall pass.* Too much is known now. You've even flagged the FBI. Your hex, yours and Jesse's." Again, he laughed. "I knew years ago you two were my only true match. But Jesse disappeared, you moved away. Then Sunday there you were, reunited with her. Seeing you up at Dennis's, I could feel it. I could feel your power emanating, and then up at Jesse's, seeing that box, I could tell that its prophecy would have to come true."

Maggie shook her head. "But you're wrong, Cody. Jesse and I didn't make that shadow box. Lora did. When she went back to the Berkeley house, the woman there gave her a box, yes—one that Jesse had made years ago, but Lora changed it, painted the Roman numerals on it herself, glued pictures in it so it would seem like a spell. She got the idea for it from the Haitian pieces she was collecting, those shrines at the gallery and the prayer flags. It was a smoke screen so her disppearance would all seem to be tied to the past in some mysterious way that no one would be able to decipher. She did it to protect Dennis, to throw suspicion off him. If you believe that box has any power, you've already killed the witch who made it."

"Clever. Even slightly plausible," he said. "But even if it was true, what difference would it make? It has a power of its own now, far past you or Lora or Jesse. It detailed a plan and the plan was created years ago. Jesse knew about it, knew that house was hexed, but no one believed her. We're all going to die. Why not die according to a plan? Have some purpose to it?"

"I don't want to die, Cody."

"Yes, you do. Everybody wants it more than anything in the world. Freud knew it. Can't you feel its pull? It's the darkest lover of all. It's just that there's so much chaos.

Everything out of control. You can't determine anything.
There's no plan, no meaning. There's only one thing that
makes sense, that's clear, indisputable, undeniable, un-
avoidable, the absolute truth, and that is death. She'll get
us all." He smiled, picked up the skull from the floor and
dusted it off.

"And she's everywhere. Every highway, house, hospi-
tal, in your car, your food, in your lungs, stomach, bowels.
She's even into sex. She'll eat you from the inside out.
She'll find you.

"In Nam she was in every tree, in the ground. She was
in the mouth of an old woman. And people thought, man,
America's so safe! There's no death back home! If I can
only make it back to America. I'll be home free, man.
Yeah, it's a fucking playground. Now the president's on
TV, he's Flash Gordon. He's a cowboy, he's going to save
us from the bad guys, radar 'em right out of the sky—pow!
Pow! But the bad guys and the good guys are the same.
There's no safe place here, just like there was no safe place
in Nam. You can't escape, but you can stave her off. You
can feed her. And that's what I do. That's what my little
temple here is all about. Death wants to eat you but what I
do is feed her first. That's how I got through Nam."

Cody flipped through the files in the strongbox and
handed her the one with the heads on the fence posts. "If
I fed her a taste of death, she left me alone. It worked
every single time. Still works. When I got home, I thought
I'd be safe just like all the others, but she kept licking at
me, wanting me, and you know what? Found out I missed
her too. Kind of wanted her back in my life, because she
was the only thing that meant anything once and for all on
this planet. The only thing final.

"When she started coming up in me and through me
and at me, at first I thought, man, I'm going to have to kill
myself. She wasn't outside me like in Nam. She had gotten
inside, see? But I found out I could feed her just as well
here as I could in the jungle. We've all got our personal
magic, Maggie. This is mine."

He held the gun out toward her and cocked it. Maggie flinched, covered her face with her palms.

"Can't you feel that? Nothing has ever made your life feel so important. No drug, no prayer, no fuck is as heavy as this is, Purey."

Keep him talking, she thought. *Let him run it out.*

"Tell me about Peter and Lily and Sandy," she said.

He hesitated, then spoke again. " 'Peter, Peter, pumpkin eater, had a wife and couldn't keep her.' Peter was a narc, Maggie. He was undercover for the FBI, watching every move we all made. He was going to bust us, so he died. He took a little of his own medicine. Lily? Just because she was there. They were my first stateside feed.

"It wasn't until the night I found out who Peter really was that I realized that I could feed her over here, too, and believe me there was no better reason than Peter String. They were sleeping when I shot them up. I sat in the room and listened to her eat them. Suck the breath right out of their bodies."

"Then you took their pictures. What was that all about?"

"Quinn taught me that. Historical documentation. Proof. Or a snack for her. When she gets too hungry, I come down here and I remind her."

He sifted through the box and pulled out pictures of Peter and Lily in the room that morning, Lily draped on the chair. Peter cheek down on the Oriental rug, that image drilled into her that would never leave.

He handed her a picture of Sandy flopped over in the easy chair beside her bed. "Sandy found my pictures in my room on one of her cleaning binges. I didn't hide things so well then."

Maggie looked around and realized he didn't hide things so well now. He wanted to be caught, it was important that others witness all of this and respond to it. It was a kind of pornography for him, same personality type as many pederasts, right down to the obsessive detail of his filing system.

He went on. "Sandy was one of the spies. She was going to call the cops. It was just like Nam again, the enemy had infiltrated us and she was the sweetest thing. The only thing was that I searched that whole house and I never found the rest of those pictures. These two were the only ones Sandy didn't hide. All of us—you, too—we would have been thrown in jail. Maggie, I saved you."

"Why don't you save me now, Cody?" she whispered. "Let me go. I won't tell anyone, I promise. Everyone thinks it's Dennis who killed Lora. He's already been arrested. You've done it perfectly."

"Ah, you flatter me. But I've got to remind you of one thing. I'm not stupid or crazy. Don't attempt to manipulate me with your therapy bullshit. Maybe you don't like my philosophy. They didn't like Christ's either. Or Hitler's. Manson's. They didn't like Westmoreland's. This is intelligence so clear the whole world is afraid. The primitives knew. They were connected. Feed her through sacrifice and you live."

"What about Lora? Did she know about all this?"

"No. Nobody knows about any of this except you. And I don't even know why I'm telling you. It's just your way. Little truth finder, our Purey, our white light. You always get to the heart of the matter, don't you? The truth is, I'm in awe of you. When I heard you were a death healer, I thought, God, it's so perfect! What medicine, what a lineage of magic! We're at opposite ends of the scale, don't you see? But with you and Jesse on the scale together, it's too fucking heavy."

Cody stood, stuffed the gun into his belt, and began picking bones up off the floor, setting them back in the lacquered coffin, straightening up the room as if he were putting clothes in a hamper. Maggie could tell he'd grown comfortable with her. Maybe he despised her ability to listen, to draw the truth out of people, but he also craved it the way people craved confession and absolution. That was the crack—he'd held it in all too long. Now he wanted to tell someone. *Go on,* she thought. *Tell me more.*

"Why did you kill Lora, then?" Maggie asked. "Just because of the shadow box?"

He went on cleaning as he spoke, words punctuated by the clack of bone on bone.

"My first mistake. I fell in love with her. I took her down to South America on a business trip and helped her make importing contacts. It was fine for a year or so, but then she started doing a little dealing on the side: white death. Powdery, pure and lovely and white, just like you. Unfortunately Lora was a somewhat gifted businesswoman. I say somewhat. She was quite successful but too talkative and gregarious. Other importers knew about her and she moved in and out of the country too often and lived too well. Eventually her name came up on a list of possible witnesses in a grand jury investigation of some murders and disappearances related to organized drug trafficking on the West Coast."

Maggie watched Cody as he talked. He turned to pick up a newspaper article that had fallen to the floor and replaced it in his files. Maggie eyed the gun inserted at the back of his belt.

"This information was leaked into the . . . community, shall we say. It would not have been beneficial for her to testify."

"You work for the mafia?" she asked.

He put his fingers together lightly and smiled. "I am not an employee of anyone. I'm an independent entrepreneur. Let's say I'm the competitor. Quite discreetly and invisibly my company brings in over twenty million dollars' worth of business to the northern California area each year." He spoke as if he were addressing a group of potential investors.

"But where are your henchmen, where's your limo, your pit bulls?"

"I said discreetly, didn't I? I live well, yes. I have a few cameras around. I prefer privacy. No one knows who I am. No one has ever met directly with me. I'm not the godfather type. The Wizard of Oz is more my style. I'm hidden behind the mask of the computer screen. I make arrangements. I transfer funds. I book flights, shipments within the international electronics community. Once in a while I go out on a pickup or delivery—incognito—not as boss, just as another hireling—to keep tabs on my people, to stay close to the nuts and bolts of the business.

"Lora knew nothing of this either. But the FBI was watching too many of my employees. They could not identify me, but they were close, the way a fever is not the disease but indicates the presence of an invisible virus. All of my people are highly skilled at what they do—all except for Lora. For all her success, she was still an amateur. I should have killed her right then—but as I said, I'd made the mistake of . . ." He left the sentence unfinished.

Of feeling, Maggie thought.

"Instead, I devised a plan to convince her to leave the country. I had my people threaten her, try to run her car off the road, shoot at her on an isolated beach, until I had her convinced that the kingpins of the Bay Area were bent on murdering her. I suggested the plan for the disappearance of the boat and she went for it. It worked in my favor that her inheritance had run out and things were lousy with Dennis. I promised her a fabulous new life in Rio after a lay-low period in Bogotá for a year or so.

"I arranged for an employee who had a boat docked at Bodega Bay to pick Lora up on *The Pearl* in the lee of the Farallon Islands. He transferred the lifeboat onto his boat, hauled *The Pearl* way out, made a couple of phony distress calls, and just let her go. When they docked at Bodega Bay, I met them and we strapped the lifeboat to the top of my car and drove up to Oregon, where I've got a cabin. Stored it out back of my garage, where it weathered all winter along with Lora's jacket, the one with the diamond stickpin from her grandmother. Then I sent her down to Mexico and on to Colombia with a fake passport. She stayed with people who work for me down there.

"The FBI didn't exactly buy it that half the people on their witness list seemed to have permanently left the country. It became imperative that there be proof of Lora's death. Thus the famous remains, a flawed idea, I admit. When I get too closely involved I lose perspective. I see now that my interests were starting to merge.

"Getting the lifeboat down to Slide Ranch took some doing. I smashed the boat up with a rock, wrapped the boards in a tarp, and rigged a sort of backpack. Then I hiked down there with the boards, the jacket, and some of . . . this." He gestured toward the skull balanced on top of the strongbox. "Besides, I realized that *she* also likes proof of death. Through another of my employees I hired two teenage kids to hike down to the cave and report their findings to the police.

"But my plan backfired. Lora got tired of life south of the border. La Gringa missed her MasterCard. She just couldn't wait it out. Plus she went back to sampling the product."

Maggie glanced over at the skull. "And who was that?" she asked. It was amazing how much he was ready to tell of this, every little detail of his ingenuity and cunning. It was as if it didn't exist until there was the telling—the proof, as he called it.

"Someone nameless and unknown. Why do you think Peter and Lily's deaths were never investigated as murders? No one gave a shit about them. They were runaways, recruited as spies. The drug task force lost people like them left and right. They were expendable."

Cody took more pictures from the box, four of them, and handed them to Maggie. Four corpse portraits, three young men, one woman. He pointed to the woman's picture, then to the skull. "That's her. Picked her up hitchhiking in Big Sur. Left her there, too, way back in the mountains. About a year later I got the urge to go back, and she was still there, so I brought her home."

Maggie felt sick and closed her eyes.

Cody continued. "No, Lora couldn't wait it out. My contacts notified me on Sunday night that she had reentered the country with the help of one of my less-than-

trustworthy employees. I received this information just
hours after I'd seen you and Jesse together. I immediately
went over to Berkeley to my employee's residence. He
had already taken Lora to Stinson Beach, he said. He was
eliminated. The next day when I saw the shadow box up at
Jesse's and heard you telling her about the death dates, I
realized that the prophecy on the hex box was correct
after all and knew I had to carry out *her* plan."

Maggie closed her eyes. He must have come up that
back path and stood at the studio window the entire time
she and Jesse were talking.

"Overhearing your talk with Jesse yesterday about going to the police also convinced me the plan was right. I
followed you to Quinn's and while you were in the gallery
I set about wiring a bomb into your car—that was my
expertise in Vietnam, you know, trip mines and explosives
—but you came back too soon. When I returned here to
Tiburon, Lora was waiting for me. She had heard from
you about Dodd's death and she begged me to protect her
—but she threw a tantrum. She needed a hit. She got out
her gun and began waving it around, saying she was going
to hurt me if I didn't protect her, if I even tried to bother
her or tell anyone what had happened between us. I took
the gun away from her. That's when I knew *she* was hungry. Lora kept mouthing off, 'Oh yeah, Big Man, kill me if
you're so tough. Go ahead. Shoot me.'

"So I did. I put her in the car—after her final portrait of
course—and dropped the film off at Quinn's. I thought it
fitting he should have the negatives in his possession.
Then I drove up to Stinson Beach. I was planning a mur-
der-suicide scene for her and Dennis, but he wasn't there.
I placed Lora upstairs in the bedroom, planted the gun on
the floor downstairs just inside the door, where it would
be handled. I waited along the highway down in town
until I saw Dennis come back, and then I called the police
from a pay phone—a concerned neighbor reporting a
possible burglary. That was when I went looking for you
and Rob. You're very athletic, you know that, Maggie?

"I did have time to wire an explosive to Garson's telephone, though. So you see, if I hadn't shot him today he was gone anyway. I just knew I couldn't wait. I can detonate the house by telephone signal—Garson's remains will not be located in the debris. How unfortunate. At least I found the shadow box. I wanted it for my collection.

"I had no idea you'd go to Quinn's, but he was on my way home. The two of you together in the kitchen through the plate glass window was a perfect chance. But you bent down just then. Witchy, Purey, witchy. Did you sense I was watching you? I watched the other night, too, after our dinner in Sausalito . . . you and Quinn."

Maggie could feel her face distort into a silent wail like one of the raging masks in Cody's collection. She drew her knees up to her chest and hid her face. *Don't show him emotion. That's what he's waiting for. Because he's so numb he can't feel anything human, he wants to feel yours. Don't let him.*

"Now, Dennis," said Cody. "I'm going to have to wait on him until he's out on bail, I guess. I still think he's a very good candidate for a suicide. Jesse's death is already arranged. We'll meet magic to magic. She's always had a strong death charge—she likes that dark power, too—but without your light she's not as powerful. And she knows it. Both of you are going to have to die by fire, of course, because of your lineage. *She* has made that clear to me."

He took out an elegant gold lighter from his pocket and held one of the clippings up, lit it, dropped it smoking to the floor. Picked up another from the files.

"Why do you call death a she, Cody? Women are the life-givers. The birthers, the mothers."

He shrugged. "She just always seemed female. Females are in charge of hunger and feeding and feasting."

"Maybe you're missing out on the real feast."

"What do you mean?" He lit another file from the folder, and smoke quickly filled the closed room. Maggie had been watching the fire. Now she saw that he was

opening a black cloth, preparing a syringe, just like the
one she'd seen in Peter's room so long ago.

"Maybe death is a hungry little boy who never got
enough to eat. Cody," she breathed. "It's your own hunger, not some she-demon with gaping jaws. It's your own
fear, not Kali."

As he bent over she lunged at him, trying to pull the
gun from his waist. He spun, sweeping her legs out from
under her. She struggled under him, scratching at his
eyes, but his arms were long. He knelt on her and inserted
the needle at her elbow. As he touched her hair, she
swiveled her head and bit his hand. He yanked back, she
could taste the salt of his skin, blood in her mouth.

"See?" he said. *"She's* hungry."

He stroked her hair again. "I want you to have time to
savor this a bit. The heightened pleasure of these last few
hours. You'll never have anything like them."

His face floated above her like a blurred moon, and then
there was nothing.

Chapter 23

It was late afternoon when Jesse finally opened the door of the squad car and stepped out into the shadows of her yard. The earth felt powdery underfoot as she walked around to the driver's side of the car. Pungent smell of eucalyptus in the air and rustle of bay laurel. They had promised to take her home by midmorning, but then Dennis had been brought in handcuffed and they'd forgotten about her and left her to wait hours on a green plastic chair.

She'd glimpsed him briefly, growth of red beard, and his sad eyes met hers once, full of sorrow and also shame. She'd known in that instant: he couldn't have done it. The shame was for having abandoned her and the sorrow was that he believed it was over between them.

The officer who had driven Jesse home gave her final instructions out the window of the squad car. "You heard what Sergeant Beale said. If you leave the Bay Area you've got to let him know."

"I'm not going anywhere. Is he going to check back with me? Couldn't one of you cruise through here every once in a while and make sure everything is all right?"

"We will if we're in the area. Call us if anything funny happens."

She nodded. *If anything more funny happens,* she thought, *I'll be dead.*

The officer glanced around the redwood grove at the green hose stretched from the house to the copper pool, a stack of pressed-wood logs next to it and the glass wands hung at odd angles in the trees overhead. "Looks like there's going to be a party," he said.

"Something like that."

The squad car pulled out of the yard, wheels crackling over dried needles.

In the house Jesse called Zoë and told her to send Ben home, thanked her for picking him up in the middle of the night. She spoke briefly to Ben and explained that Dennis had been arrested for murder. Then she tried calling Rob at work and at home. No answer. She had Maggie and Rob paged at the hospital but they did not respond. The funeral home, the coroner's office. Not there. She even tried calling Cody. His answering service said he'd gone out of town and was expected back in several days. Where could Rob and Maggie be?

As she looked out the window at the grove, the ritual space, she thought, *Everything is ready except me. If only Maggie were here. I feel so ungrounded.* Four o'clock. She'd have to do some pretty intense cleansing to clear her own mind for the ritual or the whole thing would be pointless. It would end up being an homage to darkness, just as Ben had said. If only Maggie's light and her healing presence could be here.

On the phone Zoë had urged her not to cancel the ritual. "You need us now, you need our energy."

But what about the bones, that tape in her car?

"They've arrested him," Zoë said. "They've got him in custody. You're all right."

But Jesse had not told Zoë everything. She hadn't mentioned that she thought arresting Dennis was a terrible mistake, that it was someone else altogether trying to kill them, all of them.

Jesse felt cold as she thought of that shadow box. Bad magic, Maggie had said. If only she could get her hands on that thing, reverse its message, burn it, dismantle it.

As she went out into the yard and began arranging the pressed-wood logs, Ben came running up the hill through the back of the grove, the route he always took through the woods to and from Milo's.

"Ben, are you okay?" She ran to him and hugged his bony body as if he were still a small child.

"What about you, Mom? Aren't they going to let Dennis go?"

She shook her head. "I don't think so."

"He couldn't kill anything but a fish! They must be nuts! What's going to happen?"

"I believe he didn't do it, Ben, but all the evidence at this time points to him. I'm off the hook as the main suspect, but I'm not totally in the clear either. I cooperated with all their questions—they did a nitrate test on me. They put wax on your hands and from that they can tell if you fired a gun recently. I gave fingerprints, all of it. So they know I didn't actually fire the gun. They're waiting to see what Dennis will tell them now."

"We've got to get him off!"

"It's not that easy—and there might be others involved in this. So we've got to be careful."

Ben sat down between the ring of stones and the half circle of logs Jesse had placed on the dirt. "Mom? This lady getting killed and all, her being Dennis's wife. You finding her and almost getting blamed for it—isn't that what you'd call an omen? You're always telling me to listen to the atmosphere, pay attention to what's in the ether and all that. Auras. Synchronicity. What I'm trying to say is, maybe you should call the ritual off. Have it during the full moon in September. Say you got sick or something."

Jesse sat next to him on the dirt. "Zoë thinks that I

should go ahead. That it's like a test, that spiritual concerns should prevail. Anyway, I've been thinking. I want
to dedicate the ritual as a healing prayer for Quinn and for
Lora's troubled soul, to help her move on into afterlife. I
think I ought to continue with it. Besides, everything is set
to go. Think of the work we've all done—all that you and
Cody did with the wiring to assure everything would go
according to plan."

"It's your show," mumbled Ben. "What's to eat?" He
raised his head to look at the points of the redwoods, then
rose and ambled slowly toward the house.

At the sheriff's office last night, she'd thought about just
splitting. She and Ben could take off for a couple of weeks
until school started. Rent a car or take the Greyhound
down to Big Sur. Hell, go all the way to Mexico.

Then she'd caught herself. The instinct to run was ancient in her. Fight or flight. She was the flight type. But
she was through with running. And there was no reason
to. She'd done nothing wrong. The evidence would show
she had absolutely nothing to do with Lora's murder. The
mistakes of the past had been rectified, burned clean by
the pain she'd felt. Running wasn't her way now. No,
she'd stay and face the moon tonight with all its wild
energy. Face it down, the darkness in the world. Offer her
real and imagined light.

Finally, to settle herself, she decided to do something
she hadn't done in years—make an amulet. In her studio
she cut a piece of chamois cloth and picked some clover
from the side of the road. What she wanted was sweet-
ness. Long summers, light held in, transformed into a
color and a smell. She crunched a handful of redwood
needles, pinched them into the chamois in her palm, and
then placed something at the center, an object that had
been a talisman for her from those days in Berkeley. A
tiger's eye in a comfrey leaf. The stone for proper vision
and strength, comfrey for healing.

Jesse tied the bag shut and hung it inside the charred
stump, the one right by the reflecting pool, then sat at the

center of the stump for several minutes. This tree had
always been her favorite in the grove.

But what was that? Over by the inside wall of the stump
there was a clump of dark cloth wedged behind a piece of
wood that jutted out from the core of the tree. Lifting it
out, she saw that the cloth was lace—black lace wrapped
around something. Where had she seen this cloth before?
It was familiar as a square of calico from a childhood dress
sewn into a grandmother's quilt. As she unwrapped the
small object it came to her—the canopy over her bed at
the Berkeley house. This dusty shred came from her old
room, from all the belongings she'd abandoned there.

She flipped back the corners of the lace to uncover a
small cloth doll, primitive, hand-stitched, with yellow
flowered trousers and a tiny green shirt. The face had
been burned off. The ashes crumbled into the lace as Jesse
dropped the doll to the floor of the blackened stump.

Chapter 24

The first sensation Maggie had was of being stuffed in a box, a small, square box under the ground. Dark, sharp corners. Her torso bent at an odd angle. Her mind, awake, tried to locate the home it had known—arms, legs, chest. A feeling of vertigo, of dangling sideways, hung by her feet. *Maybe I am already dead,* she thought. *This is what it is: black motion, ache, wavering stillness.*

Much later she came up for air out of the obsessive wheeling of pictures and the thick drugged sensation of not being able to become fully awake. She felt beside her in the box and touched a cold hand. Turning, she saw up close the half-opened eyes and blue skin of Rob's face, his jaw loose-hinged, the hole at the side of his temple like a bite out of bone. As she tried to jerk away, she pressed against even colder skin. Mark loomed next to her in the grave-box, his face dried close to the skull, eyes open, colorless, sad, his hand feeling for her breast. His breath against her cheek was utterly frigid.

It was then she started to feel the slow, even rock and

sway, rising up over and tilting down, up and over, lift and
plunge. She realized she was awake and alive. Beneath
her there was a dull roar that permeated everything and
above her the low rumble of an engine. She opened her
eyes. *I'm on a boat,* she thought. *I'm out on the ocean.*

When she sat up, the muscles in back of her eyes felt
jagged with pain. She was dizzy, nauseated. In the gray
she waited to orient herself. She did not hear any sounds
on the boat itself except for the even putter of the engine.
A thin light came through the dirty portholes. From the
shape of the cabin area she gathered she was in the bow of
the boat. There were four bunks built against the sides.
Long wooden crates were stacked on the bunks and on
the slanting deck.

Maggie tried to open several of them but they were all
nailed shut. She pictured plastic bags, cocaine layered
inside like small white pillows. *So this is how it's done,* she
thought. *It never comes through customs at all.* She knelt
on the wet floor next to another crate pushed up into the
bow. The top of this one was loose. Prying it open, she saw
that it was filled with boxes of ammunition, layers and
layers deep. Guns, explosives, ammunition, grenades. But
Cody had implied the dealing concerned only drugs. *Import, export. I make appointments, monitor shipments.*
The Impala wired to explode, even Rob's phone. Cody
had always been the electronic genius, Sound Man. Dope
for guns. South America had the drugs, North America
the artillery.

Stepping over an anchor, she steadied herself against
the doorjamb and peered out. She saw nothing, no one on
the deck of the boat. It appeared to be a large, elegant
cabin cruiser, all chrome and gleaming white. Maggie
pulled on the knob and the door swung back. She'd expected it to be locked.

There was no one in the cabin above her, and all she
heard was the slap of waves against the sides of the boat.
She crept slowly out of the cabin, stepping over the raised
doorjamb into the wind. The entire boat was loaded down

with crates. To her left a high rock formation jutted up from the shore. The green water swayed around her, but the ocean was relatively calm here. Was this the lee of the island where Cody had picked up Lora on *The Pearl*? But looking around, she saw they were near a long stretch of shore and other boats were moored, bobbing on the water. A large, white wooden building extended out over the water at the end of a high dock. This was not a recreational marina. The boats all had high masts sticking up, outriggers like she had seen in pictures of *The Pearl*. Fishing boats. She wondered if this was Drake's Bay, where Dennis moored his boat.

A large fishing boat was pulled up next to the high dock and some men were working in a small skiff that rode down in the waves at its side. They were hauling crates up with ropes and pulleys. The boat appeared much larger than this boat she was on.

She wanted to wave to them, call out across the gray space, but she studied them for a moment, sure suddenly that the other boat was part of this. Was that Cody down in the skiff? She wanted to climb out to the edge of the boat to get a better look. As she stepped up out of the cabin she saw out of her peripheral vision a large black bird swoop down on her, huge wings outspread. It landed hard on her back, knocking her to the deck, and she cried out. *Not bird, not shadow.* Hand over her mouth across her chest. *Cody.* He'd been up on the cabin roof, waiting for her to come out.

She swung her elbow back at his head, once, twice, raised her foot and dug back at his knee, sliding the sole of her shoe down his shin and slamming it onto the top arch of his foot.

He rolled back, stumbling against the crates, and she crouched up on the engine case, a low box at the stern. *Nowhere to go.*

Cody fell back on the watery floor and spurted out a raucous laugh. He was wearing jeans, black T-shirt, black watch cap, and heavy boots, not his usual dress at all.

Incognito. He wiped at his bleeding lip, observed the red
on his fingers, laughed again. "Oh, you like that, do you?
That's good. Maggie. Like to fight? That's right, I forgot
about all those brothers of yours."

"Keep away from me," she warned.

He stood, steadied himself against the crates and
lunged at her, first to the right, then left, like a boxer
keeping her off balance. Where could she go but backwards off the boat into the throbbing waves? Then he
crouched toward her calmly, looking at her as if she were
a small wild dog he was going to cage. Her only chance
was if she could somehow push him off. Bait him to come
at her, then push him off.

She squatted down, riding the sway of the boat with her
legs. It reminded her of skiing. She threw herself to one
side as if to jump past him and he fell toward her, snapping with his large hands. As she leapt over him, snatching
at the tall pole of the outrigger, her legs sailed out over
the water. The outrigger cracked and she swung her feet
back into the boat.

Cody was sprawled back against the boat's edge, and
she ran at him, shoving her foot against his thigh. Then,
picking up a large fishing pole, she jabbed it down at his
chest. He grabbed it and pulled, yanked it from her hands
and pulled her foot toward him, flipped her down hard on
top of the engine case. When he lowered his face down
close to hers, she spat at him.

"And I always thought of you as so nice, so pure," he
growled.

He hauled her toward the cabin and threw her back
down into the reel house at the bow. "You're just going to
have to stay down there until I finish my business. Then I
can do you like I want to. It's got to be fire, like I said. It's
tradition. But I haven't got a stake to tie you to, do I?" And
he reached into one of the crates, pulled out a grenade,
and tossed it from hand to hand. "Don't think I can build a
fire in this wind? We'll see. Purey."

When she heard the put-put of a boat coming toward

them, she cried out, screamed, and he pressed his hand over her mouth, then leaned on top of her. He fumbled at the edge of the bunk, under a folded wool blanket, and pulled out a black cloth and syringe. The grenade dropped, rattling across the deck. As he prepared the syringe she grabbed him around the neck, and he threw her full-force across the reel house, her back hitting a crate. She groaned and felt the black rise over her again.

When she came around she saw that the crates in the reel house had been removed. Her back throbbed with pain. She peered out the small porthole in the reel-house door. A man rested on the engine case holding a pistol as Cody and two other men lowered the last of the crates down off the back of the boat. Cody would come for her soon. She looked around the reel house for a sharp object, something to hit him with. Hefting up one of the bunk platforms she reached down into the wet dark. Her hand stopped just before she touched Rob's white, bloated cheek. Pressing her fist to her mouth, she slammed the bunk cover down and doubled over. A shadow moved across the porthole. There was the small rusty anchor wedged in the V of the floor. She lifted it and set it on the opposite bunk. This was the only way.

At the sound of men's voices, she peered out for an instant. The man with the gun was gone. Cody had opened the top of the engine case and was leaning down into it. He rose up then, glanced back at the cabin, gave a thumbs-up to one of the other men. She heard them clambering down the side of the boat, and she squatted on the bunk by the reel-house door, the anchor balanced on her knees. *I'll be ready. When he comes for me, when he steps down into the cabin, I'll hear his boots.* She tried to remember to keep breathing.

The sway of the water made her fall to one side, and she caught herself against the low ceiling. The sputter of the skiff's motor pulled away, and the boat was silent. *You and me,* she thought. *Come on. Sound Man.*

The anchor was heavy in her hands and it cut into her fingers. She rocked with the lifting water and he did not come. She felt superstitious: if she looked out the porthole he would come, just at that moment. Worse, he'd just be standing there, grinning through the round glass. Or perhaps he was on top of the cabin, waiting for her to come out again, waiting to leap down on her.

Well, she'd wait him out this time. That's what she'd do. Resting her head back against the wall, she remained in a low crouch, pressing herself back against the wall. The anchor sagged in hands. She rested it on her knees.

The endless roar of the sea breathed beneath her. The sky seemed darker. Dusk now. She heard nothing out there. Absolutely nothing. She knew that they were waiting each other out, that whoever moved first would die. With this thought in her mind, a spontaneous invented superstition, a rule that would keep her safe, a totem, a charm, she stayed squatted on the bed beside the door, fingers wrapped around the anchor, waiting for him to enter.

Chapter 25

Maggie did not know how long she crouched, holding the ragged anchor, riding the dip and swell of the Pacific. Out of one of the grimy portholes along the bow, she saw that it was nearly dark. Once she'd almost screamed out, "Come and get me you son of a bitch!" but she'd bitten the inside of her mouth instead. She pictured him up there standing like a sentry, leaning along the cabin wall, watching the circling gulls, simply waiting in the darkening wind. All the while she was aware of her fellow passenger in the reel house, in the space under that bunk not three feet away.

When finally, after an hour, maybe more, she had not heard a sound of movement, she set the anchor down on the thin mattress and pushed open the door to the cabin. In a cardboard box beneath a small butane stove there was a flashlight, and when she reached for it her hand closed around a paring knife. For a moment she stood listening, clutching the knife in her fist. What she would have to do would be to throw herself out across the top of the engine case, and as Cody leapt down on her, she would simply hold up the knife. She knew he'd grab for it no matter what happened, that she'd have to concentrate on holding firmly on to that knife.

Maggie sprang out of the cabin, across the boat toward the engine case, seeing too late that the engine-case cover had been removed. Down into the engine hold she fell, screaming, trying to position the knife above her, jamming her knee against metal. Her leg was caught among some tubes, between the boat and the engine. She raised the knife into the air above her, looking up at the webbed light, but nothing flew down at her, no black wings. The boat rocked gently in the waves. Gingerly she unhooked her foot from the side where it had been caught and climbed out.

Cody was not on the roof. The top of the boat was silhouetted against the dusk. Gripping the knife, she climbed out along the outer edge of the cabin to the bow and peeked around to the other side. The boat was empty. She was alone. Cody had left with the other men, left her out here alone and she'd been crouched in the reel house with that damn anchor waiting for no one.

Maggie yanked up on the rope at the bow and realized the anchor had been cut loose. Now she saw she was drifting quite close to shore, toward the large, flat rocks jutting up from the sea.

The larger boat, too, had left. A number of fishing boats were moored back by the dock but they were all dark, the dock was dark. Only one small fishing boat had a light on in its cabin. Maggie yelled, her voice swallowed by the offshore wind. For several minutes she cried out across the expanse, but there was no response.

In the cabin she fumbled in the box for the flashlight. Maybe she could drive the boat. She searched for a key, but Cody had taken it with him. Fixed to the ceiling above the steering wheel was the radio. *The radio!* She hadn't even thought of that. She tried flipping the power on but saw the lines had been torn loose from underneath, then blinked the flashlight across to the other boat. *Three short, three long, three short*— the way she and her brothers had

done on fishing trips trolling on Leech Lake with their
Dad. SOS. In their family it meant simply time to head in.

It was quickly growing dark. She crossed back to the
engine, wishing she knew how to hot-wire it. The wind
was damp and cold, and the moon rose perfectly round
over the water. Maggie shot the light down at the engine,
then clamped her eyes shut, opening them again, hoping
what she had seen was not really there.

Wired to the engine was a small black box, its digital
numerals pulsing red with the passing seconds. *Oh, my
God. Fire in this wind. Was it a timed device or could he
detonate it by remote-control command?*

Her first impulse was to yank the thing loose, throw it
over the side of the boat into the ocean. Jesus, she'd already fallen down into the engine hold, she might have
detonated it simply by knocking it loose.

She had to get to that boat across the way. Then she
remembered something Rob had told her earlier, maybe
the first night at the house when she'd been questioning
him about the logistics of Lora abandoning the boat, heading out into the open sea in a small lifeboat. The bigger
boats, like Dennis's Rob had told her, all had lifeboats on
top of the cabin. What was it that he'd said—that they
were suspended on a cable between two metal poles, that
there was a lever and when pulled, it released the lifeboat
and sent it sailing out into the water. He'd also mentioned
something about a survival suit.

The flashlight was growing weak, but she whirled it
around the cabin, looking for the lever Rob had spoken of.
There it was! Reaching up, she pulled hard on it and felt
the release. From on top of the cabin the lifeboat rode
down a coil and splashed out into the water. "That's it!"
she cried. Now, where was that survival suit? *Damn,* she
should have looked for it before she pulled the lever.

Outside the cabin window she could see the skiff still
riding up close to the boat. In another wave it washed
farther out. *There*—the survival suit folded into a square
plastic bag beside an orange life preserver. Maggie pulled

it on. fumbling, her foot stuck for a moment in a yellow fold. The lifeboat had bobbed ten yards out from the stern. Maggie yanked at the small tube at the waist of the suit and the thing inflated, puffing her into a tight ballooned vest. She hesitated at the back of the boat. It was so dark. Even if she got to the skiff over the high waves, she could sweep right by that fishing boat. She might be driven up on those rocks. For a moment she looked down at the bomb silently blinking digits. Maybe she could figure out how to defuse it.

No, she thought. This was the only way. If she stayed passively aboard the boat it would crash into those rocks and explode.

Straddling the edge of the boat, she prepared to jump off into the water when the flashlight fell from her hands, its light disappearing into the blackness. Every muscle in her body told her not to jump.

"JUMP!" she screamed, pushing herself as far out over the water as she could.

Down into the waves she was swept, holding her breath, quickly bobbing back up to the surface because of the air vest. She clutched tightly to the life preserver. The water was past cold, it stung through her bones. Swallowing salt water, she lunged, kicking with her legs, realizing she should have removed her shoes. She tried to pry them off, flailing forward with each swell, but the skiff receded farther and farther away.

After a few minutes she found a rhythm, kicking as each wave surged beneath her. When the skiff was in reach, she gave one final pump with her legs, threw her icy hands over the side, and clutched at the smooth wet wood. She tossed the life preserver over the side of the skiff, and it was several minutes before she could hoist her chest up over the stern, climbing in, exhausted and out of breath.

The small skiff tipped nearly to its side with each wave. She stayed low, crouching on the bottom of the boat, trying to start the small engine with a rope pull.

Out at the horizon the moon was coming up. She

thought of Jesse getting ready to light her wands. *"Magic for magic, I'll match her."* Isn't that what Cody had said? *The wiring, the wiring for the neon. He'd been there all that morning, the whole grove could be rigged to explode.* She had to get to that fishing boat.

The motor would not start. She pulled and pulled again on the rope but it wouldn't even turn over.

Looking up she saw that the skiff had washed about halfway to the other fishing boat. Again she began to scream out.

Finally, a dark shape emerged from the lighted cabin of the other boat. The man saw her and signaled with a raised arm. She screamed again and kept screaming as the roar of the explosion ripped through the air behind her and the boat from which she'd leapt disintegrated in a white flame that rose up over the water as the pieces began to rain down around her.

The fishing boat with the single yellow light chugged up beside the skiff. The man on board threw the rope to Maggie three times before she caught it. He pulled her up next to the stern and the skiff banged hard against the back side of his boat. The man extended a rough hand and hefted Maggie into his boat.

"What in Christ was that?" the man yelled, though he was right next to her. "I've never seen a damn thing like that out here! Nothing like that since the Pacific Theater, Big Two!"

"A bomb," she choked out, and realized she was shaking badly. "I've got to sit down."

"Here, here." He helped her down into the cabin. "Look under that bunk. There ought to be some dry clothes in there somewhere. There wasn't anybody else on that boat, was there?"

Maggie put her head on her knees and nodded, only whispering. "But he was already dead." She sat like that for several minutes before changing out of the survival suit and drenched clothes, pulling on an old sweatsuit and sweatpants, slipping her wet sneakers back on over bare feet.

The fisherman was on the radio to the Coast Guard, reporting the explosion as he rubbed his grizzled chin, the returning voices crackling over static so heavy Maggie could barely understand them. She crawled up into the cabin and leaned in the doorway, her legs weak, motioning to the fisherman that she wanted to speak.

Pressing the mike button down, she tried to keep it simple as she could. Call Beale, Marin County Sheriff's Office, tell him that explosives have been placed on Jesse Ryder's property in Fairfax and everyone should be evacuated immediately. Then she breathed out. "Robert Cody. Tell him Robert Cody is the one he wants."

The fisherman hung the mike back on the radio with a click. The rising moon turned the water to silver and the hills, to black humps along the coast.

"You're damn lucky I decided to stay out here tonight, young lady. I was just about to head back to the dock and heat up some soup. You hungry?"

Maggie shook her head. "Have you got a car out here?"

"Truck."

"Could you take me over to Fairfax?"

He spat off the side of the boat. "Do fish swim?"

Chapter 26

The moon, that cold rock-mirror, rose white over the frayed tops of the redwoods, casting a light so clean and odd that everything seemed to glow, the dim sheen of matter finally revealed. Jesse stood at the door to her studio waiting for the twelve other members of the coven to arrive. She had slept briefly and fitfully in the afternoon, waking with a sudden chill. Ben standing at her bedroom door staring in at her.

"You were talking in your sleep," he said. "Kind of loud."

She put her hand to her forehead. Slightly feverish, sweaty.

"Spirit be done with this house," said Ben. "That's what you kept saying."

Jesse had tried over and over again to get through to Beale, and she'd still not been able to reach Maggie or Rob. Now Jesse realized that although she'd left a message for Beale to call in a few minutes, she'd be turning on the answering machine. *Black out. Moon out.* No one would be able to reach her.

They were coming now, Zoë and the others, coming

quietly into the grove, all wearing white. They seemed to
glow in the moon shadows. It would have been so perfect,
so very perfect, without all this dying. Though she'd always preferred wands made of wood and crystal, tonight
she wore her knife sheathed to her thigh. She touched it
to make sure it was securely tied, then picked up the
burned doll and walked out into the grove. Just inside the
entrance to the charred stump she placed the doll in a
basket with the bones she'd found in the truck and the
ruined tape. These things she would burn during the ritual. Silly to fear a burned doll, a chicken bone. But it was
the thought form behind them. Harm or heal. Choose
your weapon, choose your wand. Jesse swallowed hard.
There had only been one place she'd seen dolls like this,
though Dennis had told her Lora imported them for the
gallery. The last time she'd seen them had been at the
home of Henry Loam back in the Haight years ago. And
Maggie had asked about Henry the other day. She'd
brushed the question aside, not wanting to think back to
those times.

*All right then, moon. You and me. This is for your
secondhand light, brilliance by hindsight.* She brought a
wooden flute to her lips and blew a single long note. The
coven members rose and came down out of the hillside,
each carrying offerings: flowers, fruit, candles, garlands,
tiny stitched quilts, crystals, scrolls with messages inscribed. The few who had been invited to watch stayed
far up in the grove on the hill. She'd prayed that Maggie
would be here, at least to watch. Milo and his father were
here, some witches from a neighboring coven, an herbal-
ist friend from Bolinas. She saw their dark shapes, and
then, as the moon rose up over the high trees and broke
through into the clear sky, she saw only shadows, trees,
stumps, humans. *Too dark to tell the difference. All
merged in the natural world.*

To go ahead with the healing in spite of everything.
Wasn't that what imagining was? To visualize peace in the

mess of the world. To say anything was possible. Envision a thing and create it, that was the essence of magic.

Years ago, when she'd first been attracted to the magic of Henry Loam, she'd thought the point was to accumulate power, to contain it. By nourishing oneself with some sort of charge to become superior and rise above. But now she knew that was an attempt to hold energy. Energy couldn't be held. Its very nature was that it had to move. Action, spun light of tiny charges and nothing between. That was why she'd had to abandon Loam's patriarchal practice.

All the witches stood around the pool, facing away from the center. One walked slowly around the group holding a white ceramic bowl filled with water into which each woman dipped her hands. A second witch followed presenting each with a sprig of sage.

Zoë spoke, lighting her sage with a match and circling the ring of women lighting each of theirs in turn. "As we come into her presence may we purify our intentions toward healing and homage to her light, leaving behind all worldly thoughts of darkness and dismay. Leave behind all fears and troubles, death and suffering. Recognize the larger self that lives in eternal light." She stood before Jesse, and the sage crackled into flame, its smoke sweet. "Let it go." Zoë whispered.

They all repeated, "Let it go."

Jesse knew that entering ritual space was not only physical, it was an attitude. It was walking into myth. The ancient body sat up and took notice. A consultation with the powers—but who was to say whether the powers floated outside of them in realms they could not touch or were within the soul, alternating emptiness and filling, slack with love, divine with decay? It was the movement that held a truth. There was no fixed point.

The coven revolved the office of high priestess every twelve weeks, and this was Jesse's culmination in that role. Tonight she would pass the priestess wand to Zoë, and in many ways she was relieved. Playing with power always brought lessons. This particular ritual had been about the channeling of power, about finding the means to pass it on correctly without the circuits blowing out.

And it was about the past—the synchronicity of seeing Maggie again, loving Dennis again, meeting up with the old group. The knot of Lora's death that had tightened around them all. The shadow box that seemed to place the blame on her. She was reminded that those who took on the role of dancing with the powers had always been persecuted—and it had always been common people, witches and midwives of the centuries, pagans and ceremonialists, alchemists and Gypsies.

It was time for the center of the ritual to begin—its circumference had begun weeks ago. The witches began humming dissonant notes, slowly finding a harmonious chord as they moved around the circle. Jesse glanced behind her into the studio at Ben, who was sitting on a high stool in front of a control panel for the lights and sound. He was under his headset, in a glory of electronics. She nodded and he nodded back. *Ready.*

The moon had moved into position overhead, its reflection already visible in the edges of the pool. As Jesse raised her arms to the east, the blue lights went on above. One by one she faced the other three directions until the woods overhead was sketched with light lines and the moon broke into the clear above. *Real and imagined light. As above, so below.* The neon radiated a multicolored glow illuminating the faces of the few observers sitting close to the grove.

For an instant a ghost face appeared in blue shadow— she could have sworn. His silver beard and steel eyes. But when she scanned the hillside, he was not there. *It cannot be,* she thought. *Stay present. No images from the past intrude. Fears fly away. Get thee behind me.*

The witches stepped back then, just behind the pressed-log ring, and Zoë came forward with a torch and lit it, flame following the drawn circle on the ground. Each witch picked up her offering, held it high, and either set it forward by the pool or placed it into the fire ring. Some of them spoke as they made their offerings: apples for fruition of a project begun, garland for continuation and healing of a relationship, coins tossed into the water for prosperity. A small hour glass for a slowed sense of time.

Jesse reached behind her into the stump for the basket, when one of the neon wands at the periphery suddenly shattered, white sparks zipping to the needled ground. The witches all turned, and a wind rose. Clouds in long fishscale stripes were moving in over the clearing.

She saw a dark figure move at the edge of the grove come down and crouch in the shadow of a large redwood. Lifting the basket, she walked around the fire ring, carefully setting the small bones into the flame. "This is for Lora," she said, "that she may move on in her journey and be troubled not by the earthly plane." Then she set the doll into the fire, the cloth smoldering into smoke. "This is for the past, that it may release its hold on us, that we may learn from its lessons and come fully into the present without fear."

Finally she took a white rose that Zoë had brought from her garden. She stepped over the fire and set the flower in the pool. "And this is for Quinn, that he may live."

Zoë raised the wand.

"Blessed be," the witches chanted in unison.

A second time Jesse felt a presence cross the grove and spun to face it. A second wand broke in air. No wind this time. Hit with a stick. Zoë held her arm, but Jesse pulled away and walked out of the circle into the darkness.

"Make yourself known," she called out.

"Jesse," Zoë hissed. "We're almost done. Let's close. It's just the wind."

Behind them an orange flare shot up into the woods with a whizzing sound. None of the witches seemed frightened or surprised. Jesse realized they all thought it was part of the installation. The witches joined hands. "May prayers offered be for the good of all," they intoned.

"And her light be celebrated and rekindled in each of us and in small ways until next we meet."

As they filed back toward the house, another flare shot up and Jesse, at the end of the line, turned back. In that instant she saw him cross the grove, his face lit orange for a moment before he disappeared into the blackness. *Loam.* What was he doing here? Why had he returned to haunt her like this? The bones, the whale tape: *he?* Another white wand cracked at the edge of the grove, sparks falling like drops of fire.

"What do you want from me?" she cried out. "Total darkness?" The wind came through the tops of the redwoods and one of the blue wands fell swaying at the end of its cord. Maybe it was just the wind, the white wands shorting out at the ends of the long extension cords. She couldn't still her heart. It filled her ears with her pulse and she held her breath.

She stood alone in the grove. The clouds moved over the moon and the wind clattered the wands against the trees.

"Jesse," called Zoë. "Come on."

Jesse walked over to the stump, the size of a small house. She peered into the thick blackness, raised her hand as a seam of lightning stitched down the sky. She backed into the stump.

"Darkness!" she called out, and in the studio Ben cut the power and the wands blacked out, leaving only the ring of fire flames slanting in the rising wind.

Then it fell over her with its slithery web, came down from above in a tangle of insect wings, a net crawling over her face and shoulders. She cried out, clawing it off her. *What was it?* Her fingers translating in the dark: *lace, the lace canopy.* She tried to scream but the cloth was pulled back against her throat, covering her face, hand over her mouth.

"So this is it, this is what all your witchcraft has come to? Golden arches? It looks like a state-fair midway. You've made a real production out of the whole thing, haven't you? But all somebody has to do is pull the plug and the whole show is over."

The voice was familiar but higher and less refined than Loam's bellowing speech. She struggled against him as he continued.

"Your magic can't match mine, Jesse. It never could. Life continues but death prevails. Light is a created thing, darkness inherent essential, the original state."

She sucked in air, her throat closing from the pressure.

"You showed promise for being a dark priestess but you failed. All this is just more materialism, a spiritual Disneyland, the fast-food goddess invoked, and all you've got left is bones."

"Jesse?" Zoë called out across the grove.

He pulled the lace tighter, mashing it over her face.

"Are you all right?" Zoë called.

"Years ago I saved you, Jesse, but that was stupid. I killed Peter String to protect you. It was you I wanted, you and Maggie, but neither of you even noticed, you only saw Quinn and Dennis, Dennis and Quinn. But now they're all dead—or will be. Lora and Rob and Maggie too. Quinn—I missed, but I'll try again. Or maybe just let him live out his time in a coma until someone pulls his plug."

She tried to scream beneath his hand, bite through the lace. She knew the voice now and the realization washed over her, the smell of death in a beautiful Italian suit.

A streak of light flaked across the grove toward them. Ben racing through the flames toward the stump. Cody dropped his hand from her mouth and she screamed out. A knife of light blasted up from the grove's edge, an explosion searing the air.

"Run, Ben!" she shouted, then broke from Cody's hold, scrambled up the small unseen steps that scaled the stump and the tree that grew from its side. She scaled up over the grove as Ben turned and fled, leaping across the fire ring. Fire crackled outside the edges of the ring and smoke stung the air where the explosive had ripped through the night, one of the small redwoods burning at its base.

Cody jumped out of the stump into the fire ring. "Your magic was always stronger than mine!" he shouted. "But not this time—now that you don't have Maggie at your side." He glanced around wildly, not knowing where Jesse had disappeared to.

High up in the tree, Jesse took the ceremonial knife from the sheath at her thigh and cut one of the electric cords that ran between two trees, feeding various of the neon lines. Carefully she lowered the line to the ground, its cut edge dangling into the pool.

Ben stumbled back toward the studio, the flashlight left dropped on the dirt, its feeble light growing dim. She couldn't see Cody anywhere, but from this height she saw the figure of the man whose eerie face she thought she'd recognized among the observers. This time she could not mistake his face, his large body lumbering through the orange light in a low crouch. For one instant Henry Loam turned back to face the grove before he entered the studio, just after her son.

Chapter 27

The road up the steep hill to Jesse's house was blocked by three squad cars, and from far down in the town Maggie heard the scream of fire engines. The fisherman jerked the truck to a halt and she touched his elbow.

"Thank you," she whispered.

"Don't get yourself hurt," he said. "Some guy in camos took over the office of a shipping company down by the airport last spring and held his boss hostage for three days. You never know when these guys'll snap. I don't know why we didn't snap after Big Two. I guess it was because we won."

Maggie didn't stay to hear the rest of his tale. She slammed the truck door and ran uphill fifty feet toward the roadblock.

Immediately she spotted Beale leaning against a squad car, his mouth close to the mike of the car radio. A police officer stopped her from proceeding, took hold of her arm. "You can't go up there, lady. The road is closed and the neighborhood is being evacuated."

Just then a small explosion ripped through the darkness above them and Maggie covered her ears. The smell of smoke drifted down through the woods.

"Beale," she gasped. "I've got to speak to Beale."

The sergeant saw her then and waved her over. "How did you get here so fast?" he asked. "I sent a car over to Drake's Bay to pick you up after the Coast Guard called us. What in the hell is going on?"

In breathless half-sentences she explained what had happened since she'd seen him at the hospital that morning.

"Jesus," he muttered. "Not Garson." For an instant he turned away, then back to her. "I heard just minutes ago on the radio that a house just went up in flames in Tiburon. They thought it might be a gas-line explosion. They're asking for Sausalito and Mill Valley fire departments to assist."

"That's got to be Cody's house. He said he was going to set it off so it would look as if he was a victim of some crime family killing, too. He said he was going to do the same to Rob's. *Where is Jesse?*" she shouted.

Beale gestured up the hill. "Some of the people have come down, but as far as I know she's still up there." He pointed toward a group of women down the road, all dressed in white.

Her coven, Maggie thought. "What about her kid, Ben?"

Beale took Maggie by the shoulders. "Look, I've sent for a SWAT team and a bomb-squad unit. They're coming up from San Francisco and should be here in a few minutes. It's useless going up there now. Explosives are being detonated every few minutes. He's set off three or four of them now. I can't even get the fire department in there until this guy is subdued. There are a few men up there now, but I can't chance anyone else going up."

"Don't you understand?" Maggie yelled. "This whole hillside could go up in flames!"

"It already has," he said.

From above they heard gunfire, several shots in succession. Maggie cringed.

"You can wait in one of the squad cars if you want," said Beale, "but I suggest you get off this hill altogether."

Maggie glanced up the dark road at the thin spine of flame that crackled up one of the redwoods several hundred feet above her. *I've got to get up there,* she thought. *Jesse's got to get out of there. I've got to let her know what's going on.*

She turned and ran down to the women in white, who were gathered at the side of the road. One woman had her arm around a teenaged boy, and Maggie addressed her. "You're friends of Jesse's," she said. "I'm Maggie Shea, Jesse's college roommate."

"Maggie," breathed a short woman. "Jesse told us all about you."

"I've got to get up there, I've got to get to her."

"There's some crazy up there firing off bombs or something. If you go up now you'll be walking right into his trap. The police . . ."

"Screw the police," Maggie said. She looked at the boy. "Are you Ben's friend?"

He nodded.

"Jesse mentioned that Ben used some kind of back path up the far side of the hill. Do you know where it is?"

He nodded. "It leads right to my house."

"Will you show me?"

"Milo," the short woman said, "show her where the path is and then get your ass back down here."

Maggie looked at the women's faces floating in the darkness like separate moons. On the hill above them there was an eerie silence. Even the sirens had stopped, the red trucks below strobing red lights across the pines. A gust of wind had sent flames to several other redwoods. As Beale turned to talk to one of the firemen, Milo shot past Maggie in the dark.

"Come on," he said. "Follow me."

The moon had been fully obscured by a thick bank of clouds, but she could feel the solid path beneath her feet. Milo had pointed the way up and she stepped carefully now, not wanting to stumble or fall in the darkness. She could tell by the flames that she was close—but it surprised her how quickly she came upon the back of Jesse's studio. Here Cody must have stood by the open window as she and Jesse talked the other morning.

Everything was black but the flames. On the ground the circle of fire had swept across the driveway in the direction of the wind. Maggie crept to the studio window and looked inside.

Two forms struggled in the darkness, rolling across the floor. Glass shattered, neon knocked from the worktable. In the thin orange light she recognized Ben. The other person was huge, but Ben was agile, squirming away from the larger man's grasp. She expected it to be Cody but knew even in the shadows that it was not.

The lights—all the hanging neon lights—were off. Jesse's words came back to her. *If the lights failed during the ritual it would not be a good omen.* What had she called the ritual—an homage to light? But if the lights were on perhaps the few cops Beale claimed were up here could see. Now it was only firelight, smoke and thick night.

The power switch on the wall inside! Maggie lifted the partially open window as the boy broke free from the man's hold and tore, half falling, out of the studio. The man stood up like a black bear and roared, "Don't go out there!" Maggie saw at once that it was Henry Loam.

From the window Maggie had a clear view straight through the studio and out the front door into the grove, the fire-ring and the charred stump Jesse had showed her. As she glanced out she saw Jesse swoop from the tree and land beside the pool, a witchy shadow in flight. Loam lumbered to the studio door, blocking Maggie's view. So he was in on this somehow. She knew he was. She slipped the window open and crawled into the studio behind him. She heard the boy cry out. "Run, Mom. Get out of here!" But Ben's voice was suddenly muffled, and then there was that hideous laugh of Cody's. Loam bolted out into the dark yard and Maggie hurried across the studio to the open door, broken glass beneath her feet.

Cody stood on one side of the pool, Jesse on the other. He held Ben in front of him, a hostage. "You think your magic is so powerful, Jesse? You can't have true power if you have your tentacles hooked to another human being."

"Let him go, Cody." Jesse spoke quietly. "Take me. I'll go with you. Take me." Cody lifted something rock-shaped in the air and held it high. Even in the dark, Maggie could tell it was one of the grenades from the crates on the boat.

"Love, Jesse? Love? See how you'll die for love?" He jerked the boy back by his hair, pulling against his throat. "Besides, there's really nothing you can do—only half your power is here. Without Purey's light, you're nothing."

"But I am here," Maggie announced, and she shoved the power switch up. Neon blinked and streamed into light, casting a blue-white glow onto the yard. Some of the rods swung in the wind, zapping like sparklers.

Cody pulled the ring off the grenade. "There's nothing like this magic!" he shouted. "Death is the ultimate disappearing act!"

From the hillside came the crack of gunfire, and Cody jerked forward. The grenade flew from his hand.

Ben dropped from his grasp and rolled to the side. From the shadows Loam ran forward, dove for the grenade and threw it toward the hillside, where it mushroomed into red fire with a sound that split the air.

The large yellow wand dangled just above the pool, illuminating Jesse frozen on the other side. Cody lunged toward her, stepping into the knee-deep water. His body lit up like blue lightning, sparks raining down. He bellowed out a ragged scream as he crumpled.

"FBI!" shouted Loam. "Everybody freeze!" He walked slowly toward Cody, gun extended. With a stick. Loam nudged the bent form and Cody slowly fell facedown in the copper pool.

Chapter 28

Maggie stood at the edge of Jesse's porch as police photographers snapped pictures of Cody's body. *How fitting,* she thought. *A final record for the archives.* Two men lifted him onto the ground beside the pool and pulled a cloth over his face and chest.

"Check this out," one of the men called to Loam. "Some sort of device strapped to his belt—a remote-control or something." Bomb squad officials were searching the area to check for any other small land mines that had not been detonated. Loam called them over and they conferred over Cody's body.

The air smelled strongly of wet smoke. A single fire engine remained in the yard, the ring of charred logs dampened in puddles. The redwoods that had caught fire like giant candles smoldered darkly. Maggie knew that in the morning the damage to the woods would look horrible, but it could have been much worse. No one else had been killed—except Cody, of course. Ironic that it was the light he was so obsessed with that had killed him, not all his weaponry and demolitions.

Jesse came up behind Maggie and leaned against her.

"It's a mess," said Maggie.

"Did you know redwoods can't seed without fire?" asked Jesse. "Burning is the only way the seeds are properly released. I always liked that idea, that nature had made a righteous place for destruction, that it's a kind of beginning."

Loam appeared at the corner of the house with Beale at his side. He nodded up at the women and a smile flicked over his face for an instant, then disappeared.

It was Beale who spoke first. "Maggie, when you mentioned the possibility of drug dealing and FBI surveillance of your house in Berkeley, I immediately called Loam here. I knew he'd worked with the Northern California Drug Task Force back in sixty-nine and seventy. It was he who informed us that Peter String had worked under him as an informer."

"It's really hard for me to believe you're with the FBI, Henry," said Jesse. "You were really spying on me back in Berkeley? But we were—you betrayed me."

He touched her shoulder. "I wasn't really *with* the FBI at that time. I was a paid informer. A fine line, I'll admit. And I crossed professional boundaries back then, too, just as Peter did, as many people involved in the drug task force did. You got pulled into the scene you were supposed to be observing. I wasn't exactly professional. We thought there was some pretty high-level dealing and that it might have been moving through your house. I knew you did a little dealing back then, Jesse."

"Who didn't?" Jesse asked.

"But I knew it was a bigger operation than what you had going. Peter's death and Lily's were both seen at the time as accidental drug overdoses. Sandy Craig's was eventually listed as a drug overdose at that time too. Accidental. Her family exerted a lot of pressure to keep it from being listed on the death certificate as a suicide. There was simply no evidence at the time that pointed in either case to murder. All three appeared to have been self-

induced. Frankly, things were pretty chaotic at that point
in the task force."

Ben came out to the porch and leaned against the railing, listening as Loam continued.

"Eventually I came to work for the bureau full-time
because I saw the wreckage of so many young lives in the
Haight. But I'd been pretty high profile in the Bay Area,
so Freda and I relocated to Miami, where we worked in
the Caribbean community—again in an undercover ca-
pacity—in the drug scene there. But we missed California, so a few years ago we came back and began work on,
among other things, this case.

"We suspected that someone in a business that did a lot
of foreign trade was also bringing a large amount of cocaine into northern California, so we began tracking by
computer anyone who went in and out of the country a
great deal. Quite a number of them were found to be
independent importers, travelers in third-world countries. Freda began making contact with them, using the
angle that she'd help them to make contacts in Haiti for
the dolls, prayer flags, and so forth. At the time we met
Lora we didn't make any connection back to your Berkeley group. Her name was Garson back then, and the name
Mayhew didn't ring a bell because her husband was never
a serious concern of ours. Actually it was Robert Quinn we
had our eye on because of his political activities—the bureau wanted to see if they could nail him on a drug charge.

"Lora was placed on a possible witness list for a secret
grand jury investigation, but then she seemed to stop
coming around to see Freda. Because she was one of many
importers we were watching and because her passport
number simply stopped coming up on our computer files
—in other words, she appeared to have ceased going in
and out of the country—we simply lost track of her until
Maggie showed up asking questions. When Beale called us
yesterday, he said her disappearance was being investigated as a homicide and asked us about other members of
that household in Berkeley, as well as another importer

named Phillip Dodd. As it turned out, Dodd was also someone that we had been watching, also a possible witness on that grand jury list. When we went to question him and found him murdered, we knew we were very hot. But I don't know if we ever would have suspected or uncovered Robert Cody as the key figure in this without you, Maggie. He must have been incredibly meticulous in his record keeping and his computer activity. Eventually we'll have access to the computer files of his companies, but we have discovered one thing. Checking into bureau files by phone tonight we found out that one of his companies had a very large defense contract for electronic explosive detonators that can be activated by computers using telephone modem devices. Let's just say he was extremely well-connected at federal levels and would have appeared in every way to have been a very prominent citizen."

"They always are," Jesse said under her breath.

Loam added, "Not to mention the fact that, frankly, unless we had caught him in the act as we did tonight, he could easily have arranged to bargain for immunity and so forth, if it had ever come to that."

Maggie shook her head. "If Lora hadn't sent me that shadow box, none of this ever would have surfaced. Everyone would have continued to think she died in a boating accident—or else Dennis would have been arrested for her murder."

"By the way," said Beale, "we found that shadow box in Cody's car parked on the hill down there. Actually it was a van. I thought he was driving a Mercedes that day at the hospital. Well, he probably blew up a whole fleet of cars in that Tiburon house."

Jesse straightened. "Is there any chance that we could have the shadow box?"

Beale thought for a moment. "I don't see why not. It's not really evidence. I'll get it for you."

"And what about Dennis?" asked Jesse. "Will you release him tonight?"

"He'll probably be released pending further questioning. I imagine that will take place sometime tomorrow."

Beale headed off into the night to get the shadow box from his squad car, and Loam looked up at the two women.

"What was all that Cody was yelling about light and darkness?"

Maggie answered, "Some weird notion he had about witches." She put her arm around Jesse's waist.

Loam smiled and bowed slightly. "I greet thee, sisters, and bow to thy greater wisdom."

"Henry, you're so archaic. Do you still practice?" asked Jesse.

But Beale was returning with the shadow box, so Loam nodded and simply said, "Not in public."

Jesse shook her head. "At least we had enough power. It's ironic that it was Cody himself who rewired the system so that it could handle more voltage."

"What goes around comes around," said Maggie.

"Oh, no," groaned Ben. "Not karma."

Beale handed the shadow box to Maggie and excused himself. The two men walked out into the dark grove.

Ben spoke. "I guess you didn't need a bunch of doves for a finale, did you, Mom?"

Jesse shook her head.

Maggie said, "It doesn't feel finished. The ritual, I mean. There's something more to do." She looked at the shadow box in her hands and handed it to Jesse. They followed Beale and Loam into the redwoods and Maggie paused for a moment at the copper pool, the water strewn with leaves and ashes. The moon had stolen over into a bank of clouds and the night sky was back lit and silver. There was no reflection to be seen in the littered water.

Epilogue

Maggie bent over Quinn's hospital bed and lightly touched his forehead. She'd had to wait several days to see him. He'd come out of the coma and had been taken off the respirator, but still the nurse would only allow her in for a few minutes, and told her not to say anything that might upset him. He probably wouldn't remember it anyway because of the drugs and it would be stressful for him.

As he blinked his eyes open and tried to give her that fabulous grin. Maggie could tell he was in pain. His words were slightly slurred.

"So that was your jealous boyfriend firing me up in the dead of night, eh, Maggie?"

"Yeah," she said. "He heard all about you."

"The cop who came to question me said it was a sniper."

"Some freak thing. I'm sure they'll tell you all about it later when you're feeling better."

Over the last couple of days she had wondered if what Cody had said was true—that Lora and Quinn were once lovers. She doubted it. Another of Cody's painful lies. When Quinn was better, she'd ask him. Beale had checked on the Bogotá telephone number on Quinn's

Pacific Bell statement and found that it was indeed the number of a craft guild. Maggie was relieved that Quinn had been cleared of any involvement with the dealing. She found herself wanting him to be clear of Lora too.

She took Quinn's hand and held his palm to her cheek.

"I didn't realize you like your men so vulnerable," Quinn said dreamily. "I'd have gotten myself blown away years ago if I'd known that's what it would take."

"Don't get all excited." She smiled. "You should rest now, babe."

"Babe, really? After all this time?"

"Quinn . . ."

"We could get engaged again. We don't even have to get married, just engaged. I like the sound of it."

He grimaced, held his hand to his side and closed his eyes. For several minutes he was silent and she wondered if he'd fallen asleep.

"See?" she whispered.

"It's only hurts when I'm in love," he said. He opened his eyes briefly to look at her, grinned. And then he slept.

They rode out to Point Reyes National Seashore in Dennis's car, Jesse up front with Dennis, Ben and Maggie in back. For two days all of them had stayed at Dennis's house, working on the memorial service for Lora and Rob. This morning Jesse had suggested a private ritual first, and they'd all agreed.

Dennis had been released the morning after the ritual with a reprimand for having left the scene of a crime. He'd been told by Beale, as Jesse had, not to leave the area without permission until the investigation was complete. Already Loam and Beale had been turning over what stones they could, looking at Cody's business files, unraveling complicated computer programs, searching for information. What really threw Maggie was the revelation that Cody had never actually been in service in Vietnam. While still in marine boot camp, he'd been given six months in the brig and a dishonorable discharge from the corps: the drill instructor he'd taken a knife to had only been saved by massive blood transfusions. But in the mid-sixties, he'd found his way to Vietnam anyway, where he had worked as a free-lance journalist and been involved in drug trafficking as well. As a journalist he'd accompanied battalions into action—to get the death hit he craved, Maggie suspected. So he'd never ever been a vet. It had all been lies and pretense. Another mask.

When they reached the seashore, Dennis pulled over to park at an overlook, and they scrabbled down a steep rutted trail. The rock shore far below was black as ancient lava, the ocean crashing up spray on craggy stones. It was desolate and barren. Jesse stopped to gaze out over the water.

"I love this place," she said to Maggie. "The human realm seems so insignificant here."

They climbed down the dirt path to the beach, and Dennis came up to Jesse as she sat by a rock. Maggie stood back a few feet, watching a single gull circle above them.

"I think I'll walk up the beach with Ben," Dennis said. He bent to wrap his arms around Jesse for a moment and then stood.

"You know. I'm deeply flawed," he said. Maggie saw that though he wasn't smiling, his eyes seemed to.

"Ben approves of you," said Jesse.

"Do you?"

"What will you give me if I say yes?"

Dennis thought for a moment. "A fishing pole?"

Jesse laughed as Dennis turned and headed up the shore.

Maggie came over and sat beside her, dark curls flying back in the wind.

"Every time I create an installation," said Jesse, "there's always a lesson in it, all the way through the preparation, all the way through to the final actualization. This one was about the past, the hold it has on us. We can't be bound by it. It has to be dismantled but only through understanding it. Only in that light. Real light, that's the present. Past and future are imagined."

Maggie pulled the shadow box, its glass now broken, out of the satchel she'd carried down the path from the car. "I think we should do something with this, take it apart or throw it into the ocean." The trinkets were all gone now, fallen out, except for Dennis's tiny cards: these had been glued onto his photograph.

The strong wind whipped loudly at their faces and through the hollows of Maggie's ears. The two women walked over to where there was a stretch of sand next to the surf and inscribed a circle with a dried stem of kelp. Maggie thought of the witches in *Macbeth* and the function of witchcraft. Clarify intentions concentrated in a metaphoric act, attain clear present vision. *The present is the point of power:* that's what Jesse had always said. In Maggie's own practice, too, she had to be wary of acting too much from the past, tilting too far into hopes and dreams and fears of the future.

In the center of the circle Maggie bent to build a small fire, but the wind kept blowing it out. She abandoned the circle, found a boulder to squat behind, and lit a tiny twig fire in the lee of the stone. She reached through the broken glass of the box and picked at the photographs that were glued to the back. Some of them ripped as she tore them from the wood and handed them to Jesse. One by one Jesse fed the faces into the thin stream of the fire.

Then Jesse dropped a sprig of sage on the flame and draped a white ribbon across the fire. The satin ribbon seemed to melt before it caught fire.

"Now it is broken," said Jesse. "The bond from the past is broken."

She sprinkled a handful of wet sand on the fire, and as she did so, a speck of one of the pictures flew up and away out of the fire, a thumbnail fleck of ash. Maggie chased it to where it drifted down. She cupped her palm over it and saw that it was Lora's face, partially blackened, as though it were a negative.

As she tried to pick it up it disintegrated, dissolving into the damp sand. She grabbed a fistful of the sand with the ashes ground into it and returned it to the smoldering fire. Together, they stirred it in.

006073234 C.2

Green
  Night angel.